Praise for Lee Brown's DARK

This is not your usual detective story...always something new poppin' out in your face.

Sleuth Pro
author of *Hip Hop Tales* • Poughkeepsie, N(

D1241895

"You ever notice how many shadows pas
"Some we can hold on to."
"Not many."
Lee Brown is a master in trafficking shadows, edges, and folds, revealing to the reader the textured glow of lives well-lived, the steady push-and-pull of chaos, and the noiseless, nuanced thoughts of those teetering along the rims of abjection, while surprising us with a gleaming undertow of humor. In his delicately interwoven stories of light and darkness, Lee succeeds in gripping our imaginations and hearts to walk us through the dark corners (so often avoided) to bring us safely to the brightly lit side of the street. This wise, new voice- as weathered and smooth as northeastern driftwood, with the melodious sweetness and warmth of a port-barrel-aged southern bourbon- mesmerizes us by conjuring a world both strange and astonishingly familiar. With chapters like Silhouettes, Drift, Rain, Shadows, *and* Sky, DARK *beckons us to enter a city in chiaroscuro. Without the shelter of a gray fedora or a curling, spiral of smoke, this thriller's heroes and antiheroes own the streets with magic and...panache. This is noir at its best.*

Ivette Romero-Cesareo
co-editor of *Women At Sea: Travel Writings and the Margins of Caribbean Discourse and Displacements and Transformations in Caribbean Cultures*

Brown's novel constructs compelling character driven webs of story you don't want to free yourself from. This is the new noir- elliptical and challenging in the best ways, with flashes of light and darkness- befitting our age but referencing and refracting others. If you like Mosley, Butler, diners, intrigue, blue notes, or the scent of books at any age, there's something here for you in this complex and rewarding read.

Mind Bullets Collective • Brooklyn, New York

DARK

LEE BROWN

Epigraph Books
Rhinebeck, New York

DARK. Copyright © 2019 by Lee Brown

All rights reserved. No part of this book may be used or reproduced in any manner whatsoever without written permission of the author.

Book & cover design: Amy Manso
Cover photos: Ian Wickstead

ISBN 978-1-948796-99-6

Library of Congress Control Number: 2019919398

Epigraph Books
22 East Market Street, Suite 304
Rhinebeck, NY 12572
845.876.4861

*To all the people
who have struggled against injustice.*

THE STORIES

Silhouettes

"You want me to run my mouth for one hour to a woman I don't know for $250?!"

He looked at me with a slight smile that appeared to be drawn on his face.

"Where's the camera?"

His look of satisfaction changed to confusion and he glanced away for a second. A grin that looked like it only involved six teeth spread tooth by tooth underneath his upper lip. He reached into his suit jacket pocket and pulled out a thin leather billfold. With a little theatric deliberation, he took out five fifty dollar bills and laid them on my desk.

"I would like you to go to 105 La Verne Terrace, apartment 4C, and speak with Susan Hart. Talk to her for an hour and you're done." He paused and added, "Obviously there is no camera."

I found my head tilting to the right and I thought maybe I looked like a dog when you speak to it and its wondering "what the hell is this human talking about." I straightened my head up and felt the left corner of my mouth pull back to about my ear.

"What am I supposed to talk to her about?"

"Anything. You pick the topic."

■ ● ■

"What's the deal here?! What kind of joke is this?"

"A $250 joke right here on your desk."

I looked down at my notes and purposely misread them.

"Why would Sarah Kane want…"

"No. That's Susan Hart."

"Okay, why would Susan Hart want to speak with me for an hour?"

"I think she might find you interesting. You're a detective. How many people each day have a licensed detective knock on their door and ask to be talked to?"

"How many people pay someone $250 to go talk to someone they've never met before for no particular reason?"

"I doubt there are any. At least not in this city."

He smiled as he stared at me, and I stared right back without a smile. His smile turned into a smirk and that infuriated me. I wanted to slap him, but then there was $250 on the table.

"Okay. What time?"

"How about now? Now would be good." He looked at his watch and nodded. I repeated the name and address while writing it down for a second time. He nodded again and stood up."

"Uhh…Not so fast Mr. Barthelme." I put my pen down and held out my right hand. "Can I see your driver's license please."

He stood stock still, like the movie reel got stuck. Then he reached for his back pocket and pulled out a different thin brown leather wallet. He handed me his license with a smile that almost seemed real. I wrote down the serial number, full name and address and handed it back to him. He slid it into his wallet without looking.

"Are we finished now?"

"Yes. Yes we are."

"Thank You." I watched him glide out the door and wished I had a suit and shoes like that. Brownish-grey. A fabric I couldn't

■●■

quite figure out and tan leather shoes that had to have been made in Italy. Every pair of shoes that I ever envied was from Italy.

I swiveled around in my chair and stared out the window at the clouds. There were only about ten of them in the sky but I think they were the puffiest clouds I had ever seen at 9:45 a.m. on a Friday morning. I stood up and stretched. I felt good. I picked up the $250 and went out into the waiting room. Two of the other three office doors were closed, so I walked into Andy's office.

"Hey Andy, did you see the guy that was just here?"

"Mr. Suit?" Andy looked up from his desk where he was writing a report. "That was a lot of suit on that guy. What did he want?"

"He wants me to go talk to someone."

"Someone for why?"

"He put down $250 for me to go talk to some woman."

"But about what?"

I started to laugh.

"Supposedly whatever I feel like talking about."

Andy put his pen down, leaned back in his chair and clasped his hands behind his head.

"Sounds like trouble."

"Of course it does. Exciting isn't it?"

Andy started laughing. I looked at the door that led to the outer hallway and then turned back to Andy.

"Where's Sharp and fucking Mojica by the way?"

"Sharp is over with Casualty and Life. I don't know where Mojica is. Why do you always call him fucking Mojica?"

I was surprised he asked that. I pondered for about a second.

"You know, he must have done something stupid sometime so I just call him that. Also because I like him."

■ ● ■

"Do you call me fucking Andy when I'm not around?" he asked with raised eyebrows.

"No. But I call your girlfriend fucking Janie. I like her."

"So you don't like me?

"I never thought about it before, but no, I don't like you. I like your girlfriend."

Andy started laughing again and clasped his hands in his lap.

"So are you going to go have a conversation with Mrs. Someone?"

I nodded.

"Took the money didn't I?"

"You want backup?"

"Nah. How bad could the trouble be at ten o'clock in the morning? But I'm going to borrow one of fucking Mojica's knives." I started toward his office. "But don't tell him."

When I got downstairs in the street I felt like I wanted to walk. It was an incredible spring morning. Everything seemed clean. Even the dirt. All of the snow and ice was finally gone and the air just felt good. I decided to walk to the bank and drop off the $250 and then get a coffee.

I went into my favorite diner on Collier St. and sat down on a counter stool. I barely managed to raise a finger to the waitress and mime "coffee" when the stale odor of alcohol and cigarettes engulfed me. I knew it was Jocko. He sat down next to me with a smile on his face like God had just given him a free pass to heaven.

"Jocko, are you drunk already?"

"What do you mean already? I have been in a continuous state of controlled inebriation for three days now. I am showing no ill effects other than my right elbow hurts, which explains why I am drinking with my left hand. I must admit that at about five a.m. this morning I was confused and the glass missed my

■ ● ■

mouth twice. However, I didn't spill a bit and my ambidextrous nature took over and I have been fine for the past five hours."

"Jocko, when are you going to stop? You look like you need sleep."

"Well, I was contemplating sleeping on Thursday."

"It's already Friday!" Jocko looked as stunned as you can look on a five day drunk.

"What?! You mean I've missed my deadline?" Jocko folded his hands on the counter and lowered his head. "What is the date today? It might be later than I thought."

"Nah Jocko. I think you're probably ahead of where you want to be."

Jocko turned his head toward me and said, "You know, that's the nicest thing anyone has said to me all morning." A smile lit up his face. "I think that calls for a drink."

"Jocko, I think that calls for sleep."

"So do I but I don't want to drift into unconsciousness without purpose. My drinking helps prime my dreams so that they will be pleasant dreams. That is the purpose of my drinking. To make all of my dreams, pleasant dreams."

"Jocko, I see my coffee coming and it will taste better if you're not sitting next to me. So why don't you go home and take a shower and go to sleep."

Jocko stood up and tried to stretch his body so that it appeared taller than it was.

"The scents of the past three days are draped across my body like a road map that reminds me of every pleasant destination I had the fortune to arrive at. Most of them bars." Jocko paused and looked around. "Maybe I do need some sleep. I'm starting to talk like I imagine that you do on Friday mornings. That, is frightening. Too da loo."

I watched Jocko slide and stumble out of the diner as I took my first sip. It was good.

I milked two coffees for twenty minutes before I sauntered over to the bank and stood in line behind a man with an uneven crew cut. I felt compelled to determine how much higher the left side of his hair was compared to the right. When he finally got up to the teller I was pretty sure the difference was at least an inch. I wondered what kind of barber gets a crew cut crooked like that. I thought maybe it was a style thing but this guy looked like he had been in the Marines about 45 or 50 years ago. When he finished his transaction he turned around and stared at me. I thought he was going to say something to me about looking at his head. Instead, in a raspy voice he said, "Today ain't no day for no punks." He nodded at me and walked past, scanning the bank in a very serious manner.

I walked up to the teller.

"Hi Linda."

She looked up at me with a huge smile.

"Oh my God. It's so great to see someone normal. What a morning. Did I tell you? We bought a house."

"That's great. When do you move in?"

"At the end of April. I have so much stuff to get rid of.

I smiled.

"Do you want any magazines? I have back issues of LOOK and Life…and Popular Mechanics."

"Naw. I don't think so. Do you have any Sporting News?"

"No. You know I'm not a big sports fan."

"Yeah, but why do you read Popular Mechanics?"

"I really like the writing."

"Do you know what they're writing about?"

"Not always."

"Maybe you should try The Sporting News. They have some good writers in there too."

■ ● ■

"I'll stick with breakthroughs in toaster technology."

"So where's your new house?"

"At 126 Cumberland Lane."

I looked at Linda with disbelief.

"Isn't that the place where those two hit men killed that guy and put him in the concrete floor of the garage?"

"Yes, but they dug up the whole floor and there's new concrete."

"Got a new tub?"

"Huh?" Linda looked at me quizzically. "We don't need a new tub."

"Well they cut the guy up with hack saws in the bath tub. They never found one of his hands. That could be any place in your new house. You could be making fried chicken and a thumb could fall from a cabinet into the batter. Of course bathing in a tub where a man was sawed apart probably wouldn't bother you. Just wash it out with Bon Ami. Gotta wonder if all the blood stains came out of the tiles. Then there's the scratches in the tub from the hack saws."

"Stop it! There's no blood on the tiles."

"Oh you may not see it, but there's residual blood in the grouting. Probably won't turn your water red, but it would make me feel creepy to know the dead man's blood was seeping into the bath water. Might take years for it to all come out."

"Stop it!"

Linda had a slight greenish tinge in her face so I knew my work was done. Linda handed me the deposit slip.

"Have a good day Linda, and congratulations on the house."

The woman behind me glanced at me and whispered, "That wasn't nice."

"This ain't no day for no punks."

Over my shoulder I could hear the woman say, "If you use Clorox you don't have to worry about any blood, dear."

■ ● ■

It was much warmer when I got outside. I looked both ways up and down the block and started off for Susan Hart's apartment. It was going to take me about thirty-five minutes to walk there. Everyone on the street seemed to be in a good mood and I found myself saying hello to random people. With a day like today they should feel exquisite, because today was not a day for no punks. I chuckled a little because I really wanted to know what that was all about. The guy with the crooked crew cut got in my brain. Maybe for the whole day.

When I arrived at Susan Hart's building I found myself looking it over. It gave me the feeling that it was in the wrong place. There was a painting of Mercury in gold and shades of yellow over the front door. There were three wide steps up to the entrance that made me feel like there should be a doorman in a green and yellow suit with gold brocades. It took me a while to get used to the idea that this was just a well kept apartment building.

I scanned the apartment numbers on the wall and found '4c Hart'. I pushed the button and the buzzer let me in after a short two seconds. The lobby was amazingly clean. A well maintained elevator took me to the fourth floor. Apartment C was to my right and I realized it must look out over the street. I decided to knock on the door instead of pushing the door bell. The door opened almost immediately. The woman who opened the door simply said, "Yes?" She was a kind of plain looking woman. Brown hair, brown eyes, very plain, conservative clothes.

"I've come to talk to you."

She looked up at me and her mouth opened but no sound came out.

"I'm a detective and I would like to speak with you."

Her mouth was open but she seemed to have difficulty saying, "About what?"

■ ● ■

"Maybe about being a detective. Or maybe about why someone would hire me to come all the way across town to talk to
you."

Her face looked like the word "surprise."

"Oh…so you're not the police."

"No, I'm a private detective."

"Uhhhh, come in. Please come in."

I entered the apartment and a large window faced me on
the wall looking out to the street. A brownish green sofa ran
the length of the living room wall to my left. On my right two
burgundy couches were separated by a very large parlor palm in
a large, tan ceramic planter. The walls were a kind of beige-pink
and there were black and white photos in groups of four on all of
the walls. The floors were a dull reddish hardwood covered partially by a red and tan carpet that looked like it may have come
from the Middle East. The place was so comfortable it made me
nervous.

The brown-haired woman stood behind me at first and then
walked into the center of the living room. She turned back to
face me and smiled.

"You're here because it's my birthday."

"I am?"

"Yes. That must be the reason."

"Okay. Happy Birthday."

"You are going to talk to me about being a detective aren't
you?"

"I suppose I could do that if you want me to."

"This is exciting. I'm going to make some tea. Would you
join me in having some tea? It's my birthday."

"That would be nice, but could I please use your bathroom? I
just walked over here and…"

"Of course. It's just down the hall toward the kitchen. Follow

■ ● ■

me. You'll see it."

I found the bathroom and a pile of the softest towels in existence on a shelf by the shower. I took Mojica's knife out of my pocket and slid it in between the two towels at the bottom of the stack.

I went back to the living room and found I was still very uncomfortable. The place made me nervous. I didn't think it was her birthday and she didn't look excited about talking to a detective. She didn't ask my name. She invited a strange man into her apartment. I was being paid $250 to talk to a non-descript woman who was making tea.

I sat down on the couch. Brown-haired Susan Hart came in carrying a tray which she placed on an end table next to me.

"Do you take sugar?"

"Yes, but I can put some in myself. By the way are you Ms. or Mrs.?"

"You can call me Susan. So how hard was it to get a license?"

A brass tacks discussion? This was weird.

"Not difficult. Had to take an exam and pay the licensing fee. We had to apprentice somewhere. We were all in policing in the military."

"Who is 'we'"?

"Me and my partners. There are four of us. Three of us were all in the army together. The fourth was the Navy but he knew one of my partners."

"That's fascinating. How long have you been in business?"

She didn't look fascinated. In fact she looked pretty bored.

"Oh, about a week."

Her head snapped toward me. I finally said something that snagged at her curiosity. So I followed up with, "How long have you been in the business? Great tea."

I smiled at her like my shoes were too small. She leaned back

■ ● ■

in her chair and crossed her legs. She was talking but the last thing I remember hearing was "Damn it! Don't spill your tea!"

I was almost awake. I could hear voices all around me. All around me. I was lying on the floor surrounded by men's voices. Every once in a while I heard a woman say something. I was nauseous and I was passing out again or falling asleep.

It was a long way to the llama farm. I was certain of that. The man walking beside me was walking backwards and I was waiting for him to fall. But he didn't. I knew he was a professional. We were walking on a sidewalk that turned into a dirt road every time I looked up from the concrete. There was a wooden fence marking off the road from the pasture. The grass was a deep rich green sprinkled with yellow dandelions and buttercups. I could smell strawberries. Where were the cows? What happened to the cows? Then I saw her. Sitting on top of the fence with her plain brown hair and that half smile of hers. We walked toward her and her smile got bigger. I asked her where the cows were and she shrugged and waved goodbye and said, "I'm not going that way." I ignored her and looked out on the rolling green hills that seemed to end at the horizon. Maybe they went on forever. Were llamas replacing cows? The guy who was walking next to me was gone. At the top of the hill I could see a pile of black and white. I could hear someone talking over the next hill.

This time I was able to raise my head. There were three men dressed in suits sitting around me. One on the couch. Two in the sofas. Two of them wore glasses. One had a receding hairline. They ignored me and my headache. I tried to sit up and made it to my elbows. A woman walked across the room, knelt on my chest and jammed something into my arm. My last impression of her was red shoes.

■ ● ■

The brown-haired woman was walking next to me. She said she wasn't going far. I could see a different man walking backwards about twenty yards away. He was ignoring us. I asked again what happened to the cows. The brown-haired woman stopped me under the only street light I knew of out in a pasture. She pointed to the top of the hill. The pile of black and white was cows. All dead. All thrown on top of each other in a heap. The brown-haired woman told me the sun felt wonderful. I was feeling cold and weird. I felt like I had to piss.

It was late afternoon and the first thing I saw when I opened my eyes were the ropes around my wrists. As soon as I saw them I was in an instant panic. They were tied to one of the radiators. I tried to get my legs under me but they were tied to the other radiator. To top it off my pants were down to my ankles and that was the real source of my panic. That and the woman with the red shoes that was sucking on my dick like a piston. I tried to roll away but it was impossible. I tried to scream but all I got through the tape over my mouth was "Ugalackuga" and that didn't sound close to "help."

"Oh…I was hoping to finish you off before you came to. I really thought I could do it." She was up on her knees smiling at me and then said in a growling whisper, "But I am going to finish you off." She stood up and pulled up her skirt and then pulled off her panties. I struggled against the ropes but all I did was hurt my wrists.

"Let's not waste that hard-on, okay?"

She sat down on my stomach and then slid back. She grabbed my cock with her right hand slid onto it smiling the whole time. Then she started rocking back and forth. I tried to think of dead people. Vomit. My worst drunk. My worst girlfriend. Me being dead. Nothing helped. Her face was turning red and I wasn't going to be able to help myself. I was in danger and why the hell

■ ● ■

wasn't I going soft. And then it didn't matter. She started laughing, muttering "I knew I could do it…I knew I could do it…" She was moving faster and I wanted her to stop. I had never felt so ashamed. Suddenly she was shuddering and slowing down and I was thinking "I hope this rape was good for you, you fucking scum."

She stood up with her hands on her hips laughing. She grabbed her panties and started putting them back on.

"I'll be back. Don't worry."

She shifted her hips back and forth as she pulled up her underwear. When she pulled her dress down and flattened it out she started laughing again. I was hoping that sicko would at least pull my pants up. Instead she just walked out the front door. I listened to her lock it from outside and suddenly realized I needed to piss very badly.

This was ridiculous. I was tied up on somebody's floor with my pants down by my ankles. In about fifteen minutes I was going to be lying in my own piss hoping I wasn't going to be killed before the end of the day. I pulled my head up a little. On the floor next to the magazine rack was a newspaper open to the sports page. Brooks Robinson had gone two for three. Vida Blue had won again. I dropped my head back on the floor and either miscalculated or wasn't capable of calculating in this state and I bounced my head on it. It hurt like hell. My head hurt and I kept thinking "what the hell is going on here?! What the hell is going on?!" When the sharp pain subsided to a dull ache I lifted my head to see how my feet were tied. Down in the corner of the room, behind the sofa I thought I saw something odd through my blurry eyes. Something really weird. I strained to get a better angle. Shoes. A pile of shoes. But not just a pile of shoes. A pile of shoes with ankles attached. My neck was getting tired and I put my head back on the floor without banging it. When I raised

■ ● ■

my head again I could tell there were three bodies stacked up on top of each other behind the sofa. I was now convinced that I was going to die with my pants down to my ankles, tied to a radiator, lying in my own piss.

The lock clicked and the door slowly opened. A huge man filled the doorway. He saw me and a look of shock filled his face. He looked down the hallway to the kitchen and then the other way toward the bedroom. He was more than 6'5 and probably weighed three hundred pounds. He closed the door very quietly and then pointed toward the kitchen. I shook my head. He pointed toward the bedroom. Again I shook my head. He stepped into the living room and looked around.

"What the fuck is going on in here?! Let me help you buddy. Are you hurt?"

He ripped the tape from my mouth.

"No. I'm okay. I'm scared as hell and I have to piss"

He started untying me.

"How long have you been here?"

"A few hours I think."

"What the hell is going on?"

"I don't know. Could you help me up?"

He pulled me to my feet. I leaned over for my pants and almost went down on my face. I was dizzy and nauseous. He must have been able to see the shape I was in.

"Let me help you to the bathroom." We started in that direction as quickly as I could go, holding on to my rescuer with one hand and my pants with the other.

"Who are you?"

"Me? I'm Bernie. Why are you here and what the fuck is going on?"

"I don't know, but I've been drugged and raped and I think there are three dead bodies out there behind the sofa."

■ ● ■

"What?! Hold on to the sink."

I almost went down again. I was trying to hit the bowl. Maybe I should have been sitting.

"Hey Bernie. Do you live here?"

"Did you see what happened out there?"

"No. I was unconscious. Are they dead?"

"Maybe you should come out here and take a look."

I turned on the cold water and splashed some in my face. Then I cupped my hands and took two long drinks of it. I shuffled out to the living room holding onto the walls.

"Bernie, we need to call the police. Where's the phone?"

I squinted my eyes up at Bernie's face and he turned toward me. I could see the right fist coming toward my head but I couldn't do anything about it.

There were llamas dancing across the horizon like sheep in a cartoon. The brown-haired woman was pulling on my arm. I looked at her and with a man's voice she said, "You're not too smart." I felt offended. I thought I was smart. My mother once said I was smart. All of my friends thought I was smart. I did really well on my SATs. Her eyes got really big and I turned to see what she saw. Bernie was throwing a punch and I fell to one knee and grabbed his arm when he missed. If I were smart what would a smart guy do? Bernie was lifting me off the ground with one arm. I let go and when my feet touched the ground again I hit him in the balls. Bernie said, "What'd you do that for?" I was scared. I hit him again and this time he bent over like he was in slow motion. When his body was bent in a 90 degree angle I punched him in the ear. There was no sound. Absolutely nothing until Bernie roared and stood up straight with blood draining from his ear and his fists clenched.

The brown-haired woman said, "You're not too smart." I looked at her like she didn't make sense. "Are your hands clean?"

■ ● ■

I examined the palms and then the knuckles. She grabbed my hands and turned them over. "No blood. Then you should run." She was right. I started running with her beside me. My head hurt, my legs were tired, but I knew Bernie was right behind me. I looked at her and asked, "Why are you running?"

She glanced at me but kept right on going and then said, "To catch up with the llamas."

"Why?" I thought. Fuck Bernie. I stopped and turned around. Bernie was nowhere to be seen. Everything was dark except the stars. When I turned back I could see the brown-haired woman still running with two llamas on each side of her. She was running into a sunset. It was still light. I looked behind and it was pitch black except for the stars. I turned back toward the llamas and it was light and there was a beautiful red-orange and pink sunset. Cool. This is very cool. I could hear a car. I turned back and under the stars I could see headlights coming. There was something wrong with the engine. It was knocking.

When I came to, the sun was going down. I was tied up again with tape over my mouth. At least my pants were up and someone was knocking at the door. I tried to make sounds through the tape but that wasn't working. I looked around to see if I could knock something to the floor. I couldn't. I was just about to bang my head on the floor when I heard voices out in the hall. I couldn't make out anything they said until I thought I heard my name. Then I heard footsteps fading away. I started to cry. I was going to die somewhere tonight for no reason that I could imagine. I wanted to scream "fuck" over and over but my mouth couldn't make anything close to that sound. I lifted my head and stared through my tears. I was stunned. I turned my head and rubbed my eyes against my shoulders. I looked again. Over behind the couch the woman with the red shoes had been added to the pile. One shoe was on the floor and the other red

■ ● ■

shoe almost glowed on her foot.

I was suddenly calm. Why wasn't I on the pile too? Why was I still lying here while there were four dead bodies behind the couch. Maybe I wasn't going to die. Maybe that had been Andy out looking for me. That's why I thought I heard my name. Andy was going to find me, but I had to find a way to make noise when he came back. I knew he would come back.

I heard the key in the lock and the door swung open. Two men entered the room and looked around. Then they both looked at me.

"Good. They got him."

"Yeah. Looks like they got him good. Look at the swelling on his jaw."

"What happened to you, fella? I didn't think the committee could get that rough."

"Somebody did. Maybe he gave them more trouble than they thought he would."

They both pulled out guns.

"We're going to untie you and then take you some place with us, okay?"

I nodded my head.

"Good. I'm going to take this tape off your mouth and you're going to stay silent. Right?"

I nodded again. He ripped the tape off and it hurt. I started to lick my lips and stopped. They were really dry and rough.

"Sorry. But I need to use the bathroom. I'm thirsty."

"I guess we can accommodate that. We don't want you peeing on the car seat. Right?"

I nodded. Then the knocking started. Andy! It had to be Andy.

"Who the fuck is that?"

One of the gunmen approached the door. Somebody

knocked again. As soon as he cracked the door I hollered "Andy, look out!" The gunman next to me backhanded me with his pistol. His partner flung open the door to a guy about 5'5 who had both hands up in front of his face, cowering, while staring right at me. The gunman at the door grabbed him by the shoulder and pulled him violently into the room.

"Get in here goddamn it!"

The man stood in the middle of the room still cowering, if you can stand up straight and still cower.

The gunman next to me said, "Well Andy, why are you here?"

"I'm...I'm not Andy."

"Your buddy here called you Andy. You must be Andy."

"But I'm not. I'm from the second floor and I'm looking for George."

My gunman started laughing. "Well, you found him. I'm George."

The terrified man got wide-eyed. "But you're not George. Panic seemed to ooze from his face instead of sweat. "At least you're not the George I know. We were gonna play cards."

"Well Andy, we're going to go for a car ride instead."

This was turning worse by the second. I had been drugged twice, raped, knocked unconscious and now I was going to die with someone I didn't know, and on top of it all I was going to die without knowing why.

"I still have to piss", I whispered.

George shook his head and took out a knife. I tried to roll away but there was nowhere to roll to. George started laughing again. "I ain't killing you here, stupid. Lie still and I'll cut the ropes." George looked at his partner and said, "Do you believe these guys. Andy came to save his partner, but for the life of me I don't know how he was going to do it."

"But I'm not Andy."

■ ● ■

George's partner started to laugh and he pushed the man I thought was Andy over toward the pile of bodies.

"Oh God! Oh God! Oh God…"

"Shut up!"

"Oh God…"

George looked at the pile and said, "That's quite a collection. Andy…if you say one more thing we'll just drop you on top of it."

Why wouldn't they do that anyway? What difference could two more bodies make?

"Get up and use the bathroom. Wow…what a face."

I stumbled toward the bathroom with George right behind me. I picked up the toilet seat and George started laughing. I could hear George's partner talking.

"What the fuck are you doing? Sick?! Don't you fucking dare get sick in here you bastard! Stand up straight goddamn it! Hey!"

Then a gun went off. I turned my head in time to see George turn his head toward the living room. I slid my hand into the towels and grabbed Mojica's knife. George took a step toward the living room and I came out of the bathroom as fast and hard as I could. I drove the blade into George's back as deep as I could and kept pushing him toward his partner. The fake Andy had a gun in his hand.

"Shoot em' again! Shoot em' again!"

George's partner was shot in the right arm. It was dangling at his side. He pulled the gun from his right hand with his left and started shooting at me. George was heavy now and I could feel the bullets slamming into his body. I rammed George's body into his partner and we fell on the sofa. I thought I heard George make a gasp for air. His partner was trying to get an angle to shoot me, but I kept trying to push George onto his partner's left arm and the same time pull the knife out of George's back.

■ ● ■

The Andy substitute was just standing there.

"Help me!" No response.

The knife finally came out and I started stabbing as fast as I could. The gun went off again as I hit him in the eye with the blade sinking up to my wrist. Everyone stopped moving. I was lying on top of two bodies, breathing harder than I ever had in my life. The bodies under me weren't breathing at all.

I suddenly heard my almost saviour say, "Are you okay?"

"Who are you?!"

"I'm Dick. Dick Brautigan."

"Why the hell didn't you shoot him again?"

"I only had one bullet."

"What?!" He looked very sincere. "What in the hell are you doing here?"

He cleared his throat and kind of cocked his head toward the floor.

"A man offered me $250 to come up here and talk to a woman. I turned him down and then I got curious about it. So I guess I was daydreaming and found myself at the door."

I looked him up and down and then said, "How come you only had one bullet?"

Brautigan opened his mouth to speak when we both heard very large footsteps coming down the hall. I motioned to Brautigan to follow me and I led him to the bedroom and out onto the fire escape. As I went out the window I heard the door open and a choking sound. I was pretty sure it was Bernie. I closed in behind Brautigan and told him to hurry up.

"The guy upstairs is a monster."

Brautigan was out of breath by the time we got to the ground, but he managed to get out, "who is he?"

"He's Bernie. You don't want to meet him. You notice my face? That's Bernie."

■ ● ■

We were walking from Susan Hart's building pretty fast and Brautigan was out of breath.

"You know Dick, there's really no reason for you to be with me. No one alive knows you were up there."

Brautigan huffed out, "You're right. Maybe I'll stay right here."

"Look…I'm gonna take off. Thanks for the one bullet. I'll look you up." I looked back and then started to run. I took exactly four steps, tripped over uneven sidewalk and fell on my knees.

"Hey. You alright? Let me help you up." Brautigan had me by the arm and on the way to my feet I noticed my pants had holes in both knees and blood was staining the edges of the tears.

"Motherfucker!" I started running again and in about fifteen minutes jogged past Eddie's diner. The street lights made the city look pretty in a gloomy sort of way. I started wondering how bad I was if I noticed how the city looked when I was panicked that I was about to be murdered. By the time I was in eyeshot of the building our offices were in, I had slowed to a very difficult fast walk. My lungs were burning. I was soaked in sweat. The air had gotten very cold or I was just scared. I started wondering why I hadn't stopped in the diner and called Andy to meet me. Maybe Andy wasn't in his office and the idea of Bernie meeting up with me alone anywhere made me realize the best thing I could do was keep moving.

I went into the lobby of our building and Ivars, the night manager, whistled when he saw me.

"Vaht the hell happen ta ya?! Ya need a doctor?"

He was staring at my stomach. When I looked down I saw it was covered in blood. Jesus! I felt my stomach and realized it was George's blood. A lot of it.

"I'm okay."

"No you not. Ven ya get upstairs look in ta mirror. I guarantee ya not okay."

I grimaced. "Ivars! Just get me the fuck upstairs!"

He guided me to the last elevator in the bank. He punched four and as we rose, so did my nausea. When the doors opened I stepped out and said "Thanks." As the door was closing I heard Ivars, "Look in ta mirror."

I bent over and put both hands on my knees. I was staring at the yellow and green floor tile and I thought I was going to pass out. I stood up and shook my head. It hurt like hell. I started moving down the hall to the office. All of the lights were on. I went into the office lobby and went for the water cooler. The water felt good and then I thought I might throw up. I heard Andy say, "Where've you been all day?" I turned around, looked at him and walked into my office.

"What the fuck happened to you?!"

I sat down in my chair. Andy came in right behind me and stood on the other side of my desk looking me up and down. Sharp came in and his eyes got big.

"Who did this to you?"

Andy looked very upset and said, "Are you bleeding?! Is that your blood?!" Mojica came in and just stared with an open mouth. I looked at them one at a time.

"Does anyone have some alcohol or a joint?" Silence. Then Mojica said "Yeah. I've got one rolled." He left my office for his and then we all paused because we heard the elevator doors open and someone, or someones, were coming down the hall toward the office. Andy turned and looked at his watch.

"Kind of late for a customer."

Sharp piped in with "Maybe it's the cops."

I opened my desk drawer and stuck my hand in it. The main office door opened and all 350 pounds of Bernie came through it followed by the non-descript woman with the brown hair, Susan

Hart.

I yelled, "Look out!" and I stood up and put four bullets in Bernie's chest. His right knee buckled and he tilted. He looked around with concern on his face and hit the floor so hard the windows rattled. The brown-haired woman stood perfectly still looking down at Bernie. Then she looked at me. A smile, a soft, gentle, real smile spread across her face. My next slug hit her square in the forehead and her smile stopped.

■ ● ■

Drift

The city seemed dark to me. I hadn't passed many people after leaving the bus station. I was hoping I'd be able to figure out where I could make some money. I was thinking it might be Main St., if I could find it. I sure wasn't going to make any money over by that bus station. Cops everywhere.

After about ten blocks I saw a shiny metal diner with a green and yellow neon sign that said "Last Cap r Diner." It looked like somebody put the diner right in the middle of the street, but then I could see that the street I was on ended and you had to go either right or left. The diner windows looked like they were about eight feet off the ground and one of them had a red flashing sign that said "Open 24 hours." I kind of was hoping that would be a good place to try to make a little money. Then I saw the man running and almost hopping down the sidewalk. He kept looking back behind him and when he got close and ran beneath the street lamp I could see his face was all busted up and it looked like he was bleeding to death. He went by kind of fast, even though he was way out of breath. I watched him run and stagger down the street and then I saw the other guy staring at me.

■ ● ■

I knew that stare. If I stood out here for a little bit I was pretty sure he was going to ask for something. Then maybe I could get something to eat besides scrambled eggs and toast. Up in the diner window there was another sign that said "Breakfast all day $1.09." That would leave me with twenty-eight cents. The diner looked really clean. Maybe I was in the wrong part of town. But I knew that stare.

I crossed the sidewalk and dropped my bag right next to the diner wall. I turned around and leaned my back against the metal. Then I looked over at the guy staring at me.

"You got a cigarette?"

Now he smiled, but not at me. It was more like, "okay, so we're going to do some business." He walked over to me and stood about two feet away.

"So you got a cigarette?"

"Not for you."

I looked away from him, but he kept staring at me. I hated this routine.

"How much?"

This was the really stupid part. I kind of hesitated before speaking. I looked up and down the street before I spoke.

"How much for what?"

He started to laugh a little and then stopped.

"How much for what…how much for you to suck my dick?"

"Ten dollars."

"Ten dollars?! All I have to do is walk fifteen minutes down the street and I can get my dick sucked for five dollars."

"So go wherever you go and let some scuzzie suck you off for five dollars."

He didn't say anything at first. He just kept staring. Then he threw his cigarette on the ground and crushed it with his foot.

"Who the fuck could you call scuzzie?" Then he was quiet

■ ● ■

again and I was wishing he'd just go away.

"Okay. Ten dollars."

"Let me see the money."

"Not until I see your lips on my dick down that alley over there."

"You ain't seein' nothin' until I see ten dollars."

He stared at me again real hard. God I wished he'd just go away. He pulled his wallet out and handed me two fives. I made a big deal of putting them in the back pocket of my jeans and then bent over and picked up my bag.

"Which way?"

He started walking in the same direction the beat-up man had gone. This was a mistake but I followed him, switching the ten dollars to a front pocket of my jeans. We passed a couple of buildings and he stopped at an alley.

"In here, cunt."

Jesus. I needed the money and I followed him in. It wasn't as dark as I thought it was going to be.

"Right here." He leaned against the alley wall. "Well…"

"Well what?"

"Don't be stupid! Unzip my pants and get busy."

Let me get this over with and go get something to eat. I put my hand inside his BVDs to grab his dick. I thought he might already be hard but he wasn't. I bent over and put my mouth around his dick and he started to grow. He put his hand on the back of my head and I knew I had to get my hand around the base of his cock so he couldn't try to shove the whole thing in my mouth when he came. I didn't want to be out in this alley gagging on this jerk's dick right before I ate. I could feel his hand start to put pressure on me to get more of his dick in my mouth. He was rubbing my back now and his hand was sliding down toward my back pocket. My pocket was empty and I had to be

■ ● ■

ready to run if he went ape-shit or something.

I pulled harder and just like I thought, he was going to try to shove his whole dick in my mouth. I pulled harder because he was going to cum.

"Swallow me baby…swallow all of it…you…you…fucking bitch!..swallow…

He relaxed and I grabbed his pants and pulled them all the way down. I snatched up my bag and started to run out of the alley. He tried to grab me and I could feel his hand fly past my head. I ducked and kept going.

"You fucking bitch!"

Then I heard him laugh. I ran down to the diner and stopped at the stairs to see if he was close behind me, but he hadn't come out of the alley yet. I climbed up three or four steps and pulled open the door. A guy was on the pay phone talking about a horse race. He never turned to look at me. I turned left and took two more steps up and pulled open another door. The diner was deserted except for two old people in a booth down at the far end and one guy sitting at the counter. There was a waitress a few stools down filling sugar jars. I passed the guy at the counter and took a seat about three stools away. The waitress turned around slow, and without looking at me asked if I wanted a menu.

"Yes, please."

The man at the counter glanced at me and then looked back down at the paper he was reading. The guy who was on the phone came in.

"Hey Phyll…give me a coffee to take home."

The waitress filled a paper cup and put a top on it. The guy put thirty-five cents on the counter.

"Thanks Phyll." He left.

"What'll you have, hon?"

"I'll take a cheeseburger with onions…a…a cherry coke."

■ ● ■

"Want fries?"

"No. Just the cheeseburger." Phyll walked away and then started hollering through the kitchen window.

"Eddie! One burger in the sun with onions!" The man at the counter started laughing.

"I thought a burger with tomato on it was in the sun, Phyllis."

"You're in here enough that by now you should know that's a California. When the hell are you gonna learn somthin' anyways?"

The man laughed some more and looked at me. He shook his head and looked back down at his paper.

"Phyllis…could I get some more coffee? Or could I have a heater on my java?"

"Ya want another cup of coffee or what?"

"Yeah…but can it be hot this time?"

The waitress poured the man his coffee. He turned the page of his paper and the waitress put a plate in front of me with my cheeseburger, some coleslaw and a pickle on it. I hadn't eaten since yesterday and I took a bigger bite than I should have and kind of choked. The man with the paper got up and started patting me on the back. The waitress was holding my cherry coke and looking at me like when was I going to stop the commotion or at least choke to death.

"Try some of this and wash it down. Eddie's a good cook so go slow and enjoy it."

I had tears in my eyes, but I managed to swallow and take a sip of my coke.

"Thanks."

"Phyllis is right. Eddie makes good food. I've never heard anyone complain about it." The guy sat back down.

I reached for the ketchup and heard the door open. I saw Mr. Ten Dollars coming through the door and right toward me.

■ ● ■

"Get up. You're coming with me." He grabbed my arm and started to pull.

"I ain't going with you." I sounded like a whining cat.

"Get up. You owe me ten dollars." I tried to pull away from him but I knew he was going to win. Maybe I'd just go with him.

"She's not going anywhere. Take your hands off her."

"This is got nothing to do with you. She owes me ten dollars."

"I don't care if she owes you a hundred dollars. Take your hands off her."

"You better go back to your business."

The man stood up and took a couple of steps toward us. I held onto the ketchup bottle like it was anchoring me to the counter. My ten dollar trick let go.

"So what are you gonna do gimpy?" It looked like the man with the newspaper had one leg shorter than the other. He didn't look afraid, but now I was, so I slid two more stools away. I looked at my left hand. It seemed like I was squeezing the hell out of the ketchup bottle, but I couldn't stop.

"Let's go outside so we don't mess up the diner."

"Naw. Let's do something right here because I'm getting my ten dollars."

"You're getting nothing but trouble and you can get that out-side and we don't have to mess up the diner."

"Fuck you! What do you think about fuck you."

"Hey!" I turned around so fast I almost fell off the stool. The cook from out back was standing right behind me.

"Get out of the diner before I call the cops."

"Go back in the kitchen pops, and if you call the cops you're gonna get hurt." He turned back to the man with the limp. "And you sit the fuck down gimpy."

I felt the ketchup bottle leaving my hand.

"Hey!!"

■ ● ■

My trick just said "what" and didn't turn his head. The ketchup bottle hit him right on the side of his face. He stumbled a little and went down on one knee.

"You look at me when I'm going to hit you with a ketchup bottle you son of a bitch." The cook put the ketchup bottle back on the counter. "Good glass. Didn't even break." The cook started to go back to the kitchen.

"Phyllis, did you call the cops?"

"No."

"Why the hell not?!"

"I thought you'd handle it."

"Well I still don't want him in here."

"Christ Eddie…look what you done. He's bleedin' all over the place."

My trick stood up and started screaming, "I'm gonna get you for this!"

The cook charged out of the swinging doors and then Mr. Ten Dollars started to run out of the diner.

"If you come back the only thing you're going to get is another headache, stupid!"

The trick was gone and we were all looking at the door waiting for something to happen. It didn't and the cook turned around and looked at Phyllis.

"Did you call the cops yet?"

"No."

"Jesus Christ, Phyllis! Why not?"

"Cause you were handling it."

"Tell Brady to mop the floor when he comes in."

I heard a voice behind me and jumped about ten feet. When I turned it was the old man and old lady.

"That was exciting, but can we have our check now?"

Phyllis looked embarrassed.

■ ● ■

"Oh my God! I'm sorry. I forgot you were over there. Do you need anything else?"

"Nope. Just the check."

I kind of crawled back over to my food. The man with the newspaper was smiling at me. I shrugged my shoulders and started to eat again. Slow. The two old people left and the waitress went down to clean their booth. A young kid came out of the kitchen with a mop and started to clean up the floor. The man with the paper moved over to the stool next to mine.

"Do you really owe that guy ten dollars?"

I leaned away from him.

"Noooo…"

"How do you know him? He a friend of yours?"

"No. I don't know him." The man was looking at my plate.

"We were outside talking. He's a jerk."

The cook came out of the kitchen and walked right at me.

"If you're working out there I don't need your shit in here. If you're working these guys I don't want you coming in here. I don't need that kind of trouble."

"I'm not."

"She's okay, Eddie."

"Uh-huh."

The cook turned away and went back to the kitchen. I started eating again really, really slow. The guy next to me folded his hands on the counter and was looking at them.

"Mind if I walk you home?"

I glanced at him.

"I can make it on my own."

"Well, yeah…maybe. What if Mr. Toughguy is out there waiting for you?"

I didn't say anything.

"I thought you might feel better having some company."

■ ● ■

"I handled guys like that before."

"I'm sure you have. Well, if you're sure. I'll see you then." He got up, walked over to his coffee, and finished it off standing. Then he threw a dollar bill on the counter.

"Take it easy Phyllis. Tell Eddie to be careful."

I stared at the dollar bill and wondered how he could leave such a big tip. I finished my cheeseburger and sucked up the last of my cherry coke. I made a noise so loud that the waitress turned around. I felt kind of stupid and said, "I guess I'll pay up." I left a quarter tip and started to get nervous about going out on the street, but I thought my trick probably went to the hospital.

"Be careful out there, hon." I turned around and smiled at the waitress.

I went out the first door, down the two steps, and stood on the landing next to the pay phone. I looked at my reflection in the next door for a couple of seconds. My hair needed washing. I had to get out of this sweatshirt. One sleeve was kind of dirty. Then I tried to see through the glass for anyone waiting on the street. I took a deep breath and pushed through the outside door and went down the steps. I turned left, away from the alley and started walking. I didn't really know how big this city was, but I'd have an idea by morning. I passed about three storefronts before I saw his reflection in a window. He was across the street and he was following me. I made a left at the corner and half way down the block I crossed the street. I walked fast to the next corner thinking I should have gone back to the diner. I made a right and started running. In just a couple of seconds I heard someone running behind me.

"Hey! Hold up!"

How did he catch me so soon?! I stopped and turned. I wished I had a knife.

"Why're you running?" He looked around. "Did you see that

■ ● ■

jerk again?"

"Oh shit. It's only you."

He started laughing.

"Yep…It's only me." He laughed some more. "Why are you running?"

"I thought that creep was you."

He looked back toward the corner.

"When did you think you saw me? I heard someone running and I turned around and saw you turn the corner."

"That wasn't you back by the diner?"

"Probably not."

Maybe I could make some money from this guy. I didn't get the feeling he wanted anything, but maybe I could talk him into it.

"Maybe I should walk you home now. What d'ya think?"

I shrugged and looked around.

"I'm not from here. I'm not kind of sure where I'm going. I thought I'd just walk until I can get a bus out of here."

"So let me walk you to nowhere."

"I don't know. I do better when I'm alone. I don't like crowds."

He started laughing again.

"So Eddie was right."

"Who's Eddie?"

"Eddie owns the Last Caper Diner where you tried to choke yourself to death. He swings the really mean ketchup bottle"

I didn't know what to say. I didn't really know where I was, but I was getting a pretty good feeling that I wasn't going to get anything out of Mr. Limp.

"What's your name?"

I pushed the hair back from my face and wondered for a second if I should tell him anything.

"Sharon."

■ ● ■

"Well Sharon, let me walk around with you for a while. If you think you find someone more interesting, I'll just go home."

He started walking toward me and I shied away from him. He smiled and just walked right on past me. His limp wasn't as bad as I thought. I had to walk fast to catch up to him.

"So Sharon, I'm Bryce. Bryce Jacob."

"Bryce? What kind of name is Bryce?"

"The kind of name Scottish beatniks give to a son. You don't like Bryce?"

"I don't know. I never heard it before."

"What kind of name is Sharon?"

"What d'ya mean? Just a regular name."

I got the feeling he was walking somewhere in particular.

"Are we going somewhere? I thought we were kind of going nowhere."

He started laughing again and it pissed me off.

"Why are you laughing? Am I funny or something?"

"No Sharon. I wasn't laughing at you. I was laughing at the juxtaposition of us going somewhere that is actually nowhere."

I had no idea what he thought was funny, but the idea of us going somewhere that was nowhere kind of made me feel strange.

"Kind of like 'Nowhere Man,' right?"

He looked at me kind of weird. I didn't say anything and just kept walking along with him. I saw some lights up ahead and then realized we were getting close to some bars. One of them had yellow and orange lights like an old time movie theater. I liked the way it looked.

"You like the Beatles?"

"Sure. Everybody likes the Beatles don't they?"

"No. Not everybody. I do, but I like Jimi Hendrix better."

"He's cool. Too bad he died. How'd you get that limp? Were

you born that way?"

He stopped walking and started staring at something. I started looking around to see what he was staring at.

"Vietnam. I got shot in the leg and shot in the shoulder. I have a metal rod in my left leg that seems to be going bad. I'll probably need another operation. I'm putting it off as long as possible."

"I'm sorry Bri...Brian...what's your name again?"

He started laughing again like everything I said was funny.

"Well I'm sorry. We just met back there."

"Bryce. My name is Bryce."

What the hell was so funny. Every time I said something he started laughing. Did he think I was a clown or something?

"Let's go in Calhoun's. Sometimes they have a good band playing in there."

With all the lights outside I guess I expected more inside. It was just another regular bar. The band wasn't playing, but they had all of their equipment on stage. We went up to the bar and sat on stools. Bryce ordered us Schlitz beer. I had heard Schlitz was terrible, but I thought this was pretty good. The band started playing and they were okay and the place was filling up.

"I gotta go. Thanks for walking me, but I gotta go."

"Saw someone more interesting? So take it easy, Sharon. Nice meeting you."

I had to make some money and there were a couple of dorks I thought might give it up. I was right so I left with them for a while. But after that it was real slim pickings. About two hours later when I went back into the bar, there was Bryce still sitting on the same stool.

"You're still here."

"Listening to the band. How's business?"

"What business?"

■ ● ■

"That slow, huh?"

"What's it to you?!" This Bryce guy could really piss me off.

"You're right. What's it to me. Did you make enough to get out of town?"

I wanted to tell him to mind his own shit, but he asked so matter of fact like, I just said "no."

"Well Sharon, here's my proposition. I'll give you one hundred dollars to spend the night at my place. Then you'll have enough to get away from here."

"What time is it?"

Bryce started laughing so hard I thought he was going to fall on the floor.

"It's fucking 1:30 a.m. You're trying to figure out if you can make more money out here or more money with me. Do you need a few minutes to figure it out? This place closes at 3 o'clock. That bit of information may help your calculations."

He really pissed me off this time, but he kind of scared me too.

"I need to see the…"

"You have to shower, though."

"What?!"

"Look kid, I'm not trying to be rude, but you need to get some of that trail dust off you. Might help business."

So first he pissed me off. Then he scared me. Now I was just plain embarrassed.

"We're not doing anything. You're going to shower and then we're going to sleep."

Now I was really worried he was crazy.

"For one hundred dollars?!"

"I don't have all of the money on me. The rest of it is back at my apartment. I can let you have forty right now."

He picked up his beer and finished it off. Then he got down

■ ● ■

off his stool and smiled.

"Coming?"

The way to his apartment was the way we came to the bars. Bryce's apartment was only a couple of blocks from the diner. I was kind of surprised by that, but I didn't know why. It was up on the second floor and it was very clean. But not like somebody dusted every day. He had real paintings on the walls and books stacked up on the floor. His kitchen table had a really cool red and white tablecloth. He said it was from Guatemala and he laughed when I told him I knew where that was. Then he threw me a towel and big t-shirt.

"You can try to wash some of your things out in the sink. If we hang them on a rack by the window they should be dry by morning."

The shower was great. The front of the t shirt said "Baltimore Bullets." When I came out of the bathroom 'Bitches Brew' was playing. I was drying my hair with a towel and Bryce said that he was going to shower and that my money was on the kitchen table. I went to get my brush from my bag and instead of just picking it up I knocked it on the floor. Everything went everywhere. Bryce picked up my lipstick and said "nice shade." I took it from him and then he picked up my prescription. He held it up and I tried to grab it but he pulled his hand away and started reading the label.

"Give that to me."

"Clozapine. Hmmm." He shook it. "Empty. How bad do you need this stuff? This is usually for schizophrenics. Are you a schizophrenic?"

"I can get it refilled tomorrow. And no, I'm not schizo."

"How long since you last took it?"

"None of your business. I don't know. Just give it to me." He gave me the bottle and then started picking other things off the

■ ● ■

floor.

"You know Sharon, you actually have beautiful hair."

He said it so weird, I didn't know if I should be mad or embarrassed.

When Bryce got into bed I could see the scar on his leg. He laid down on his back and I was sitting cross-legged on my pillow.

"This is a big bed."

"Uh huh."

"This is a nice apartment."

"Thanks."

"You get a lot of girls up here?"

He didn't answer for a while and then he said "no." I layed down and put my hand on his chest.

"We're going to sleep."

"We don't have to."

"Yes we do."

We were both quiet for a while and I heard a truck go by.

"Do they still hurt?"

"What?"

"Your scars."

"Sometimes."

"Can I feel the one on your shoulder?"

I put my hand under his t-shirt and slid it up to his neck. I could feel the edge of it and I moved my hand across it. He grabbed my hand.

"That's enough."

"That's a big scar but you don't have to be ashamed of it."

"I'm not."

"Do you want to take your clothes off?"

"No. We're going to go to sleep. I'm paying you to go to sleep."

I should have been tired but I wasn't. I wasn't so good about

■ ● ■

sleeping at night.

"Were you in the war a long time?"

"I guess I was in the war long enough or too long, so I suppose that would make it a long time."

I could hear people out on the sidewalk. It was kind of like a train going by. First you hear the whistle and the train gets closer and then you hear the wheels slamming the tracks over and over like a rumble. Then you hear the caboose go by ringing a bell; ding, ding, ding, ding, ding, until the sound fades away and you just hear crickets.

"Maybe if I get you in the mood." I started to rub his leg and he pushed my arm away. "Don't you want to feel good? Come on." I grabbed for his cock, just fooling around and I screamed. He snatched my arm and twisted it hard.

"Don't touch me! You hear me?! Don't touch me!!"

I fell off the bed when he let go. I skidded on my butt across the floor into the corner. I was scared and I didn't know what to do. I had never had this happen before. I looked over at Bryce and now he was sitting on the edge of the bed looking out the window.

"Bryce?"

He didn't say anything. I was afraid but I had to say something.

"I didn't know you didn't have a dick."

He started laughing again, but he didn't sound like anything was funny.

"Bryce…I didn't mean anything. I just didn't know."

He wasn't laughing and he wasn't talking. I had to get him to say something, but I didn't know what to ask.

"Did that happen in Vietnam too?"

I could hear him sigh. I was thinking maybe I should get my stuff and just get out of there.

■ ● ■

"Yeah. It happened in Nam. My life got completely fucked up in Vietnam."

"I'm sorry."

"Nothing to be sorry about."

"Is that thing always there? Oh shit…never mind. I don't need to know that." Stupid, stupid. Why did I have to say that? Maybe I should get out real quick.

"You want me to leave?"

"No. I paid you so you have to stay."

"I'll go if you want."

"Shut up. Shut up! Goddamn it shut up!!"

I went half way up the wall. I was ready to run and then he laid back down on the bed and pulled the covers over him. I thought he might try to kill me. What was I going to do about that?

"I'm going to lay back down with you…okay? I'll just go to sleep…okay?"

I laid back down. He had his back to me. How could I get out of here? I knew I shouldn't be here.

"I'm just going to rub your back a little…okay?"

I rubbed his back and in a little while I could tell he went to sleep. I was surprised by that as mad as he was. I knew he wanted to kill me and I had to do something. I looked at the clock over and over. Finally I knew what I was going to do. I slid out of the bed and tiptoed into the kitchen. I found a knife in a drawer with a really good point. I went back to the bed and knew I had to kill him before he killed me. His back was to me and I got up on my knees.

"Sharon? You okay?"

I laid down on the bed and hid the knife under my stomach.

"Yeah. I'm okay. I had to use the bathroom."

I heard him start to sleep again and thought soon I would have my chance.

■ ● ■

Eyes

I sat down and put my gun on the desk. Nobody said anything. Andy, Mojica and Sharp were staring at me. Then, like they were the Rockettes, they all turned and stared at the two bodies on the floor. Andy put his hands on his hips and shook his head. Mojica was the first one who really moved. He disappeared from view for a second and when I saw him again he tossed a couple of pairs of latex gloves to the other two. While Andy and Sharp were putting their gloves on, Mojica went down on one knee and started frisking Bernie. He came up with Bernie's piece. Andy put his hand out and Mojica gave him the gun. Andy turned around toward me. "Move to your right." I must have been in a daze because I didn't respond. Andy yelled at me, "Move over that way!" Andy pointed and without getting up I rolled my chair a few feet to my right. Andy lifted his arm to shoot.

Mojica said, "Higher, Andy." Andy lifted his arm higher and then shot my desk. Some papers flew up in the air. He gave the gun back to Mojica. Mojica put the gun in Bernie's hand and pointed it at my desk and pulled the trigger. A second shot hit the wood front, tore through it and ended up in the wall.

Sharp was checking out the woman.

■ ● ■

"I don't think she has a weapon."

Mojica nodded, stood up and disappeared again for a couple of seconds. He came back with a small pistol and I watched him empty the chambers. He went down on one knee again, took the brown-haired woman's hand and pressed her forefinger and thumb on each bullet. Then he reloaded the pistol and put it in her right hand. Mojica stood up and looked down at her.

"Do you think she was right-handed?"

Sharp bent over and looked at her left hand.

"Let's go with the odds. I don't see any calluses from anything on her left hand."

"Give me the gloves."

Andy and Sharp took off their gloves and handed them to Mojica. He disappeared from view again.

I knew I was losing it. I thought I was watching a TV commercial. A woman, who sounded like Lauren Bacall, said, "Coverup…when you need the wrinkles and scars of life smoothed over…Coverup." The sirens out in the distance interrupted the commercial broadcast. Ivars had probably called.

Andy walked into my office, snapped his fingers, and snapped me out of my daze.

"What's going on?"

I shrugged.

"Is that an 'I'm not going to tell you' shrug, or an 'I don't know' shrug.

"I don't know. I went over to that apartment. I was drugged, some woman sat on my cock, I was drugged again and knocked out cold. I killed two guys and there are four extra bodies behind a couch where this all took place. A short guy who was supposed to be there in my place helped me get out. I don't know why this happened or why Bernie and Bland are here."

Sharp and Mojica were leaning in the doorway listening.

■ ● ■

Andy turned to them.

"The big guy came in firing, went down, the brunette pulled a piece and she went down." Andy looked at each of us to get confirmation. We could hear the elevators coming up.

Suddenly it was like the gates opened up at Fenway Park. They were everywhere. I was asked about fourteen times if I was shot or hurt and whether that was my blood on my shirt. When I finally said it was George's, all of the cops started looking at Bernie. About five or six of them were milling around the bodies, probably wondering how that much blood could get on me after I shot Bernie. When I said that was Bernie on the floor and George was at another apartment, the cops in my office got real quiet. When I told them there were six other bodies in another apartment the quiet swept through the other offices like a wave. After a few seconds a lieutenant gave orders to have Susan Hart's apartment checked.

The first cop to start the real interrogation winced when I turned toward him and he saw my face. I noticed my eye was starting to close up. The second cop was more like fascinated.

"Ever see Mathew Saad Muhamed fight?"

I looked at this cop with as much wonder as I could muster at one o'clock in the morning and just nodded.

"You look just like him now."

The first cop tried to be all business without looking at my face.

"Did you shoot both of them?"

"Yes."

"Why?"

"Because they were going to kill me."

"Why would they do that?"

"I don't know. Do you?"

"So you just killed them."

■ ● ■

The second cop piped in.

"If this was a fight we'd probably cut you, you know what I mean?"

"Shut up Larry. We have a lot of work to do, okay?"

The second cop gave the first cop the finger. I was looking at Larry now, wondering if he was really a cop or just somebody's younger brother.

"So what made you think they were going to kill you?"

"You know...I didn't think about it very long. Maybe I should have. Maybe they didn't come to kill me. Maybe they just came to wound me. Jeez, now that I think of it, they probably just came here to wound me and Bernie missed." I stuck my left index finger in the hole on my desk. "You know, officer, what if they made a mistake while they were trying to wound me and they missed and killed me...christ, what would you do?"

Larry started to chuckle.

A lieutenant, who was apparently in charge, came into the room and said, "You two go downstairs and talk to the elevator operator. On your way out send Phelps and Jones in here. As far as I could tell with one eye, the two cops both looked sheepish. My left eye was closed now and I reached up to feel the swelling and the first cop said, "Don't touch it!" Larry said, "You need to get some cold presses on that. Panama Lewis uses a cold metal plate." The lieutenant popped up at that point sounding pretty exasperated.

"Larry, will you get the hell out of here."

The lieutenant looked me over and when the two new cops came in he said "Just give these guys your story and then we'll get you over to the hospital, okay?"

The phone rang and I heard Sharp holler from his office for Lieutenant Callahan.

The Lieutenant came back to my office and put his hand up

■ ● ■

for me to stop talking.

"You killed how many people tonight?"

"Just these two and the two gunmen at the other apartment. Why?"

"Just making it clear in my head. You didn't kill six people over there did you?"

"No. Just two. Only God kills that many people at one time…and the U.S. Army."

The lieutenant left the room and I ended up telling my story three more times to three different sets of cops. I could see they didn't believe it. While I was on the second telling, Mojica came over and leaned in the doorway. Photographer's flashes were going off. Medical personnel came in and went out. On the fourth telling, when I stared explaining about the bee farm, Mojica said, "That's enough. We need to take him to the hospital." One cop said, "We have more questions we need to ask, especially about the bee farm." Mojica yelled, "Sharp! Call our lawyer so we can get over to the hospital. These cops don't want to let us get medical attention."

Lieutenant Callahan, who seemed to be invisible most of the night, walked back into my office.

"Let him go."

One cop said I should get some ice on my forehead. Another cop said I should rub alcohol on it. Callahan said, "Forget that shit. Get a couple of shots in you. A drink will probably make you feel better."

Andy walked in.

"When will you guys be out of here? The bodies are gone. The slugs have been recovered. The photographers are gone. We've all given our stories about ten times."

Callahan got real sarcastic. "Look, we don't get eight bodies all in one night, so forgive us for hanging around for such a long time. Eight bodies in one night, all tied to one guy will make most police officers curious. So…"

Andy interrupted Callahan and through one eye I could see that Callahan was pissed.

"My partner needs to see his own doctor and get some sleep."

"And a shower."

Andy shot a look at Heeks. "Thanks Mojica…I'm sorry Lieutenant, but if you need more you're going to have to wait a few hours."

I saw Daniels, our lawyer, coming through the door. I swiveled in my chair to look out the window. Some birds I couldn't identify flew past. The sun was coming up and the city looked a little pink. I was suddenly astounded by how much bad could be fit inside twenty-four hours.

"It's going to be a beautiful morning, I think." I swiveled around and everyone was looking at me.

"What?"

Mojica said, "Sharp, let's get him to the hospital. Andy can fill in Daniels."

We were in Sharp's Barracuda heading toward County Hospital. Mojica was in the back seat complaining about the radio station. I was in front getting tired. Very, very tired.

Bernie was right in front of me. He was asking someone to let him slap me again. About five yards away a man was walking backwards. He dipped his left shoulder and waved at me with his right hand. He started singing, "Ees dee leemone, ees dee li-hime." Then I couldn't see him anymore because Bernie was in the way. I looked into Bernie's eyes and could see that he had decided to hit me without getting permission. He threw a punch at me and missed, even though I was tied with ropes to a chair. I kept moving my head and Bernie kept missing. While I was moving my head I could see we were in a warehouse. But

■ ● ■

it looked like a football field. Down at the other end of the warehouse at the five yard line, was a pile of black and white I had seen before. Somewhere down in the shadows there was a marching band. All I could hear were the drums. Really good drums.

Mojica was shaking my shoulder while the drum solo from Inna-Gadda-Da-Vida was playing on the radio.

"C'mon, man. Let's go see a doctor."

I forced myself out of the car and stood facing the doors of the emergency room, wondering if I really needed to go in. I could hear Sharp and Mojica talking about my clothes and then Sharp drove away.

Mojica and I went in and I let him do all of the talking. At first everyone was excited at seeing so much blood on me, even if it was dry. When they understood it was someone else's blood and that someone else was dead, everybody calmed down. Mojica answered some questions and I went and sat down. Just as I did a guy staggered in with a gunshot wound and fell down on the floor. A couple of orderlies and a doctor put him on a gurney and I started to think it might be a while before anyone would give me a look. Mojica sat down next to me.

"How're you doing?"

"Fine, for having a head that's twice its normal size with only one functioning eye and a headache that's bigger than the world's fair."

Mojica was looking around the room.

"Well, you've never been clever, but maybe in a week or two you'll be beautiful again...or maybe in a month or two with enough rest...or..."

"Screw you man."

"Let's just say you'll look better after a while, because I always thought you were ugly."

■ ● ■

"Your girlfriend doesn't."

"Hold on Capitan, don't push that shit."

"Okay…then let's end the conversation here with fuck you Mojica and what in the fuck do you keep trying to look at in this goddamn emergency room?"

Mojica smiled for a second and then he stopped.

"I know you're hurt now if you ask me that question. Who were those two people who came for you? Will there be more of them? How many more? Where did they come from?"

My head felt like it was turning to ice. I began to look around the emergency room. Mojica started laughing.

"Just sit still. I got it covered."

"Mojica?"

"What?"

"Fuck you."

"Watch your mouth, man. There might be kids in here with crocodile bites and shit."

"Well fuck you anyway."

"I'm glad you're feeling better, but I want to ask you a couple of serious questions. Why didn't you tell the police the name of the guy who helped you escape?"

"I couldn't see a good reason to keep him involved. I kind of feel like if I name him I might be putting him in danger. I mean somebody offered him the same deal they offered me. He had the sense to say no and I didn't. I was almost killed. Two of these people came after me at the office and I don't know why. I don't know anything and neither does he. Maybe he should just be a blank face for a while.

"You know the cops are going to be looking for him."

"Well, they'll be looking for a short guy who likes to play cards."

Sharp came into the emergency room and tossed two shirts

■ ● ■

in my lap.

"Maybe you should go to the men's room and change so you don't scare all of the women-folk and confuse the medical staff into thinkin' there's something wrong with you besides that bump on your head."

"My almost best friends…" I went to the Men's room and took off my shirts. From one eye I stared at myself in the mirror. I was a wreck. At least from the neck up. I threw some water on my face and that hurt. I wiped my face with a paper towel and that hurt. Putting my t-shirt on hurt. I looked in the mirror again and felt pretty sure that hurt too. I spit in the sink. Blood. Christ, Bernie must have loosened some teeth. I went back out and sat next to Mojica.

"The other question I had is why didn't you give the cops the name and address of the guy who hired you?"

I turned my head so I could see both Mojica and Sharp. They were both looking at me.

"I want to go get the guy myself."

Sharp turned his head away and slid down in his chair. He stretched his legs out straight and then crossed them. He crossed his arms on his chest and then whispered, "That's a bad idea."

"Look, Sharp, you don't have to be involved."

"Ahh didn't say I wasn't going to be involved. I just said it was a bad idea."

Someone touched my shoulder and I jumped. "Excuse me… we're going to examine you now. Would you please get in this wheelchair?" I could see the look of concern on the nurse's face when she saw my whole face. I shook my head and she got the idea that I wasn't going to ride. I followed her and I heard one of my best friends say "wheelchair?" and then two of my best friends started laughing. I wanted to turn around and give them the finger, but now I realized my 'daze' was clearing and I was

■ ● ■

actually in a lot of pain.

An hour later I left the hospital with a small pile of pain pills, a prescription for ice and a diagnosis of a concussion. The sun was up and it was going to be a good day. A good day for sleeping. Mojica and Sharp walked me upstairs to my apartment and we agreed that we wouldn't give any information to the press. When they left I unplugged my telephone, brushed my teeth, took a pain pill and promptly passed out in my clothes on the bed.

■

I was back in the warehouse at the ten yard line. Bernie was tied up in a red wooden chair. Down at the other end of the warehouse, in the shadows I could just make out a man dancing backwards. A woman was trying to hide behind him. I patted Bernie on the shoulder.

"Is she coming for you Bernie?"

"Maybe, but don't hit me buddy, okay?"

"Don't worry Bernie, I won't hit you."

"You did once, remember?"

"Yeah. I remember. But you were going to kill me."

"Don't kill me, buddy. Please."

"Bernie, a lot of people love violence. Killing you would be something a lot of people would love to see."

I couldn't see the woman anymore. Maybe she was hiding in the stands. I started walking toward the fifty yard line. I could hear Bernie behind me yelling, "Hey, buddy, don't kill me. You'll regret it." No I won't.

The afternoon was brighter than I expected. I walked to the bathroom expecting my head to pound in pain, but it didn't. I stood at the bathroom mirror looking at my swollen head and partially closed eye. It was much better than the morning. Now

■ ● ■

I could see a little out of my left eye. The spot where the woman with red shoes stabbed me with the needle was sore. But it was time to talk to my partners and go find Mr. Suit.

When I got downstairs I had a craving for pizza. A lot of people were on the street. Some coming home from work. Some just out because it was Spring. I decided to stop at Carl's Pizzeria before I went to the office. I didn't even know if I could chew a slice, but I'd be satisfied with sucking little pieces if they had pepperoni on them.

When I sat down at the counter Carl came over with a big smile on his face.

"Did ya get them?"

"Yeah. I got him alright."

"Ya know…you need to put a steak on that."

"No ice, huh…"

"Steak's better. I used to do some prizefightin'. Did I ever tell you that?"

"I think you did about fifty times and can I have a slice of pepperoni and a lemon-lime?"

"Coming right up." Carl threw a slice in the oven and then moved over to the cooler. "But I had one fight where I got tagged pretty good. My face got big and when I got home my sister started to cry and then she went out to get a steak for my eye. Took the swelling right down."

"Really…did you win the fight?"

"I should'a won. My corner told me to round him off. If they had told me to go knock him out I could'a knocked him out."

"So why didn't you just go knock him out?" Carl put the slice in front of me and I took a swallow of my favorite pop.

"My head was fuzzy and my corner told me to stay away from him."

The pizza was good even though my jaw was aching by the

■ ● ■

time I finished. That was when Carl whispered, "What happened up there?" I shrugged, left Carl a big tip, and went to our building. I went into the lobby and there was Ivars.

"Don't you ever go home Ivars?"

"Not today. It's been very exciting around here. Ya just missed ta last news crew. Ah'm gonna' be on T.V. tonight!"

"What for?"

Ivars looked at me like I just got off the boat.

"Ya killed some people. The news people want ta know vhat I tink."

"Oh yeah? So what do you tink?"

"If they come here to kill you, it was probably a very good idea that you kill them first."

"Ivars…what did they say when they came in?"

"Good afternoon. We are from channel…"

"No, Ivars, I meant the man and the woman last night."

"Andy ask me the same question. They did'na ask me anything. The big guy said they were takin' the elevator. When he close the door I call police. I knew there is trouble somewhere so I think maybe I can get a head start on it."

Ivars had a big smile on his face.

"Can you take me up?"

"Sure. Come on. You know, you should put something on your eye."

"Yeah, I know."

I walked into the office and saw Andy sitting on the edge of his desk talking on the phone. He waved and I went into my office. I looked at the bullet hole trying to visualize how Bernie shot at me and I plugged him three times in the chest. Self-defense all the way. Three witnesses. I didn't give them a chance. If it happened again I would have waited by the elevator and did them there instead of having them bleed in the office. I could

■ ● ■

hear the elevator coming. I stepped around my desk, opened the drawer and reached for my Colt. It was gone. The police took it and I was going into a panic. I heard Andy put the phone down.

"Andy! Do you have a gun handy?"

"Why? What's up?"

"The elevator's coming! Don't you hear it?!"

Andy came around the corner. He looked at me funny. "Yes. I hear it and it's probably Sharp and Mojica."

"But maybe not."

"Wow. Calm down." Andy reached behind his back and made a .38 appear in his hand. "Feel better? Want to hold it?"

The elevator doors opened and I could faintly hear Ivars, Sharp and Mojica joking around. Andy looked at me and shook his head.

"You're sweating. You need to calm down. We've been through worse than this."

"Yeah, but not stateside."

I sat down and watched Sharp and Mojica walk into the office. They both stood in the doorway and Mojica spoke. Andy went back to his office.

"You feeling better?"

I nodded.

"Funny…you don't look better."

"Fuck you, Mojica."

Andy hollered from the other room.

"Hey Heeks! You got a piece you can spare?"

"Sure." Mojica looked at me with a smile. "You feeling naked?"

I ran through everything that happened again for my partners. Sharp asked when we were going to drive over to see Mr. Suit. The three of them agreed that I couldn't go up to the door and they all seemed excited about going and seeing if we would get lucky. Maybe Mr. Joseph Barthelme would be home and we

■ ● ■

could find out what was going on. Or maybe I'd just kill him.

When I thought about killing him, I shuddered a little. How did I get to the stage of "let me kill somebody and everything will be alright?" Maybe I needed to see a shrink. Maybe I just needed to kill someone. I heard Sharp say we probably should hire a secretary. Andy agreed and pointed out that Casualty had renewed their contract with us. Mojica said it was fine with him and wanted to know what I thought.

"I think Joseph Barthelme will not be there. I think he is gone."

Everyone was quiet for a few seconds and then Andy said, "Daydreaming a little? We'll have to check it out. Maybe we'll be able to find out where he went, if he is gone."

When we got to Barthelme's house, Sharp went to the door and came back quickly.

"Okay, he's gone. He moved. Maybe he didn't think this escapade would turn out right, because he moved a week ago." Sharp smiled.

I said, "Is his mail being forwarded?"

Mojica thought that would have been stupid.

"Maybe not. What if he thought whatever they had going on would turn out right. So he didn't move because he was scared. He moved for another reason."

"So how does that help us find him?"

"People love free shit. Even suits."

Andy turned around to face me in the back seat.

"So?"

"So we send him something free…like a $100 dinner that he thinks he won in a contest."

"And then what? Wait for him to show up? He's not going to come back to town after all of this stuff hits the papers. If the army doesn't blow up something big, this story will probably go

■ ● ■

national."

"The dinner prize won't be in town. I'll sit there the month of June, every night, and wait for the son-of-a-bitch."

Everybody was quiet. I could hear the seat leather squeak when Andy turned back around. Then Mojica spoke up.

"You know, that just might work. I heard some cops did something like that out in California and quite a few knuckleheads showed up."

Andy and Sharp were still quiet.

Then Mojica said he thought we could use Rosita's.

Sharp frowned. "Naw, that's too close. I know a place that's perfect."

I closed my eyes for a second and the left side of my face hurt.

Andy said, "Are you okay?"

I opened my eyes and saw Andy looking at me from the rear view mirror.

"Probably not, said the one-eyed man."

We were going to use Helen's Impala because it wouldn't be noticed so easily. She wasn't real happy about it when we told her that she couldn't come with us. Just because we were using one of her cars didn't mean she could hang with us on the job. Helen looked at the four of us standing around her and said "Someday you're going to wish I was there."

Everyone but me started laughing. I was opening and closing my eye and realizing it didn't hurt so much. Then everyone started laughing again and I wondered what they were laughing about, but I laughed too, and my eye didn't hurt.

■ ● ■

Twig

"What're you doin', Twig?"

Twig didn't move at first. He was just leanin' over another pile of garbage. Every time he saw a pile of garbage he had to look in it. He was gonna be twelve years old, like me, in two months, and sometimes he acted like he was ten. Sometimes he was real embarrassing, but he was my best friend.

"Twig, come on."

Twig reached down into the garbage and pulled out a pipe. At least it looked like a pipe.

"Con! Look at this! Do you think it might be gold?"

"Let me see that."

"It might be pure gold…"

"It's not gold or it'd be heavier."

"Well maybe it's gold on the outside."

"Ya mean gold-plated."

"Yeah! What do you think?"

"Twig, you're crazy. Why would someone throw gold out in the garbage?"

Twig took the pipe from me and started swinging it around.

"It's shiny though isn't it?"

■ ● ■

"Yeah. It's shiny. Now c'mon and let's go get those sodas and get back to the tent."

I started walking down the alley by myself and finally Twig caught up, still waving the pipe around like a sword.

"Con. You know if I put tape on this end this could make a good weapon."

"Yeah." Twig was always making weapons. His closet was always full of them until his mother made him throw them out once a month. Then he would hide half of them under the front porch. One time his father found them there while we were standing out in front of his house. His father started yelling about all the junk under there. I thought Twig was gonna get it good. Then his father picked up one of the pieces and sat down on the front steps. His father stared at this stick and he turned it over a couple of times. I thought he was gonna hit Twig with it and then he said, "This might make a good weapon." And he got up and went in the house with it.

Twig was the skinniest kid I knew. He was always eating but he was always real skinny. I think that's why he was always making weapons. I think he was planning on gettin' revenge on all the guys that made fun of him and pushed him around. Well, used to push him around. I got into a couple of fights because of Twig and I guess guys figured that if they made trouble with Twig, they made trouble with me. Really it was kind of like I got mad because they were makin' fun of me for being friends with Twig. Well, mostly they kind of stopped pushing Twig around so much after the fights. I was glad 'cause I don't like fightin'. Some guys like fightin' for some reason. I guess it makes them feel like a big man or somethin'. But some guys fight even if they're gonna lose. Over nothin'. I don't get why guys would fight over nothin'.

Like Danny Patterson. Him and Petey Bradley were talking

■ ● ■

about their mothers and Petey said, "Your momma so fat she hurt the economy." That didn't make no sense.

Danny's mother ain't fat, but Danny said he was fightin' Petey. Everybody knew Petey was gonna win, but Danny fought him anyway.

Twig didn't fight anybody. He'd just mumble "Wait 'til one day." I think I heard him say that more than anything else.

We were almost at the end of the alley. We could cut through the back of Fortunato's and go to the soda machine outside Paley's garage and my parents would never know we were gone. I looked back down the alley and Twig was looking at another pile of garbage.

"C'mon Twig! Yer slowin' us up."

Twig kept starin' at the pile and then he said, "Conrad."

"What?! You find more gold?"

"You better see this."

Twig never called me 'Conrad' except in school, so I walked over to Twig's garbage pile and partly covered in the garbage was a woman. She wasn't moving.

"Con...do you think she's dead?"

"I don't know Twig. We should get somebody."

All of the sudden Twig poked her with his pipe and she moved. I jumped back. Twig was over against the wall on the other side of the alley in about one second. We were both kind of frozen, but somebody had to do somethin' so I stepped up close to her.

"Lady, can you hear me?"

"Con, is she alright?"

"Jesus Christ Twig! 'Course she's not alright. If she was alright would she be lyin' in this pile of garbage?"

"Ask her if she's alright, Con."

"Shut up, Twig!"

■ ● ■

"Help me."

I could barely hear her say it, but I jumped back away from her and then I felt stupid. Twig walked back over to her and was staring down at her. He wasn't sayin' anything though so I said "Lady?"

"Help me." She lifted her arm up and I took her hand. I thought she wanted me to help pull her up, but when I pulled she moaned and went limp. I let go of her hand and her arm fell back in the garbage.

"Connnn…"

"We need to get help."

"Con…you killed her."

I felt my stomach get funny when he said that and I was really scared.

"Shut up Twig! I didn't kill her. She might not even be dead."

Twig poked her again with his pipe. I shoved Twig really hard.

"Stop that stupid! We need to get help. Maybe we can find a cop car."

"There ain't none around here."

"Well we gotta find help, Twig."

"Billy Force! Let's go over to Billy Force's house. He'll know what to do."

I don't know why I did it, but I started walking toward Billy Force's house. Then I started runnin' because maybe she wasn't dead and she needed help bad. If there was one thing Twig was good at, it was runnin'. Once we started runnin' he was ahead of me the whole way. It took us about five minutes to get to Force's house. When we did, the only light on was in Billy's room.

Twig went to the side of the house and bent over and scooped up some gravel. He threw a handful up at the window. I thought the glass was gonna break.

"Twig! What the heck are ya' doin'?"

■ ● ■

"Trying to get Billy to come to the window."

"Whyn't ya' just call his name, stupid."

Twig looked at me funny, but I kind of whispered and hollered up at the window.

"Hey Billy!" I waited a couple of seconds and repeated "Hey Billy!"

Behind me I heard Twig say real low, "Wait til one day." I turned around and looked at him. Twig was staring at me. Then I heard the upstairs window slide open.

"Who the fuck is out there throwing stones at the house?"

It was Pauline. She was Billy's older sister.

"It's me, Pauline. Twig. Where's Billy?"

"Twig?! What the fuck are you doing down there?!"

"I got to talk to Billy. It's an emergency."

"Emergency?! I'm going to have Billy come down there and kick your ass for throwing stones at our house! Then you'll have a fucking emergency."

The window slammed shut and then I could hear Pauline screaming, "Get your ass up! That fucking Twig is downstairs throwing stones at my window!"

A minute later the front door opened and Billy came out pulling a T-shirt over his head. When he had it on he put his hands on his hips and looked at both of us.

"What the hell is going on? It's two o'clock in the goddamn morning!"

"It's an emergency. We found a dead woman."

"What?!

"In the alley by Fortunato's."

Billy was looking at us like we were queer.

I said, "I don't think she's dead. We need to call the police."

"I think…"

"Shut up Twig!" When Billy said 'shut up' usually you shut

■ ● ■

up. He was one of the toughest guys at school. Twig knew Billy better than I did and Twig got real quiet.

"Conrad…is she dead?"

"She moved until she tried to sit up."

"She's probably just unconscious or something."

Twig said, "Yeah, maybe."

"Twig! Shut the fuck up!"

"Billy, maybe we should just call the police."

"Not from my house. I don't want no cops over here when my Dad gets home from work. Plus, if she's just unconscious maybe she doesn't want no cops involved."

I didn't know if Billy made sense, but he made me feel better. This was Billy Force and he was fourteen. He was arrested twice. Once for fightin'. Billy was one of those guys that liked to fight. At least I understood why Billy liked to fight. It made him famous. Everybody knew who Billy Force was.

"Hey Billy. How come Pauline is in your room?"

Billy came down off the porch and walked right up to Twig. Twig took a step back.

"Because that's not my room, dummy. Me and Pauline switched rooms."

"Why?"

Billy stared at Twig and then he looked at me and then back at Twig.

"For the last fucking time, shut the fuck up Twig! And don't bring your ass over to our house throwing stones at it!" Billy looked at me again. "Why the fuck do you hang with this fucking needlehead anyway, Conrad? Jesus H. fucking Christ! Where is this woman? Let's get over there so I can get my ass back in bed before my Dad gets home."

We started walking back toward the alley.

"Maybe we should run."

■ ● ■

"Twig? Did I tell you to shut the fuck up? I'm not running half way across the East Side to help some drunk woman, who fell down, get back up."

That made me feel better than I had for the last half hour. She was probably just drunk. Billy was experienced and knew about this stuff.

When we cut through by Paley's, Twig took off runnin' toward the alley. When he turned the corner I heard Twig's pipe rattle on the ground. We both stopped. I looked at Billy and he had a really serious look on his face.

"Hold up, Con."

I looked back toward the street and saw a faint red light appear and disappear over and over. Then Twig came around the corner with a man holding his arm. I was really scared now. The man pulled Twig along with him as he came closer.

"Okay, boys. Get over here and let's have some names."

I knew it was the police and I was going to be in trouble.

"I said names."

Twig shouted. "She's dead, Con." Twig looked up at the policeman and said, "He's the one who killed her, officer. Conrad killed her."

I couldn't believe it. Twig said I killed her. Behind me, in a really quiet voice, Billy said, "Run."

I turned around and Billy was flying. So I took off too.

I was a little ways behind Billy and after two blocks I saw him turn into a parking lot.
When I caught up I couldn't see him.

"Con…over here."

I saw him crouched down by a Krowley's milk truck. I started walking over to him and Billy whispered, "Get down!" I bent over and squatted down next to him.

"That fucking Twig. You tell him if he tells the cops anything

■ ● ■

about me I'll break his balls with my Dad's claw hammer. You tell him that!"

We were both quiet for a little while, kind of listening to see if anyone was coming.

"We need to get out of here, Con. Why the hell did Twig say you killed that woman?"

"I didn't kill her!"

"No fucking clue, but what the fuck was Twig trying to do?"

"Get even?"

"What?! For what? Being the only guy on the whole east side that can stomach his ass?"

"I'm going back Billy."

"Back?! Are you crazy?"

"I won't say anything about you, but I know Twig told them everything about me. If I don't go back they'll just go to my house."

Billy and I were quiet again. He stood up for a second and looked around. Then he squatted back down.

"That fucking Twig. You tell him about my Dad's hammer. I'm not kidding. I'm going to beat it home. Good luck, Con. See you around." Billy took off running and disappeared.

I stood up and walked back. I didn't kill her but Twig was the only witness. When I got back to the alley there was an ambulance and three police cars. One cop ran over and grabbed me by the arm and started hollering.

"I caught one, Lieutenant! I caught one!"

One of the cops in a suit walked over to me and looked at me like he wanted to slap me in the face. If I was a condemned man, I wasn't gonna be scared anymore, so I just looked right back at him.

"You can let go of him, Stevens." I looked past the cop in the suit and saw Twig sitting in a cop car. He waved at me, but

■ ● ■

I didn't wave back. The cop in the suit asked me a lot of questions about who we saw walking around when we were heading towards Paley's. He wanted to know what the woman said. He asked me about Billy but I wouldn't say anything. He kept telling me to look him in the face, but I wouldn't. I was condemned. I didn't have to do nothing. He said that was okay and he called me a 'little shit.'

"Your friend, Arnold, over there told me all about him."

I jerked my head up at that because at first I couldn't remember Twig as Arnold.

The cop in the suit made another cop take us back to my house. I wasn't speaking to Twig, but Twig said, "She had beautiful brown hair when they got her out of the alley, Con." I didn't say nothin'. I just looked out the window.

When we got out of the car I looked at Twig and said "Why'd ya' tell the cops I killed that woman?"

"I thought you did, Con. I was going to tell them you killed her by accident though."

I couldn't believe how mad I was at Twig. How could he just rat me out over somethin' that wasn't true?

"Billy told me to tell you that you had better not say anything to the cops about him."

"I had to say something, Con. The cops had me."

"I didn't. I stayed quiet. Billy said that if you told the cops about him he was gonna get his father's ball-peen hammer and smash your balls so you can't walk straight."

I heard Twig whisper, "Oh shit."

We walked around the corner of the house back to the tent. Twig went in the tent and I walked back to the corner of the yard to piss in the bushes. When I got back to the tent Twig was leavin' with all his stuff. His sleepin' bag was draggin' on the ground, but didn't say nothin'.

■ ● ■

"See you around, Con. I'm going home to sleep."

I didn't say anything. I got in the tent and laid down in my sleeping bag. I was layin' on my back listenin' for crickets, but I didn't hear any. Then I started thinkin' that Twig wasn't gonna be my best friend anymore. Wait til' one fuckin' day.

■ ● ■

SUITS

The sky was turning purple and orange. The inside of Helen's Chevy Impala was quiet. Mojica was in the back seat sleeping. He could have been dead. Andy was reading some magazine. We had been here every night for almost three weeks. Mojica slept. Andy read. I stared out the window at everyone who went into the restaurant.

"Bent Larsen."

I looked over at Andy behind the steering wheel. He was staring at the magazine hard.

"What?"

"Bent Larsen. He's my favorite chess player."

"Oh yeah…why's that?"

"He's a great player and he doesn't draw all the time. He also wears those great Danish sweaters."

"Uh-huh. I have to piss. I'm going back in the pizza shop."

Andy was looking over the top of his magazine. "Oh yeah?… what about him?" Andy pointed toward the restaurant with his chin.

I stared hard into the sunset and shadows of the four people approaching the restaurant.

■ ● ■

"Bingo!" A cold shiver ran up my back.

Andy said, "Heeks! We got business."

I told Andy I was going to make the phone call from the pizza joint. I watched the four people enter the restaurant and then I got out of the car. I leaned in the window.

"We should give them ten minutes to get settled and get their salads on the table." Andy nodded. Mojica yawned but looked wide awake.

"Check this out. Two more coming right behind them… maybe three."

I watched the pair follow the four in. The single guy went in and came back out. He looked around and left in the same direction he came from.

After I made the call I found myself standing over the toilet bowl with my hand shaking. I couldn't pee fast enough and I felt bad because this was the cleanest bathroom I'd ever seen in a Pizza shop. I kept missing the bowl. On the way out I gave the owner fifty bucks to be blind.

"I ain't seen nothin' in two or three years."

When I got outside the sky was just turning a light blue-black. Mojica was leaning against the car with a smile, wearing his sunglasses and holding a three foot long flower box under his arm. Mojica and Andy were talking about something but I didn't make out a word they were saying. Andy started the car and Mojica stood up straight.

"So, shall we?" Mojica was still smiling. I nodded and we crossed the street. Mojica said something but I really didn't hear him and just said "yep." Mojica said "okay" in a funny kind of way. I glanced at him and kept on walking.

We went into the restaurant with me in the lead. The lighting was subdued and the walls were covered with a beautiful yellow and tan wall paper that gave you the feeling you were

■ ● ■

walking through an atmosphere of yellow syrup. Everyone in the restaurant was seated next to a wall except for Barthelme's party. They were seated in the middle of the floor all laughing. Right where we wanted them to be.

I walked straight up to his table. Barthelme saw me and grew straightfaced. He forced a borrowed smile onto his face and tried to ignore me.

"Get up."

"I'm having dinner."

There was movement to our right. Mojica pulled his sawed-off pump out of the flower box. I heard him say, "Contemplation is the best thing you two can do right now." I could feel the two bodyguards relax. One of the women at the table squealed "Oh my God!" Mojica reached across the table for a baby tomato. He said "excuse me" and popped one in his mouth. Mojica seemed to be looking at a man on the other side of the restaurant. The man was watching, but just kept right on chewing and never put his fork down. I looked down at Barthelme.

"Get up."

"I'm not…"

I raised my Colt like a hammer and brought it down on Mr. Suit's forehead. Blood immediately began running down his face and he started sliding toward the floor like a strand of wilted spaghetti. I grabbed his shirt collar and began to drag him toward the door. His chair fell over and I heard Mojica say "Good tomatoes this season." He leaned over and grabbed Barthelme's jacket and together we dragged him out to the car. I got in first and then pulled Barthelme in by the collar of his shirt. Mojica jumped in the back seat with us and slammed the door. Andy pulled away from the curb slowly and then floored it.

The three of us were quiet for about ten minutes. We left the town without being stopped, with Barthelme lying on the floor.

■ ● ■

Mojica tossed me a rag.

"Wipe his face off."

"Why?"

"So the blood doesn't get everywhere." Mojica sounded annoyed.

I wiped his face and then we pulled him up onto the seat. Mojica undid Barthelme's belt and unzipped his pants. I started slapping him in the face.

"C'mon goddamn it. Wake up!"

"Don't hit him so hard or he'll never wake up."

"I don't give a damn! Wake up you bastard."

Barthelme started to move.

"Okay, c'mon. You're going to answer some questions." Barthelme moaned. "C'mon, goddamn it all!" I slapped him again and put my Colt to his forehead. "Can you feel this?" I pressed harder. Barthelme's eyes opened wide and he almost started to struggle. Mojica took his sun glasses off and put them in his front pocket.

"Getting dark out. Gosh…didn't think it was that dark yet."

"Who set this up?" Barthelme was quiet and I jabbed him with my Colt. "Who set this up? What the hell is going on?"

"I don't know."

I put Barthelme in a choke hold with my left arm. Barthelme pulled at my arm with both hands.

"Pull over." Andy slowed down and then stopped. He turned off the engine, swung around and got on his knees in the front seat and pulled out a .38.

"Okay. Let's cut his balls off."

Almost instantly Mojica made a blade appear that was so long it startled me. I snapped my head back and hit the car window. Barthelme went nuts. He was kicking and struggling like a madman until Andy hit him in the stomach. Barthelme lost

■ ● ■

his breath and Andy ripped Barthelme's pants down. He was crying now and gasping for air.

"Susan Hart hired me to get you there."

"Why?"

"I don't know." I heard cloth ripping and knew it must be Mojica slicing his way through some $100 pants. Then Barthelme jumped.

"You want your balls? Did the knife blade just cut you?"

Barthelme cried, "Oh God please!"

"Motherfucker you better tell us who hired you to hire me and why. What the hell is going on?!"

"No! Oh God no!" Mojica must have made contact again.

"Well?"

"James Sturgeon. He's part of the commission."

"What commission?"

"They were planning something. I don't know what." I could hear more cloth tearing. "I just procure things for them. They pay me. I don't know what they're doing. I don't know what they want with you."

I looked at Andy in the semi-darkness and it looked like he raised his eyebrows and then his shoulders.

"Take his shoes." One after the other I heard the shoes hit the floor of the Impala. I opened my door and pulled Barthelme out after me. He had no pants, shoes or socks on. His jacket was torn. He had blood on his shirt. I grabbed him by the tie and laid one of the best punches of my life on his jaw. He went down in the middle of the road with both hands trying to support his weight on the pavement. I got back in the car. Andy started the engine and we pulled away at about 40 mph. Mojica was looking back.

"Headlights."

I turned around. Someone was coming and then they

■ ● ■

stopped. Andy slowed down.

"Looks like they could be the lights to a Barracuda."

Andy said, "Think it's Sharp?"

I turned back around. "Better be."

"Did you make the guy across the room?"

I turned toward Mojica. "Some kind of cop?"

"Yeah…but not local. A local guy probably wouldn't have been so calm. He just kept on eating."

"FBI?"

"F something. He was too cool."

"Not the greatest bodyguards."

"Naw…but they cost money."

"I wonder if they made the guy across the room."

Andy hollered back. "So either the two bodyguards are fired, or they're probably going to come looking for Barthelme."

"I wish they would." I could feel Mojica staring at me, so I rolled down my window. The breeze felt good and I realized I was drenched in sweat. Mojica was talking but I wasn't hearing him. I was listening to the wind rush past my ears. I felt relaxed. Mojica grabbed my arm.

"What?"

"At some point we have to consider what the police response might be. Are you listening to me?"

"Yeah."

"You didn't hear a word I said."

As we passed street lamps I could see Andy glancing at me from the rear view mirror.

"Heeks…let him cool off and we'll talk back at the office." Andy and Mojica started talking again but I couldn't hear them. At one point I concentrated really hard and heard Mojica say "…just wants to kill some…" but I couldn't make out the rest. I knew they were talking about me. The breeze from the open

■ ● ■

window felt so good and the sound in my ears was so relaxing I wanted to sleep, but couldn't.

When we got to the office building an hour later, Ivars took us up. On the way he said, "You running in a race tonight?"

Mojica popped off with "He's entering menopause."

"Not vit all of the blood all over him." Ivars and Mojica laughed. Andy looked like concern was dripping off his face and puddling on the floor around him. When we got into the office Andy asked me if I felt okay.

"You just drenched your shirt and jacket. You look like you've been out running full court. Do you feel alright?"

I looked at both of them and shook my head.

"I feel like I did when you and I went across those paddy fields the first time. I can't seem to shake the feeling."

"Maybe we should call the V.A. tomorrow. Maybe…"

"They won't do shit! They got a thousand guys that can't walk! They don't need me over there!" Andy and Mojica both had their eyes locked on me. I felt foolish.

"I'm sorry. I didn't mean to bitch at you like that. The truth is…I wanted to kill Barthelme."

Andy put his hand on my shoulder. "That would have screwed things up if you had."

"I know. That's why I didn't."

Mojica looked at me, smiling. "All that time out in bumfuck would have been wasted."

I snapped my head toward Mojica. "That's the best three weeks of sleep you had since we've been back in the states, you bastard!"

Mojica grinned. "See, Andy. He'll be okay. He needs to get out of that bloody, rancid shirt though. I think I have one that'll fit in my office." Out of the corner of my eye I saw Andy glance at Mojica like he didn't believe something Mojica said.

■ ● ■

I was feeling confused and a little scared. I felt like I was in a panic so I said the first thing that came to mind.

"Why does fucking Mojica have everything over there in his office? Guns, knives, clothes, reefer. Hey, Mojica! Do you have some BVDs in my size?"

"I have a pair of women's panties in yellow that would probably fit you. Everything else is too small."

I forced a deep chuckle and caught Andy staring at me with a smile on his face. Mojica slid back into my office and threw me a shirt.

"How was that tomato, really?"

Mojica laughed. "It was good. Really good."

"Do you think we'll see Sharp?"

Andy shrugged and walked out of my office for his. Mojica looked at the floor and then up at me.

"I got to get the car back to Helen. See you in the morning."

I sat down in my chair and leaned back, wondering when we'd see Sharp.

■ ● ■

Scuzzie

I woke up looking out the window. The city looked like it had probably been awake for a couple of hours already. The sky was blue and filled with wispy clouds that reminded me of a dead zebra. Someone had thrown a green army blanket on me and I realized I never changed into the clean shirt Mojica gave me the night before. I heard paper rustling in another office and I swiveled around in my chair to face my desk. The morning newspaper was sitting in the middle of it.

I picked up the paper to see if there were any headlines about us. Two articles caught my attention. One was about homicides in the city being up 210% so far this year. A Lieutenant Callahan sounded like he was in a lot of trouble because over half were unsolved. That wasn't my fault. Half of the homicides related to me I did myself and confessed to them. So fifty percent of mine were solved. The other article that got my attention was about another woman found in an alley in the downtown area. She was five-five with brown hair, about twenty-five years old. The fifth one.

I heard the elevator open and I pulled out the top drawer of my desk on the right. I slipped my hand in and felt slightly

■ ● ■

relieved to find Mojica's Colt inside. I gazed at the door and felt myself breaking into a cold sweat as Mojica came through the outer office door with three coffees pinned between his hands.

"Want a coffee?"

"Does the Pope drink wine?"

Mojica smiled. "Andy…black with sugar?"

"Yeah."

I heard Andy's chair squeak and then all three of us were in my office.

My second question of the morning was, "Anyone heard from Sharp?"

Andy shook his head. "No, but I have a meeting with Castro Engineering this afternoon at three."

I heard Mojica ask Andy what they wanted. Mojica and Andy were talking, but nothing seemed to register with me.

"So what do you think? Is that okay?"

I looked up from my coffee. "You mean about Castro?"

Andy and Mojica looked at each other.

Andy said, "No. About the secretary. Can we interview her at ten tomorrow?"

I nodded, but cared less. I wanted to see Sharp to find out if that was his Barracuda that came down the road last night. How many Barracudas could there be on that road out in the middle of almost nowhere? One?

I looked up at Andy who was now sitting on my desk. I quickly looked at Mojica who had a quizzical expression on his face, and then back at Andy.

"Why don't you go home and get some more sleep? We'll call you if Sharp appears. You need the rest, brother."

The way Andy said 'brother' snapped me out of a stupor I didn't realize I was in. I shook my head and said, "You're right. I should get out of here."

■ ● ■

Mojica started laughing. "Yeah. Go home. Make friends with a bar of soap for a while, okay?

"Fuck you, Mojica." I picked up my coffee and silently left the office.

I hailed a cab outside the office. The cabbie did a double-take when I got in.

"You butcher your own meat, mister?"

I didn't say anything.

"I wouldn't have stopped if I saw you looked like that."

I looked at the cabbie's tag. Dominic Petrillo. "Look, Dominic, I had a tough night. I'm not in the mood for conversation."

"Well, all I got to say is I don't see any bruises on you, so this must be a 'you should see the other guy' moment."

At that, I laughed. "Definitely."

"City's getting crazy, ya' know?"

I looked out the window. "Definitely."

"Every time I turn on channel 13 somebody's been shot."

"If it bothers you, I wouldn't turn on the T.V. then."

"I feel bad for those women though. I hope they catch the guy soon."

We were both quiet after that. I wondered why I still hadn't changed into a clean shirt. We pulled up right in front of the door to my building. I paid the fare and tip and said "so long" to Dominic. On the way in I noticed a guy with blond hair leaning against the wall down at the corner. He seemed awfully disinterested in everything. So disinterested that he made me interested. I checked my mail and went upstairs.

My apartment was on the corner of the third floor. If I stuck my head out enough windows I could see up and down two streets in four directions. Blondie was gone. He either was in a doorway close by or he got a ride. Or maybe he was sitting in a car. Whether he was somebody or nobody, I needed a shower.

■ ● ■

I took off the shirt, which was stiff with blood. I held it up and then decided to just throw it away. The pants I would salvage.

The shower made me feel drunk. I grabbed onto the shower head and just let the hot water run over my face and down my body. I must have stood in there, frozen in place, for half an hour. I replayed the past three weeks over and over. But when I got to last night, instead of trying to think things through, it was like there was a skip in the record and I kept wondering where Sharp was. What the hell was he doing? I couldn't analyze anything. I just kept wondering where he was, and then I'd replay the events until at one point I wondered if it was possible to drown yourself standing up in the shower.

When I came out of the bathroom I knew I couldn't sleep. I went downstairs and decided to walk over to Eddie's diner. I looked around for Blondie and instead I saw a guy on the other side of the street with brown hair and a mustache. I went four blocks with him matching me stride for stride and then he turned a corner. I decided to head for the park for a while and hit the diner later. As I was crossing the street I saw him again, except the mustache was gone. I walked into the park about forty yards and sat down on a bench. I turned my head a little, but I couldn't see my tail. Two kids were playing catch with a hardball about fifty feet away. I saw clouds rolling in at the horizon. Then I heard one of the kids say something about Carew. The sun was so bright it made me squint.

"A Lucky Strike is the only car you'll need this year. It's toasted. Our toasting process gets 28 miles to the gallon." The T.V. announcer came walking across the ball field and sat down on the bench next to me. The sun was still so bright I couldn't stop squinting. "I forgot my lines. Had a lot of work lately. I'm mixing up products. Just like you. All of those cows being killed gets under your skin doesn't it? It would me. Want a Lucky?" He

■ ● ■

pulled out a pack of black and white Chesterfields. I had never seen that packaging before. Looked like spots on a cow. "I always keep my Luckys in another package so people don't know I've got them. Good trick, huh? This field out here all used to be cows once. Black and white Holsteins." Out at the edge of the field I could see Bernie and the brown-haired woman walking right at me. Bernie and Bland. "I better get going. You're going to be busy." The announcer stood up and walked away practicing his lines. "New Luckys are road-tested and they're toasted and you…" The brown-haired woman fell down and Bernie just left her there and kept on coming. Why doesn't he help her up? Help her up, Bernie! Bernie just kept on coming across the field. I was going to run but I couldn't get up. Bernie was right in front of me, glaring and then he sat down. His voice sounded scratchy. "Yeah, Buddy, I used to play in my mother's closet. I was just a kid, ya' know. One time I found a box with some negatives in them. I held 'em up to the light and I could see people in them. That's how I learned what a woman looked like without her clothes on. My mother was in just about all of them with some men I didn't know. Took me a while to figure out what they were doing, but I didn't figure out why 'till I was older. One day my mother found me in there and she asked me what I was doing. She grabbed the negatives from me and started holding them up to the light one by one. Then she started laughing. She was looking at different ones and would start laughing again. She was laughing so hard I started laughing too. Then she asked me what I was laughing at and slapped me across the face. I was small, if you can believe that, and I started crying. She tossed the negatives at me and walked away. Then I heard her laughing again out in the kitchen. Every time my mother laughed after that I'd put my hands up in front'a my face so she wouldn't slap me again. But she never did. By the time my Dad was dying she

■ ● ■

was long gone. He wanted to leave me somethin', but we didn't have much money. I had a really good paper route. People said it was lucrative. But it was only a paper route so we were still poor. My Dad really wanted to leave me something so he spent a few days writing me absentee excuse notes for school. He wrote 'em so all I had to do was fill in the dates. He told me to keep his death quiet and nobody would be the wiser. I was seventeen when my father finally died. I made it to eighteen before the guidance counselor found out my father was dead. I used nine of those notes. They came in real handy. Child services…are ya' payin' attention?" "Ow!" Bernie kicked me in the shin.

"God Damn!"

"Sorry, mister. That one got away. You okay?"

I looked down at my foot and saw the hardball. Then I jumped because I thought Bernie was sitting next to me. It wasn't Bernie. A street bum was sitting there hollering at the kid.

"You God Damn kids ought to be more careful! Can't you see two adults here havin' a conversation?

I picked up the ball and tossed it to the kid. The bum was still hollering.

"Maybe you need more practice so you know how to play!"

The kid's face turned red. "I know how to play. I made the All Star team this year. I know how to play."

The kid was embarrassed and defensive.

I smiled. "It's okay. One'll get away from somebody every once in a while. You made the All Star team, huh?"

The kid stood up straighter. "Yeah. It's my second time."

"Oh yeah? What position?"

"I play outfield."

"Uh huh. Who's your favorite player of all time?"

"All time?!"

"Yeah. All time."

■ ● ■

"Musial. You know who he is?"

"Aren't you a little young to be a fan of 'Stan the Man?'

"Well, my Dad told me everything about him and I have his cards."

"Do you cut your eyelashes?"

"What?"

"You didn't know that? Musial used to cut his eyelashes so one of them wouldn't fall in his eye while he was batting."

"He did?"

"Hey, Con! C'mon! Throw it!"

"Sounds like your friend is looking for a game. What's his name?"

"Game? We got practice." The kid turned and threw the ball to his friend. "That's Tommy. He plays second base. We're best buddies." Con ran toward his friend and caught Tommy's throw back on the run.

"Damn kids."

"You were a kid once too, weren't you?"

"Yeah! But we had respect! We didn't go around throwin' baseballs at people."

I smiled again. "What's your name, bud?"

"Scuzzie. Forgot already, huh?"

"Scuzzie?" I started laughing.

"What's so funny? It's short for Scozzolini!"

"Come on, Scuz. That's a pretty unique nickname. They call you that on the paper route?"

"Paper route? What paper route? What the hell are you talkin'about. I thought you was a regular guy. Paper route…"

I looked around the park. I didn't see anyone else. "How long have we been out here?"

"I dun' know. Don't you know? Hour maybe. My watch dun' work so good." Scuzzie took a watch out of his pocket and looked at it. He shook it and put it up to his ear.

"Doesn't tell much time anymore, I see."

"It's good some days. When it's damp out the gears get all locked up."

"Oh yeah?" I looked at Scuzzie's hair close. Pretty thin, with a few scabs spread out here and there. Might have been blond hair once. Had very blue eyes. Some crusty, dirty, smelly pants.

"Where's your stuff, Scuzzie?"

He looked up from his watch with a start. "Some place safe. I got someplace safe." His eyes fell back down to his watch. Scuzzie clearly didn't trust me.

"You see anybody come out here and just stand around?" I looked over my shoulders both ways.

"No. Just you." The sun was in Scuzzie's eyes now and the lids were fat slits. He wrinkled his forehead like that would keep the sun out of his eyes. "You waiting for a friend?"

"No. Just wondering." I kept looking around.

"Well, as I was sayin', when I…"

I stood up and Scuzzie peered up at me with one eye closed. I pulled some money from my pocket and handed Scuzzie one dollar and fifty cents.

"Get yourself a sandwich, Scuz."

"Tanks. I really mean that. It was good conversing with you. You're a very good listener."

I chuckled and walked away with Scuzzie's praise following me down the street like echoes. A block away I heard him holler again that I was a very good listener.

■ ● ■

Rain

I didn't get too far before the rain started coming down. I ducked into an apartment building entranceway and shook the rain from my sleeves and hair. I looked up at a gray sky that was shooting out raindrops like pistol pellets.

Once upon a time I would have lit up a cigarette and blown smoke at the rain. Instead I rubbed my hands together and started wondering if Sharp was really still with us. Why didn't he come back last night? Maybe they bought him off. Maybe he needed money. Maybe he was always against us. Why am I thinking like this? Maybe… My brain froze.

When I turned around and looked in the lobby they were there. Two of them. Talking to each other like they didn't have a care in the world. How'd they get behind me? How'd they know I'd stop at this building? They must have circled around to come in the back. I looked up and down the street. The rain was bouncing off the sidewalks like sleet. They were empty except for one guy with a black umbrella a couple of blocks down.

When I glanced back, one of the tails inside the lobby lit up a cigarette. He did it to taunt me. I'll taunt that motherfucker down at the corner. I'll wait around the corner and when they

■ ● ■

get there I'll nail both of them!

I was leaning, with my head out in the rain, looking down the length of the building to the corner.

"Excuse me."

"Jesus." I jumped back. It was a mailman coming from the opposite direction.

"Didn't mean to startle you, buddy. Sorry." He had a smile on his face. I nodded.

"You okay?"

"Yeah. Yeah. Got to be somewhere."

He looked at me funny and went into the building. I heard the mailboxes open and then start slamming closed. I looked back and one of my tails was gone. Did he go out the back of the building and he's waiting down the street? I started looking up and down the street again to see if I could spot him. The door opened behind me. I turned expecting to see the mailman. It was the two tails. Except they were teenagers. One of them had an umbrella and he was opening it. They were both laughing. The umbrella went up, they both huddled under it and they wandered off in the direction of the park, still laughing.

The mailman came out and looked up at the sky.

"Hell of a rain, ain't it?" He was smiling.

I looked him over. "Yeah it is." He was wearing sneakers. I looked at him hard. "You guys can wear sneakers on the job now?"

He looked at his feet. "My issues split and these were all I could come up with. That, or wrap my shoe in shipping tape. These are not much good in the rain, but in this kind of rain it doesn't matter." He shook his head. "Take it easy." He stepped out into the rain and crossed the street to another building.

I was alone again. I looked up at the sky. The rain was letting up a little. Thunder. It came rolling through the streets like a

■ ● ■

woman slapping some jerk's skinny face. Another thunderclap. I was feeling sick to my stomach. Maybe there was something wrong with me. Maybe I just needed to eat something.

I decided I'd get wet. I stepped out into the rain and listened closely to the thunder while I walked. I stopped at the corner and looked to my right. The mailman was walking away from me half a block down. I felt sorry for him in his sneakers. I did a spin like I was one of the Four Tops, looking for anyone who might be looking for me. But the streets were deserted.

I started walking toward Eddie's diner again. It wasn't my favorite diner, but it was close to the office. I liked walking. I liked walking alone. I looked over my shoulder. No one. The rain was dripping off my eyebrows now. The sound of thunder was coming from far away. Kind of sounded like a bombing run, but not as crisp.

I looked over my shoulder again. There's no one there! There really was no one there. I had to talk to Andy because they were there, somewhere.

I went about ten blocks and turned the corner. There at the end of the street, right in the middle, was Eddie's. I wonder why Eddie didn't like me so good. He liked Andy and Sharp. He was okay with Mojica. He loved Helen. Maybe I criticized his food too much.

I stepped off the curb to cross the street to the diner and landed in a puddle that went up to my ankle. "Fuckshit!" I jumped out of it, but my right foot was soaked. As I crossed the street I saw about two heads up in the windows in Eddie's. You couldn't see the counter from this close. Eddie's was almost six feet above the sidewalk. Shining silver with green trim and with water running down the sides, it looked like the walls were melting.

I wondered why Eddie gave up the business to run a din-

■ ● ■

er. Maybe he couldn't stomach some of the problems he came across. Some people say he was very good once. Some of the older cops told me that he was in over his head once too often. I suppose if you feel like you're drowning in shit you reach for any preserver you can get to. Maybe the diner was Eddie's preserver. At least the diner was clean and the food was edible.

I climbed the two sets of steps into the diner with my right foot making squishing and sucking sounds. I was dripping wet and immediately began to shiver. Air conditioning. There was Phyllis with her hand on her hip looking down at a newspaper she had laid out on the counter. She looked up and smiled as I walked past her.

"Forget your swimming trunks?"

"You ever go home, Phyllis? Every time I come in here you're leaning on the counter."

"What do you care?"

"You're right. I don't. But can I have a very hot coffee and a burger?"

"I thought you were so god damn health conscious these days. Thought you'd order a glass of water and a stick of celery."

"Nothing wrong with being healthy."

"What the hell are you eating in here for then?"

"The company, Phyllis. The titillating conversation."

Phyllis turned and yelled to the back through the kitchen window. "Hey Eddie, a burger neat on the coals, hold the celery!"

Phyllis turned back toward me. "Titillation, huh? Shot anybody over in your office recently?"

"Naw. Not this week." I turned away from her and looked out the window down at the sidewalk. Phyllis slid my coffee onto the table. I didn't look at her, but she didn't move. She stood there hovering over me.

"I'm sorry. I didn't mean anything. I was just foolin' around

■ ● ■

and I guess it wasn't funny."

I turned, caught her eyes and smiled. "I'm cool, Phyllis. I guess you had to be there for it not to be funny. We're okay." I looked away and noticed a guy walking across the street with a limp.

"Sorry." Phyllis was walking back to the counter.

"It's okay. Can you get Eddie to burn my burger a little?"

Without turning she said, "That's what I told him already. That's how you always eat it, ain't it?"

The guy with the limp came in and sat on a stool about four seats from my booth.

"Darling Phyllis. Can I have a mother and child reunion with cryin' Johnnies?"

"You finally learned something! You're slow, but yer getting' it. Hey Eddie, a mother and child cryin' Johnny."

Phyllis came over with my burger. She gave me a short smile and let the plate roll in a circle on the table like a coin. When it finally came to rest she turned away and focused her attention on the limper.

"Hey Bryce, you seen that little girl around at all?"

The guy at the counter didn't say anything. He picked up his coffee with both hands and just looked at it.

"Ya hear me? You ever seen that girl around?"

"What girl?"

"C'mon. You know the one." Phyllis came over close to the guy and lowered her voice. "You know...that working girl you were with a little while back. The one you had breakfast with."

The guy sipped his coffee and then put it back on the saucer. "She left town as far as I know."

"Really. That's too bad in a way. She was kind of cute...you know...for her kind'a girl."

The guy looked around to see if there was someone else Phyllis could bother, and then said, "Is my food up yet, Phyllis?"

■ ● ■

Phyllis looked hurt. "If it was up, I'd put it in front of you."
She slid away.

"I didn't mean anything, Phyllis. I'm just hungry."

"I'm sorry, Bryce. I'm pissing a lot of people off today. I should just keep my damn mouth shut." A man and a woman came in and sat in a booth by the door. Phyllis went to greet them in her own inept way. I kept watching the guy at the counter.

I glanced out at the street again. The rain had almost completely stopped. Pieces of paper and a kid's pink shoe were making their way down the gutter to the drain. When I looked back, the guy at the counter was eating his chicken and egg sandwich like he had to catch a bus. The onions were falling out the sides. In less than five minutes he had cleared off his plate. I wondered if he could have even tasted the food. I watched him pay and leave and then Phyllis came over to my booth.

"You gonna even try that burger?"

I looked down and then back up at Phyllis. "Yeah. I was just thinking."

"Must have been interesting."

"Phyllis, the guy with the limp…he a regular?"

"Bryce? Regular? He eats here two or three times a day. Does that qualify?"

"Really? Why's he limp?"

"Think he got that in the war. He was pretty bad when he first started coming in here. Some days it seemed like the best he could do was a slow shuffle."

"Who was the woman you were asking him about?"

"Why are you so nosey today?"

"Kind of my business, isn't it?"

"Yeah, except I don't think no one hired you to be curious about him."

"Oh come on Phyllis. Just a vet curious about another vet."

■ ● ■

Phyllis stared at me for a second and then bit her lip. "Well, he doesn't ever come in here with anyone, except this one morning. There was this cute, little dark-haired girl with him. Beautiful hair. He was laughing a lot. I think she had eyes for him, but I'm pretty sure she was a working girl. He probably didn't need that kind of girl around, but I have to admit, he sure looked happy that morning."

"What happened to her?"

"Don't know. Never saw her again. Bryce said she left town. So I guess she left town. You can't really say about a girl like that."

"Interesting. Bryce, huh...interesting."

"What's so interesting about a pro?"

I looked up at Phyllis and smiled. "Depends on your perspective I suppose."

"You must mean that having the clap is an interesting perspective."

"Not for me. Uh-uh. Not me."

Phyllis chuckled.

"By the way, what color hair did she have?"

Walking away Phyllis said, "Dark. Dark hair. Think it was brown. It was a little greasy that night...yeah...but when she was cleaned up she had real nice hair. Beautiful hair actually... but yep, brown. Brown hair."

I took a five out and tossed it on the table. I grabbed my burger and walked out of Eddie's as fast as I could. When I got in the street I could see him limping about a block and a half away. I picked up my speed until I was twenty yards behind. I started eating my burger while I walked and soon I had catsup dripping down my sleeve.

The Bryce guy turned at the next corner. I went by the corner and crossed the street. Then I turned back and took a quick look around the edge of the building to see where he was. He was

■ ● ■

looking in a Thom McCann shoe store window with his hands in his pockets. I looked around slowly to see if I was noticed. Bryce started moving again. I followed him from the other side of the street for three blocks and then he made a left. I ran over to the corner in time to see him enter a building. I went over to the entrance and looked at the mailboxes. 'Bryce Jacob, second floor' I stepped backwards toward the street and looked up. So he lived up there. Second floor. Our serial killer.

■ ● ■

Elaine

I watched him fly into the office space where my new desk was sitting. He didn't acknowledge me and I didn't have a chance to say anything except "Hi…"

"Andy! We have to talk!"

Andy came out of his office slowly. "I'd like to introduce you to Elaine, our new secretary."

He turned and looked at me standing there like I was a concrete pillar. Then he turned back to Andy.

"Andy, we have to talk. Now!"

The phone rang and I answered, stating the name of the agency I was now working for. I took a message for Mr. Mojica, put the phone back in the cradle and watched them drift into Andy's office. At first I couldn't hear what they were saying, but then, "Andy, I know who the killer is, I'm telling you. I followed the guy back to his apartment and I know he killed one of those women."

I could see Andy put both hands on his hips. "Sit down."

"I'm telling you I followed him and I know where he lives and we can trap the bastard."

"Sit the fuck down, goddamn it!!"

■ ● ■

I sat down even though Andy wasn't talking to me and listened to a ramble about tails and a serial killer.

"So on the basis of one burger and a short conversation between Phyllis and a man with a limp, you figure him for three or four murders. Tell me the whole story from the time you left your apartment, but talk under the speed limit this time."

I heard the elevator doors open and close and footsteps in the hallway. The office door opened.

"Hi, Elaine. Any messages?"

I looked up at Mr. Mojica and handed him the note. He read it frowning and then smiled at me.

"So you met everyone?"

"Yep. It was love at first sight."

The smile left his face, replaced by a look of mild confusion and uncertainty.

"Hey, Heeks. Come in here for a second."

"Excuse me, Elaine."

I watched the three of them move into the office with the curved window. They got real quiet and I didn't know if I should leave for the women's room or not. I guessed if they didn't want me to hear, they would close the door.

I looked around the offices. My desk sat in a large waiting room. It was the largest space in the offices and was totally functional and embarrassingly bare. Nothing on the walls. No carpet. Two nondescript wooden chairs. At least there were two windows across from me. From my desk I could see into everyone's office. It was kind of like their offices lined mine on two sides.

The office with the big, curved window looked like it was modeled on a room from a bad detective movie. Stark. Nothing on the walls except a calendar. The desk was basically clean. Two chairs. One on each side of the desk.

■ ● ■

The next office to the right seemed smaller and belonged to Mr. Mojica. He had so much stuff in it. It looked like someone had moved a Five and Dime in there and mixed it in with a hardware shop.

Sharp's office was next to his. His walls were painted light beige and he had black and white photos of Texas on the walls. He had one of those green library lamps on his desk and a couple of small stacks of papers next to a leather bound Oxford English dictionary. He had two nice, leather chairs in front of his desk, on top of a red and yellow rug that looked like it came from the Southwest, or Mexico. Over his window he had those old style wooden blinds. In one corner he had an L shaped bookcase.

Down at the end of the waiting room to my left I could see into Andy's office. It was cluttered with stacks of paper everywhere. On the chairs. On his desk. On the floor. He also had a bookcase. A large one. And on every shelf, on top of the books, he had papers. I guessed that's why I was here.

I could still see the three of them. Andy was standing and had his arms crossed on his chest. Mr. Mojica was standing next to him.

"Well, yeah…somebody was tailing me. Probably two guys at least."

I could hear Andy's voice rising. "Bro, let's get this straight. So you were being tailed by two or three guys and then you happened to fall upon the serial killer and you follow him to his apartment."

Mr. Mojica looked at Andy and said, "Could happen."

Andy did a double take and then pushed Mr. Mojica in the shoulder. "Knock it off! We have a real problem here. Were you tailed while you followed the limping serial killer?!" I could hear Andy's sarcasm bouncing off the walls.

"What the hell you talking, Andy?! I'm not crazy!"

■ ● ■

The door to the office swung closed. Voices were raised and I started to wonder if I really wanted to work here. Just because I wanted an exciting job didn't mean I necessarily wanted to work with creeps. I listened to the dull roar from the office for twenty minutes and then the door opened.

The three of them walked over to my desk. I stood up and Mr. Mojica said, "This is Elaine, our new secretary. She'll be here from ten until six, Monday through Friday. And this is…"

"Oh I know who this is. We went to high school together. A little heavier now. Hair's a little thinner. Could use a shave."

"Elaine Gottfried."

"Amazing. You even remembered the last name."

"Andy, I really think he's the guy. It's a hunch, but what if we can nail the guy?!"

I was a concrete pillar. "Glad to see you're so glad to see me after all of these years." I sat back down.

Andy was staring at Mr. Mojica. "Do you believe this shit?! What the hell is wrong with you?"

"What?"

Mr. Mojica started laughing. "You are being one rude son of a bitch, Capitan. Slow the fuck down. We're trying to introduce you to our secretary. We haven't had one before. Andy has done most of the bookkeeping up until now, remember?"

"Yeah. I know! We should all appreciate Andy. I do. We have a secretary and I know who's killing all of those women."

"When are you going to get me a gun?" They all turned in my direction. "I told you I'd work here if you got me a permit and a gun. My high school chum here obviously doesn't give a fuck, but if you two want me to stay, I want you to hold up your end of the bargain."

"Andy, Heeks…you told Elaine here, the kid who used to sit in the front row of Mr. Hobb's homeroom and make eyes at him, we'd get her a weapon? Really?!" He looked from one to the other and in a really squeaky voice repeated himself. "Really?"

Since no one was defending me I thought I should. "My desk is sitting on top of the fading chalk outlines of two dead bodies. You try to find someone else who would take this job. The only way I'm staying is if you get me a gun. Period."

"If this bitch shoots one of you, you can crawl to the hospital because you are on your own."

Now I was angry and I stood up again. "I don't think Andy or Mr. Mojica will have to worry about that. If I shoot one of them, I have a drivers' license and I will take them to the hospital myself. You, however, if you ever refer to me as "bitch" again I will blow your fucking balls off from behind. Once you get me the permit...you got that?!"

He just stood there staring at me and then he turned away and went to his office. I heard his chair squeak so I knew he was sitting down.

Mr. Mojica had a big grin on his face. "So was Mr. Hobbs a looker?"

I sat back down and looked up at Mr. Mojica. "At fifteen? To die for."

Mr. Mojica's grin stretched from ear to ear. "Maybe we could go like Tuesday for that permit application. What do you think, Andy?"

"Yeah." Andy frowned. "Elaine, it's not always crazy around here, but right now you may have dropped into a firestorm."

"I took this job because I wanted an interesting job."

Andy lowered his voice. "Heeks, what do you think about this serial killer stuff?"

"I think he's a little off."

"I'm serious."

"So am I. I think our man might be losing it a little. You do

■ ● ■

too, don't you? The way he talks."

Andy looked at the floor and then back at Mr. Mojica.

"We have a real problem here. Something weird is all around us. There could be tails. Who knows what we've had dropped on us. There's a serial killer in the city and our partner keyed on him while eating a hamburger?"

Mr. Mojica's face looked as serious as I had ever seen it. "The problem really is, that it's possible. Right now anything is possible." Mr. Mojica turned to me. "What do you think, Elaine?"

"Me?!"

"Yeah, you. The secretary of four hours."

"Well, Mr. Mojica…"

"Elaine…I have a legal gun. I have illegal guns…untraceable guns. If you call me 'Mr. Mojica' one more time, I will take one of my untraceable weapons and…"

"And what?!" I growled at him.

"I'll pretend to threaten you or something. What do you think of that?"

I didn't want to laugh, but the look on his face made me crack up. Both of them started laughing along with me.

"Andy, I like our new secretary."

"I could come up with a list of psychologists if you want."

Andy stopped laughing first. "Yeah, why don't we do that."

■ ● ■

SKY

I was going to catch the guy. I knew we had to do it even if Andy thought I was wrong.

The sky was clearing really fast. There were only a few fluffy clouds left from the storm. I stared out the window at the jet trails. A pigeon flew past. An old piece of newspaper was dancing on the wind currents, up and down and then it disappeared. I felt someone behind me. I spun around in my chair and found Andy staring at me with a frown on his face. Mojica had a grin on his.

"What? Round two?"

"No. We have to try to figure something out about the guys following you. We're going to put you down in the street and we're going to try to pick up on your tails."

Finally. I felt excited.

"Okay. When do we start... and what the fuck are you grinning at?"

Mojica just kept grinning and then he said, "You liked her, didn't you?"

"Who?!"

"Elaine. You liked her back in high school, didn't you?"

■ ● ■

"Fuck you, Mojica." His smile got so big it had to borrow space on both sides of his ears.

"Yep. You was diggin' her, and she was diggin' Haps."

"Hobbs, asshole. Hobbs. And no I didn't dig her! Why the hell did you guys hire her? She was fucking crazy then and she's probably still fucking crazy now."

Andy put his right hand up like a traffic cop. "First of all, you didn't pay any attention when we discussed her. Second, you didn't make the interview and we needed to make a decision. Third, she was the only applicant who was fluid in English."

"Fluent."

"Fuck you, fluent! And she seems to be smart. I'm not going to do the books all the goddamn time. We have too much work now. Fourth, we had two dead bodies on the floor out where she's answering the phones. Lastly…you say she's crazy? Take a good look at us, stupid!"

We were all quiet, looking at each other and pondering our collective sanity. I spun back around to the window, looked out at the sky, sighed, and got up. I walked past Andy and Mojica out to Elaine's desk. I extended my hand.

"Elaine, I want to apologize. I don't know why I acted like I did. I'm glad we have a secretary and I hope it works out here for you. I'll never refer to you as 'bitch' again and I'm ashamed I used that word in regards to you. I hope you'll accept my apology."

Elaine stood up and shook my hand. "Accepted."

"Thanks. But quit standing up and down all the time. You make me dizzy." I turned back toward my office. Andy and Mojica were staring at me. Andy's eyebrows were raised. Mojica was frowning.

"What?"

Andy shrugged and walked into his office. When I got close, Mojica wiped a fake tear from his eye and I took a swipe at his head. He ducked, gave me a backhanded slap on my butt and ran toward his office. Before I could turn I heard him say, "Sharp! What's shakin?"

I turned around and there was Sharp standing in the doorway.

"Hi, Elaine. Glad you could join the company." He walked to the center of the floor. "Gents, let's have a talk."

We all went into my office. It seemed like all of our meetings were in my office.

At first Sharp made me feel uncomfortable. I couldn't understand why. He was one of my best friends. He caught me staring at him and said, "What's up with you?"

"Nothing.Nothing...how come you didn't come back here last night?"

"That would be because Ah was making friends with Mr. Barthelme. After you guys left him bleeding to death in the road, I stopped and picked him up as planned. That laundry bag idea you had, Heeks, worked out good. I gave him a pair of pants and offered to give him a ride to the police station. He told me he had been robbed, but he didn't want to see the police. He did, however, want to make a phone call. Heeks, those little infra red opera glasses or whatever they were, were perfect. I stopped at a gas station so Joey..."

Andy looked up, "Joey?"

"Yeah. Joey. We're good pals now. I bandaged his head. Loaned him a pair of pants from the Salvation Army that he bled all over and thought they were mine. Gave him a pair of flip flops to wear, drank with him until four in the morning, slept on his couch and listened to him tell me how we should get together. How I was such a great guy. I think he was lying about those parts, but I went on smiling. The number he called from the gas station was an area code just north of here. That woman I know over at the phone company will have the address for me by four

■ ● ■

o'clock. I got most of a second number he called from his house. That area code was Chicago. I missed the last two numbers so that will probably have to wait until we have time to figure out what we think we're looking for. When I left at noon there were two pugs sitting out front in a grey Chrysler with a black vinyl top. Did you guys get anything out of Barthelme's pants?"

Andy said, "Not much. Twenty dollars, a driver's license under the name Barthelme, a license for the name Holloway, some keys and a security card for a company that's not local."

We were all silent for a couple of seconds and then Sharp went on. "If there's a real organization behind this bullshit, and it seems there is, maybe Mojica should call up Raoul and see if he can give us a line on what we're dealing with." We were all quiet again. I knew Andy wasn't going to like that idea.

"I hate going to Whitfield. Every time we ask him for information we end up owing him something."

"We have to trade something, Andy. He doesn't do this for money."

"I know that Heeks, but I always feel like we come out on the short end. We ask for a little information and end up spending days doing something for him. Like that time he asked us to take those twin brothers to D.C. and those mob bastards were after them. They shot up the car and it wasn't even my car!"

I piped in then. "Yeah, that was fucked up, but if anyone is going to know about a committee, or commission, or some bizarre organization on our side of the fence, it's going to be Ray."

Andy shook his head. "Yeah, well I don't trust the guy."

"That's because he doesn't like you and you don't like him."

"I don't like him because I stopped at a gas station to take a piss and when I came out there were two dead guys in the back seat, four flat tires and more holes in my mother in law's car than I could have counted if I had wanted to. And what did Raoul say

■ ● ■

when I called him before the cops took me into custody? 'Oh shit, is Mojica okay?'"

I couldn't help but start laughing. Andy glared at me.

"And then the bastard started laughing just like you! That shit's not funny."

I tried not to laugh, then Sharp broke up and Mojica said "Shit's not funny" and then he was laughing.

"Go ahead. Call the bastard, but he is going to get one of us hurt some day. I don't trust him. But on top of that, if Sharp has a chance to be Barthelme's buddy, he should disappear from here for a while. We shouldn't chance one of his guys seeing Sharp come in here, especially after we beat the hell out of him."

"I'll have Ivars let me out the basement."

Andy looked at me and said, "So you go down in the street and we'll see if we can spot someone."

I nodded and stood up. "I'll head north up toward Palmer."

"Give me five minutes. Pause for thirty at the fourth corner. Where do we go static?"

"I'll stop at the Post Office."

"Okay."

Mojica said, "I have to serve those papers for Forster and then I'll try to set up a meeting with Raoul for tonight."

We all left my office at the same time. I had my hand on the knob of the hallway door when I heard Mojica.

"Elaine, you said you know how to shoot."

"That's right."

"How about a Smith and Wesson .38?"

"That would be good."

I turned back toward Elaine's desk and involuntarily a "Jesus" escaped from my lips.

Elaine was opening mail. She looked at me and then back at the letter she was opening. I heard her whisper, "I will blow your balls off."

Sharp walked up to me and slapped me on the back. "Open the door, Agatha." I gave him a pained smile and then he said, "You know you have catsup all over your shirt sleeve?"

"Yeah. I know."

Sharp tilted his head. "Okay. As long as y'all know."

I shook my head, went out in the hallway with Sharp and rang for an elevator. Andy and Mojica joined us and we stood there looking at each other until we started laughing. When the elevator doors opened Ivars stared at us and then started laughing, too. After we dropped two floors Ivars asked, "Vhat so funny fellas?"

I looked at each of my partners and said, "I don't think any of us knows."

The elevator bounced when we hit the lobby. "Glad you're getting good at this, Ivars." He looked embarrassed.

"Dat vhas not so bad."

"You're letting Sharp out in the basement. Heeks and I are riding down with him and coming back up."

"Okay, Mr. Andy."

I stepped out into the lobby and without looking around. I walked straight to the doors and went out on the sidewalk. I turned left and walked close to the building, looking in the street level sales windows. Andy would pick up my tails so I didn't bother looking around. I went to the corner and glanced to my right. That had to be one. He was looking all over like he was lost. Andy would pick him up like a snap.

I crossed the street and bent down to tie my shoes. My right foot was still damp. I went to the next corner and stared in a window at a little red fire truck and an old Robot Commando. Andy should be out on the street by now. I couldn't see the guy across the street in the window reflection. People were starting

■ ● ■

to go home from work. A lot of women. Probably from the new garment factory the mayor was all excited about. I wondered if the mayor ever worried about someone shooting him. If I was mayor, I'd worry about it.

I started walking again. I went north about a mile and then took a left. I went into the Post Office and bought some stamps. About twenty minutes later I was back at the office building. I took the elevator up with two men I vaguely recognized. I was sure they had offices on the floor above ours.

I opened the door to the office and stopped like my feet were frozen to the floor. I didn't expect Elaine to be there. I didn't know what to say so I just said, "hi." She said "hi" and I said "hi" again and felt like an idiot. I started walking to my office and said "yeah." I had no idea why I said that. As I passed Elaine I saw the smirk on her face just before she said, "You men have a meeting tonight at 9:30."

"Okay." I closed the door to my office and sat down thinking that I felt like one of those kids from the gallery of the Officer Bill cartoon show. That wasn't good.

About five minutes later I heard the outer office door open. I heard Andy say hello to Elaine and she relayed the message about the meeting. I heard Andy walk to my door and then he came in.

"Don't you ever knock, goddamn it?!"

Andy looked stunned.

"Who the hell are you talking to and since when do you close your door?"

"So did you make them?"

"No."

"What do you mean 'no'?"

"I mean there was no one following you."

"You didn't see the guy in the grey suit?"

■ ● ■

"There were a number of guys in grey suits, but none of them was particularly interested in you."

"You didn't see anybody?!"

"No. I didn't. But let's send you home in a cab and Mojica and I can be over there when you come out of your building. Or, maybe we'll clue on somebody staking
your place out."

I gave Andy an unforgiving glare and then turned my chair to look out at the sky.

"So we'll pick you up at 8:45, unless you plan to stay here."

I didn't say anything and Andy didn't leave my office. I felt so angry I wanted to cry. Finally I said "okay." Andy got up and left. I concentrated on the sky.

■ ● ■

RAOUL

Raoul Whitfield had a repo business out past the train tracks called "Emerald Repossession." Once, when I asked him why he called the place "Emerald", he just said "1930." I thought, "Okay, that's good enough for me, whatever that means."

The lights were on when Mojica knocked. They immediately went out except for one dim light that seemed to shine dully from Ray's office. Behind me I heard Andy mutter, "Great."

We were all probably thinking the same thing. Ray was taking precautions against a hit.

I heard Ray's deep, bass voice say, "open." The door buzzed and the four of us went in. I heard the door click when it closed, but I couldn't see Ray. Suddenly a very large man stepped out from the shadows to our right. Raoul Whitfield, all six feet, six inches of him, smiled while holding a Remington pump action shotgun across his chest.

"Gentlemen. Come into my office." When Ray spoke it felt like we were in the take-off path of a 727. It seemed like the furniture rattled every time he took a step. We went into his office where he had four wooden folding chairs set out in front of his desk. He turned around and smiled at Mojica.

■ ● ■

"Heeks. How you be?"

They embraced and then Ray stuck out his hand to Sharp. He looked at me and a big, welcoming smile spread across his face. "What it is, brother." He squeezed me half to death with one arm. Then he backed away and with full moon eyes said, "That was some nasty shit over at your place of business."

Ray looked at Andy and merely nodded. Mojica wandered over to the opposite wall where six television screens were sitting on a table. It looked like they showed every angle of the building outside. Mojica was enthralled. He looked over his shoulder at Ray and asked if the setup was new. Raoul said he put it in about three months ago. "It serve its purpose." Ray smiled.

"What's this panel on the table, Ray?"

"That's an SEG…Special Effects Generator. I got it from one of the guys over at the Experimental Television Co-op. Let's me change to whatever I need to see real quick."

Mojica was already playing with the levers and on one T.V. screen I could see images fading and reappearing.

"Gentlemen, have a seat." Raoul sat down at his desk and laid the shotgun on top of it. Andy picked up one of the wooden chairs, carried it over to the far wall, and sat down in the shadows. We were all turned around looking at him.

"If they come through the door I want to be out of the line of fire."

Ray looked really annoyed.

Just before he sat down Mojica said, "Ray, what kind of company you expecting?"

"Something nasty. One of my clients didn't like the way I did my business. So if he and his friends want to get into some bad craziness, all they got to do is come ovah' here."

Sharp started laughing. From the look that appeared on Whitfield's face I thought the gates of hell were going to open.

■ ● ■

But he looked at Sharp and a smile broke out like he saw his mother cooking Thanksgiving dinner. Ray started chuckling right along with Sharp's laughter and then said, "That's right. That's right."

Raoul had been in naval intelligence before Vietnam. That always amazed me. A black man in naval intelligence way back then. That was how Mojica and Ray made their connection. Ray had intended to be a lifer, but he got disgusted with the work and walked after his fourth stint. The Patrice Lumumba murder still bothered him and he hated Eisenhower for it with a passion. While he was in he tried to make as many connections as he could, inside and outside of the Navy. He was probably pretty close to being a walking one man CIA. As a result he would often be quizzed by the FBI, the State Department, the CIA and other government ghosts. It was a good thing his sister's husband was an excellent lawyer or Ray would either be broke by now or in jail on some phony charge.

Since he'd left the service I knew he'd been involved in shootouts with some Neo-Nazis; had been close to the Black Panthers, but never joined; helped get some people to Cuba; and was generally involved in some crazy shit after hours. He ran this auto repo business so he could have his own time.

Mojica piped up first. "We have some problems we need to ask your help on, Ray."

"I know. As soon as I saw the papers about that shit up in your office, I knew I would eventually see my boys. That shit sounded weird."

"You know anything that could help us?"

I said, "Especially about some thing called 'The Commission.'"

Ray looked very serious. "First of all, the…"

Andy interrupted. "Should we be talking in here? Is this place bugged?"

■ ● ■

RAOUL   107

Ray looked really pissed. "Of course we can talk in here. Think I'm some punk doesn't know how the enemy works? I check this place out every day just like I eat my breakfast. So, first of all…" Ray paused, frowned and his eyes danced from Mojica, to me, to Sharp. In a sing-song voice that sounded like a diesel truck warming up, Ray said, "Is little Andy still pissed? He still upset about his car? I reimbursed him for the car and…"

Back in the corner Andy said, "No, Andy's not pissed about the car. Andy's pissed about the two days he spent in jail because the FBI thought little Andy set up those two brothers to be wacked at that gas station."

Everybody was quiet.

"First of all…" Ray started again like Andy wasn't in the room. "…These are bad people. They are the enemy."

I said, "Are they Feds?"

"They're connected, but they're a little different. Look, this is how it is. Back in the 60s the states of Mississippi and Alabama had some people create organizations to help stop the Civil Rights progress. They wanted secret organizations that could do things the states couldn't get caught doing…if you can imagine that, since the troopers were doing a lot of backward shit. But these organizations prodded people in the Klan, or what have you, to kill some people, to hurt some people, to disrupt. What was expected was that there would be no tracks to discover, at least not the tracks of the government. But these people had access to state intel and in some cases federal intel. Basically they had a free hand to get into whatever they wanted. If they could get some idiots from the KKK to ice the man they wanted dead, the FBI would look the other way. That's the way it was. No tracks that led to the staties and the Feds went blind.

"Now this Commission is set up the same way only at the Federal level…and these people are slick. Hoover was a little

■ ● ■

pissed about it, and he never identified all the players, so he just rolled with it. Webster's pretending like he doesn't know anything about it."

Sharp tilted his head, "But the FBI seems to have a pretty free hand to do what they want. Why tolerate an organization like that?"

"That ain't been true since Nixon went down. Imagine an FBI that's not the FBI, that's set up to function without rules. If they decide to pop someone…he gone. FBI can't do that anymore."

"How do you know this, Ray?" I had seen crazy things in Vietnam that had been kept quiet, but this sounded too big.

"It's pieces, man. Just pieces. But this is just the beginning. The incident that made me and some other people take notice was in a small city called Binghamton, in upstate New York. A guy hid out in a building one day and that night he became a sniper in the downtown area. Now, he didn't kill anybody, but when he was pulled out of the building a reporter was there and heard this guy say 'Did it start yet? Did it start everywhere else?' About a year later something similar happened in Kankakee. One of my sources found out that the Kankakee sniper disappeared while in custody. My source then decided to check up on Binghamton and found his records were gone too. The reporter who was there when the first sniper was arrested died of a heart attack at forty-two one year later. That was when the Commission first got our attention. These were training exercises."

"Lousy training exercise. Trainee goes to the clink for ten years." I really wasn't being convinced.

"The sniper wasn't the one being trained. Anybody can pull a trigger. The trainee was the one putting the sniper in place."

"Sounds like a bad sci-fi thriller, like The Manchurian Candidate." I was really skeptical, but this was Ray talking.

"Uh-huh. Some people may be training assassins. But they're

not just into that. They be in robbery so that they can be independent of the government. They have sit downs with the Feds, but they set their own agenda. There are suspicions that they have been concentrating on breaking certain types of leftist organizations and especially black community organizations. But they might be a little more than that. It's almost like they're a corporation that's trying to figure out what their product is going to be. Like maybe they want to be a shadow government."

No one said anything. We were all shifting in our seats trying to process this information and you could hear the wooden chairs creak.

Then Raoul said, "Boys, these are bad people. They're like a group of junkies who don't know how to get their fix, but they're going to do anything to get it. See, in a way this is not new. You know there's an organization called the Trilateral Commission. Y'all know it?"

Sharp and I shook our heads no.

"The Trilateral Commission is an international organization in the industrialized countries that invites certain powerful people to come together to discuss how the things in the world should go. These are men like Jimmy Carter… the chairman of BP…the Prime Minister of Japan. Barry Goldwater was enraged because he said these people were trying to create a world government. He was also pissed because he didn't get invited, but that's beside the point. This organization is making decisions about how the world is going to run and hardly anybody knows who these people are or what the organization does. You can find out who's in it. Republicans, Democrats, Social Democrats, captains of industry, professors. But the Commission is different. You may have run into a couple of people working for the Commission, but we don't really know who they are or really what they intend to do. It's all speculation…and I admit that.

■ ● ■

"Look, I'm not even gonna pretend I know everything about this Commission. But my sources say these people got some foul ideas. You got dragged into something and it sounds like they made a mistake somehow. I don't know what it is, but I would bet my business it's something they think they have to straighten out. Stay loose, gentlemen. Stay loose."

Sharp was staring at me.

"What?"

"What?! What did you get us into?"

"All I did…" Sharp started smiling. Then Raoul started laughing. I could even hear Andy laughing.

"My man Sharp. Always acting like he on the outside just lookin' in…and he always right there in the middle of it with a devilish smile on his face. My man Sharp!"

I heard Andy's chair scrape on the floor behind me. I turned and he was standing. Ray stood up, so I guessed we were done.

Mojica said, "Ray, you need our help with this problem you got?"

Andy popped off with, "Yeah Ray, you need two or three of us to hang around to get killed with you?" Raoul glared in Andy's direction.

"Heeks, if I need your help, I'll get you on the horn."

"Well you might want to make sure you got my correct number right now, because it looks like serious trouble up on the roof."

We all walked over to the monitors.

"Damn! Their mommas didn't teach them nothing! First one through that door up there is dead."

On another screen we could see two cars parked about a block and a half away. Men with weapons were getting out of the cars and were slowly coming our way. Up on the roof the four men were talking to each other.

■ ● ■

Andy was the first one to speak up. "Raoul, what do you have heavy?"

Ray walked to the other side of the room and pushed buttons on a combination pad. Part of the wall swung open and Ray reached in and came out with an AK-47. Andy walked over to Ray, grabbed it like he was pissed off and then looked up at Ray's face.

Ray said, "On the right hand side at the first landing there's a closet. You can lock it from the inside. When they're all past you, hit the switch by the door. There'll be lights shining down the stairs so bright they won't be able to see you. But don't step out into the hall in case one of those motherfuckers gets stupid."

Andy opened the door that led to the roof and went up without saying anything.

Ray went to the door of his office, closed it and dropped a metal bar across it. Then he opened slots in the walls on each side of the door.

"Gentlemen, help yourself to whatever you want. I suggest the pump action."

Sharp strolled over to the arsenal in the wall and tilted his head. He started chuckling. "Jesus Christ, Ray, you have an old Thompson?"

"You can use that if you want. It's dependable."

I walked over to the wall with Mojica. Sharp passed us, pointing the Thompson at the ceiling with a big smile on his face. "Do you believe this?"

Mojica grabbed a pump action, handed it to me and took one for himself. I looked over Ray's collection for a brief second. Rifles, grenades, some tear gas.

"Ray, what the hell?! You've got a rocket propelled grenade launcher in here...what the hell?"

"Need to be prepared."

■ ● ■

"For what?!"

"For whatever I need to be prepared for."

"For what, a tank?"

Ray ignored me. "These boys got no training and they mommas didn't teach them how to think. They are all coming in the front door. Do you believe that shit?! They all comin' in the front doe."

On a T.V. screen we watched them congregate in front of the outside door.

"When they're all in I'm gonna drop the front gate. They can't get through this interior door without explosives. Heeks, if they leave anybody outside can you go out the back door and go get them?"

"No problem, Ray."

"You two can…" The first shot went off up on the roof. Ray quietly said, "He dead." A small fusillade followed and Ray muttered, "What you shootin' at boys…" He said it almost like he was sad about it. Then the glass of the outside front door shattered. I looked through the slot and they came pouring in the door. One of them said, "Break that motherfucker down!" The little battering ram that they used on the glass front door started thumping on the office door. One of them screamed, "Hey!" and I saw the gates drop on the front of the building. They were trapped. It sounded like they were all screaming. The light behind me got my attention. It was shining out of the stairway like it was the sun rising. I heard Andy say "put your weapons on the floor." Ray walked over and stood at the side of the doorway. Again I heard Andy. "I said, put your weapons on the floor! Raise it and you're dead." The AK-47 went off. One man came out of the door running and Ray hit him square in the forehead with the butt of his shotgun. The man's legs buckled and he slid across the floor on his knees like James Brown. And then he didn't move. Andy hollered, "Pick him up and go down the stairs." Two men came out of the stairway. One had blood running down his right leg. Ray said, "Sit down ovah' there in the middle of the room." They did as they were told. The light in the stairwell went out and Andy came out with a very grim look on his face.

Ray turned around to us and said, "That pounding is an annoying sound, ain't it? Sharp, why don't you show them what's what."

Sharp looked out his slot and then put the Thompson in it pointed up at the ceiling. When it went off all I could think was that there are few other weapons that just sound like death. It got real quiet, real fast, in the next room. I heard one of them whisper in a very high-pitched voice, "motherfucker."

Then Ray yelled, "You put your weapons on the floor or there are gonna be a lot of cryin' mommas in town tomorrow." You could hear metal meeting the floor and in the clatter there was one uncertain voice that said, "fuck that motherfucker."

I looked at Ray and his eyes got big. "Did I really hear what I thought I just heard?! Oh no." Ray walked across the room with his head shaking. He peered through Sharp's slot.

Sharp whispered, "Two of them. The one in the corner and the one hanging behind the one that's crying."

Ray said, "Look out!" We all stepped aside from the slots. One of the two fools started shooting with a semi-automatic pistol. After about ten shots, one round managed to come through the slot on my side.

"Let me straighten this out." Ray pulled a .45 from the back of his pants. He looked in the slot, raised the pistol and fired once. I saw the guy standing behind the crier hit the floor. The one in the back corner bent down and put his gun on the floor.

"God Damn! They shot me again."

■ ● ■

I turned around and the one bullet that made it through the window port hit their own man. He was sitting on the floor wide-eyed mumbling, "They shot me again...they shot me again...goddamn they shot me again." I could see from where I was standing that the wound was superficial. It got him high in the shoulder. The shot Andy put on him would need a doctor pretty soon though. Andy got him just below the ribcage in the side. A couple of more inches to the center of his torso and we would be dragging his body down the stairs like Andy was doing now for the first guy who opened the door on the roof.

Ray was taking the bar off the door. "All of you get your foreheads on the wall and then lock your hands behind your head." Ray looked at me and then Sharp. We both nodded. Ray opened the door and went in. Sharp moved into the doorway with the Thompson pointed at the floor.

"Now then...when I get done collecting these weapons, y'all are gonna walk into the other room and sit on the floor with your friends."

"They shot me again...they shot me again..."

"I told you to stay down. You shouldn't a stood up. I think it was Ickey shot you, Dill."

"What?..Ickey?..Ickey shot me?"

I turned around and told them to shut up. The one bleeding on the floor said, "but I was just standin' there and you shot me again."

Maybe he had lost more blood than I thought he did, because he didn't seem to have a clue as to what was going on. Andy was getting closer. The thump, thump on the stairs was pretty loud now. All of the men had filed into the room and were standing in the middle of it staring at the stairwell. When Andy came through the door, the AK-47 was in his left hand and in his right he was pulling the corpse by his t-shirt, which was up

■ ● ■

under his chin by now. Everyone was staring at Andy and then Andy let go of the shirt. The corpse's head hit the floor with a thud. One of the tough guys let go with a sorrowful moan. Ray slammed the office door closed and a few of them jumped. I looked over at Sharp and did a double-take. He had a toothpick in his mouth that seemed to slide from one side of it to the other side like a pendulum. I wasn't sure but it looked like he had a smile on his face.

Then Ray started. "Now then, we are going to have a conversation."

The guy bleeding on the floor said, "Ickey, did you shoot me?"

The one who was Ickey said, "Wha' chu' talkin' bout? Shut the fuck up, man."

Ray slid over to the talker. "From now on you don't speak unless I talk to you."

The talker looked at Ray and said, "Fuck you."

Ray's fist landed on the side of his jaw so fast I wasn't sure if I saw the punch. I saw the result though. The talker wilted like a flower that hadn't seen water in a month.

Andy hit two of them in the shoulder with the butt of his weapon to push them out of his way. They both staggered and then Andy said, "Ray, you want to kill them all now?"

One of them said, "Oh God!" and he started crying. Ray stared hard at Andy. I was getting a sick feeling in my stomach. I glanced at Sharp and his eyes were just slits. The toothpick was sliding side to side faster than the last time I looked.

Ray said, "No, not yet. Maybe we don't have to kill them all."

The crier was sobbing now. The kid next to him had a tear dripping down his cheek. Andy's head was bobbing back and forth like one of those dolls everybody had in their car windows.

"You sure, Ray?"

"Yeah. Let me talk to them first."

■ ● ■

Andy moved away and stood by the stairway to the roof again. I looked over at Sharp and his eyes were still slits, but he had a smile on his face and the toothpick was rolling from one side of his mouth to other.

Ray was moving back and forth through the eight men still standing. I noticed how young a couple of them were.

"Who wants to live?" They were all silent. Then Ray roared, "who wants to live?!!", so loud I almost answered, "I do, I do." They almost all murmured, "I want to live."

"Then y'all sit on the floor."

All of them sat, except I noticed one of them was on one knee and he didn't flinch when Ray spoke. His eyes just kept moving from Ray to Andy. I walked over to him and his eyes locked with mine. "Sit on the floor." His eyes shifted to Ray. I repeated, "Sit your ass on the floor, right now." Ray looked at him and said "you think I'm crazy? Get hinky with my man there and you be in some trouble." He looked at me again and slowly lowered himself to the floor and crossed his legs. I moved back to the wall. Ray started walking again and then stopped in front of the crier.

"How old are you?"

In between sobs he said "seventeen."

Ray moved to the next one. "How old are you?"

"Sixteen." Ray shook his head.

Ray stopped in front of the next man. "Do you think it was a good idea to come up in here?"

The man looked around the room and seemed to hesitate before he spoke. "Well, I own't know."

Ray's voice shot out like the sound of a cannon. "I don't know?!!" Mr. 'Own't know' flinched and put his hands up in front of his face like he thought Ray was going to put his lights out.

■ ● ■

"You don't know? Ain't you got any sense?! You got one of your friends over on the floor dead. You got two of your friends bleeding on my floor. You standin' here in front of that man over by the door who is gonna kill everybody in here when I'm done talking if…"

It was like a wail. The crier went up on his knees with his arms flailing like he was at a revival meeting. Then he slid onto the floor. "Oh God! Please don't kill us all…Oh God…please don't kill everybody…" His body heaved with sobs.

Ray looked down at him and finished his sentence, "…if I don't stop him."

The sixteen year old picked up the crier under his arms. "Get up, Germaine. Be a man. Come on, get up. If we dying, we dying on our feet like men."

Ray put a hand on the sixteen year old's shoulder and said "sit back down."

"Now then, let me repeat the question. Do y'all think it was a good idea to come ovah' here?"

They all started muttering "no," except the crier, who said, "no, no, no, no it was a bad idea, a very bad idea, just bad."

At that, one of the others started to laugh. Ray's head snapped in his direction. "Are you high, fool?"

Our fool stopped laughing and then said, "Yeah, a little."

Ray snorted in disgust. "Course you are." Ray's head scanned the rest of them. "You, you and you…all high, ain't you?" You could see they were confused, like 'course we're high; what did you expect?'

"A couple of you are men. Most of you act like boys." Ray pointed at the sixteen year old and the crier. "You two go in the other room."

"Come on, Germaine." They left with Germaine still weeping.

"Now then, who gonna come back across town with Ickey

■ ● ■

and Baron when Baron decides he's ready to do something stupid again?" Four men looked at the floor and didn't say anything. One of them suddenly broke for the stairway and Andy hit him in the stomach with the butt of his weapon. The runner fell to his knees coughing.

Andy looked at Ray. "Can I shoot this one now?" He almost sounded desperate.

Ray's voice sounded funny, like he wasn't certain of Andy. "Come on, man. You can't be killing everybody that does something stupid. Okay?" The way Ray said 'okay' it was almost like he was pleading with Andy not to kill anybody.

Andy bent over the runner and said, "What the hell did you think you were doing?"

The runner was gasping for air. "I don't know. I'm sorry."

Ray walked over to him and said, "You sure is sorry. You one sorry motherfucker. It is surely sad how sorry you are." Ray pointed at the man bleeding on the floor and the man next to him. "You two go in the other room, and you two take that body in the other room and come back out here."

Ray walked over to me and whispered, "What do you think?"

I turned my head to Ray's ear. "That one on the floor is a problem. He's hard core."

"Yeah. That's Baron. I'm going to have to deal with him." Ray walked away. "Who has the car keys?" From the other side of the room I heard, "Germaine does."

"Who else?" Silence. "Come on. Who else? Y'all came in two cars so there had to be two drivers." One of the men next to Baron took the keys out of his pocket and handed them to Ray.

"Now then, the boys in the next room are going to the hospital, aren't you?" All of the voices from the next room said "yes."

Ray went to the door and held out the keys. "Germaine can't drive, so you and you go get the cars and pull them up to the door. When you are at the hospital you say the Rangers did this to you. If I hear anything different, I will have to come find all of you. Understand?"

I could feel the understanding flood through the door.

Ray turned to Sharp. "Can you hold these four here while we load the cars?"

"Be my pleasure."

"You gonna leave us in here with this cracker?"

Ray turned around and stared at Baron. "You so stupid you will never understand how stupid you are. You got two of your friends shot, one dead and that's only so far. Now I say I'm a hav'ta kill you out in the woods and I know you gonna say 'what you mean?' That's dumb, Baron. Ignorant dumb. Yes, I am leaving you with my favorite cracker son of a bitch and if he kills you before I do, I will only be slightly disappointed."

Ickey was moaning now and trying to sit up. His face was so swollen, I knew he had a broken jaw. He tried to speak, but when he did it sounded like his teeth and lips kept getting in the way of his words and most of what came out of his mouth was blood and saliva.

Andy and I followed Ray out of the office. He had raised the front gate and the two cars were backed up to the door. Andy and Ray grabbed the corpse and tossed it in the trunk of the Lincoln. Germaine and the sixteen year old were just starting to get into an LTD when the Thompson went off. Ray and I ran back into the office. Sharp was sitting in Ray's chair behind the desk with a big grin on his face and the toothpick still wiggling between his teeth.

"Sorry to disturb you. They apparently got the idea they could rush a Thompson sub-machine gun."

Ray looked around, confused. He bent over and picked up a piece of plaster and then looked at his ceiling.

■ ● ■

"Why the fuck you shootin' up my office, man?!"

"Had to give these knuckleheads a little warning."

"Warning my ass! Shoot the motherfuckers next time. Put the bullets in them. Not in my office! I run my business in here. Damn. This my place of business."

Ray and I walked back out to the cars. Germaine was on his hands and knees crying. The sixteen year old was trying to get him back up.

Ray said, "Why are you runnin' with Baron? You seem like you got more sense than that."

The sixteen year old stood up straight. "What are you going to do with them?"

Ray crossed his arms. "Why?"

He stared right into Ray's face. "They my friends. I don't want 'em dead."

"Y'all should'a thought of that before y'all came across town."

"They won't come back."

"Hell, Ickey'll be back here before the clock strike twelve."

The sixteen year old didn't say anything.

Ray put his hands on his hips. "Baron's crazy and he ain't stupid. Eventually he'll probably be back too. I can't have that."

This kid had balls. Not the crazy, 'I don't give a fuck'attitude. Guts. He never took his eyes off Ray's face.

"He's my cousin. I don't want him dead."

Wait a second. Was this kid threatening Ray? I was looking at this kid like I was witnessing childbirth. I looked at Ray and he had a frown on his face deep enough to plant corn in. Then Ray said, "I'll see what I can do. You get your people to the hospital."

I said, "Hey kid…what's your name?"

He turned on me like a chained tiger who hated me because I was holding the chain.

■ ● ■

"Marcus. Marcus Williams."

"Is that Germaine Williams?"

The look disappeared from his face. He nodded and got in the car.

Ray stood next to me and we watched both cars pull away. "You believe that boy?!"

"Maybe he's a miniature you."

"Naw. I wasn't that foolish at his age."

"What are you going to do with the other four?"

"I'm going to take them for a ride in my van and drop 'em off over on 71st and Daler. Then I'm going to call somebody."

"That's almost an execution, Ray. That's Ranger territory."

"Either I do it or somebody else does. But I'll give 'em a chance. Ickey got to go, one way or the other. He got no sense. No sense. Maybe the others can get home if they get lucky and run fast." Ray eyed me for a few seconds. "Andy was funny in there. He was really playin' his part."

"What makes you think Andy was playing?"

I had never seen Ray look this confused before. It seemed like he was recalculating his assessment of who Andy was while he stood there staring at me. Actually, so was I.

Ray's eyes scanned the neighborhood, such as it was. "What do you think Heeks is doing?"

"I was wondering that myself. It's not like him to disappear when something like this is going down."

We both turned around to see Mojica come out of the empty front door of Ray's office. He did not look happy.

"Ray, does your SEG record?"

Ray shook his head. "Not yet."

"While you guys were getting ready to welcome visitors, I noticed something on the top of that abandoned building next to that old switching terminal. I went out the back and made my

■ ● ■

way down there. Two of them; one black, one white; up on the roof checking things out. When I was going up they heard me. They put a wire and cans across the stairwell. I couldn't see it in the dark. When I got to the roof , they had already gone over the side. They left in a black town car. The black guy smoked Parliaments."

Andy had been listening and walked over to us still carrying the AK-47. We were all staring at the two buildings barely lit up by train yard lights. Then Ray breathed out, "Damn."

Twenty minutes later the four of us watched Ray pull away in his black van with four men tied up in back. As the tail lights disappeared around a corner, Andy said, "He's going to get one of us killed some day."

Mojica came to Ray's defense. "Come on Andy. Ray didn't know there was going to be trouble."

"Bullshit! Why do you think he set our meeting up for tonight. He needed help and you're telling me we just happen to be there to get stuck in the middle of it. He knew this shit was going to break. Raoul Whitfield knows everything that's going on in this town."

Sharp started chuckling. "Then you should have stayed home."

"And miss all of this stupidness?!"

I said, "Andy, I can't wait until you're fluid in English."

Andy looked down at the ground and muttered, "He's going to get us hurt some day."

We were all silent for a few seconds, then Mojica said, "Hey, what do you say we boogie?"

■ ● ■

Ears

I had to get out of the office. I didn't understand Andy. He was supposed to be my friend but he wasn't acting like one. I had to clear my head so I just started walking again. Over here the sidewalk was uneven. Cracks in the pavement rose up like teeth. One part looked like an ear. I was walking quickly. It felt good. I picked up my pace like I had somewhere to go. After about eight blocks I stopped. Under a tree two kids were flipping baseball cards. One kid looked up at me. He had ears like Gregory Peck. All of those ears. Just a pile of ears.

I started walking again. Hurrying on about ears. Those God Damn fucking ears. It felt good to walk like this. Really striding and sweating. Ears. God, it was hot that night.

Part of the floor glowed red from the lights across the street. The woman was lying on the bed, cut open from her vagina to her throat. Her ears were missing. She had long black, shiny hair, spread out around her head like a halo from one of those medieval paintings. The lamp next to the bed had a yellow bulb, and the parts of the sheets that weren't blood red, looked yellow. They were probably filthy. I could hear voices drifting up from downstairs and the street, mixed in with the sounds of whiny,

■ ● ■

little motor bikes. I wiped the sweat from my forehead.

Andy cracked the atmosphere saying, "The three MPs are convinced it was a GI."

I walked over to the window and looked down into the street. It was crowded with whores, GIs, some sailors and people hawking shit. I turned to Andy and nodded. "Yeah… If they weren't sure, and this wasn't like, what, the sixth one, they probably would have said 'some gook did it.'"

The next day we were brought before a cigar smoking general, who said that as far as he was concerned, all Andy and I were going to do for the rest of the war was catch the killer. There was pressure on from everywhere. From Central Command, to way, way up above. From the Vietnamese, all the way to the top, wherever that was. The Vietnamese army was screaming for the American files on the murders so that they could snag the guy. Yeah, like that was going to happen. Give us your files. Right. But if this story got out, it would have been very, very bad PR and probably bad for us. Me and Andy. The general made it real clear that we had to have the perp before the ARVN or the Vietnamese police did. He said we had carte blanche.

I remembered the look on Andy's face when we started to read the file and realized we had been lied to right at the start. Actually, did they lie, or just not tell us the whole story? I had been surprised at how angry Andy was when he read the file and found out that some poor grunt had already been arrested for the first three murders. When the fourth popped up, they didn't know what to do with the soldier they'd already convicted. The biggest shock though, was that there weren't six murders. There were eleven. I was reading the reports and glancing up at Andy while he kept flipping through the photos. Andy looked like he was on the verge of an uncontrollable rage. I half expected him to turn into that green monster from the comic books.

■ ● ■

"Andy...calm down. We just need to catch this guy. We've done this type of job before."

Andy glared at me and pushed the photos across the table. I had seen dead bodies many, many times. I'd seen autopsies performed. But when I saw these photos I almost heaved. It was three of the photos that really got to me. All of the women had been sliced open, but three of them had been tied up on a bed. These three were cut up while they were still alive. There were rags stuffed in their mouths and their eyes were open. Dull, dead eyes that looked like they had been trying to scream, 'help me!'

I had to do something or I was going to be sick. I looked up at the ceiling, shook my head, drank some water and grabbed the Chesterfields off the table. Through the smoke I blew at the ceiling I said, "Andy, how can there be so many? How can someone get off base this much...get so much leave? How could he be alone so much?" We sat in silence for about thirty seconds, and then the looks on our faces must have been reflecting off each other. We hit on the idea at the same time. He wasn't with a base unit. He did office work somewhere in the city and he was able to move around whenever he wanted to. And he was connected.

We had our list of suspects narrowed down in two days. After we checked out and crossed off the first name on our list, Andy said, "you know, they didn't want to catch this guy. They were going to let him just finish out his tour and go home and let him start over in Detroit, or Texas somewhere. Not their problem any longer."

"Give me the file Andy." He tossed it to me and I went through the suspects again and then pointed to a Lieutenant Roberts. "He's our man."

Andy stared at me. "What? Why are you so certain?."

"Because he wants to re-up."

Andy was mulling it over. Then he started nodding his head.

■ ● ■

"Let me see that."

Just to emphasize the point I said, "Why go home. He's having too much fun here. At home somebody would come after him. Here, he's in the sand box."

"And we get called in because somebody realized the scumball wasn't going to leave."

The next day we tracked him down to a big, miserable-looking, shit-hole bar. He was sitting in a corner in the shadows with a prostitute. Andy had brought along four MPs. Two of them he sent to the alley behind the bar before we went in. When Roberts saw us coming across the bar room floor he didn't even flinch. The prostitute, though, knew it was trouble and she moved away so quick it was almost like she'd never been there.

We stopped in the middle of the room. Andy was real formal. "Lieutenant Roberts, you will come with us to division HQ." The two MPs walked past us. "You will be…"

"Grenade! Grenade!"

The MP right in front of me crouched down like a baseball catcher just as it went off. He slammed back into me like a log. People were screaming through the dust in the air. I couldn't get the MP off me. Then I heard Andy hollering, "Are you alright?! Soldier, are you…" He pulled the MP off me. I sat up on the floor and looked over to see blood pumping from his open chest. Then it was like somebody snapped their fingers and the dull flow became a trickle and stopped. Andy ran out of the bar. I got up as quickly as I could and limped out of the bar just as the MPs, who were supposed to be in the alley, passed me on the way in. I ran down the street limping, wondering what was wrong with my leg, but not looking to see what.

When I got to the alley, Andy was looking at the bathroom window. "Roberts is damaged. He cut himself up pretty good getting out. Lots of blood on the window sill.

■ ● ■

If those MPs had held their position, we'd have him right now."

Suddenly it was loud in the bar. Andy and I both slid to the sides of the bathroom window and peeked in. The tenor inside had changed. No screaming now. It was yelling in Vietnamese and English.

Five or six Vietnamese plain clothes were milling around in the bar. One of them was arguing with the three MPs. Another one was slapping the prostitute and yelling questions at her.

Andy looked down at my leg. "Can you run on that?" I nodded. "Are you sure?" I nodded again. "Don't just fucking nod! Are you in shock or something?! Can you move on that leg? They're going to be right behind us. If we stop fast they're going to be four months up our assholes. Can you go?" I nodded. "Oh fuck you!" Andy took off running and I tried to keep up. When we got to the end of the alley finding Roberts seemed hopeless. It was a market street that was jammed with people. We both looked up and down the street. Mopeds and scooters were flying by. The sidewalks were filled with heads bouncing up and down as far as we could see. I heard Andy say, "We don't have a cha… There!" Andy pointed and about three blocks down a jeep was pulling out into the street. I saw him now, too. Andy growled, "We'll never catch that motherfucker."

I walked out into the street with mopeds dodging me and their riders cursing at me. Two GIs and a colonel were coming toward us in a jeep. I stepped in front of it and leveled my Colt at the driver. He slammed on the brakes and the colonel stood up and put his hands on his hips. Before he could spit out any of his officer bullshit, the two grunts slid out of the jeep with their palms up. The colonel glanced at his two escorts and quietly stepped over the side. A few people pointed, but most people just went on about their business like this went on every minute of every day.

■ ● ■

Andy ran past me and swung himself behind the steering wheel. I limped over and took the passenger's seat, never taking my eyes off the colonel. He seemed like he might be stupid enough to try something. We lurched forward with Andy laying on the horn every three seconds. I kept my eyes trained on the colonel until we were out of range. He might have been a good shot.

The road got dusty fast. Lt. Roberts was about a half mile ahead of us and the dust from his jeep just seemed to hang in the air. We were going around a hill and then at one point the road curved back like a horseshoe toward us. We passed so close I felt like I could have reached out and grabbed him. He disappeared around the bend in the road and when we went into the same curve I could see them. About a mile back were two jeeps with the Vietnamese cops in them.

When we got to the other side of the hill the road straightened out and we started going downhill. The road became bumpier and Andy started cursing and he slowed down. But not Roberts. We could see his jeep bouncing up and down. And then Andy yelled, "Whoa! Did you see that?!" Roberts' jeep flipped forward and to the side. You could see Roberts hanging on to the steering wheel with one hand, trying to grab anything with the other and his legs running in mid-air. Then he was loose and he disappeared from view over a bank. A spray of water shot up like it was in slow motion.

We pulled up quickly at the spot where Roberts flipped his jeep. Andy hit the brakes so hard I had two hands flat on the windshield trying to keep from going over it.

Andy was out of the jeep and out in the rice field before I could step down. When I finally got out I looked back up the road and saw two jeeps just getting to the downhill part. Where we stopped, the road was about four feet above the field and I

■ ● ■

stumbled down the bank trying to follow Andy as best I could. The sun was hot as hell. The air felt sticky. I hopped about twenty yards out in the mud. Then I stopped and crouched down. I suddenly felt very naked. What the fuck was I doing out here?! For two hundred yards, if somebody wanted me dead, I was dead. My head spun around looking for someone who wanted me dead. I started twisting at the waist trying to see where the shot would come from. Over to my right, about fifty yards away was a row of palm trees and about fifteen yards away was a two foot high dike. I was squinting, trying to see if anything was moving over there. I was waiting for a shot, or maybe many shots.

Up ahead I could see Roberts and Andy splashing through the field. I started moving again slowly, tentatively. I kept looking to my right expecting to take fire. I tried running. It looked like Andy was close to catching Roberts, but the sun was so bright I couldn't be sure. I was stumbling, my leg hurt. I knew Andy was going to need me. I kept going and kept stumbling. I thought I saw Andy dive and tackle Roberts. I wanted to run, but all I had in me now was a stumble and a limp. It looked like Andy was struggling with Roberts in the mud and water. A feeling of desperation started beating in my chest. I had to get up there with Andy and I was closing too slowly.

When I finally reached them, Andy had his arms wrapped around Roberts' legs. Roberts was on his back trying to kick free and was hitting Andy in the head at the same time. I fell on Roberts, planting both of my knees in his chest. I punched him in the eye and his fight was over. While gasping for air I asked Andy if he was okay. He didn't say anything. He crawled up to Roberts' arm and we cuffed him. We both stood up, pulled Roberts to his feet, and started dragging him toward the road.

"Motherfucker!" Andy was pissed. He glanced over at me

■ ● ■

and then at Roberts. "We got you, you cocksucker."

The three of us all had our heads down, making sure we didn't stumble and trip in the mud. I glanced up and was surprised, even though I shouldn't have been. There were about ten Vietnamese police of some kind, milling around our jeep.

I said, "Andy…"

Through gritted teeth he almost screamed, "What?!"

I nodded toward the jeep.

Andy looked up. "Jesus Fucking Christ. Just what we needed to complete the day."

We stopped walking and stood there out in the field staring at the ten men who were staring at us.

I said, "Maybe we should just let Roberts walk up there by himself."

Roberts screeched, "What? I'm trying to win the war just like you! I stopped fifteen gook bitches from killing any of our guys. How many have you stopped?" There was desperation in Roberts' voice. I looked at him and then at Andy. Both of them were looking toward the jeeps. One of them was almost perfectly sane. The other would never come close in this lifetime.

One of the Vietnamese yelled, "Send him up here GI."

I tried to figure out if we had a chance to make it to cover. The palm trees or the little dike.

In a very respectful voice I heard Andy say, "I can't do that you short motherfucker, sir."

The first shot came about two seconds later. I screamed, "This way!" You would have thought we'd walked into an NLF ambush. The air was full of every American caliber bullet known to man. We dove behind the dike with dirt flying up all around us. I rolled over on my back. "Andy, are you okay?" His reply scared the hell out of me. "How bad are you?!" I ran my hand over my chest and started hollering, "Where am I hit?!" Roberts

■ ● ■

started laughing and I swung my elbow into his face to shut him up.

"Your leg!"

I looked down at my leg and my panic disappeared. The water around my leg was pink. My leg hurt like it had a piece of metal in it. But it was just the leg.

"Did that happen back in the bar? Christ! Looks like you're bleeding to death."

"Fuck my leg, Andy. How the hell are we going to get out of here?"

"Christ! I can't believe I'm going out in friendly fire."

"It's not friendly fire, Andy. They're not even on our side." We were quiet for a couple of minutes and the shooting died down. A pop every once in a while and a spray of dirt and mud that splashed in the water.

"You know they're going to try to flank us."

Andy looked at me like he had been born full of hate and it only got worse the older he became, because he didn't know what to do with it.

"Hey short motherfucker."

"What you want faggot GI?"

"I'm coming up to the jeep and we're going to talk."

Silence.

"Okay faggot GI. Come on."

Roberts went into a panic. "You can't let them have me! You can't do that! I'm U.S. Army! I'm in your custody!"

I started smiling.

"Shut up, God damn it! Give me your hands." Andy removed the cuffs. I stopped smiling. "I have no intention of letting that trash get you. Stand up." Roberts didn't move. "Stand up!" Roberts got up slowly.

"You're going to let me run for it?"

■ ● ■

Andy didn't say a word. In one motion he raised his Colt, shot Roberts in the head and before he could fall, Andy pushed him over the dike.

Andy dropped down for protection behind our little dirt wall. It was stone cold quiet. I felt like my skin was on fire. I started smearing mud on my arms and face.

"We have to do something about that leg." I glanced over at Andy. He was lying on his stomach, peering just over the top of our little dike.

"You know if they haven't left by now, we must have pissed them off so much they've decided to do us too."

Andy sighed. "I know. I was just thinking that."

"You know, Andy, I don't think I've ever been this scared before." Andy was still squinting over the top of the dike.

"You?! Scared?! Right. This is you being scared? Smearing mud all over yourself and gazing up at the sky? You seem more concerned about sunburn than anything else."

"Are you scared, Andy?"

Andy ducked his head down and stared at me. "Scared?! I'm fucking terrified, stupid! I don't want to die out here in this piss-hole. I'd like to get laid at least one more time. Why the fuck are we talking about this shit now?"

"Just trying to get us in touch with our emotions."

"What?!" Andy was looking at me like I had lost my mind and then he turned back to squinting over the dike at our Vietnamese comrades.

I raised my head a little. "Hey Andy…"

"What?"

"This is really going to piss them off."

"What?" I aimed my hand gun in Andy's direction. His eyes got huge. "What are you doing?!"

My Colt went off and Andy couldn't have dug any deeper

■ ● ■

into the ground if he had a bulldozer.

Andy looked at me again like 'what the hell are you doing?'

"One of their assholes was crawling up the other side of our dike over there." Andy looked the other way and poked his head up quickly over the top of the dike. "Shit. Good shot. You iced that motherfucker."

The air was now filled with Vietnamese voices trying to find out if their friend was anything less than dead. He couldn't have been more dead. Those sons of bitches opened up like we had raped their grandmothers.

After about a minute Andy's eyes looked crazed. He shook his head. "We're not going to make it out of here. Let's see if we can take more than one of them with us!"

Then the shooting started from behind us in the palm trees. I curled into a fetal position almost immediately. I wanted to cry. I was going to die out here in this mud puddle. They had us completely surrounded! How?!

It took me a few seconds to realize the shots were not aimed at us. They were lighting up the jeeps. It was NLF guerillas behind us with two heavy caliber machine guns. The Vietnamese police who were left standing were trying to escape in one jeep. They didn't make it. Their vehicle got hit so bad the tires blew out and you could hear the gasoline running onto the ground when the shooting stopped.

It became nerve-wrackingly quiet. No movement over by the jeeps. I could hear Andy breathing. I could hear the water move around my feet. We laid there for about an hour without speaking. Trying not to move.

Finally Andy said, "What do you think?"

"I think we're not dead."

We both got up on our knees and looked around. Especially over at the palm trees. We got to our feet and in a crouch we

■ ● ■

both walked toward the jeeps like we were on tip-toes. The mud kept making squishing, sucking sounds and it drove me nuts. I wanted to be the quietest man in the world and it wasn't happening.

"If six were nine." Andy looked behind us.

I whispered, "What?"

"I want to hear Hendrix play 'If six were nine' one more time before I die."

When we got to the bank in front of the jeeps I stood up straight and looked around. I was sweating like a pig.

The ears. All of the fucking ears. The next day we found Roberts' little, one room apartment. On a table, right in the middle of the room, was a pile of thirty-two ears. Different sizes. Some still had earrings in them. I got dizzy when I looked at them. One of them had three cuts in the top. Was that one of the first ones and he didn't know what he was doing…or was the woman still alive and struggling while he was cutting?

The crash snapped me awake from my daydream. Two freight cars slammed into each other. I jumped and stumbled sideways. I looked around. Where the hell was I? Railroad tracks? Damn! I walked all the way to the other side of town. I was soaked in sweat and it wouldn't be any cooler hiking back. I could hear more freight cars slamming together off in the distance. I looked up at a brick red car that read "The Chessie System" in white paint, and below it in yellow chalk, "suck my dick."

■ ● ■

Dicky's

I was hoping it would get busy in the afternoon. If it did I'd be able to get a new pair of slacks. I needed some tips. I had my rent paid. The electric bill was paid. I had my pads. I picked up my medicine yesterday. I needed some milk.

If I could get some new slacks, then I'd go see him. See what he thought. The coffee was done. I had to set up a new pot. A customer came in sweating kind of hard.

I watched him sit down in the corner booth by the last window. He looked out at the street both ways as I walked over. When he looked at me he kind of forced his smile.

"Hi. What can I get you?"

"Can I have two raspberry jelly donuts and a coffee, please?"

"Sure can. Be right back."

The guy's shirt was soaked. He's outside running in shoes and pants? I put his donuts on a plate and poured his coffee. When I took it over to him he was still looking up and down the street. I said, "Hot out there today."

"It's not that bad but your air conditioning feels good."

"It's nice. Good for the summer."

The AC was good for me. The windows were good for me.

■ ● ■

The whole front of Dicky's Donuts was a big window. Everything open. Booths next to the windows and a long counter with
red stools. I liked it here. Reminded me of junior high school
when I used to work in that Chock Full of Nuts on the corner.
Two walls of windows. Gosh, that was a long time ago. I looked
at the racks and noticed the powdered only had one left. When
I went to the back, Alex, he was only seventeen, and Barry the
owner, were working on the donuts for the evening. Barry was
almost powder white from head to toe with flour. Alex just came
in, so he was still clean.

"Wha'dya need Sharon?"

"A tray of powdered."

"Just finished them."

"What time do you stay til' tonight, Alex?"

"I'm only on until nine. Barry doesn't need me to stay."

Barry looked up from the table through a cloud of flour.

"Julie'll be in at six, honey."

I picked up the tray and went back to the front. When I
came out the guy in the corner was holding a donut in his left
hand halfway between the plate and his mouth like he was frozen. He was staring at something across the street. I put the
powdered rack up and then walked over to his table.

"See something good-looking out there?" He turned his
head toward me so fast, he scared me and I took a step back.

"What was that?"

"More coffee?"

"Yeah. Sure."

Then he turned back to staring across the street and took a
bite of his donut. While I was walking away I heard him say, "I'll
need more cream here."

When I came back with the coffee and a new creamer he gave
me a real smile. I almost asked him if he needed any company

■ ● ■

later, but I had to stop that shit. I had enough money. I wasn't going to do that stuff any more. When I went to see Bryce again, everything in my life was going to be clean. I was thinking I was going to ask him if he wanted to take me to breakfast again. Maybe he'd think that'd be fun. Maybe it could be our thing.

I kind of winced. What if he didn't even remember me. He was kind of weird. Really, really nice, but weird. I guess a war could do that to you. I doubt he could ever have a girl friend the way he is. Maybe we could be friends. We could share an apartment together. That could be really cool. Shit. Maybe he wouldn't even remember me.

"Hey Sharon!"

I pushed off from leaning on the coffee stand and went to the back. It didn't take Alex long to get flour all over himself.

Barry smiled at me. I really liked his smile. "I'm going over to Toney's for a late lunch. I'll be back in an hour. Those honey donuts can probably go out."

I took the tray out through the swinging doors and noticed that the guy in the corner was staring into his coffee with his head down. A new customer had come in. He was sitting at the counter, right in the middle, looking at the newspaper.

"I'll be right with you."

"Okay, but just a coffee."

I put the tray of honey donuts up and poured a coffee for the new customer. He was still looking at the paper. I put the coffee down on the counter and he grabbed my wrist. He looked up and said, "Remember me? You owe me ten dollars, bitch. And maybe a freebie. What do you think? Huh?"

I tried to pull away but he held on grinning like a carved up pumpkin.

"I need some milk, too. Get me some milk."

He let go and I backed away. I kept my eyes on him and

moved down the counter to get a creamer. I went back to him and put it down fast so he couldn't grab me again and he started laughing.

Another customer came in and sat down by the register. I walked past Mr. Ten Dollars in a wide curve away from him. He watched me the whole way and started laughing. The new customer looked at me funny. I kept looking over at Ten Dollar even though I was standing in front of the new person.

"I'll have an ice tea and a honey donut. Make that two more to go."

"Okay." I walked toward the donuts, keeping as far away from the counter as I could. When I was right across from Ten Dollar he suddenly flinched like he was afraid of me, but I was afraid of him. I tried to jump back but I was already against the coffee stand and all I did was knock over some cups and make a big noise. He started laughing again. I went to get the iced tea and I noticed the man in the corner looking at me and then he started looking at Ten Dollar. I had the tea and the donuts and I was determined to walk past him normally. When I just passed him he slammed his hand down on the counter and said real loud, "That Gil Thorp is something else!" I turned around quick and spilled some of the tea. I told the new person I'd get him a new tea, but he said that was okay. I picked up a rag to wash the counter on the other side of the register, even though it was clean. Ten Dollar started laughing again.

The sweaty man down in the corner was walking toward us. I thought he was going to pay. Then he stopped and sat down right next to Ten Dollar. The man with the to-go donuts stood up and dropped two dollars on the counter.

"Keep the change." He walked out with his bag.

I was watching the other two out of the corner of my eye, but I couldn't really hear what they were saying. The sweaty man

■ ● ■

spun around on his stool like a little kid. Then I heard, "Bitch owes me ten dollars." I couldn't hear them again until, "So go back to your table," and then, "I'm not done with my coffee." I heard Sweaty say something about a "blood transfusion." Sweaty spun around on his stool again, but when he came around this time his left hand shot up really, really fast to Ten Dollar's throat. I heard a thud and then Sweaty pushed Ten Dollar off his stool and pinned him to the floor. I was leaning over the counter to see what was going to happen and then I heard Alex say, "What the hell is going on out here?"

Sweaty said, "Do you really need that coffee?"

Ten Dollar didn't say anything. Sweaty stood up and backed away. Ten Dollar stood up and started to turn away.

"And you better pay for the coffee."

Ten Dollar put some change on the counter.

"Better leave a tip, too."

Ten Dollar stared at Sweaty and then put his hand back in his pocket. He slammed some more change on the counter and started backing away.

"I'm not going to forget you."

Sweaty got a big smile on his face.

"Well I hope not. That's why I hit you."

Ten Dollar turned around and on his way out he pointed his finger at me. I leaned away from him.

Sweaty said, "You better put that finger back in your pocket."

Ten Dollar turned and spit in the direction of Sweaty, but most of it hung on his chin and dripped on his shirt. Then he sailed out the door.

Two guys I recognized from the night shift at Philco came in the door laughing and sat at the counter. Alex was standing by the swinging doors holding a flour sifter, "What's going on out here?"

■ ● ■

Sweaty laughed and said, "We had a disagreement over Gil Thorp."

Alex looked at me. "You okay?" I nodded and hoped Ten Dollar wouldn't come back. I didn't want Barry to find out about me. I served up two coffees and noticed Sweaty coming back from his table. He walked right up to me.

"You owe that guy ten dollars?"

I shook my head.

"You work until closing?"

I shook my head again. He put three dollars on the counter.

"Don't worry about me. I'm okay."

"Uh-huh. No change."

He left and I started thinking, "what if he was the guy who was killing all of those women...why was he asking me all of those questions...maybe I should call the police...what if Ten Dollars was...naw...Ten Dollar just wants a free blow job...but he's scaring the hell out of me...I can't have Barry find out... maybe I should just quit and try to find another job...maybe there's a Chock Full of Nuts here, too."

■

I had been walking a long time now. It wasn't that warm but I was drenched in sweat. I needed some place to cool off, but I wasn't that familiar with this part of town. I knew I was walking in the right direction just by going east. Eventually I'd get somewhere.

I kept looking for my tail but I wasn't seeing anyone yet. I knew there were some shops over by the Philco plant. Maybe I could find a place to buy a soda over there.

When I saw the Dicky's Donut shop I knew it had to have an AC so I immediately went in. Nice little shop. The façade was all picture windows. Nice booths. I took the booth in the

■ ● ■

farthest corner from the door. I looked up and down the street to see if I could spot my tail. He must have been laying back so I'd think he'd lost me.

The waitress was kind of small, brown hair, nice smile.

"Hi. What can I get you?"

"Can I have two raspberry jelly donuts and a coffee, please?"

"Sure can. Be right back."

I thought I must look ridiculous. It was like somebody poured a bucket of water on me. The waitress had brought me a coffee and donuts but as I took the first bite I couldn't remember her bringing them to my table. I looked around the place. I was the only one here. Even the waitress was gone. For half a second I wondered if I was dreaming. I started to take another bite and I saw him. Leaning at the corner, watching the front of the donut shop. How does he keep changing his look?! Maybe it's a couple of guys. Maybe...

The waitress said something and startled me.

"What was that?"

"More coffee?"

Whatever she said before that didn't register. "Yeah, sure. Going to need more cream over here." I looked back out the window. There he was. Wasn't doing very good at not being noticed. That guy crossing the street. He just passed him. Was that a signal? Here comes my tail.

I lowered my head so he wouldn't think I made him. He must know I'm on to them. He's looking in the door. Looking around like he doesn't know I'm in here. He's coming in and he's sitting at the counter. Why are they pushing this now? What the hell do they want? He's grabbing the newspaper. Great cover. Obviously they don't care if I know they're behind me. The waitress came back out carrying a tray of donuts. She's got that smile going.

■ ● ■

"I'll be right with you."

"Okay, but just a coffee." He doesn't even look up.

I checked out the street again to see where the other guy was. Some women walking by. A couple of kids further down.

"Remember me? You owe me ten dollars, bitch. And maybe…"

'Maybe what?' I couldn't hear that last part. What the hell was he doing? He needs to let her go. He started laughing.

"I need some milk, too. Get me some milk."

The waitress seems to be afraid of this guy. She's afraid he's going to grab her again. Another customer has come in and he sits down slowly. I looked out the window to see if I could spot his partner. I looked both ways and then there was a crash. My head snapped back to the counter. The waitress looked like she wanted to climb the wall, but some glasses and silverware got in the way. She's backing away from him. He's not here for me. He's in here for her.

I watched her pick up a rag and start cleaning the counter down by the doors. The other guy with the bag got up.

"Keep the change."

That screwball started laughing again. I got up and walked over to the jerk and sat down on the stool next to him. I whispered, "You know, you're acting like a real jerk."

"So who the fuck are you?"

"Keep your voice down." I spun around to my right on the stool. I hadn't done that in a long time.

"Keep my voice down? Who the fuck do you think you are? Bitch owes me ten dollars."

"I told you to keep your voice down. You couldn't do that, so now I think its time to for you to leave. You're disturbing the customers."

"So then go back to your table."

■ ● ■

"I said, I think its time for you to leave."

"I haven't finished my coffee yet."

"I don't care if you haven't finished your blood transfusion yet. Take your ass out of here pud-face."

"How about fuck you? How's fuck you?"

I spun around hard on the stool and when I was facing him again, I grabbed him by the throat with my left hand and threw a punch to his kidneys. I slammed him to the floor and waited for his eyes to open after he registered the pain and the embarrassment.

"Do you really need that coffee?" He didn't say anything so I squeezed his neck harder. He barely shook his head, but he shook it, so I stood up. He got up slow and turned to leave.

"And you better pay for the coffee." He reached in his pocket and then put some change on the counter. He took a step to leave, but I couldn't resist.

"Better leave a tip, too."

He was staring at me like he was trying to think of something to do. He put his right hand in his pocket and came up with nothing. His left hand jammed into his other pocket and he came out with some change. He threw it on the counter and some of it fell on the floor. He started backing away.

"I'm not going to forget you."

I almost started to laugh. A kid in junior high said that to me once. I didn't see him again until my senior year. He was huge by then. We both got suspended over that one. I couldn't quite understand holding a grudge that long. Maybe this guy will hold one, too. But I won't have to worry about him eventually being huge. He was a punk jerk who would never grow larger than his ego was right now. 'He won't forget me.' Uh-huh.

"Well I hope not. That's why I hit you."

The jerk slid kind of sideways to the door and then he pointed his finger at the waitress. My assessment of punk-jerk changed. I

■ ● ■

hadn't seen that kind of rage in a long time.

"You better put that finger back in your pocket."

He turned his head toward me and spit. I almost started laughing again. The spit didn't seem to make it past his chin and then hung down to his shirt like a rope. I stomped my foot like I was going toward him and he banged out the door. I watched him run across the street. His face was an ugly red.

I guess I finally heard the kid behind me asking what was going on, like he couldn't figure that out.

"Ever read Gil Thorp, kid? We were having a disagreement over Gil Thorp."

He asked the waitress if she was okay and she nodded while looking at the floor. The kid disappeared through the swinging doors.

I went back to my table and finished off my coffee and donut while standing up. I scanned the street. A couple of guys came in and sat at the counter.

I turned back to the counter and walked over to the waitress. She looked apprehensive, even though I had slammed her boyfriend on the floor and threw him out. I put my hand in my pocket.

"Do you owe that guy ten dollars?" She shook her head. She looked scared. "You work until closing?" She hesitated and then shook her head again. I put three dollars on the counter.

"Don't worry about me. I'm okay."

"Sure. Uh-huh. Keep the change."

I walked out the door thinking the tip was too big, but she probably didn't make squat. I looked both ways up and down the sidewalk. It was empty for a few blocks in both directions. Now it was hot. Up ahead I could see guys crossing the street heading toward the Philco plant. I needed to get back to the office to talk to Andy. I had to tell him I had found the serial killer.

■ ● ■

Traffic

"Heeks, let me borrow your car."

Mojica stood up, tossed me his car keys and then sat back down. I stood in the doorway to his office wondering how he managed to have so many things in a space this small. It was like looking at a PX full of contraband. The walls on both side of his desk were fake. There were shelves in front of both of them filled with stuff. Just stuff.

He'd spent days building the walls when we first moved in here. I didn't know him so good back then and at first I thought he was crazy. But when he finished, and I couldn't tell that his walls could move, and then seeing that behind those false walls he had things I could easily imagine we would be using in the future, my whole perspective on Mojica changed. He was really smart, even if he was a smart-ass sometimes. He quickly became one of my three closest friends.

Every once in a while I think you meet someone who you're pretty sure will be in your life until you die, even if you don't see them every day, or even for years. Just some random meeting and somehow that person ends up being there forever. Fucking Mojica was one of those random persons.

■ ● ■

"How's Helen?"

Mojica looked up from the report he was writing and smiled. "She's still pissed that we didn't let her come with us when we were setting Barthelme up. She says she knows she's better behind the wheel than Andy."

"Jesus Christ. Everybody wants to do the gangster shit."

"I don't think it's that. I think she wants to show off her skills. She won the last two pylon competitions she was in out at the Flatts."

"Doesn't she realize that driving through pylons is a lot different than wading through some craziness at sixty miles per hour?"

"Dude, it's hard arguing with your average, everyday, common medical student."

"Whoa! So nurse Helen got into medical school? That's great! When is she gonna dump your ass, now?"

Mojica started laughing. "You really are an ignorant son-of-a-bitch. I'm good to last at least until she interns."

I felt really good for Heeks, but I really didn't know what to say.

"Congratulations, man. Congratulations."

"It's not like she's pregnant, but thanks, Mr. Enthusiasm. Are you leaving anytime soon, because I need to finish this report."

I waved and stepped out of his doorway. I counted to three and then stepped back in.

"Mojica…" He looked up. I gave him the finger.

"Damn. You're ambidextrous."

"You're an idiot."

"Don't wreck the car, A.J."

I got downstairs and stopped in the middle of the lobby. Only a few people were passing through at this time of day. I looked at the yellow-brown marble walls. I turned around and

■ ● ■

looked at the four art deco-trimmed elevators with the silver clock over them. The guy who sold papers over against the wall was long gone for the day. There was a bronze door to the left of the elevators that led to the basement. To the right was the one that let the health conscious climb the stairs. I looked up at the round globe lights hanging from the ceiling.

"Vhat's wrong? Everyting okay?"

I looked down at Ivars, who was looking up at me with concern on his face.

"Nothing wrong. Everything's great." He looked up at the ceiling to see what I was looking at and then looked at me.

"Everything's cool, Ivars." But I wasn't. I had no idea of why I had stopped there. I tried to smile and then went out to the sidewalk. I stopped there, too, and just looked around. I shivered and made a right around the corner toward Mojica's car.

Mojica's cars always purred. Helen saw to that. Whether it was his Fairlane or his Rambler, when they started it felt like you had the wheel of a Corvette or a Jag in your hands. I had no idea how Helen acquired so much automotive skill. She said she wanted to be a doctor, but maybe she really should have been a car mechanic.

The big thing I couldn't figure out was why Mojica had a red Fairlane. The two-tone green Rambler was cool. The seats reclined until they were flat with the back seat. Every sixteen year old's dream car. Mojica liked the screens that were factory fit for the windows. He could go fishing, sleep out in the country without a tent and be free of mosquitoes. The Fairlane he said was inconspicuous. Inconspicuous my ass. A glowing fire engine red is not inconspicuous.

I was daydreaming about cars, so it took me a couple of turns to spot them. They were pretty far back, but they were making all the turns I was making. A grey Chrysler. I decided to

■ ● ■

make a left and then I took another left and parked in front of a truck. Kids were coming up the sidewalk from a movie theater. There was a lot of laughing and a little shoving. A late model black Chevy cruised by. No Chrysler. I started the car, pulled out and made the first left. I pulled up at the light and watched the Chrysler I thought was tailing me go through the intersection. How could they be so far back? I put my directional on, deciding I would follow them. The light changed, I turned, they were gone. I squeezed the steering wheel. The guy behind me honked. "Okay! Okay!" I was going about two miles an hour.

Traffic was still light and parking was easy when I pulled up in front of my apartment building. I stepped out of the car just in time for them to pass ten inches from me with the windows up. They made a right at the corner. I pulled my pen out and wrote down the plate number. Why was it a black Chevy? I felt weird and confused. I couldn't tell cars apart from each other now?

I went into the building and took the elevator to my floor. When I got out Mrs. Culletti was waiting to go down.

"Hello, stranger. A friend of yours was here a little while ago."

I looked down the hallway to my door and felt a little nervous.

"Really? How long ago?"

"Oh, twenty minutes. I was taking my trash…Jake isn't home or he would have taken it. It wasn't much, but we had fish last night and now the smell. Jake should have taken it then, but he had to watch the fight. I said Jake, take it after the fight, but I think he fell asleep, because I was talking to my niece's brother-in-law's wife's sister and she was telling me…."

"Did he have a name?"

"Who?"

"My friend."

"I'm sure he did, but he didn't mention it."

"How do you know it was a friend?"

■ ● ■

"He said so."

She looked at me like I was missing parts. I held the elevator door and moved back a little to give her the hint that she should get in. She stepped in and I tried to gently close the door, which she must have taken as a sign she should start talking again. She switched her pocket book to her right hand and held the door open with her left.

"He seems like such a nice man."

"Who?"

"Your friend! That's who we're talking about here."

I tried to push the door closed, but I think she put a foot on it to keep it open.

"He was a big man. A very big man and we were talking about rigatoni. He really knows Italian food. He's not...."

"How big?"

"Oh my. He looked like the size of that monster." She started laughing. "You know, Rodzilla."

"That's Godzilla, Mrs. Culletti." How could someone living in America not know Godzilla. But then they say one to two percent of Americans don't know who the President is.

"And all of this time I didn't know that. Godzilla you say, not Rodzilla. I never saw one of those movies. All of those frightened people running and screaming."

Mrs. Culletti's eyebrows raised about a foot and her eyes got so big I was worried they would fall out of their sockets and I would have to catch them before they hit the floor.

I could feel my face begin to screw up. It was time to leave Mrs. Culletti to her free association thought patterns. I started down the hall wondering who 'my friend' was.

"He was very dark and big, like Godzilla."

I stopped in my tracks and turned around.

"Who was? My friend?"

■ ● ■

"Of course your friend. Who do you think we have been talking about? He was African-American. That's the correct term, isn't it?"

I nodded. "Thank you, Mrs. Culletti."

"You're very welcome. Have a nice day." I could hear the elevator start to go down.

Raoul. I walked to my door and stared at the grey paint. Why in the hell would Raoul come to my place? Why did it take me so long to figure out it was Raoul? My mind started running over all of the characters in the case. Case?! What case?! There was a 'thing' happening. I had to figure out what this 'thing' was. Bernie and Bland. Barthelme. Brautigan. How many B's were there in this 'thing?'

I shook my head, opened the door and went straight to the windows. Were they there? I looked down into the street but I couldn't be sure if their car was down there or not. I went into the kitchen and grabbed a hammer from under the sink. Then I picked up a file from my bedroom and started down the stairs. When I got to the sidewalk I looked around. Two girls were playing hopscotch in front of the next building. One white. One Black. They looked happy. No school. Sunshine. Hopscotch. Friendship.

I slipped into the Fairlane, put the hammer under the seat and headed back toward the office. Those two GIs playing with stones by the drainpipe. My head started drifting toward that time with Andy when we were sent to check out a unit where an officer had been fragged. Somebody high up thought we were going to be able to find out who did it. Yep.

Most people who weren't blind knew how the war was going over there. But when we walked into that Quonset hut it became crystal clear that the war was definitely heading toward an end that Washington wasn't going to like. There were rumors that Walter Cronkite was coming and if he spent five minutes with these soldiers, he could just turn around and go back home with the knowledge that the U.S. was not going to win this war.

On one side of the hut all of the black soldiers and one white soldier were huddled together smoking and whispering. One black soldier and the one white soldier were tossing little stones at a drainage hole in the floor. It looked like they had made a game out of it. On the other side, all of the other white soldiers stood milling around.

The sergeant walked toward us, glancing at the black soldiers a few times like he expected one of them to do something.

"Bout time you got here. We been sittin' on our asses here all day. We're tired of sittin' around. We want to do somethin', so I hope you figure somethin' out right quick."

Andy said, "We'll do our best, Sarge."

"He was a good officer." The sergeant looked at us like he expected us to agree with him. Then he turned and walked away.

The Sarge was a gung-ho, duty-bound lifer. Andy looked at me and made an "O" with his mouth.

"Why don't I start over here and you take those guys and we'll get a feel and then switch." Andy nodded.

I moved over toward the black men. I squatted down with them and the first thing I heard was, "what the fuck you want?"

I took a slow stare at the one who spoke and said, "I want to know who killed the cracker Captain and why." A couple of guys to my left chuckled. To my right someone with an accent that sounded like he was a television news anchor started speaking.

"The Captain was in fact a cracker son-of-a-bitch." To my left I heard chuckles again and one 'thas right.' The anchorman continued. "He sent black man after black man out on point and three men are dead. Only one white man ever took point while he led us. When we stood up and protested, he said he would

■ ● ■

make sure we all took turns at the point. He meant the brothers would take turns. That man was an Alabama cracker and that motherfucker deserved to die." The 'uh-huhs' and 'that's right' spread to the other soldiers. "But I didn't do it. Someone else tossed a grenade and beat me to it. But I will tell you this. If that person had asked for my grenade, he would have had it." Off to the left I heard chuckles again.

I had been looking around at the other soldiers while the Anchorman spoke. I looked back at one soldier and said, "Is your safety on?"

"Fuck no! I don't trust those mothers to waste us all if they get the chance. I want to be ready. Period."

Combat usually dragged grunts over the racial barrier out of the necessity of survival. If these men survived, they would be taking home some emotional scars that might stick for a lifetime. While they were here they probably wouldn't mind if the other half of the unit died.

"Who's that one white soldier over there?"

A soldier with black rimmed glasses answered. "Who? Two-tone? He the only one of them got any sense. Plus, he stood up in front of ever'body and asked the Captain why only blacks were being put on point. The Captain said, 'Why damn if y'all ain't next, white-boy. Didn't y'all know that?' Two-tone walked point and didn't complain or say a thing when he was on point more than ever'body. He a stand-up motherfucker. He should'a been a brother."

A man standing outside the circle said, "He is a brother. He's white, and I don't care. That man is my brother."

Another soldier spoke up. "Man, it wasn't just point. The Captain would do stupid shit. Like that time he said 'Webster, walk out there to the tree line. See what you can see.' Webster started out across that field and Captain Collins turned to the

■ ● ■

Corporal and said 'We need to draw their fi-ah.' Draw, their, fi-ah?! Shit…all we needed was to lay some rounds in those trees and we'd a drawn their fire!"

It felt like I was at a church revival meeting. Everyone was agreeing by adding 'that's right,' 'uh-huh,' 'like it was.'

"What happened to Webster?"

"He back in the States by now. Charles tore his ass up. He prob'ly never walk again, but he out of this shit hole."

I looked over towards Andy and saw him talking to one soldier off to the side. Then the mortar rounds started falling in. Everybody dove on the floor and we could hear shooting outside. They missed the Quonset hut, but nobody wanted to talk after that. Everyone was expecting action.

Andy and I drifted off to the side. Andy whispered, "I don't think one of the black soldiers did it."

I looked past Andy toward the white troops. "Why not? They all wanted him dead."

Andy started walking out of the hut and I followed. When we got outside he turned around so he could see anyone coming out the door.

"Two of the white guys think one of the white soldiers did it. One of them said he was sure of where all of the, as he put it, 'dudes of a darker persuasion' were when it happened. The other one said the Captain and the Corporal had words that morning.

I noticed them again about three blocks back. The grey Chrysler. I squeezed the steering wheel. Two minutes later I was wondering where they went. I had my eyes in the rear view mirror so much, I was surprised I didn't rear end someone before I got back to the office.

By the time I parked around the corner and got upstairs, it was almost rush hour. When I walked into the office I immediately noticed that Elaine had a new addition to her desk.

■ ● ■

"What's this?"

"My new computer."

"Really. What can it do?"

"Keep track of accounts, cases, all kinds of things."

I nodded while wondering how much it cost us and when we decided to get her one.

"Some day they're all going to be able to talk to each other."

I looked at Elaine like she was crazy. "You mean all computers will be hooked up to each other?"

"Sure. If you want to be. Some day pretty soon, almost everyone will have a computer."

"Are we suddenly wiping out poverty? How will people afford them?"

"Just like people can afford cars. Eventually they'll be mass produced." Elaine paused and seemed to look off into the distance. "We'll still have poverty though. Poverty is too valuable for the rich."

I stood there staring at Elaine while I held my file in front of me with both hands like I was handing in my assignment for biology. I felt kind of off balance by what Elaine had just said. It was like she had stabbed a nerve in me.

"What college did you go to, Elaine?"

"Why?...Princeton, until they kicked me out."

"Oh."

"If you had read my application, or been at the interview you would probably know this, if you were capable of listening that day."

My head snapped up. "What's your problem? Fuck you... you...." I wanted to say 'bitch,' but that was out. I wanted to say ten other things, but if 'bitch' was out, so were the other ten.

Elaine was looking at me with fire in her eyes. "Brilliant. Let me give you my address, so that when you get out of the hospital

■ ● ■

and have gotten used to not having gonads, you can come looking for me."

"Fuck you...fuck you, Elaine! How's that?!"

Elaine stood up and put both hands on the desk and leaned over it towards me.

"Hey! You two playing house again? I'm gonna watch, okay?"

We both turned to Mojica who stood there with the second biggest grin on his face I had ever seen anywhere. His eyes went from me to Elaine, back to me and he never stopped grinning. "Don't stop now. You were on the verge of bloodshed."

I looked at Elaine slightly embarrassed. All I could say in a normal voice was, "asshole."

"Pussfuck."

"Twat."

"Twat?!" That was one of the ten things.

I started walking away expecting to take a bullet at any moment. Instead she yelled, "Creon!"

I turned back. "Creon? You called me Creon?"

"Yes I did and I'm amazed you were listening."

I turned my back on her again and went into my office. As I sat down hard, I hit my thigh on the arm rest. "God damn it!"

Mojica bounced into the office all smiles. "That was fun. I love our office atmosphere." I was looking at an adolescent who had recently been let out of his cage. His face suddenly got serious and he said, "what's a creon?"

"Nothing."

"No. Seriously. What's a creon?"

"Nothing. She made it up. She went to Princeton. They do shit like that over there. They make shit up."

Mojica paused. "Okay...Do you have the Brighton file?"

"Yeah. That's what I went home for. Jesus, I can't believe I almost forgot, listening to Elaine run her mouth. Raoul was at

■ ● ■

my place today. I missed him, but maybe we should go see what he wants."

"Let's wait for Andy. He should be back any minute."

"Then let's wait for him downstairs."

When Mojica and I left, Elaine was typing away on her new computer. Mojica told her when to expect us back and she gave us a wave with her right hand without looking up.

One of the other elevator operators took us down. I didn't recognize him. I didn't see Ivars and I hoped he wouldn't have a conversation with "Mr. Andy" about my standing in the lobby in a daze.

When Mojica and I went out to the sidewalk I immediately saw them one block away. Car running; windows up. I was just about to point them out when Andy strolled up.

"What's shakin' guys?"

I spun around. "Raoul was over at my place looking for me. We think we should go see what's up."

Andy put both of his hands in his pockets and turned his face toward the sky. "Jesus H. Christ. Does he need somebody dead today? No bodies over at his place in a couple of nights?"

Mojica said, "Andy, you know as well as me that Raoul wouldn't come looking for us unless it was important."

Andy lowered his head until he was staring at the pavement. "Alright. Let's go." When he looked up he stared at my face. "Do you sleep any more at all? Where's the car?"

I pointed and said, "I'm driving."

Mojica took shotgun and Andy sat in the back. I pulled away from the curb and started taking side streets to avoid the traffic. After about five minutes Andy said, "Where the hell are you going? We won't get across town until after breakfast tomorrow morning."

I didn't say anything.

■ ● ■

I heard Andy mutter, "Jesus H. Fucking Christ."

I saw them. Two blocks back. A black Chevy. I turned a corner.

Andy erupted. "Where the hell are you going now?! Pull over and let Mojica drive."

I ignored him. Then I heard Mojica say, "You don't want to go this way. We'll get tied up in traffic with all of the buses."

I went that way anyway. In one minute we were dead stuck in traffic with buses trying to get people home from work. They were stuck, too.

Andy was beside himself. "Do you believe this?! It's too late now to switch drivers, but it would give me a great deal of satisfaction to see someone else behind the wheel."

I slammed on the brake, put the car in neutral, grabbed the hammer from under the seat and flung my door open.

As I got out of the car I heard Andy say, "Good. Heeks, you drive."

Then I vaguely heard Mojica say "He's got a hammer."

Horns started blaring. A few people cursed me. I could hear Andy yelling at me. I walked back four cars and the two men inside the black Chevy were acting like they didn't see me. I tried to yank the door open but it was locked. The driver looked up at me with a frown on his face.

I smashed his window in with the hammer and the glass sprayed all over him. He leaned away and I stuck my hand through the hole and unlocked the door. Some of the horns stopped honking. I ripped the door open and grabbed the driver by his sport coat and pulled him out of the car.

Andy's arms were around me in bear hug. He lifted me off the ground and started carrying me back toward our car.

"Let go of me, God damn it! Those are the guys!"

"What the hell do you think you're doing?!"

"It's them! It's fucking them!

■ ● ■

"What the hell are you doing?! Have you lost your mind?"

Mojica was out of the car, walking parallel to us on the other side of the cars jammed up behind us. I could see him looking all around as Andy carried me back to the Fairlane.

Andy yelled, "Get in the goddamn car!" He pushed me in head first and I halfway fell on the floor. Andy slammed the door and then got in the driver's seat. Mojica got back in front.

I was in a rage. I wanted to smash Andy's head now. I screamed at him, "Those were the guys, goddamn it! I had them!"

Andy hollered back, "Shut the fuck up! Just shut up!"

Mojica was turned around in his seat looking out the back window. After a couple of blocks Andy took a left out of traffic. Mojica looked at me and frowned. He reached over the seat and grabbed my arm.

"Put the hammer down, bro."

I looked down at my hand squeezing the handle of the hammer so hard it looked like my veins would pop. I put it on the floor and then, in a frustrated voice, said, "We're not heading toward Raoul's."

"Raoul's?! We're not going to Raoul's. We're going back to the goddamn office where I am going to pick up a phone and get you a doctor."

"What?! You think I'm crazy?!"

"You're damn fucking right! That was normal? You get out of the car, smash some random guy's window in with a hammer. Pull him out of the car. What were you going to do then? Beat him to death with the hammer? Who did you think they were, anyway? More serial killers? You've already identified two. Was that two more?!"

It got quiet in the car.

"Heeks, what the hell are you looking back for?"

"Just drive Andy, okay?"

■ ● ■

I stared out the window until we got back to the office building. No one said anything as we went up. When we walked into the office Elaine said, "You have visitor waiting in Antonio's office."

We all walked over to Mojica's door and saw Raoul sitting in the chair behind Mojica's desk. Andy and Mojica walked in. Raoul said, "Heeks, what it is?"

Elaine's hand grabbed my shoulder. "Are you alright? Do you want me to get you something to drink?"

"You're not my servant, Elaine. You're our secretary. No thanks."

"No, I'm not your servant, but what happened? Are you sure you don't want me to get you something?"

"No." I pulled her hand off my shoulder and started into Mojica's office but stopped. I turned to see Elaine walk over to her desk and sit down. She glanced up at me and then started typing on her computer.

I moved over to her desk, leaned over it and put both hands on it for support.

"Elaine, I didn't mean to be a jerk just now to you. Something bad happened and I'll tell you about it after the big guy leaves. I'm sorry."

Elaine whispered, "Don't worry about it, but I'm all ears when you come back. That's only if you want to talk."

I pushed away from her desk and turned around. Tears started welling up in my eyes. I was wiping them away with my palms when suddenly Elaine was in front of me.

"Here, use these. I hate it when something gets in my eye and I can't get it out." She handed me some tissues to use and then slipped back toward her desk again.

"Creon." I spun around and pointed at her. She started laughing. I threw the tissues at the waste basket and missed.

"Had to get you back on track."

■ ● ■

I took a few steps backwards away from her while she shooed me off with the backs of her hands. Then I heard Raoul's rumble of a voice. "Creon was a king in the Aristophanes plays."

Andy said, "Excuse me. Can my partner and I get back to our topic of conversation?"

"Heeks asked me who Creon was."

I walked in and leaned against the wall. Raoul looked at me like he was concerned, and nodded.

Andy turned his head toward me. "There's someone...."

Mojica interrupted him. "Andy, where are the cops?"

"What?"

"I won't get behind you on this unless you can tell me where the cops are."

"What the hell are you talking about?"

"We've been back twenty minutes. After what our partner pulled, you don't think fifty people had our plates and descriptions? Don't you think one of those two guys would have crossed the street to the phone booth and called the cops? Why aren't the cops here?"

Andy was looking hard at Mojica.

"I think there was someone back there. I'm not sure there weren't two cars."

Two cars! God damn it, what was wrong with me? The Chevy and the Chrysler. I could see Andy was looking at things differently. He leaned back in his chair and put his hand up to his mouth.

"Who has a lunatic smash his car window, gets dragged out into the street and doesn't get the cops?...besides Raoul."

Raoul chuckled.

Andy looked at Raoul and locked his hands behind his head. "Raoul, why are you here?"

"If you have business you have to take care of, I can wait up to

■ ● ■

fifteen minutes. But I have to catch a flight."

Mojica said, "Where are you heading for?"

"The Bay Area."

Then Andy asked impatiently, "Raoul…why are you here?"

Raoul stared at Andy. Andy started glaring back. Then, like he never saw Andy, Raoul looked first to Mojica and then to me.

"I decided to call in a favor for some information. I was thinking about our man here fighting his way out of that apartment and all of that craziness. I wondered if there was a connection between that man who said his name was Brautigan, and you."

I stopped leaning and stood up straight. There was a buzzing in my ears.

"Did you find one?"

"No. Not directly with you. My source came up with a connection to Andy."

Andy sat forward like he was going to fly out the chair. "What connection?!"

Raoul leaned back in Mojica's chair and pursed his lips. Andy stood up. "What connection?"

I said, "Raoul, what in the hell are you talking about?"

Raoul looked at Mojica. "Heeks, you want to stand up, too?" Mojica chuckled. Andy sat back down.

Mojica said, "Raoul, what connection? Quit screwing with Andy."

Raoul looked at Mojica and then at Andy. He turned back to Mojica and said, "That is the last thing on my mind, brother."

I was starting to get annoyed again. "What fucking connection, man?!"

Raoul looked at me like I had gone crazy and said, "You need to get this boy some sleep. He almost out'a his mind, talkin' to someone like that."

Andy muttered, "Don't we know it."

■ ● ■

Raoul started laughing and Mojica joined in. When they stopped Raoul looked at Andy. "You ever work on a case with a serial killer who was mutilating women?"

I looked at Andy who was directing all of his attention at what Raoul was saying, and not saying.

I said, "Andy and I were partners on that case."

"Well, Mr. Brautigan was there first. He was a postal clerk who brought it to the attention of the Military Police that there was a pattern to some killings. When you two were brought in, Andy's name was linked to Brautigan's by the circumstance of a report. I put out feelers for Brautigan, but I don't think he's in the city. If he's still here he's probably deceased."

The room went silent except for the slow squeaking of Mojica's chair as Raoul rocked back and forth. Andy looked at me and then at Raoul. "Thanks for the information, Raoul."

"Gentlemen, I got's to roll." Raoul Whitfield stood up, completely blocking the window behind him. "You know, you have a very nice woman out there working as your secretary. Seems real smart. Don't abuse her."

Raoul shook our hands and then stopped on his way to the elevators for a couple of words with Elaine. When the elevator took him down, it felt like the world was suddenly empty.

Mojica spoke first. "We need to have a meeting to talk this out. We need Sharp here, too."

Andy was looking at his hands folded in his lap. "The sooner the better." Andy looked at me.

"How long do you think they've been behind you?"

"For days."

Andy looked back at his hands and shook his head.

I said, "Raoul has given us some serious information and we need to weed through it to see what it might turn up."

Andy sighed and looked up at Mojica. "Heeks, see if you can

■ ● ■

get in touch with Sharp and see if we can all get together somewhere tomorrow…since our office is probably being watched."

"Cool."

"So we better keep our eyes open and if you're going to knock
somebody out during rush hour, do you think you could tell us
what you're doing and even maybe a 'why?'"

"Yeah…yeah. That was stupid."

"That, my friend, was out of control. You're not working alone,
you know."

"Yeah. I know. I'm sorry."

It got quiet again.

"Guys, I have to leave. I'll let you know what Sharp says."

We both watched Mojica leave the office and we heard him
say goodbye to Elaine. I sat down in a chair next to the desk.
"Andy, I'm sorry about what I did out there. I feel like I couldn't
control myself."

Andy leaned forward resting his forearms on his knees.

"You're under a lot of stress and I'm worried about you. I'm not
really helping the situation either. I feel like I haven't been your
friend. A hell of a lot of stuff has popped off here and I don't know
what to think."

I leaned forward and my head was almost touching Andy's.
"Brother, I think I may be losing it. Every time I turn around I
think there's somebody there."

"Damn, maybe there is and I haven't wanted to see it because
you keep finding serial killers." I turned my head and saw Andy
smiling slightly. "We're going to have to figure this out and I have
to have a more open mind. Right now I don't think you're crazy
and I was wrong for thinking that."

"No you weren't. Andy, you know me better than anyone I
know. I'm not completely wacked, but there's something wrong
with me. I don't know what it is. I feel like I'm on edge all the time.

■ ● ■

If you were serious about me seeing a shrink, maybe I should."

We were both silent for a while.

"If you need to talk to a pro, I'm behind you all the way. If you want me to go with you, I will. Whatever you want or need, I'm there." Andy slapped me on the shoulder. "I have to head home. Why don't you let me give you a ride?"

"Naw. I'm gonna grab a taxi after I get some pizza."

"Okay. We have a lot to talk about tomorrow. Come clear-headed." Andy left and I heard him say 'good night' to Elaine.

I shuffled out to Elaine's desk and told her what I did with the hammer. Then I told her about the donut shop.

"You know, you can still get out of here before something really bad happens."

Elaine smiled. "So what are you doing tonight? Are you going to home and get some sleep?"

"I will, but first I want to go over to the donut shop and see if I can pick up on anything."

"Like what? A Bavarian crème? Is that where you were last night? You should go home."

"Eventually I will, but Elaine, do you think you could lay off the Creon bullshit?"

"That depends upon your attitude in the future, o' great thespian."

"Fuck you!" I could hear her giggle as I stepped into the elevator.

Carnival

I watched guys come out of the donut shop and head back to the Philco plant for the rest of their shift. The waitress was counting her tips at the counter and changing them in for bills at the register. She'd be coming out soon, too. Earlier I'd found out her name was Sharon.

I stood as far back as I could in the corner of the lobby of the insurance company across the street. I was surprised the door was still open this late. When somebody came down to leave, I would duck under the stairwell and I only managed to crack my skull once.

Now there was a woman at the counter with Sharon talking to her and laughing. She must be the nine to one replacement.

A blue Valiant station wagon pulled up outside. Four teenagers got out, crossed the street, went in and sat down at the counter. They kept punching each other in the shoulder like they were the Four Stooges. They probably couldn't think of anything better to do on a summer night than find some waitress, somewhere, to bother.

Sharon came out and turned left. I moved up to the lobby door to watch her. She made nervous glances over her shoulder

■ ● ■

for the first block. After that her walk became more relaxed, like she was strolling. I let her get a block and a half ahead before I stepped out to the street and followed. It was a beautiful night. Warm breeze, not humid like the afternoon.

After four blocks Sharon took a right. I crossed the street to her left. She never glanced in my direction as far as I could tell. I wished there were some other people out besides us. I looked behind and saw a blond two blocks back.

After I had crossed to the other side of the street I noticed a guy and a girl locked arm in arm coming at me. Sharon was watching them come down the block all the way.

I passed an open window where a ball game was on the television. The guy and his girl went on by with Sharon's eyes locked on them. I dropped into the entranceway of the apartment building I was passing and pulled off my dark shirt and tucked it in the back of my pants. I took a quick glance up the street to make sure I kept contact with Sharon and heard, "It's a two and two count on Dave Kingman." I stepped back out to the sidewalk and out of the corner of my eye I saw the blond still coming, swinging her pocket book like 'come steal this from me.'

After about six more blocks Sharon started to cross over to my side of the street and then she paused. She was looking down the block to her right and I slowed down. I could hear it now, too. Some kind of music. Actually, it sounded like a jumble of music. Sharon started walking toward it. Some people were coming out of the street to my left and were also heading toward the sounds.

When I got to the corner I could see her silhouette in the lights of one of those traveling, summer carnivals. I sped up to get closer to her because now there were people getting in and out of cars. A family passed me while I put my dark shirt back on over my white t shirt. The two kids were crying because they

■ ● ■

didn't want to leave yet. "We don't have school tomorrow." The
mother was smiling. The father looked pissed. I still didn't notice
anyone with an interest in Sharon.

When I got close, I realized this was a pretty big fair. Much
bigger than I remembered them. Maybe I hadn't seen one in a
while. Half of the lights in the world seemed to be moving. The
Ferris wheel had orange and yellow lights twirling around in a
circle. The Whip had purple lights coming at me and snapping
away again. The Salt and Pepper shaker had red lights and was
starting to rotate in the opposite direction. There was a ride I
never saw before going straight up and then dropping. It seemed
like everyone on it was screaming. Past a carousel with yellow,
pink and green neon tube lights, I could see at least part of the
midway. It seemed like we were going to drown in colored lights.
This had to be larger than the usual carnival. It had to be two or
three of them put together.

The ground was already soft and spongy. I remembered this
area as a football practice field for one of the local high schools.
Wouldn't be much grass left by the time this was over.

Sharon stopped at a cotton candy vendor and bought a huge
puff of blue sugar about the size of a large cloud. I moved over
to the ice cream stand and bought a small vanilla.

Sharon continued down the midway looking left and right
with a big smile on her face. She kept sucking the fingers of
her left hand, probably trying to clean off the sugar. Two guys
walked past me complaining about how bad the spook house
was. Sharon stopped at a concession where you picked ducks
out of a waist-high pond of water to win prizes. I stopped a little
ways away, dropped my empty cone in a trash can and leaned
on a counter, looking around to see if there was any interest in
Sharon. I kept expecting to see donut boy appear in the crowd.

Now that I was stationary, a barker was asking me if I want-

■ ● ■

ed to shoot. I looked to the back of his booth and saw about twenty balloons pinned to the wall. There were small pellet rifles chained up, lying on the counter.

"Naw. No thanks."

Just as I looked back toward Sharon she turned to me. I looked back at the balloons. The barker had turned his attention to some young kid, trying to suck him in to trying his luck with one of the air rifles.

"Hey! Let me take a shot at this." The barker tried to look at me like I was his best friend, but in his smile all I could see was "sucker."

"Changed your mind, huh? Five shots for a dollar. Twelve for two dollars."

"I'll just do five." I handed him a buck and he handed me a rifle. I took the first shot and missed bad. I looked over my shoulder to the left and Sharon was back to watching ducks. I heard some odd screams to my right and looked toward the Ferris wheel. For whatever reason, it had stopped. When I looked back at the balloons, the barker was staring toward the Ferris wheel with a frown on his face. Then he looked at me with his greedy smile and said, "Haven't done this in while, huh?"

I took two more shots and missed with both. I looked down the barrel of the rifle and grinned at the barker.

"I'm going to take twelve shots now." I handed the barker two more dollars and then I grabbed the barrel with both hands and put it to my knee. The barker yelled, "Hey! What the hell you doing?" I kept grinning and then ran off ten hits in a row.

"Got enough balloons? What can I win now, huh, pal?"

The barker looked at me like I was an asshole for blowing his little scam. He'd just bend the barrel back after I left though.

"Yer that guy." I didn't turn. I lifted the pellet rifle to shoot again.

■ ● ■

"Hey...yer that guy."

I turned around and Sharon was staring at me. I really screwed this up, trying to prove I was Dead-eye Dick instead of paying attention to my job.

I frowned like I didn't know who she was, then tried to smile my brightest 'what a surprise' grin. "You're the waitress from the donut shop, aren't you?"

"You following me? I'm calling the cops."

"Wait a second, I'm..." Her face suddenly looked very pale and she dropped her cotton candy.

"Look, I was..." She squatted down screaming, put her arms over her head like she didn't want anything to fall on it. I turned to put the rifle down on the counter and wondered where the barker went. I started to turn back to Sharon and a spot on the counter about six inches from my hand exploded. I pulled my hand away like I had touched a hot stove. There were screams to my right and people running.

"He has a gun!" People were running with their kids in their arms. Some were dragging them in the dust. One guy, with a huge beer belly, staggered by holding a four foot long, lime green teddy bear under his right arm. In his left hand he was sloshing a large container of beer that he didn't seem to have the time to drop.

My head snapped left because now people were screaming and running in a panic from that direction, too. Sharon was still squatting with her arms covering her head. A man tripped over her and she fell sideways into the dust. I dodged some people while I tried to get over to Sharon. I grabbed her by the arm and pulled her up.

When Sharon was standing, an old man fell right in front of us like he had been shot. When he completely collapsed on the ground I could see he had been. I looked a few booths past the

■ ● ■

duck pond and could see the shooter looking right at me, and then he started coming.

"Grandpa! Grandpa!" Two young teens were on their knees trying to get their grandfather back in life. It would never happen.

I yelled and pointed, "Run that way! Now!!" The girl took off. "Come on, David!" David had tears streaming down his face. He grabbed his grandfather's arm and I screamed, "Go!" He looked up at me and then he bolted after the girl.

I was dragging Sharon toward the BB gun booth when the ground kicked up in front of me. Two shooters. I paused for half a second, then flipped Sharon over the counter. As she sailed through the air I thought, 'I hope she doesn't break anything.' I dove over the counter just as I heard three shots go off from a pistol. I landed on my right shoulder and thought I broke it. I lifted my head and saw the barker. He was lying against the wall of the counter with a big red spot in the middle of his white tee shirt. He looked stunned, like how could this happen to me. I rolled over and saw Sharon crab walking backwards toward the end of the booth. I got to my knees and crawled as fast as I could to catch up with her.

"Go under the tarp! Go! Go! Go!"

Sharon flipped over and looked like she dug her way out of the booth. When I lifted the tarp a shot went off and a hole appeared next to my hand. I went under the tarp thinking, 'He needs more time on the practice range.'

When I got under the tarp Sharon was squatting again. She looked like a terrified squirrel holding an apple in her hands. I grabbed her wrist, pulled her up and started running. She was a good runner once she got going. We jumped over generator cables. Knocked chairs over. Ran into a clothesline. There was chain link fence all around the fair, and I couldn't see a hole in it.

■ ● ■

For a brief moment I thought maybe we could climb it. Another pistol shot and I knew the shooter was too close for us to do that.

"This way!" I pushed Sharon in between two booths. We were right across from the spook house. I grabbed Sharon's arm.

"When I say 'now,' we run for the spook house and hide until the police get here." Sharon was pulling away from me.

"I can't go in there." I looked at her and could see flat-out terror on her face. Her eyes were wide and crazed. I hoped it was from the shooters, but it seemed it was the idea of going into the spook house.

"Are you kidding?! You're a waitress. You can do anything!"

I started running across the midway toward the spook house dragging Sharon behind me, when the sound of a rifle retort split through the carnival sounds and the screams. For two seconds Sharon slingshot her way in front of me. We made it to the front entrance when the pistol went off again. We ducked inside and I glanced behind just in time to see a shooter with a pistol and one with a rifle.

"Are we gonna' take a cart?"

I glanced at Sharon. "Are you nuts?! C'mon!" We started into the darkness, stumbling on miniature train tracks.

"What if…"

"Be quiet!" Almost as soon as I said that, a screaming witch jumped out of the wall at us surrounded by yellow and green flashing lights. Sharon was hysterically screaming. She was half bent over and she was bending at the knees bobbing up and down. I grabbed her and pulled her further down the tunnel into the darkness. I had Sharon in my left hand and I was touching the wall with my right as a guide. A heavy gust of air hit us and I jumped around in time to see a ghost drift past us into the wall.

When I turned back for Sharon I couldn't see her at first.

■ ● ■

She was muttering, "oh God…oh God…oh God…" The damn witch was screaming again and I could faintly see Sharon on her knees. I pulled her up and said "Shut Up!" There was a sound approaching. It took me a second to realize it was a cart coming down the tracks. Would someone with a gun be in it? I tugged on Sharon's arm and felt the wall to see where the ghost went through.

"In here! Quick!" We went through the hole in the wall just in time for the ghost to slide out across the track and another burst of compressed air made Sharon jump. "Hold my hand. Don't let go."

We were walking very slowly. Actually it was more like we were just sliding our feet. I could hear screams, evil laughter, ridiculous cackling and metallic sounds, like a hammer hitting an anvil. Then I thought I heard water. "Water?" At the end of the hall a red glow appeared and disappeared. In the glow two girls sitting on the floor appeared for a brief second. They were terrified with their knees up to their chins.

"You should come with us. It's not safe here." Like it was safe anywhere.

In the periodic red glow I could see one of them shaking her head. The other one just said, "No."

I didn't think we had time to discuss it, so I pulled Sharon behind me. We stepped out into a new passageway and Sharon said, "Maybe we should stay with them."

"We can't. It's too close to the front. We have to find…" A figure jumped at me and I swung my fist on instinct and managed to break the ear off a devil holding a pitchfork. My hand hurt like hell and then the devil started laughing. Sharon said, "Don't break it."

"What?! C'mon! We have to find a place to hide. If we can find a place a little further in we might be okay until the police

■ ● ■

get here."

We started down the tracks and I went, "Shit." I was standing in water.

Sharon whispered, "There's water in here somewhere. I can hear it."

"Yeah. C'mon. I'm standing in it."

I pulled Sharon behind me by the hand and half-way through our puddle a purplish light started coming up slowly. Snakes were coming down the walls and Sharon let out a scream that made me duck. She couldn't slip out of my grip, but she went down in the water trying to get away. I was panicking now. People for twenty blocks would be able to hear her screams. If there were gunmen still after us they knew right where we were. I jerked Sharon up and clamped my right hand over her mouth. The light faded out. I took one step and the light came back on and the snakes started sliding down the walls again. Sharon's legs were moving a mile a minute with water splashing everywhere. I started dragging her away from the snakes with legs and arms flailing. I stopped moving. I thought I heard, "over here." They saw us?! My head snapped in both directions.

A whisper. "Over here. Hurry!"

I moved toward the voice. Sharon was ripping at the hand I held over her mouth. Her legs were still kicking, but not as violently. A hand reached out and grabbed my T shirt and guided us through another space in the wall.

"Do you need a gun?"

"What?! Yes, I need a gun!" I was as confused as I could be. "Elaine?!"

"Yep. Here." She pushed what felt like a .38 into my left hand.

An empty cart went rumbling by in the dark. Then we could hear the screams of the girls back in the hall. Two shots. I could

■ ● ■

hear the witch again.

"Elaine, what the fuck are you doing in here?"

"Trying to help save your ass, I think." A light pulsed through the cracks in the wall next to us and I could hear a scream on the other side of it that I thought was a person. In the dull light I could see Elaine staring up at me wide-eyed.

"What do we do now, boss?"

I couldn't believe this. What in the hell was going on here?

Then Elaine whispered, "Honey, if he takes his hand away, are you going to scream again?" Sharon shook her head. "Okay, honey, that's good, because if you scream again I'm going to shoot you." Elaine held up a .45 in front of Sharon's face. "Understand?"

Sharon nodded her head yes. I slid my hand off her mouth slowly. Elaine put one finger in front of her lips and went, "shh-hhh..."

It was Sharon's turn to whisper. "Why is he trying to kill us? Why did he follow us? Why does he want to kill me?!" Sharon grabbed Elaine's arm with both hands and I could see Elaine struggling to get loose.

Elaine ignored Sharon's questions and looked up at me. "What are we going to do?"

"You two stay in this hall. I'll go down the tracks and see if we can get out safely."

"What?!" Sharon grabbed my shirt now with both hands. Elaine took Sharon's wrists one at time and pulled her hands off me.

"He'll be back. He won't leave us here. I have a gun, too. We'll be okay until the police get here."

I hoped that was true, because I was beginning to think it may be a while before the police got to the spook house. I started to think that maybe they would set up a perimeter around the

■ ● ■

whole place and then methodically work their way through the booths and trailers, after they pulled in enough off-duty cops for some overtime.

The spook house screams and laughter suddenly stopped and it scared the hell out of me. Then twenty watt bulbs came on in the ceiling changing the way I felt about being in the spook house. It was like there was no place to hide now. From outside I could hear the muted music of the other carnival rides mixed in with police sirens. In here, mixed with the quiet, it sounded like death.

I kept looking in both directions as I walked until I came to another hole in the wall that opened to another maintenance hallway. But in this one I got lucky. Down at the end of this hallway I could see cracks in the floor that were actually the edges of what looked like a trap door. When I got closer I could hear a generator outside.

I turned back to get Sharon and Elaine. When I stepped out of the hallway, three pistol shots went off and I jumped back into the hall. Then a shot from the other end of the hall away from the trap door. I was pinned and the only reason the guy with the rifle didn't hit me was because of the angle he was shooting from. The guy with the pistol missed me because he was a bad shot. If I was shooting my way out of this it was going to have to be against the guy with the pistol.

Two shots went off. They sounded like thumps. I peeked out in the direction of the pistol shooter. He was crouching down, twisted, looking back to his left. I took one shot and hit him in the stomach. He fell back against the wall and slid down to the floor. I moved down the tracks thinking that wasn't a patrolman's weapon I heard.

I got to the gunman and kicked his pistol away. I kept looking for the rifleman to come out of the hallway behind me. I heard Elaine whisper. "Is it safe now?"

I realized it had been Elaine who had let off the two rounds that had distracted the pistol shooter.

"No. But come on anyway. We have to get out of here. It might be hours before the cops get here."

Elaine came around the bend pulling Sharon by the arm.

"I think there's a way out back in that hallway. When we get in there, get down on one knee against the wall and cover the other end. The guy with the rifle has a bad angle. He'll have to go all the way into the hall to get a decent shot at us...unless he's left-handed."

Elaine and Sharon both stopped moving when I said that. I was nervous now, instead of just alarmed. I wanted to chuckle, but all I could do was tell them to keep coming.

We got into the hallway and Elaine went down on one knee against the wall with her weapon pointed toward the end of it. I took two steps toward the trap door and looked back. Sharon was standing in the middle of the narrow hallway looking over Elaine's shoulder like she was calling balls and strikes at a baseball game. I went back and pushed her down against the wall.

The trap door actually lifted easily.

"Elaine, Sharon, c'mon."

Sharon started to run down the hall, tripped and got back up running like it was a dance routine. She started to go out the hole in the floor but I grabbed her.

"Wait." I kneeled on the floor and stuck my head out. Upside down, the world looked safe. I dropped down to the ground.

"C'mon Sharon." She dropped down, started to stand up straight and then realized we only had about four feet from ground to floor. Elaine came down and just as her feet touched the ground a rifle shot hit the wall above us and wood splinters flew everywhere. I yanked Elaine down by her blouse and stuck

■ ● ■

my hand up in the hole emptying my revolver blindly. Elaine was getting up and for the first time she looked scared.

"Run for the fence."

Sharon was gone in a second. I had started to say "I'll help you over," but she went over all eight feet of it like she had trained for that her entire life. When she landed on the other side she took off running again. Elaine and I stood at the fence staring after her for a second, we shot a glance back and forth and then covered for each other as we climbed over.

"I'm going after her."

"Give me your gun."

"What?" Then it dawned on me that I wouldn't get farther than jail if a cop stopped me chasing down the street after a terrified woman with all of the craziness at the fair.

I held out my weapon and Elaine opened her purse. I stared into it and then stared at Elaine. "What the fuck?!" Inside there was a blond wig. I dropped my .38 in her bag and took off in the direction that Sharon had gone.

As I ran I became aware of people coming out of their porches and into their front yards. News must have made its way to their televisions and radios. I stopped at a corner for a state police car to roar by on its way to the fairground. I heard a mother scream, "Get back in here and lock the door!" One guy, barefoot, asked me as I approached him, "You see anything down there?" Nope. Not me. I slowed down.

"You see a young girl run past here? She's my sister. We got separated." He squinted at me with his hands clasped in front of his throat. "Well, did you see her?"

"No. No. I didn't. Did you see anything back there?"

I started running again. I went a couple more blocks and made a left just in time to see three Sheriff's cars fly through the next intersection with their lights flashing but no sirens. I made

■ ● ■

a right for some reason at that corner and saw Sharon walking at me wringing her hands. When she looked up and saw me she stopped and started backing away. Her hands fell to her sides. She was looking quickly left and right like she wanted somewhere to go but couldn't see where somewhere was.

I stopped and put both of my hands up with my palms facing her. She slowed down.

"I just wanted to make sure you were alright and maybe see if I could help you get home."

She looked around in a circle. When she finally looked at me tears started running down her face.

"Can you help me? I don't know where I am." She began wringing her hands together again. She sobbed, "I'm not from here." I walked up to her and when I was close she said, "Don't touch me."

I was surprised. I don't know what she thought I was going to do out here, but I started replaying all of the times I had touched her tonight. Tossing her in the air. Crushing her hand. Probably almost suffocating her by the snake pit.

"Where do you live?"

"18 Elmwood."

"I know where that is. Let's go."

She stayed as far to the edge of the sidewalk as she could. People were passing us on their way to the fairgrounds. Both of us were dodging people. Some teens jogged past us in the middle of the street. It seemed like every fourth house had people on the porch or in the yard, holding discussions about something none of them had any information about. Except there were shootings. That's all they knew.

"Why did they want to kill me?" Sharon kept crying as we walked. She didn't look at me. She just cried.

"I think they were trying to kill me." That would make her

■ ● ■

feel better. She didn't even turn her head. Yeah, that helped.

"Then why couldn't you leave me alone?" She said it with so much anger I almost felt like I needed to apologize.

"It didn't occur to me until we were over the fence. I'm not positive they were after me, but you saw what happened to grandpa."

"Who?!"

"The old man who got shot with his grandchildren right in front of us."

"And those two girls who wouldn't come with us?" She put her hands in her hair and started sobbing. I took a step toward her. She started bobbing up and down. "Don't touch me!"

I walked past her and said, "C'mon."

Three guys approached us from across the street. "Hey, Lady. Are you okay?" Two of them were looking at me like they thought they were going to do something. I definitely wasn't in the mood for this. I started staring back like, 'when?'

Sharon said, "No, I'm not okay. We were at the carnival."

Apparently these three hadn't been watching T.V. or listening on the radio because all of them were debating who was coming after me first. Then from behind me I heard, "Did you see the sniper?" I turned around to an old man leaning on a cane.

One of the three said, "Sniper?"

"You didn't hear? A sniper shot up the carnival and there's bodies all over the place. People were jumping from the Ferris wheel and getting stomped on. Bodies all over!"

"Holy Shit!"

"Maybe we should get over there. Maybe we can help."

"Help with what? That's what the police are for."

The old guy was getting his fix. Right now he was as important as Walter Cronkite. "They didn't catch the guy yet. T.V. said he might'a had a machine gun."

■ ● ■

"Holy Fuck. Maybe we should get over there."

"Yeah, and maybe we can see something."

"We'll just be in the way."

"Maybe we can see the guy ourselves. He's got to try to get away. Maybe he knows where that hole in the fence is over by Boylston St."

"Are you kidding me? A guy with a machine gun is not going to crawl under a fence to get away."

I felt like I was looking at two geniuses and the guy who took them out for walks every once in a while. Sharon walked past me with her head down. I stepped in beside her and heard the third guy say, "He'll shoot his way out." Three geniuses, not two.

I led the way to Elmwood. We were both silent. I felt like my brain was filled with an ocean roar. But every time the waves broke I'd hear, 'Barthelme.' He was going to have to die. The roar didn't let up until we stepped onto Elmwood and I remembered how seedy it was over here. When we stopped in front of her entranceway I looked around the street. Not quite empty, but not busy for a summer night. I looked at my watch.11:15. People needed to go to work, so they wouldn't be out wandering around on a Thursday night.

"You wanna' come up?" Sharon said it like she was afraid to go up by herself.

"Sure."

We climbed two flights of wooden stairs with squeaks that sounded so loud I wanted to call the landlord to complain right then. Like a complaint would get you anything in this place. Sharon put her key in the lock and I couldn't figure out how she saw the keyhole. The hallway light was so dim, it looked like a ten watt bulb that somebody had painted with grease.

I followed Sharon into her room and it was pretty much

■ ● ■

what I expected. A table with a yellow plastic table cloth and two chairs by a window. A small sink with a hot plate on the counter. A single bed with a green army blanket on it. Over in the corner there was one of those old bakelite radios plugged in sitting on the floor. Probably got it at the Salvation Army.

"You wanna' sit down?" Sharon sat down on the bed wringing her hands together.

"I think I better get going."

Sharon started crying. "Why did they do that?! Why did they hurt those people?! They're all dead, aren't they? Why did they want to kill you?!" She was sobbing uncontrollably now.

I sat down at the table. A light from a passing car glided across the wall behind her. Then another one went across the wall in the opposite direction. A light breeze started coming in the window and I imagined white curtains starting to billow over her table. Except Sharon didn't have any curtains up, but it felt like they were moving in and out and catching the light from the street lamps.

Sharon looked at me, her face struggling against her stomach spasms. "Why do you know my name?"

Her question surprised me. I almost stuttered when I answered. "I asked somebody."

I was expecting her to say 'why' or 'what's your name.' Instead she just looked at the floor and said, "Oh."

"I was worried after that guy bothered you in the donut shop." She kept looking at the floor. "Maybe we should go to the police."

She looked up at me slowly. "I can't go to the police. I don't need the hassle." There was a pause, and then she said, "How do you know they were after you? When are you going to go to the police?"

She had me there, because I wasn't. I was going to go snag

■ ● ■

Barthelme and then work my way up the food chain.

Sharon started crying again. "This ruined my day." I almost started laughing. "I lost my wallet. It had all of my tips in it. I knew I should have stuck some of the money in my pockets. God Damn it! God Damn it all! All I wanted was to get a new pair of slacks so I could go see this guy.God DAMN it!"

"Who? Your boyfriend?"

She sniffled so loud I almost said 'why don't you blow your nose in something disposable?'

"No…just this guy. He'll probably forget who I am before I can see him again."

"No he won't. I don't think it's easy to forget you."

She looked at me and wiped her nose with her arm and then rubbed her arm on her jeans. I would not be forgetting that move.

"Guys forget me all the time. You'd be surprised how many guys forget me…at least I hope they do."

"That's ridiculous. I'm sure the guy you want to see will be glad to see you."

"How the fuck would you know? You think you know him or something?"

"I didn't mean anything. I'm just saying that the guy would probably be flattered to have a pretty woman like you come to see him."

"That's funny. I don't think Bryce even cares what I look like. Maybe…"

I stood up. "What? What's his name?" I was staring at her through a cloud. The dull, ocean roar came back to my head.

"Why? Bryce. He's this guy I met…"

I couldn't hear a word she was saying. I was starting to feel sick. Bryce?!!

"I think I have to go." I pulled ten dollars out of my pocket

■ ● ■

and put it on the table. "I meant to give you a better tip this afternoon. Maybe you can get those slacks after all." I was feeling dizzy and lightheaded. A car light drifted across the wall again.

Sharon snapped me out of it. "We almost got killed tonight."

I looked at her sitting on the bed clasping her hands in her lap. I wanted to tell her everything would be alright, but I didn't want to lie just then. Instead I said, "Yeah, but we survived. That's what we had to do and we did it." It was as simple as that. We had survived.

"I didn't help much. I was so scared." Tears were running down her cheeks again. It was time for her to worry about dehydration.

"Sharon, why don't you try to go to sleep?"

"I don't think I can. I'm too scared."

I felt sorry for her, and more sorry for me. I sighed. "Alright, I'll sit here at the table and you lie down."

Sharon put both of her hands on the bed by her hips. I thought she might say that I should go, but she didn't. She curled up into a fetal position and I turned and sat down at the table wishing I still smoked Chesterfields.

Sharon whispered, "Thank you."

■ ● ■

Sleep

The street looked like someone had painted it and used only one color: dark. Everything that wasn't a tone of gray was black and the grays seemed sparse. There was only one street light working on the block and that threw off more shadow than light. It still managed to attract a couple hundred bugs that either circled the lamp like drunks or darted through the air at odd, schizophrenic angles.

The street was quiet though. If you were going to work tomorrow you could get a decent sleep. The only sound was the hum from that last street lamp and since it flickered every once in a while, it was probably on the verge of shorting out.

A car had come through about an hour before and its tail lights made everything in the street glow a dull red for about three seconds before it made the corner. That was the last time I saw anything close to color.

I was nodding and the thought slipped across the table that I should try to go to sleep. My head suddenly snapped up. I thought I saw a figure come around the corner. I rubbed my hand across my face and it froze covering my mouth. A figure was coming down the opposite side of the street. He was mov-

■ ● ■

ing normally along and when he entered the alley across from me he disappeared in blackness. I thought maybe he was just going home, until I made out his shadow climbing up the side of the building. I squeezed my face with both of my palms to make sure I was awake. It looked like he was using pipes to climb. I started wondering if he going all the way to the top and then he stopped at the third floor. I could only see half of his body. He disappeared momentarily, into the black except for part of his leg. I could hear him tapping on a window. A couple of seconds later he seemed to go head first into it. I chuckled to myself a little and stared back down into the dark.

The air was getting cooler. The curtains were moving like snakes. The wind was picking up and sometimes the curtains snapped and popped. Across the street a guy was walking backward away from the building. Was it the climber? Suddenly he waved and I waved back, sharing his secret. I could see him smile. He looked oddly familiar. Where did I see him before?

Then another figure came around the corner. He came slowly. He'd take two, maybe three steps and look back over his shoulder. He was big. I couldn't make him out. The damn curtains kept blowing into my face. Or was that smoke?

Who was smoking and blowing it into my eyes? I wanted to turn to find out, but I had to concentrate on the figure. He was huge. I couldn't make out his features. I felt my eyes squinting. I'd be able to see his face when he passed under the street lamp.

Bernie! There were so many moths now and they all seemed to circle Bernie when he walked toward me. Then I noticed her across the street. My stomach felt sick. Madame Bland was gazing up at my window. I had to hide. I tried to lean back out of her line of vision. If I could lean back a little she wouldn't be able to see me.

A yellow light went on. Sharon was using the bathroom, but

■ ● ■

all she was doing was brushing her hair. I looked back out the window and Bland waved.

Bernie was coming and I had to get out. My body was stiff. "Wake up! Wake up! Goddamn it, Bernie's coming. It's a dream!" I started crying and laughing. I didn't want to be tied up again. I couldn't be gagged. Not again! I could hardly move, but I had to fight and get up.

I must have sounded like a truck hitting the building when I landed on the floor. I tried to look up at Sharon. In the pale light from the window it seemed like she didn't even stir. Her knees were still up to her chest and her hands were clenched by her mouth.

But I did manage to wake up some other people in the building. Someone below us was yelling, "Chill that shit!" Across the hallway I could hear a door open and close. Somewhere else I could hear an agitated discussion begin, and then fade out. This was the kind of building where you could hear someone in another apartment swallow a pill if you wanted to listen for it.

By the time I made it back up to the chair the place was quiet again. I rubbed my elbow which I had banged on the floor. I crossed my arms on the table and put my head on them. I was looking out the window waiting to sleep. A misty rain was beginning to fall. It was so light I wouldn't have noticed it if it weren't for the street lamp. A couple of buildings down a yellowish light went on for a second and then went black.

What the hell happened tonight? I'd have to sort it out in the morning. I needed to get three or four hours of sleep. Jesus Christ! What is going on?! We have to figure this out. We can't let stuff keep happening.

I shifted my head on my arms and noticed him. Another figure coming down the opposite side of the street. It was okay if I was dreaming. He was smaller than Bernie. A cold chill swept

■ ● ■

across my back. Bernie was dead. A lot of them were dead.

He stopped at the building across the street. Is he going to climb up the pipes, too? She can't let them in the front door? I wonder if anybody ever fell? It's got to be free if guys are climbing up walls to get to it…or else they're teenagers.

He started crossing to this building and paused in the middle of the street. I sat up straight. He was trying to see if this was the address. He started coming again and disappeared from my view. I heard the front door screech open. I listened for the stairs. I could definitely hear the groans and squeaks of the wooden stairs. The guy was coming up slow, like he didn't want to be heard. I was hoping he'd go past this floor, but he didn't. I could faintly hear him tip-toeing down the hall. He stopped right in front of Sharon's door.

I stood up and took a step. The goddamn chair was stuck to my pant leg by a nail and I stumbled. I grabbed the chair to pull it from my pants, stumbled again and fell. The chair must have spun up into the air, because when it hit the floor it was twice as loud as me. I could hear someone taking the stairs two or three at a time. I'd never catch up to him. I got back up and moved quickly to the window. I could see him come out the front door running. He passed under the street lamp. Donut Boy? He disappeared around the corner and I never saw his face. Why did I think it was Donut Boy? I only saw his back.

"What are you doing?"

I turned around, picked up the chair and set it back by the table.

"I'm sorry I woke you. I had to use the bathroom."

The door across the hallway closed. From downstairs I could hear someone yelling again, "Cut that shit out up there!" Someone else was banging on a door. I could pretty clearly hear the argument when the apartment door below us opened.

■ ● ■

"What the hell are you screaming about?"

"You can't hear all that commotion upstairs?"

"No! I hear you screaming and some asshole running down the stairs."

"Well that's what I'm yelling about."

"The guy's gone so shut the fuck up. I need to go to work."

"So get the hell back in your apartment."

Then it got quiet. The guy below us raised his voice and said, "Poughkeepsie? What the hell are you talking about?"

Now I could only hear one side of the discussion. The other guy had lowered his voice. The door across the hall opened again.

"What the hell are my toes to you? Are you nuts? I'll call the cops. Picking my toes?! Are you queer or…"

The sentence stopped and I heard a thud. A door slammed closed and then another. The door across the hall closed quietly again.

Sharon moaned, "What the hell is going on? What the hell did that guy mean about picking his toes with a pikipsi?"

I chuckled. "I don't know. Sounds like the guys on the floor below don't like each other. "Why don't you go back to sleep?" Before I could say "sleep," Sharon started snoring again. I thought maybe now was a good time to try to sleep, but too much was going on. I sat back down. I had to make some sense of it. I was out before I could finish my second thought.

I woke up with a start. It was morning and some cars were going up and down the street. People were out. It was partly sunny and felt cool. My neck was a little stiff. I must have slept sitting up somehow.

I turned toward Sharon's bed and nearly jumped over the table, except my knee banged into it. Sharon was sitting cross-legged on her bed staring at me with huge, horror movie, zombie eyes.

■ ● ■

"Hi." She said it like she didn't see me jump.

Now my knee hurt and my elbow hurt. The elbow must have been scraped when I fell on the floor during the night. I looked at my watch. Ten o'clock.

"It's ten o'clock."

Sharon said, "I don't have to be at work until one."

"Oh yeah? Well I've got to be at work earlier than that."

"I got us some coffee and donuts." I looked at the bags and coffees on the table.

"You went all the way to Dicky's?"

"You were sleeping pretty good, so I didn't want to wake you up."

I looked at the bag on the table. It looked like she got about four dozen. One of the paper cups was leaking at the bottom. Sharon got up and came over to the table.

"I didn't think you'd be here when I woke up. I slept better with you here, I think. They're both regular. I got a lot of donuts. The walk ain't far. I can warm them up and pour them back in so they're hot. What's your work?"

I looked up from the donuts and coffee to Sharon's newly inquisitive face. "Are you related to someone named Culletti?"

Sharon looked confused. "Huh? No, I don't think so. I'm not from here."

"Yeah, I know. Did you see a newspaper while you were out?"

"I didn't get one. I'm tryin' to save money, but the headline was about the carnival bad stuff."

"I'm a detective."

Sharon took a step back away from me and her 'which way do I go look' spread across her face.

I was slightly amused. "I'm not with the police. I'm a private detective."

I could see her relax a little, but she took another step away.

■ ● ■

I think her imagination suddenly went into overdrive.

"Why are you following me? Who could care where I am beside the cops?" She started shifting from one foot to the other.

"Sharon, why don't you calm down, and you know what? Warm up that coffee. I'm going to use your bathroom and then have a donut. Are they all the same?" I opened the shopping bag and looked in.

"No. I got as many different kinds as I could. I didn't know which kind you liked. They're a day old but they're still good."

Sharon stepped back over to the table and looked in the bag. "I like the crème filled ones. I thought you liked the jelly ones. That's what I remembered you getting."

"How about the coffee, Sharon?"

"Huh? Yeah."

She pulled a yellow pan with a black rim out from under the sink. Thankfully she rinsed it. She poured the coffees into the pan and put it on the hot plate. Then she took two dusty cups from a shelf over the sink. One was white with a yellow flower on it. The other was just yellow, but it had a nice gray crack and a chip in it. Mercifully she washed those out as well and then came back to the table for a crème filled donut.

"There are some napkins on the side of the bag somewhere." She started rummaging around in the bag and pulled out about two months worth of napkins. I smiled and found the raspberry jelly donut tasted really, really good. Powdered sugar dropped on my pants and when I went to brush it off I saw where my pants had been ripped by the nail in the chair. Then I looked at the nail. Son of a bitch.

I shook my head and looked out the window. Amazing. I was able to get five or six hours of sleep. I felt like a new man. What a night. Well, this was where I was going to ruin Sharon's day. She was acting like she didn't remember what happened at the carnival.

"Uh, Sharon…"

"Why are you following me? If you're really not the fuzz, who's paying you?"

Sharon made me smile again. "Nobody's paying me. Last night when you were asleep, someone came up here and tried to pick the lock."

Sharon took three steps away from me, her eyes got big and she stopped chewing with a mouthful of donut. When she finally spoke, part of her donut fell out of her mouth onto the floor.

"Who?!"

"Hey, swallow that, okay? I don't know for sure, but I think it was Donut Boy."

Sharon's eyes darted all around the room for a few seconds then landed on me. "Who? Who's that?"

"Oh, sorry. That's what I call the guy who was giving you trouble in Dicky's."

"The guy you threw on the floor, ya' mean. Jesus. It was only a ten dollar trick! What the hell?!" She was still dancing from one foot to the other like she was standing on hot coals.

"Trick?"

She stopped moving and stared at me. "I didn't mean that. I meant something else."

Before my eyes it looked like her personality was dripping out of her body. She'd accidentally revealed a secret about herself and looked like she was collapsing. She couldn't keep her own secret and felt worse for that than she did for whatever she had done. At that moment I felt as sorry for Sharon as I ever did for any person I'd ever known. It all fell into place for me. Sharon was a hooker who was trying to change her life around because she met a guy in a diner. If I was going to ruin someone's day there was no reason to stop now.

■●■

"So that's what Donut Boy is all about. He paid you ten dollars for sex." Sharon had the tears running now. "Turn off the coffee. It's going to boil over." She didn't move. I got up and turned off the hotplate. I poured the coffees and set them on the table.

Someone's past domestic training took over and Sharon said, "I'll take that one. It's got a crack." And then they flowed. She stood next to the table crying with her arms at her sides squeezing a crème donut that was now dripping onto the floor. The tears rolled down her face like all of the good dreams of her life were running away and she had to water the bad ones to have any dreams at all. I handed her a napkin.

"Blow your nose, Sharon."

She took the napkin and tried to blow her nose while she held the crème donut. Naturally she got the crème all over her cheek. At least her nose wasn't running down to her lip anymore.

"Sharon, sit down, okay?"

She didn't move, so I got up and guided her into the other chair.

"He's gonna hate me. He's gonna fuckin' hate me." She slammed the donut down on the table. The crème squirted out onto my arm.

I looked at her annoyed. "Really?"

She stared at my arm for a couple of seconds. "I'm sorry. I'm really sorry. I'm a fuck-up. Just a fuck-up." She grabbed my wrist and with a napkin began spreading the sticky crème filling all over my arm trying to clean it.

"C'mon. Wait. Let me wash this off." She started to get up. "Sharon! Just sit!"

Her head snapped toward me. I thought I scared her and felt bad about it. "He's going to hate me. He probably doesn't even remember me."

■ ● ■

"That guy from the diner?"

"Yeah. Bryce."

I felt waves of stupidity and confusion fill my stomach and head while I ran water over my arm.

"Sharon, I don't care what you've been doing or with who. I don't know Bryce and I am not going to say anything to him. I'm more concerned about the guy who came to your door in the middle of the night."

I wiped my arm off with a clean napkin and Sharon looked at me like I had just promised her everlasting life. She clearly thought I was connected to this Bryce guy.

"You won't say anything?"

"Sharon, you pursue Bryce however you want to. We are right now going to talk about someone trying to come into your apartment last night. You should talk to the cops."

She shook her head. I sat down to the coffee and grabbed another donut.

"Wipe your face, Sharon. Bryce is not going to dig a woman who shows up with Dicky's donut all over her face…or a runny nose." Christ, another virgin-whore. I looked around her room again. What a hole. She was definitely determined.

"I can't tell the police. What do I say? Hey fuzz-face, I gave some a guy a blow job and now he's bothering me. Cop'll probably tell me to give him another blow job." New tears started running down her face, but at least she was looking at me.

"Then you have to be careful. When you walk home at night you have to look around and be aware of your surroundings. For the next two weeks, when you go home after a late shift, you walk the same route every time."

"The same way? Won't that make it easier for someone to find me?"

"If they really want to they're going to find you no matter

what. They already know where you work. But if you go the same way you'll also notice if something weird is out of place."

The tears had stopped and she kept staring at me. The wheels were definitely turning.

"You're going to watch me, aren't you?"

"Maybe." I smiled.

"I don't know if that's good. You might be bad luck."

My jaw clenched. I was kind of speechless and now I was having a hard time chewing the damn jelly donut. When I finally managed to swallow I said, "What?!"

"I could have been killed last night at the fair. I might have been able to get rid of that guy in the donut shop. You don't know who was trying to get in here last night. I handled guys like him before. I don't even know if there really was someone trying to come in here. Maybe its bad luck to be around you."

Maybe she was right. Maybe I was bad karma for her. I put my donut down and took my chair over to the door.

"Sharon, you see this?" I wedged the chair under the door handle. "When you come home at night, or before you go to bed, I think you should do this with the chair. Your lock isn't worth spit."

She started laughing. "Isn't worth spit?" For some reason she thought that was the funniest joke Don Rickles never told. I walked back to the table and finished off my coffee standing up. I picked up a glazed donut to take with me and went back to the door. When I grabbed the handle Sharon said, "Don't take me the wrong way. I'm sorry. All I've ever had in my life is bad luck and I guess you're just more of it."

I nodded and then said, "Gee, thanks. And get some curtains, or put a sheet over the window." I stepped out into the hall. "See you around."

As I closed the door I heard her say, "Okay." She reminded

■ ● ■

me of a mouse squeaking.

I took one step and stopped. Downstairs I could hear pounding and wood splitting. It was coming from the second floor. I went down the stairs and peeked around the corner. A guy was hitting a door with a hammer. On the next blow the hammer got stuck and the guy was having a hard time ripping it out.

When I came around the corner I said, "Need a hand?" He was in a multi-colored bathrobe and slippers and he jumped half-way down the hallway when he saw me. He clenched the robe together like there was some reason for him to be modest. The hammer was still sticking in the door, but when I grabbed it, it slid out easily. I offered it to Mr. Modesty and he took it from me like I had just pulled Excalibur from the stone. He had a black eye. A nice one.

"Who are you?"

I looked at the door and laughed. "What're you doing?"

"What's it to you?"

I shrugged and headed for the office. I wondered how he was going to look with two black eyes.

■ ● ■

Morning

How many mornings have I opened this store up in all these years? Maybe I should have tried to buy this place from Hanratty a year ago. Doesn't matter. I'm a pharmacist with twenty-five years experience. Of course, they're all in one store... all right here. I know I'll find something, but Mary was right. I should have made a move a couple of years ago when the big buy-out came.

I will not miss that bell over the door, though. One of the boys from upstairs.

"Como si siente hoy, Antonio Mojica?"

"I'm fine, Morgan. How about you?"

"Well. You need some aspirin or something?

Antonio smiled, and said in a louder voice, "Condoms, Morgan. I need condoms."

"Hey. Keep your voice down. There might be a woman or a kid in here." I looked around sheepishly to see if one had snuck in when I wasn't paying attention.

Antonio started laughing. "There's no one in here, Morgan. I saw that when I came in."

It was a little upsetting having Antonio point out that he was the only customer in the store.

"So you guys are closing up in three weeks I heard."

"Yep. All of the Rexalls seem to be going down the tubes."

"What are you going to do?"

"Go to church."

Antonio started laughing. I couldn't help smiling.

"I'm a little too young to retire, so I'll find another druggist to work with. I don't think I'll have too much trouble. It's not like pharmacists are out of date. Just Rexalls."

"Well Morgan, I want to wish you all the best in the future. It was nice getting to know you and having you down here, even if it was only for a year."

"I'd say it was nice meeting the four of you, but that would be a lie." Antonio did a double-take and then grinned at me.

"Hold on, turkey. You're not blaming us for putting you out of business, are you?"

"The way you fellas carry on up there, you may drive the whole neighborhood out of business."

Antonio started laughing again.

"I don't think any of us expected anything like what's happened so far."

"What do you mean, 'so far'?"

Antonio shrugged.

I couldn't imagine trying to do the job they were pursuing. Confrontations all of the time. Trying to serve papers on people who don't want them. They're all young men. Are they really going to spend their whole lives always fighting someone? Always chasing someone down? Trying not to get killed? I can admit it. I'd run to avoid a fight. Korea was enough for me. I couldn't be like them. They probably look at me and say 'how could he spend twenty-five years doing what he's doing?'

"I see you have a secretary up there now. Maybe she'll calm

■ ● ■

you boys down a little."

"Doubt it. I get the feeling Elaine may be crazier than all of us put together. But she sure knows how to run an office."

I turned toward the door when I heard the bell ring. Two men walked in and I said, "Good Morning."

"Looks like the afternoon rush got here early, Morgan. Let me wander over here so you can make a sale, and later I'll ask you a question."

The two men and I converged on the counter.

"Hi. Can I help you with anything?"

One of them was wearing a light summer blazer and a brown fedora pulled low over his eyes. The other one was wearing a Cardinals baseball hat and was carrying a gym bag. The baseball fan said he had a sore throat. The man in the fedora kind of slipped away. I walked down the aisle and took a bottle from the shelf.

"Cepacol."

"Uh-huh." He started reading the label and slowly wandered off.

It was the man in the fedora who got my attention and made my skin tingle. Twenty-five years of experience in this store taught me a shoplifter could be any age. He was in the same aisle as Mojica and he kept glancing at him out of the corner of his eye. Then I noticed the guy with the baseball hat was acting like he was looking at the Cepacol bottle, but his eyes seemed to be resting on a spot beyond it. Then he started down the aisle that his friend was in. Probably try to have his friend drop stuff in his gym bag while it looked like he was reading the bottle.

My eyes went back to the man in the fedora when he turned toward the street. He pivoted back toward Antonio and raised something above his head. I yelled, "Look out!"

Antonio turned quickly as the man with the fedora swung

at him. Antonio threw his right hand in a funny way and hit the man in the throat. The man went red in the face, started choking and disappeared from my view. I was running to the aisle and grabbed a bottle of something just when the guy in the Cardinals hat swung a club at Antonio. He put his arm up to block the blow. I could hear something snap.

The Cardinal fan raised the club again and I hit him from behind with the bottle. He staggered forward a step and dropped his arm, but I hit him again. The bottle shattered and I could feel my hand was cut. So was his head. The baseball fan tripped past Mojica, who was down on one knee holding his arm. He helped the guy in the fedora to his feet and they staggered out.

"I'm calling the cops! Antonio, are you alright?"

He looked up at me like he was in excruciating pain. He mouthed the word 'no' and then said, "Call up to my office. Tell them I need help. Then call the police."

He slowly rose to his feet and told me the number. I spoke to the secretary and she said someone would be right down. I called the police and wrapped some gauze around my right hand, since I was bleeding all over the receiver. When I went back to Antonio I checked his arm. Definitely broken.

Mojica tried to smile and then said, "Morgan, you got anything for pain? Some weed? Morphine? A case or two of aspirin?"

The door opened and their new secretary came in looking all around. When she entered our aisle I could see she had a gun in her hand.

Antonio was bending over in pain, but he managed to say, "It's clear in here."

"What happened?"

"Elaine, I think you need to take me to the hospital. Someone in a baseball cap broke my arm with that pipe on the floor."

The girl kicked the pipe and then said, "What team?"

■ ● ■

Mojica said, "Cardinals, I think."

"I was always a Cubs fan."

Antonio started laughing, but you could tell he was laughing through pain. I wanted to get him something but I didn't want to lose my license.

The girl said, "Mr. James, are you okay? I see blood."

"I'll be okay."

"You want to go to the hospital with us?"

"I'll go later if necessary. Someone has to be here for the police. You had better put that away before the police get here."

The girl put the gun in her pocket and then took Mojica by the arm and led him out of the store.

I went behind the register, rewrapped my hand and wondered where the police were. Then I called Mary to tell her what happened and that I was okay.

When the police finally came, they kept saying it was probably a robbery and that I had stopped it. I asked them what kind of robbers don't try to rob the register and on top of that try to beat a customer with lead pipes. One of the detectives said they probably had a grudge. The other detective nodded in agreement.

I said, "They were trying to kill him."

One of them replied, "Now that wouldn't make sense in a common robbery, so it was probably a grudge."

'Astounding' was the only word I could think of. "Do you really think that makes any kind of sense?"

Neither of them said anything.

I stood behind the register waiting for Hanratty so I could go get stitches. My hand was throbbing now. I shouldn't have told them to cancel the medics. One of the detectives held up a broken bottle.

"This looks like it might'a been the bottle you hit that one

■ ● ■

guy with. Has blood on it."

I felt angry and disgusted. "Yes. That might have been it, dee-tec-tive." He glanced at me and then read the label out loud.

"Swamp Root...a diuretic to the kidneys."

Swamp Root?! We still had bottles of Swamp Root on the shelves?

■ ● ■

Sharp

When I heard the phone, I was reading a crazy newspaper article about a sniper at a carnival over at Haley Field. I ignored the phone and expected the answering machine to pick up. I had a hard time figuring how they would stop a guy if he decided to go crazy at a place like that. One guy could hurt a lot of people. Seemed the guy ended up committing suicide in the Haunted House. One guy with a rifle. Some people thought there were two shooters, but the police said the second person was someone who was actually shooting back at the sniper.

The phone kept ringing like it was a Sunday morning church bell and God couldn't wait for me to answer the call. I guess I forgot to put the answering machine on. With a sigh I got up from the couch and walked toward the kitchen. I looked out every window on the way. A lot of people don't like railroad apartments, but mine had five rooms, and every room had a window with a view I liked. I didn't really care if people had to walk through my bedroom to get to the dining room.

Today looked great. The sky was blue. The air was cool. I had all of my windows open.

The kitchen always gave me satisfaction. It was all yellow and

■ ● ■

white, and even on a cloudy, rainy day, it made me feel like the sun was coming up.

I pulled the phone from the wall expecting bad news. I couldn't seem to shake the feeling that whenever I picked up a phone there would be bad news coming from the other end. But we all needed phones I guess, even if they were only messengers of bad news.

"'Lo?"

"Sharp?"

My skin began to crawl. "Who's this?"

"Elaine."

A feeling of sweet relief flooded my body. When I was still a boy, pretending to be a man, I knew a woman in Amarillo who sounded just like Elaine. Evil as they come. Ran from her one night with just the clothes on my back and joined up. Stupid, I guess, but they'd a got me eventually anyway. Uncle Sam wants you, ninety-nine times out'a a hundred he will get you skin and bone. Still, it's funny that at seventeen the Army was the only way I could think of to get away from her. All through my first tour I expected to see her come walking through the front door of some gin mill with discharge papers for me in her hand. "He lied about his age! I'm taking him back with me!" Fifteen years later, just the thought of the woman's voice still made me nervous. I wondered how long it would take me to get used to Elaine's voice.

"Mojica was attacked this morning. He has a broken arm and we're at the hospital."

I should have brought my coffee with me from the living room. "Where did this occur?"

"Down in the drug store. Two men with pipes."

"Pipes?!"

"Mojica apparently knocked one of them down, but the other

■ ● ■

one broke his arm. Morgan hit that one with a bottle, but they got away."

"The pharmacist?"

"Yes. He'll probably be here soon, too. His hand was cut pretty good."

"Are you hurt?"

"No. I was up in the office."

"Where are you calling from, Elaine?"

"I'm in a phone booth down the street from the emergency room."

"Have you spoken to anyone else?"

"No. Not yet. Nobody was home. But Sharp, there's something else. Have you seen the papers yet?"

"Why? What should I be looking for?"

"Did you see anything about the carnival?"

"Jesus walking barefoot on a river of flaming shit, are you telling me that had somethin' to do with us?"

"Yes."

"Damn. Okay. Look, don't use the office phone for anything having to do with the location of any of us. Any meetings we have, postpone. Be vague with our regular customers. We'll call everybody back. Use pay phones when you call the boys. How bad is Mojica?"

"He was in a lot of pain, but the x-rays showed a clean break."

The operator interrupted us to ask for more money.

"Hold on, Sharp. I have to drop another dime in."

As soon as I heard the 'ching,' I said, "Get in touch with the others as soon as you can. I'll let you know about where we should meet today. You understand what we need with our customers?"

"Yes. If necessary, I lie."

"Like a cat with a comfortable spot in front of the fire. Now

■ ● ■

fill me in about what happened."

About seventy-five cents later Elaine finished up by telling me who she thought Sharon was. We said our goodbyes while I finished my third cup of black coffee. I put the phone back on the wall slowly while I watched a cat chase a squirrel down in the yard.

This was not how I wanted my morning to start, but we were going to have to do some figurin' out in a small hurry. Mojica, and the carnival had to be connected.

I went into my bedroom and grabbed a pad, a pen and then I sat down on the edge of my bed.

Raoul had said there was an organization of some kind. Somebody trains people as assassins. They conduct other business but they don't know why. Barthelme finds things for them and seems to have three connections…two close and one in Chicago. Barthelme has bodyguards, but everybody who procures for the Commission can't have a few bodyguards. He's got to be more connected than he lets on during a castration. Bodyguards is serious money.

Two attacks. So different. Did they want Mojica dead, or were they trying to do something else? If you really want somebody dead you tap him on the forehead with a fast moving bullet. I have to believe they wanted him dead, though. If you're trying to kill somebody you can't really scare him much with pipes if you're already shooting at him. Did that make sense, my man?

I shook my head. The boys and I had gone over the incidents in the apartment and the office quite a few times. We tried to figure out why the connection between Brautigan and us was so important. Especially now. Mostly we were hoping for a break with Barthelme. He was our only real connection. We had three phone numbers but we were hoping to find one more contact through me being buddies with him.

Out the window I could see three boys, with hair longer than mine, walking across the old factory foundation. One of them had a basketball under his arm wedged between his chest and his bicep. Another one was smoking. He wasn't passing so I assume it wasn't weed. I love watchin' basketball. I wonder why I never really played. I guess too much whorin' around at a tender young age. Funny how you find something early in life and it just takes over.

Okay, cowboy, work this from the other end. We have a connection between us and Brautigan. Brautigan and a serial killer. We have bodies all over the place. Two in our offices. Six in an apartment. One was maybe a psycho. Two were killers. Maybe the psycho in the red shoes was a killer, too. Who were the other three? Why didn't the big guy know what was going on? Everybody had a key. It had to be a place where people met. So many keys. But why didn't the big guy know what was going on? He had a key, so he belonged. Red shoes had a key so she belonged, unless somebody was just passing keys around. What about the three bodies behind the sofa. They must have belonged. They were having a conversation. Only the big guy was upset. The two killers weren't. They acted like their team was winning or something.

Whoa…

I stood up like I'd just got bit by a skinny snake. What the hell?! Teams! There were different teams and they were competing with each other. Very fucking crazy, but this whole thing is crazy. If there are teams, what are they competing over? Points for murders? But then why would the connection between Brautigan and Andy be strong enough to kill over now? Actually, Brautigan and us. We probably have to assume now, that they want to put all of us on ice.

■ ● ■

I rolled that over for about five more minutes and then thought about a place for us to meet where I wouldn't be seen with the boys. Probably have to be comfortable. This discussion was probably going to go on for good while.

I grabbed one of my boots and slid a knife into the sleeve inside it that Mojica had sewn in. I decided to take my shoulder bag so I could carry a few more clips for the .45. Might as well be loaded for bear, even though it really felt like there was a weasel running around. I put on a white, short sleeve cotton shirt. Tied my hair back. Grabbed my shades, and the cowboy was ready to roll.

I looked out the peep hole and then opened the front door with the security bar still in place. No time like the current time for being careful. Just as I started to step out, the phone rang again. The answering machine was on and I was going to let it handle the call unless it was one of the boys...or Elaine.

It was Barthelme. "Hi there, Tex. I was wondering if you could stop by this evening. I have a favor to ask of you. About seven."

So we have reached the 'favors level.' How does that hog slime know how to dress in such fine threads?

By 11:30 I had called Ivars and told him to tell Andy, "President 15, 4."

Corey Buchanan was a friend who owned a quiet bar just outside of town. He let us use his house to meet in when we fell into some bad craziness. I first met Corey outside a movie theater where he also met his future wife. I had been at a bar a little ways from a movie theater and I was in a little dust up with some locals who all got real drunk and decided they didn't like people from Texas that particular night. The dance started in front of the bar and drifted toward the movie theater.

When Corey came out of the theater, I had already put one

■ ● ■

hero on the ground. Corey told me he was just going to watch at first. Later he said he thought it was a fair fight when it was two on one, but when the third guy jumped in he started throwing punches because he didn't think three on one was fair. But when he got involved the last three came at us and it was basically three on one anyway, but I appreciated the company.

When the cops showed up we were amazed they didn't take us in too. But that was mainly due to the movie theater ticket taker who said we were randomly attacked "by these drunken thugs." Unfortunately one of the drunken thugs heard her and called her a "fat whore." At that particular point she ran over and kicked him between the legs so hard I shivered and closed my eyes for a second. One cop started to laugh, but when she kicked him again the other cop said, "Okay! You too!" And then he dropped some bracelets on her while she tried to get one more kick in.

Corey and I became friends that night back in the bar, trying to get enough alcohol in us to mask some of the pain where the bruises were forming. After the bar closed we sat in an all night diner and decided to bail the ticket taker out of jail in the morning. We were feeling proud of ourselves when bail was posted and we waited for our heroine to come through the metal door. Well, she came out and the first thing she said was, "You let me stay in there all night?! You animals!"

Corey started laughing and said, "Gee, and I was going to ask you out to dinner and see if we could get married." She took a breath so deep I thought the buttons would rip off my shirt.

"You think I'm a common tramp? You think you offer me dinner and you'll have your way with me?!"

Corey looked at me smiling. She stood there with her hands on her hips, just fumin'.

I said, "Corey, I think I gotta' leave. This is gonna' get nasty."

■ ● ■

Corey turned to her and said, "Okay, I lied. I figured if we posted your bail you'd just give it up."

At that particular point I moved away from Corey as quickly as I could manage. She went after him like a brakeless freight train on a downhill grade. She'd a like to beat him to within one week of his death. They got married six months later. Two years later they were divorced. One month after that Denise died of ovarian cancer. Corey was devastated. He had signed on for thick and thin. Denise decided she didn't want him to see the end, so she hid with her family and they called him when she was gone. I stayed with Corey at his house for quite some time. I don't know that I had to, but he seemed to appreciate it anyway. It was funny that all that time I was there, neither of us had a drink. He went to work six days a week and didn't drink in his bar either. One night, about nine months after the funeral, we were sittin' on his porch and suddenly I smelled weed. I wasn't really surprised, but when I turned toward him he said, "Friendship is like a pair of pants that you really like. Sometime they might wear out, but if you're serious about them you put a patch on them and wear them just as proud as before." Then he passed me the joint. I sat there lookin' at it, and then I looked at him. I kind'a squinted at the smoke and then looked back at him.

Corey said, "Are you going to take a hit off that or not?"

I looked at the joint again and said, "I don't know. I don't think I want to be as high as you are. What in the hell are you talkin' about some pair'a pants?!"

Corey started laughing. "Damn, I am pretty high. Watch yourself with that stuff."

I was almost as close to Corey as I was with the boys. Corey was a good man and a better friend. Denise was a good woman.

I walked into Buchanan's at 3:45. Corey gave me five and then tossed me the keys. I told him we'd be a couple of hours at

■ ● ■

least. He said we could stay until breakfast. And then he said if we needed his help don't hesitate to ask. The last thing on earth I was gonna' do was get him mixed up in this shit.

I walked up the stone path from the parking lot toward Corey's house. The hedge obscured the patio, but the part of the house that I could see looked great. Corey did a lot of upkeep on it. I think the place was built in the 1870s. Funny, that's something I'd usually remember.

I slid through the opening in the hedge and all of the boys and Elaine had beaten me here. Three of them looked grim. Mojica didn't, which surprised me. I went to unlock the door and said, "Anyone want a beer?" Three sodas and a water and I knew we were going to have a very, very serious conversation.

■ ● ■

Talk

There were three ways you could get to Buchanan's house. You could walk up the hill from the bar parking lot, or you could take one of the two driveways. One came from the highway. The other came from an old, gravel covered, dirt road that led to a county road that went over a hill and through a valley that looked like a Disney cartoon when the leaves changed in autumn. Whichever way you came, you had to go about a hundred yards into the woods, so the house was pretty isolated.

Andy and I came in off the highway at about 3:30. We were the first ones there and by the time I had told Andy the whole story of the night before, Andy was charged up. About ten minutes later we heard Mojica and Elaine pull in. We were sitting on the patio when they came around the corner of the house.

Andy immediately stood up and launched into Elaine like a viper. "What the hell did you think you were doing?! You're a God damn secretary and that's what we hired you for! You're not a bodyguard! We didn't hire you to play detective! What the…"

I stood up and interrupted Andy's tirade. "Chill out, Andy. Why didn't you scream at me on the way here instead of stewing? Elaine may have saved a couple of lives last night. Yeah, it was dumb stupid, but it turned out right."

Andy's face was beet red and then he unloaded on me. "What the fuck are you talking about?! This is serious shit and we don't need amateur secretaries…"

Elaine spoke up then. "Wait a second! Don't scream at him because I did something stupid. I'm sorry. I won't do it again. If you want to fire me, just fire me and quit yelling at people."

"Andy, she did something foolish but it turned out right. If you don't want to fire Elaine, why don't we sit down. Somebody wants us dead and if we don't figure it out, one, or all of us is probably going to get hurt."

Andy took a step toward me and said, "See how you sound?! You get some sleep and you sound almost normal!"

"Well, what the fuck is with you?! You're usually the voice of reason."

Nobody said anything until Mojica said, "Mojica's okay by the way. If anybody was wondering. Just his arm is broken."

We all looked at him as he sat down with a Buddha smile on his face. Andy shook his head and said, "Jesus," and then he sat down.

Elaine and I exchanged glances and we both sat down.

Andy started staring at Elaine. "Where'd you get the two guns?" Elaine turned to Mojica, who was still smiling, and pointed.

"Jesus H. Christ! Why did I bother asking." Andy stood up and started pacing. I watched him for thirty seconds and then I said, "Hey, Andy. Sit the fuck down will you? You're making me seasick."

Andy turned toward me, pointed a finger at my face, opened his mouth to let some silence out and then he sat down again. Andy looked upset. Elaine looked upset. I probably looked upset. Mojica though, was smiling like a happy idiot.

■ ● ■

I said, "Heeks, are you just on the pills the doc gave you, or are you self-medicated?" He just nodded and kept on smiling.

Sharp came through the hedges then and looked at each of us. "Heeks, you okay?"

"Nothing that a couple of pills can't fix."

Sharp went to the doors to unlock them. "Anyone want a beer?" Everybody ordered either soda or water. Then Sharp said, "Mojica, why'nt you let everybody in?"

"I thought it would be rude, plus I'd probably need two hands on that lock."

Andy said, "And we were comfortable out here on the patio." Sharp looked at Andy and then at me. "Uh-huh. Little tense, Andy?"

"Yeah I'm goddamn tense."

"Well let's sit down in the living room and figure this out."

Sharp started talking and we never made it out of the kitchen. Sharp told us his idea about the Commission teams. Andy was staring at Sharp and I could see the wheels turning like they hadn't turned in quite a while. Sharp ran through his ideas and ended up with Barthelme. "He wants me to show up at his place at seven. If I leave here by 6:30 I'll be good." Andy started to say something and Sharp cut him off. "Maybe we should just pop Barthelme. See what comes out of the woodwork."

Andy did a double-take. "Something is already out of the woodwork. Killing Barthelme now just eliminates our only palpable lead to these people."

"I love that word. Palpable. Great word." Everyone looked at Mojica. He had a very serious look on his face. He glanced at each of us and started smiling again.

I said, "Andy's probably right. If Barthelme is dead, as much as I'd like that, it doesn't necessarily mean another Commission guy is going to appear."

■ ● ■

Sharp nodded. "Just a pleasant thought."

Elaine spoke and I could see Andy's hands tighten into fists. He was really pissed at her for following me the night before.

"Sharp's idea about teams might be on to something. Maybe they're having an internal housecleaning like the Nazis did during the Night of the Long Knives."

Andy's hands opened up and he put them flat on this thighs. "Let's say they are. Did we somehow start the split? Somehow we're related to whatever and why they're killing people."

Sharp said, "Let's not forget Brautigan. Our connection to the Commission is through the case you two and Brautigan were involved with. What if…"

Mojica's voice suddenly drifted through the air. "Guys, let's make this simple. Somebody in their organization, one guy, has a tie to those murders you investigated back during the war, and he doesn't want anyone to know about it. Is there another soda in the ice box?"

Sharp started laughing. "Ice box? Yeah. Help yourself."

Andy chuckled. "Heeks, how high are you?"

"Not sure. I can follow the conversation and I'm enjoying it on an intellectual level." He paused and then said, "I don't know if I can make it to the refrigerator though."

Elaine stood up, but I grabbed her arm. "I'll get it. You sit. Anybody else want one? I'm going to make some coffee."

We all thought the split idea was important but we weren't sure how that helped us. Then we discussed our problem with the police. Maybe the papers could lie a little, but to distort what happened at the carnival meant someone, or some ones, in the police department had the juice to feed distorted information to the papers. Sharp said he thought if the papers were printing false reports, we had to assume the Commission had some kind of control inside the police.

■ ● ■

The conversation went on. We couldn't trust the police or news reports. It was likely some people in the police were working with some people in the news to distort the story. If Sharp couldn't get farther with Barthelme soon, we were probably going to have to squeeze him again.

"You know, fucking Mojica is probably right. One guy is connected to us and the war. The split, the teams, or whatever is going on in the Commission is just being used as a cover to wipe out something from his past. We never knew who actually issued the order for us to go after Roberts. If we can make that one guy our target, maybe we can get through this. Instead of us worrying about their internal problems, we just think in terms of finding one guy."

Andy leaned back in his chair and put his piss green Cliquot soda on the table. "And what if our target has to be bigger than that? How do we know it wasn't three or four generals who knew what was going on and they're all in the Commission? What if…"

Elaine interrupted. "What if the guy you want to be looking for was actually connected to the murders? What if he participated in some way?"

Andy shot me an annoyed look. "There was no evidence anyone else was involved."

"What if he was a voyeur?"

Everyone was silent. Why did that seem to strike a chord? Andy was looking at the floor. Sharp was looking at Elaine. I couldn't tell what Mojica was looking at.

Sharp said, "We can do a full load of speculatin,' but I'm gonna go see my pal Barthelme and see if I can shake a little information out'a his shoes. I'll toss the keys back to Corey and you all lock up."

Sharp stood up to leave.

■ ● ■

Andy looked at Elaine and then me. "Look, before we leave, we have to get something clear. We are all relying on each other and we can't have you two off on your own private expeditions. We need to know what everybody is doing if we're going to get through this. Elaine, that goes double for you."

"I know. I'm the secretary."

Andy smiled. "Thank you for not saying 'just.' You might want to rethink whether or not you want to stay with us. You might have to be more than a secretary before this is all over."

"I thought about it all last night when I couldn't sleep. I thought about it most of today. I wanted an interesting job… and we have the new computer. I really like the new computer."

"I love our office atmosphere." We all looked at Mojica, who was smiling like Alfred E. Newman.

Andy looked more annoyed if that was possible. "Are you still high?! How many of those damn pills have you got, anyway?"

"I can spare one or two, if that's what you're asking."

Sharp was dying by the door. "You just one high motherfucker, Heeks." We all started laughing except for Andy.

I said, "You know, Elaine, when we get through this, the job will probably get really boring. You sure you want to stay?"

"I really like the computer."

"I gotta boogie. I'll call in later."

Andy said, "Yeah. It'll be a 'johnson' after Mojica checks out the office for bugs and taps."

Sharp waved and walked out.

"Heeks, when do you think you'll be straight enough to do an office sweep?"

"Come on, Andy. Don't be insulting. I'll be ready by the time we get back to the office."

Andy looked up at the ceiling and rubbed his face with both

■ ● ■

hands. "Jesus H. Christ."

When Andy asked Mojica that, I felt elated. We were going to take care of business. We were going to bring these fucks down!

Elaine touched my shoulder. "Are you okay?"

"Huh? Of course I'm okay. We're going to get these sons of bitches. Ooops. Wrong word. We'll get these bastards! Why are you looking at me like that?"

She had a really concerned look on her face and then she turned her head toward Andy. I stood up and saw Andy staring at me with a frown on his face.

"What?"

Andy crossed his arms. "Nothing. Ride back with Elaine. Heeks will ride with me."

"Okay."

Elaine and I went back to town by way of the country road. Once we hit the valley Elaine took her time. It was beautiful out here and probably relaxing. But I wasn't feeling relaxed. I started to feel annoyed and uncomfortable. I thought if I talked I'd feel better.

"Elaine, I want to thank you for last night. It took a lot of intestinal fortitude to react like you did. Thanks."

Elaine wasn't speaking. She just kept staring straight ahead. After about a mile she said, "I was scared shitless." I turned toward her expecting more, but nothing came.

After about another mile I said, "So was I."

"You didn't seem like it."

"Actually neither did you."

"What would you think if I quit this job?"

I chuckled. She glanced at me, and then put her eyes right back on the road. "I would think you were normal. It would completely destroy my assessment of you."

■ ● ■

"What do you mean?!"

"In high school I thought you were bananas and now I know you are."

"Fuck you…seriously, would you think less of me if I quit?"

I wanted to say 'I couldn't possibly think less of you no matter what you did,' but I held my tongue. Elaine was obviously going to take this discussion somewhere that she thought was serious.

"Elaine, are you trying to work yourself up to quit?"

"No."

"Then why are we talking about this?"

"Because I want to know why you haven't quit this. You love this, don't you? You can't shake loose of the feeling."

I looked away from Elaine and watched a stream curve toward the road and then away from it. A few crows were moving off towards some farmer's corn field.

"You're stuck on this, aren't you? The violence."

I started looking at the road. "It's not always like this." I was feeling a little confused and I could feel myself start to get angry. "It's what I know…and these are my friends. This is my job. These are people I know I can rely on, and I can see in their faces that they know they can rely on me…this is my job, and these are my friends."

"And is this when you get to test their friendship?"

"I don't have to test anybody's friendship! It just is, and every once in a while our job gets weird. That's all. Why are you trying to make something bigger out of this? We are not in a Princeton psych class." I was getting pissed. We needed to change the subject.

"I'm just trying to understand." We rode in silence for a couple of miles.

"You really ought to think hard about being with us. I think this is going to get pretty bad."

■ ● ■

"Worse than last night? Thanks for the warning."

Elaine glanced at me. "Keep your eyes on the road, Ms. Secretary."

"Fuck you! Andy said I was probably going to be more than that."

"You're smart enough to realize that you should be hoping you aren't forced to be more than the secretary. If you didn't hear me the first time, I think this is going to get very, very bad."

"Well then you guys had better just TCB."

I started chuckling. "TCB huh?" I looked out the window. "This is a weird conversation, Elaine."

We rode most of the way back to town in silence, until I suggested we stop at Carl's and get a pizza. We took it back to the office. When we walked in Mojica was up on a ladder with one of his wands checking out light fixtures. I barely got "anyone for pizza" out of my mouth, when the phone rang. Andy picked it up and said, "Mr. Johnson was here." From Andy's tone I could tell something serious happened.

"Sharp wants us to meet him at Barthelme's. He said Mojica should bring enough gloves. Elaine, I think you should go down with us and then go home."

I grabbed a slice and held the box open for Mojica. Andy shook his head 'no.'

Ivars took us down in the elevator and didn't even try to make conversation. As soon as he saw us he went silent. Mojica and I ate pizza. Andy stared at the floor. Elaine had a look on her face that seemed to say 'what am I doing here'…or 'why the hell aren't I going with you?'

The drive out to Barthelme's in Andy's car was pretty quick and mostly quiet. We knew Barthelme was dead. We were probably all considering how and why. I was wondering if Sharp had done it, even though we told him it shouldn't be done. Does he

■ ● ■

want us out there to set us up?

I heard Mojica say, "He's not listening."

"What?"

Andy said, "Forget it. Not important."

"What?!"

"Never mind, dude." Mojica at least said it with a smile. What the hell had they been talking about? I went back to looking out the window.

When we pulled up at Barthelme's, I mentioned that the bodyguards' car was gone. Sharp's was in the driveway. We pulled in behind Sharp's car and followed Andy in through a side door. From the description of the house layout we had from Sharp, we didn't have any problem making it to the den. When we walked in the first thing I saw was Sharp with his arms crossed on his chest, his boots up on the desk and a .45 clenched in his right hand. His eyes were just slits and he was working on a toothpick.

Then I saw the Christmas tree lights. They were wrapped around Barthelme's neck blinking randomly. There was a hole in the middle of his forehead. His mouth looked full and slightly open. Andy walked over behind the desk and started assessing the damage.

I said, "Does he have his pants on?"

Andy didn't even look up. "Yeah. But they're on down around his ankles."

"So those are his balls in his mouth?"

"Well whose did you think they'd be?"

"Maybe one of the bodyguards."

Andy stood up straight and nodded his head like that was a possibility he hadn't thought of yet.

Sharp said, with a Texas toothpick accent, "Bodyguards are in the basement by the pool table. They're whole."

Andy turned to Sharp. "Did you do this?"

"Nope. Christmas tree lights were on when I got here."

"Okay then. We've got some work to do real quick."

Mojica tossed gloves to each of us and we split up the house. Sharp and I went upstairs. Andy and Mojica started downstairs. It was one of those searches where we didn't know what we were looking for, but we'd toss the house and see if we could find anything helpful. After about fifteen minutes I heard Sharp say, "Beatin' down the doors…"

I hollered, "What?"

"I have come across his pornography collection. It's German…"

"Did Barthelme know how to read German?"

"Don't have to read German. The photos are pretty explicit."

"If he wanted to order a blow-up fraulein, wouldn't he need to know German?"

"Maybe…"

From downstairs we could hear Andy. "Bingo!"

Sharp and I went back down. The rug in the den was ripped back. Andy said, "Heeks found a safe in the floor." Andy was looking at a sheet of paper. He handed it to Sharp.

Mojica was on his knees counting money. "Looks like about twenty grand."

Sharp's toothpick was sliding from one corner of his mouth to the other. "Good. Take it. We're gonna' have expenses."

I thought that maybe we should leave a little. We all looked at Andy for some reason. He looked at each of us. "Naw, take it all."

Sharp handed me the sheet of paper. It had five names on it. One was familiar to me. A. Paulie Bargas. Paul Bargas. "Andy… Bargas. Isn't he the asshole who owns that bar over by Davenport?"

"Yeah. The Shield."

Sharp knew a bartender there. "You know this Bargas guy? That's quite a hole over there."

■ ● ■

I said, "No. I know of him." Andy nodded.

We stood in a semi-circle looking at Barthelme and the flashing Christmas tree lights.

I felt disappointed. "You know, I really wanted to pop that bastard myself. And you know what else? Whoever these guys are, they have some sick minds."

Sharp patted me on the back.

Mojica was smiling. "So are we all heading across town tonight? I'm getting tired and soon it will be past my bedtime." I could see the Christmas tree lights reflecting in his eyes.

"I have to get something to eat first."

Andy shook his head. "Sharp, you're always hungry. Can't you eat after this?"

"He's dead. Ah'm hungry."

Sharp sounded reasonable to me.

■ ● ■

Dance

We were standing outside a club called "The Shield." It was a bar with a reputation for violence. The kind of violence that would stop a police officer from going in by himself.

It reminded me of a place that I went to once called "The Luanna." When I was eighteen I went in to see what that kind of place was like. I wasn't at the bar five minutes when some guy sat down on my left and told me he didn't like me. I bought him a drink and before he finished another guy sat down on my right and told me the same thing. Pretty soon there were ten guys between me and the door and I couldn't buy enough rounds to make one friend among the daytime patrons. I slid out the bathroom window into an alley to get away. I had a friend on the force who told me the place was such a pain in the ass they just burned it down one morning.

"The Shield" was a little different. From what I heard the place was usually filled with red-neck, skinhead, Nazi types and a large sprinkling of hardcore drunks. Fridays and Saturdays were a little different. Somebody had the idea of having music in the place, so the crowd was a little more diffuse. The board by the door had three bands listed. The Matter Babies, Killtakers and

■ ● ■

Scumscreech. Whoever was up now was loud and playing fast. I didn't recognize the music at all.

I heard Mojica say, "We have a plan?"

Andy said, "Nope, but I'll pay the cover."

Andy and Sharp went in first. When Heeks and I slipped by, Andy and the big guy at the door were both looking down at the money. The place was packed. A lot of women were dancing to the Matter Babies. Actually it was more like they were jumping up and down. I liked it.

Mojica was in front of me. When he turned around I heard the big guy at the door bellow, "You brought a spic in here?" I turned quick, ready for a fight. "And a nigger?! We don't have any niggers in…" I took half a step and saw an arm like a piston connect with the big guy's jaw. When he hit the floor I thought I could hear a thud, but I couldn't have. The music was too loud. Sharp was standing over the guy with a slight smile on his face. He hollered at Andy, "Help me get him under this table." They pushed him under it. Andy stooped down and bent the guy's legs so no one would trip over them.

Sharp hollered, "What's the cover, Andy?"

Andy yelled back, "He charged me five dollars a head."

Sharp bent over and picked up the bills from the floor. He sat down on the stool.

I yelled, "What are you doing?"

"I'm gonna work the door for a while. Call if you need help."

I could see Mojica start laughing. Andy hollered, "Let's go find this Bargas guy."

The music stopped, but the buzz from the crowd was almost as loud as the music.

Then I heard, "Hey Sharp! How the hell are you doing? Hey, where's Donnelly? He's supposed to be…" Sharp's friend saw me and Mojica and he frowned. Then he saw Donnelly under

■ ● ■

the table and I could see he was about to drown in fear. "What the hell did you do?" He looked around real fast and put his hands up with the palms facing the guy on the floor. He was shaking his hands real fast, "I didn't see nothin'! I didn't see shit! You guys are fuckin' crazy!" He hurried back behind the bar like a pack of Dobermans were biting at his ass. Sharp took a tooth pick out of his pocket and slipped it into his mouth. He looked past me.

"Hey. You two. Cover's five bucks tonight."

I saw Andy smile just before he hollered, "Let's go."

We were weaving our way slowly through the bouncing crowd. Every once in a while Mojica or I would get a stare, or someone would do a double-take. I was glad we were packing. Coming out of here might be a problem.

We started making our way down a long hallway that had four doors. Andy stopped in front of the one that had a German flag on it. He knocked and then pushed the door open. A guy was sitting in a chair leaning back, staring at us.

"What the fuck do you think you're doing?!"

In his most polite voice Andy said, "We need to talk to you." Then he turned to the women. "You two get out."

Bargas sneered. "Don't move."

I walked up to the two women and looked at them with a smile. "GET THE FUCK OUT!" I watched them run for the door. "And don't say anything to anyone."

Behind me I heard Andy say, "Don't do it."

When I turned back Andy had a pistol out aimed at Bargas. Bargas froze but he kept his hand inside the desk. Mojica grabbed a chair, dragged it across the floor and jammed it under the door handle. I walked around behind the desk. Bargas still had his hand in the drawer. He was watching Andy. I slammed my knee into the drawer. He jumped up choking. His hand was caught

■ ● ■

and he couldn't pull it out.

"Fuck you. Fuck."

"You want your hand broken?"

"Fuck. Fuck."

"You want your hand broken?"

I thought he was going to cry. He whispered, "No."

I put my knee down. "Sit down." He didn't move. "I said sit down. You don't want a suicide in your office do you?" He looked at me wide-eyed. He obviously didn't understand. I started smiling and then I could see in his eyes that it clicked. He sat down rubbing his hand.

Andy took over. "I want you to look at the names on this list very carefully. Then I want you to tell me who they are and where they are." Andy handed him the paper. Bargas glanced at it and tossed it on the desk and started rubbing his hand again.

Andy glared at him. "Pick it up. Look at it again. I'll take phone numbers, too."

Bargas didn't even make a move for the paper. The next sound we heard was very odd. We all looked at Mojica. He was holding that damn knife again. I wondered where he kept it when he wasn't terrifying people with it. Mojica started to move around the desk. Andy jumped in front of him and put his left hand on Mojica's chest. "Not yet. Not yet. Did you take a pill, man? Did you take a pill recently?"

I really had to fight to stop from chuckling at them. Andy and Mojica were struggling almost like they meant it. I was hoping that Andy wouldn't get cut by accident. The thought immediately flashed in my brain like it was lit up in neon, 'That's Heeks with the blade. Nothing will happen by accident.'

Suddenly Mojica stopped moving. I had my pistol laying on Bargas in case he was a lot dumber, or braver, than I thought. Mojica was staring past all of us at the wall.

■ ● ■

"That's a door!"

I looked left. "What? The bookcase?"

"Yeah." Mojica moved past me and looked at the wall up close. "Help me move this desk." We jammed it in between the bookcase and the wall, making sure someone didn't interrupt us.

When I turned back to Bargas and Andy, Bargas's head was tilted to one side. Andy's gun was planted in his ear. He was talking very calmly about why Bargas had better go over the list again.

I picked the paper up off the floor and walked over to hand it to Andy. Whatever Andy said while Mojica and I were screwing around with the desk, had now gotten all of Bargas's attention. Andy tucked his piece in the back of his pants and then took a small pad out of his shirt pocket. Bargas started talking. Andy took notes while Bargas talked and kept glancing at Mojica. I looked at Mojica and he had that smile back on his face. He looked close to half crazy.

"I don't know those two." Andy slapped him in the back of the head. "I'm serious. I don't know who they are."

Andy looked at me. I shrugged. Andy said, "Let's hope this information is good, even though we all know it didn't really come from you. Right?" Bargas nodded. "Let's go."

Mojica pulled the chair away from the door and opened it. Andy walked out, followed by Mojica. I stared at the bookcase. Then I saw what Heeks noticed. The black mark on the wall where a rubber wheel, or something, ran across it when the door opened. Damn, I missed that.

Out in the main room the next band was sound checking. Sharp was still on the door, only now he had a large wad of money in his hand.

"We all done, boys?"

Andy nodded.

■ ● ■

"Hold on while I give my petrified bartender buddy the cash." Sharp made his way over to the bar and leaned across it trying to get his friend's attention. A woman with friendly intentions turned on her stool, saw Sharp and broke out her very best Redbook smile. She immediately tried to start up a conversation, but it didn't seem to go very far. First, the smile disappeared and then the frown appeared. Finally she turned away from him. Sharp glanced back at us, stuck his lower lip out, shook his head and then turned back to wave his friend over.

His bartender pal kept looking around like 'is there something else I can do besides go over there.' He wouldn't make eye contact until Sharp grabbed his wrist and put the money in his hand. The other two bartenders were now watching, probably wondering what the hell was going on.

The Killtakers started up loud. Then they got louder. The crowd seemed to go nuts all at once. They started banging into one another. Weird. It was kind of like watching a football game without a ball. Then I thought, 'Here we go.' From across the room a gang of about ten knuckleheads were coming right at us. They looked like the kind of guys who have fun on holidays by hitting each other in the face with baseball bats. Some of them were wearing suspenders over white tee shirts. All of them, except for two, had buzz cuts, but I didn't think they got them from the military.

I yelled, "I think we should go, unless we want to be in the middle of a riot."

Mojica yelled back, "What?! Some guys are coming for us!"

Sharp slid up to us and hollered, "We need to go!"

Mojica screamed, "What did Sharp say?!"

We started backing up toward the door. Andy pushed me and Mojica out the door. Then he grabbed Sharp by the arm and guided him out to the sidewalk.

■ ● ■

Sharp said, "I'm ready to go. We should get out of here because it'll be those ten and whoever wants to jump in on their side."

When Sharp wasn't willing to knuckle up he either knew the situation was hopeless or he was hungry. Right now it was probably both.

We were walking away from the club quickly. Mojica was talking about his hearing. The air felt really good after being inside. It felt like everything was far away. I was paying a lot of attention to the light and shadows on the sidewalk. I saw a flower pot up on a window ledge. Then I walked into Mojica's back.

"Damn. Sorry."

"What's up, dude? There's room for all of us in the car." He was smiling and I couldn't figure out why. Why was Mojica smiling? Everyone got in the car but me. I stood outside wondering if it was safe. Sharp stuck his arm out the window and slapped the side of the car.

"What're ya' doin'?"

I didn't know what to say.

Andy said, "Get in the car so we can get the hell out of here."

They thought I was a punk. They thought I was afraid to get in the car. I could deal with Andy and Mojica. Sharp would be a problem. When they made their move I'd have to get Sharp first.

Mojica leaned over and pushed my door open. "Come on, man. Let's go get something to eat." He smiled. I wasn't afraid of him. I just had to watch them and keep my eyes open. I got in and slammed the door. Andy turned and looked at me. "What the..." His eyes slid toward Mojica. Mojica shrugged.

"What?" They were thinking about me. I knew it.

Andy turned around, started the engine and we pulled away from the curb. "I don't think we should sleep at home tonight. We should get rooms."

Sharp said, "We have expense money, so of course we should

■ ● ■

do that. Some place with room service."

"Hey, I'm going to have to call Helen."

Sharp turned around in his seat. "Heeks, maybe she should meet us. Whad'ya think?"

"What? You thought I'd just call home and say, 'Helen, honey, I'm not coming home tonight because there are some crazy bad men who might come to our apartment to try to kill me. I'm going to stay in a hotel tonight. So you keep the doors locked, don't forget about the shotgun if someone breaks in, and you call me in the afternoon to let me know if anything happened. Okay, hon?' What the hell is wrong with you?"

Sharp was laughing, close to hysterical. "You call her 'hon'? Are you kidding me? You call Helen 'honey'? Andy, does Mojica really call Helen, 'honey'?"

"I believe he may, though I've never actually witnessed it."

"You guys go to hell. My arm hurts. I'm tired. I need to call Helen. I need a phone booth."

Andy sped up to make it through a yellow light and pulled over to the curb.

"There's your booth."

Mojica got out of the car and waited for a truck to go by before he crossed the street.

Sharp hollered, "Talk to her before you take one of those pills again. You sound stupid when you're on them."

Mojica went into the booth and shut the door. The light inside it went on and he flipped Sharp the finger.

Andy and Sharp both chuckled. Sharp said, "Andy, what about Janie?"

"I convinced her to visit her sister for a while. She left this evening, I hope."

"What about her job?"

"Screw that job. She hated it anyway."

■ ● ■

A couple of cars went by.

"What about Elaine?"

Sharp turned toward me. Andy made eye contact with me in the rear view mirror. Then Sharp said, "Maybe we should go get her. What d'ya think Andy?"

We were quiet until Mojica got back in the car and said, "Helen will drive her car over to the hospital. We'll pick her up there."

Sharp said, "Goin' to be crowded in here, but that's okay."

Mojica looked curious. "What are you…"

"We're going to snag Elaine, too."

Mojica shifted in his seat. "Cool. I'm glad you guys thought of that."

Sharp was still facing the back seat. He flicked his thumb at me. Mojica got that big, 727 grin on his face. "What was that dude's name? You know, the teacher dude."

"Screw you, Heeks. Take a pill. Take two God damn pills." I started staring out the window.

Andy said, "Maybe we should take two cars."

Everyone agreed. I agreed because everyone else did. Then I watched street lights fly by.

■ ● ■

Rooms

We met up with Helen in the hospital parking lot. While Andy was inside trying to call Elaine, Sharp and I listened to Mojica and Helen discuss his broken arm. I was leaning on a red Caddy. Sharp was sitting on the fender of Helen's Impala facing me. She wanted to know who set his arm. What kind of break was it? How much bruising was there? I noticed Sharp had a toothpick in his mouth again. His smile was being camouflaged by his hand holding the end of the toothpick. Finally Helen said, "Are you in pain? What prescription did they give you?" Mojica started to speak and she said, "Take a pill. You'll feel better."

Sharp laughed. "He sure will."

Andy came out of the hospital and walked over to Helen's car. He looked at us and put his hands in his pockets. "She said she'd see us all in hell tomorrow morning if we came over there."

Sharp hopped down off the car with a very serious look on his face. "Doesn't she understand how bad this is? We just kicked a good size hornets' nest tonight."

Andy shrugged.

I said, "I think we should go over there and get her."

■ ● ■

Andy spun toward me. "We're not going over there."

"Why not?"

Andy didn't respond and then Sharp echoed, "Why not?"

Andy took his hands out of his pockets and crossed his arms. "Why not?"

I nodded my head.

"Why not? Because she said she would shoot me on sight if I woke her up again. She said she didn't sleep the night before and she was going to sleep tonight. Then she cursed me and my mother's mother and dared me to come over to her place."

"Well what did you say?"

"Nothing, stupid. She hung up."

"Call me stupid, but I think we should go get her."

"Did you hear what I said?!"

"Yeah. She said she was going to shoot you! So?"

Helen interrupted us. "I'll go up and talk to her. I doubt she'll shoot me."

Now I was juiced. "Fuck it! Leave her ass up there. We can get another secretary."

Andy's facial expression changed in a quick second. "I'm not doing the goddamn books again. Get in the car!"

We made it over to Elaine's apartment in about ten minutes. Before Andy could park and turn off the engine, Helen and Elaine came out. Andy pulled up next to the Impala and Helen said, "The Cranston, right?"

Sharp said, "That's right. We have expense money."

Elaine was in the back seat holding her head up with her hand and not looking at us. Mojica was looking right at us with that big grin on his face again.

Sharp had picked the Cranston for us. He knew they had room service on the weekends until 3 a.m. He didn't care if the rooms were clean, the beds were firm, or if they had T.V. He just

■ ● ■

wanted to be sure he could get a steak on a French roll with a Rheingold.

While Andy checked us in, Sharp and I stared at Elaine in silence. At first she just stood there stone-faced. Eventually a slight frown appeared. She wouldn't look at either of us.

A little ways away, over by the elevators, we heard Helen say, "What the hell are you doing with these?! I could have gotten you something that wouldn't beat your brain into putty." Everybody near the night desk turned to listen. We could hear Mojica mutter something, but not the words. Helen responded, "Of course your arm would hurt. You need some rest and sleep. I'll get you something tomorrow that will let you think." Mojica had his 'all around the globe' smile going again. Helen noticed everyone looking at her and she cocked her head. "We're discussing his medication if you don't mind!"

Everyone turned away and pretended they didn't hear anything. I heard Andy tell the night manager, "She's a nurse." The kid at the desk nodded like he understood, and if we needed to keep a secret, he was not going to be the one to tell.

Just as we started to walk away from the desk I heard the kid say, "Do you have any of those you can spare?"

Andy looked at the kid. "When is your shift over?"

"Seven."

"If you took one of those now, you'd be asleep by 4:30."

We were on the twelfth floor with five rooms. In the elevator Andy started to question Elaine. "You were going to shoot me when I called. We stop at your apartment and you come out with Helen in about thirty seconds, dressed and packed."

Elaine looked around the elevator and then said in a haughty voice, "It looks like tomorrow Helen and I will have clean clothes. I assume Anthony will also since I'm sure Helen had the foresight to pack for her boyfriend." Andy clearly wanted her to

■ ● ■

say more, but Elaine was silent. Sharp started laughing.

Elaine shook her head. "As soon as I hung up I knew you were going to come bother me, so I thought I might as well get dressed so we don't waste time. It sure took you long enough to get over there."

Andy appeared to be a little confused. "It only took us ten minutes."

"It's two o'clock in the damn morning! I was not out at a club!"

I popped up with, "We were."

She looked at me hard. "So?! Why the hell should I care?! I want some God damn sleep! Will you guys eventually let me do it here?! Please." She was almost crying.

After we had shuffled out of the elevator, Andy began to describe our evening to Elaine. It seemed like she was all attention, but at one point I thought I saw her swaying.

When Andy finished Helen said, "Good night. I want to get Mighty Mouse into a bed. We all said 'good night' and watched them stop at their room. Then we heard Mojica say "Wait, wait. Let me pick the lock."

Helen pushed him away and said, "Get the hell out of the way before I break that good arm." Heeks stepped back. Helen unlocked the door with her key, waved to us with a "do you believe this" look on her face, and then pulled Mojica into the room by his shirt.

Elaine turned to Sharp and said, "How much did you keep from the door?"

Sharp smiled. "That was for the musicians."

Andy looked dumbfounded. "That's all you've got to say?"

Elaine turned on Andy like a fanged snake. "No, that's not all I've got to say! I want some goddamn sleep. So let me get to my room and see if I can forget the story you just told me." Elaine walked down the hall, her head turning from left to right looking

■ ● ■

for her room. Sharp started chuckling. Elaine stopped, turned around slowly, and with fire in her voice said, "Why the hell didn't one of you bastards tell me I was going the wrong way?!" Elaine came back down the middle of the hall and the three of us plastered ourselves to the walls until she went by. When she opened the door we all mumbled something like 'good night.' She glared at us, went into her room and then slammed the door.

Sharp said, "Hey Andrew, you be careful when you go for breakfast. That woman might be out here by the elevators layin' for you." We all started to laugh, but the door to Sharp's left opened. A guy in sky blue pajamas stepped out into the hall.

"Can I get some sleep, please? I have an important meeting tomorrow morning."

Sharp said, "It wasn't us mister. It was that crazy lady down the hall. We're gonna' go down and talk to the manager about her. Hollerin' like a banshee in the middle of the night. You want, I'll bring up your room number while I'm down there."

The man in the pajamas turned around. "Yes. If you want I'll give you a business card." Sharp put a new toothpick in his mouth while we waited for the man to reappear. When he came out he handed each of us cards.

Sharp was clearly amused. "Trampolines? Wow. I might be able to use me some trampoline back home. Whad'ya say we go down to the bar and discuss it?"

The pajama man could barely hide his smile of good fortune. "Let me get dressed."

"Naw. Just grab a bathrobe. The kitchen'll close in 45 minutes."

"Okay. I'll be right with you."

Andy was leaning against the wall staring at the floor. Sharp had his arm around the trampoline salesman as they got on the elevator. Andy put his hands in his pockets and pushed off from the wall with his elbows. As he walked past me he said, "Lunatics.

■ ● ■

I'm surrounded by son of a bitchin' lunatics." He stopped a little past me and added, "I think we need some sleep. Especially you." Andy turned around, punched me lightly in the arm and wandered off to his room.

I was standing in the hall alone. I thought I should be thinking about something, but I didn't know what. I looked both ways in the hall and slapped my hands together. I was smiling. I started jumping up and down like those women in the club. I spun around. I was breathing hard. I thought I should go to bed. But I suddenly felt responsible. Sentry duty. I should do sentry duty. I started walking up and down the hall with a purpose. It took me an hour to go to my room for sleep.

At about noon I sat up on the edge of my bed surprised that I could remember any of my dreams. It felt like I slept good. While I stretched I thought I had been annoyed by someone the previous night, but I couldn't remember who. When I looked out the window, the sky was wearing its grey, away uniform. Maybe we'd get rained out.

On the way down in the elevator I felt like something was gnawing at my stomach. I almost unbuttoned my shirt to look. Instead I just rubbed it and realized I had lost weight.

When I entered the dining room it was obvious that our crowd was going to take over one corner of it. Sharp was sitting over by the windows with a fork in his left hand and a knife in his right. He was reading the newspaper and he had two plates piled with food. On one plate he had a steak and parts of three eggs, toast and home fries. On the other plate he had a stack of pancakes covered in strawberries and whipped cream, with sausages on all sides.

"From the look of your plates I'd say you've only been here twelve minutes. You still have some eggs…your coffee is only half gone…waiting for your food was ten minutes. Yep. I'd say twelve minutes."

Without looking up, Sharp glanced at his watch. "Eleven minutes, tops."

"You know that stuff will kill you."

Sharp chuckled. "The way we're livin', what do you think our life expectancy is anyway?"

"Seriously. That steak and sausage will eventually kill you."

Sharp started cutting his steak. "So what are you gonna have"?

"I don't know. Bacon. A lot of bacon."

"Sit down, asshole. Grab a table."

Andy was sitting two tables away reading a book.

"Hey, Andy."

"Hey. Listen to this. 'The nation-state as a fundamental unit of man's organized life has ceased to be the principal creative force: International banks and multinational corporations are acting and planning in terms that are far in advance of the polit-ical concepts of the nation-state.' Amazing. Zbigniew Brezinski wrote that in 1971."

Sharp had a mouthful of steak, but still managed to get some words out of his mouth cleanly. "Isn't that sum-bitch in charge of something?"

I said, "Just the country…you know, the nation-state."

Sharp smiled. "I knew it was somethin' important like that."

Elaine slipped in next. She looked like she slept well, but she didn't have any smiles. I thought maybe she had realized what our situation was.

At one, Helen and Mojica walked in. For some reason we all applauded. I think we stopped when we saw how pale Heeks was. He sat down like a tree falling in the woods. Helen read our concern and told us not to worry, that he would be fine.

After another hour we all managed to gather around one table and make some decisions. We decided that we would stay

■ ● ■

here a few more nights, but we were going to have to show up at the office some time. We decided 'some time' would be to-day, since we had a business to run. We agreed that we would conduct our business in pairs, no running off to do things solo without the rest of the gang being told.

We dropped Helen off at the hospital for her shift and told her not to come outside when her shift was over. We would be there waiting for her in the lobby. If we weren't there, stay inside until we contacted her.

In the car, on the way to the office I said, "You know that list? Does anyone think we can figure out who the guys are that Bargas didn't know?"

Andy looked at me in the rear view mirror. "Why?"

"Well, I was thinking, if he doesn't know them, they don't know him." I could see Andy's eyes start to smile. "We might be able to do a little imposter thing and get some serious informa-tion. Especially if they're in a tizzy right now."

Sharp turned around in the front seat to give me five. "Bar-thelme was not very loose with his tongue, but I don't think he was feeling any real pressure. This really might work since Joey-boy is dead."

We drove downtown past the entrance of our building and went around the corner. As Andy, Sharp and I got out of Andy's car, Elaine and Mojica cruised past us and parked a little ways down the block. We waited for them to catch up and then we all kind of marched off toward the office. When we got to the corner everyone went left except me. I went straight.

■ ● ■

Arcade

A ndy started to yell, "What the hell did we just talk..." His
voice trailed off and when I glanced back, the four of them
were heading into the lobby. I crossed the street and walked toward the old arcade that was about a third of the way down the
block. I entered the passageway and saw Lt. Callahan leaning in
one of the doorways. He looked different than he did up in our
offices. Maybe it was the context.

My brain ran back to when I was a kid, hiding on a gray,
rainy day like today in this curving hallway that seemed like the
most exciting place in the world then. A hundred kids would
be hanging out in this hallway that went from one street to the
next block. Some of them would be playing pinball in Manny's.
Some of them would be hanging in Ron's Barber Shop talking
basketball with Ron. Even the shoe repair guy had some fans
who talked to him about anything and everything. Some guys
just wanted a place to smoke and talk loud around the girls.
Seemed like the center of the universe. Now it was just a grey
hallway with one or two businesses selling cigarettes and gum. It
was hard to believe it was this grey then.

I walked past Callahan and he looked behind me until I was

past him. When he caught up to me I asked him what he wanted.

"I didn't think any of you would see me."

"Then why did you stand there if you didn't think we'd see you?"

I stopped in front of the double doors that used to open into 'Marty's Ping Pong Emporium." It was just an empty store front now. Somebody told me Marty ripped the name off from someone else, but I could never imagine who that could be.

"I've been transferred."

"Huh?"

"They sent me to bunko."

"Well, I hope it's the job you've always wanted."

He cleared his throat. "I was transferred for raising a small stink about the shootings over at Haley." He stopped and grabbed my arm. "There wasn't one shooter. There were at least two."

"Yeah. I know."

He let go of my arm. He looked as stunned as if I told him the Cubs had won the World Series and he missed the television broadcast.

"You were there?"

"Apparently I was a target."

Callahan's mouth opened, but nothing came out. He shook his head and started shuffling his feet. "I knew it. I don't know what's going on. Maybe it's better for me if I don't. As soon as I mentioned that possibility with a couple of the others…you know, that the incident up at your office and Haley were connected, everyone in the room froze. The next thing I knew I was being transferred out of homicide."

I didn't mean to be sarcastic. I guess it was in my genes. "Good work, Holmes." Usually I would expect a cop to get real pissed off at me for that kind of quip. Callahan just raised his

■ ● ■

eyebrows. He looked around and when he began speaking he sounded like he was talking to himself. "There's something going wrong in the department. Right now I don't think I can do much about it. As soon as I said there was more than one shooter I felt like I was on the outside. If I can see it, why can't the others?" He paused and looked right at me. "Why couldn't the others?"

"They did. That's why you're in bunko. Callahan, do you have kids?"

"What? Yeah. Three. Two boys and a girl."

"You better think about that. We're pretty sure this is going to get worse than it already is."

Callahan sounded desperate. "Well what is it? What's going on?"

"We don't know either. We have some ideas, but nothing solid."

Callahan ran his hand through his hair. "I've got kids, but I have to do something." Now he sounded scared.

"Why'd you want to meet with us?"

"I had to figure out if there was a connection between Haley and you."

"That's it?"

Another pause. "No. I was going to tell you I'd feed you information."

"But now you're not sure. That makes sense. You have kids."

He was standing still, but every limb connected to his torso was moving. He may have been the first cop I ever felt sorry for. "Callahan, you haven't done anything yet. Why don't you just go hide yourself in Bunko until this is over?"

He froze. I felt like I had just given him permission to ignore everything that was going on in the world around him. He no longer had responsibility for anything. He looked like he was

■ ● ■

deciding the direction of his life right in front of me. A kid slid past us on a skateboard. Callahan looked at his shoes.

I took a step away from him. "Take it easy, Callahan. Try to stay out of trouble."

"Chief Croyle has been meeting with two men I thought were FBI. Now I'm pretty sure they're not."

I moved in close to Callahan. "Do you know what they've been discussing?"

"No. The only thing I heard once was 'North Carolina.'"

"What about North Carolina?"

"That's all I heard."

"Christ, they could have been talking about taking a fishing vacation. Why do you bring that up?"

"Because of the way they looked at me when they realized I was close." I was wondering how this guy ever survived in homicide.

Two men in suits walked by. Callahan acted so nervous they looked at him like he was a dealer or an addict.

"I have to get out of here." He started to move away.

"Wait. Callahan, you can help me right now, I think. Can you tell me anything about the guy who's killing the women?"

Callahan looked confused. "They're related?"

I decided to lie. "Yeah. We think they're connected."

Callahan's head snapped back like he had just walked in on the worst murder scene of his career.

"How?!"

"I can't really tell you yet, but as soon as we work it out, we'll come to you." No cop in the world should have accepted those words from me. I felt stupid even saying them. But not only did Callahan accept what I said, he seemed to drift into some kind of state of paralysis. I decided to ride with it. "I swear that as soon as we put a little more together, we'll give you everything we have."

Callahan had been a homicide cop for a while. He probably saw ten or more murders a year. His view of reality was certainly different from most people. But he probably had a grip on it. Right now he looked like his understanding of reality was crumbling all around him. I wondered what kind of crazy connections his mind was making if he thought what I had just told him was true. I wondered if this was how I looked sometimes when I saw Andy or Heeks staring at me.

"Callahan?..."

"It's been driving us crazy. The guy seems to operate any time of day. Then, what he does to the women is weird. On some of them he draws circles with lipstick. Some of them he ties up with wire. A few he beat in the left side of their face. The others, the right. They all have brown hair, about five-four. Three were prostitutes. Three weren't. Then there are these interconnected squares he draws on the floor. There are six of them now, in two sets of three. But they went from two, then three, another three, then five and six. At first, all of them were interconnected. Then with the six, there were two sets of three. Whatever that message is, we're not getting it. It made me feel like maybe we didn't find all of the bodies yet. I don't know. All of the other info was released to the newspapers."

"The papers suggested all of the murders occurred at night."

"That was someone's brilliant idea of luring the guy out into the open."

"What?"

"How is this connected anyway?"

I ignored Callahan's question. "This is not a good place to meet. If you have any info you think will help, call our office and ask for Jack Levine."

"But where do we meet?"

■ ● ■

"Hawley St. Bridge. Bring a pole."

Callahan nodded, turned and walked away. I wondered if he was walking away feeling like a blind man.

I walked across the street, looking up and down the block to see if anything would catch my attention. The street seemed clean. I walked into the lobby and Sharp came over to me from the side of the phone booths. We rode the elevator up with an operator we didn't know. When we got out, Sharp said, "I'll talk to Ivars about that." I nodded.

In the office the five of us stood around Elaine's desk while I gave a brief run-down on my chat with Callahan.

Andy said, "We can't trust him any more than we can trust anyone else on the force. But maybe we can get some info that'll help us."

I said, "Andy's right. The transfer could be bullshit. And even if he's on the level they could feed him all kinds of misinformation. But I think he's really scared and confused."

"Heeks, you said you thought you could get those cameras functioning in three days?"

"Probably two, Andy. I want to do it at night so we don't have anyone accidentally stumbling through while I'm installing them. Raoul found us a place that will have the screens and the cameras. We'll be able to record whoever visits, and the cameras are almost invisible once they're installed. We'll also have a microphone out in the hall."

I almost asked how much it was going to cost, but I figured everyone had already talked about it. We started discussing the business and which clients we had to see and how soon. Elaine had been working on a schedule for us, which kind of irritated me, because she had assignments laid out. Who was going where, when. The others seemed to be fine with that, but I was annoyed. Were these her new secretarial duties? It should have

■ ● ■

been discussed. Then I thought, maybe it had been, so I kept my mouth shut.

The arcade was depressing. Almost all of the businesses were closed. One kid on a skate board. Just gray. And Callahan frightened so that he couldn't stand up straight. When was the last time I was in there? Before I enlisted? Maybe I…

"You comin', partner?"

Sharp was moving toward the hallway. I nodded and waved goodbye to no one in particular.

■ ● ■

Two

It was our fourth night watching the donut shop. Elaine was the only one willing to sit with me. Andy and the guys wouldn't have let me go unless I had company. Sharp and Mojica were on a stakeout. Andy was doing paperwork at the hotel. So that left me with the joy of Elaine.

Right now, it was quiet for a change. Not that the change was necessarily good. It was more like a surprise. For three nights Elaine had managed to start conversation after conversation. It felt like I was in a car with Scheherazade. I found myself kind of amazed, and slightly amused, that I kept getting drawn into them and liking it. But tonight it looked like Elaine had finally run out of gas. I couldn't shake the feeling that I was disappointed.

Elaine was sitting in the passenger seat slouched down with her arms crossed over her chest. For about two hours I thought she was going to fall asleep, but she just kept staring at Dicky's Donuts with her eyes half closed.

"I'm going to call in." I started to open the car door.

"What time is it?"

"Eleven forty-five."

"Maybe I should get a coffee."

■ ● ■

"Can you wait until I get back?"

"Course…do you want one, too?"

"Yeah, and get me…"

"A raspberry jelly donut."

Elaine the mind reader kind of annoyed me. "Actually I was thinking Bavarian crème."

Elaine never moved except for her lips. "No you weren't."

I got out of the car and hit my head on a tree branch. We were in a corner of the insurance company parking lot, under a maple tree. It was so dark in that corner that even if you knew we were out here, and you were looking for us, we'd be hard to see.

I stuck my head back in the open window. "Bavarian crème, Elaine. I'll be right back."

As I walked away I heard her murmur, "Raspberry jelly."

The phone booth was a block and a half from Dicky's. I walked past on the opposite side of the street and saw Sharon bring out a tray of donuts. On the way back I'd go down the street and cut through two alleyways, then walk behind the insurance company building back to the parking lot. Elaine would take the same route after she bought the coffee.

The phone booth light didn't go on when I closed the door. I dropped in the dime and read the cover of what was left of the phone book. "For a really good time call Sylvia blah, blah, blah." I had a dream once that I was shipwrecked. Everything seemed so crisp and clear. I was lying in yellow sand when I opened my eyes. The beach was covered with blue and green shiny glass bottles. I spent most of the dream stumbling along, looking to see if there was anything in them. Finally, from one of them, a message slipped out. "For a really good time call Fred Murtz." What a lousy dream. Every time I see someone has written "for a really good time," I get a flashback to the beach and Fred. What a lousy dream.

■ ● ■

"Hello?"

"Hey, Andy. We'll be out of here in about an hour."

"I'll be down in the bar getting my ass kicked. Look for me."

"Ass kicked in what?"

"Chess. Met a guy who is taking me to town. He's toying with me. He suggested we play for money. Fortunately, I had the sense to say 'no.' He kind of reeked of 'hustler.' Like those guys we used to run into in the pool halls. Never met a chess hustler before. I'm trying to get him drunk. I don't think it will matter. The guy is great."

"Well, don't hurt him."

"See you in an hour and a half, right?"

Wow. Somebody was 'toying' with Andy in chess?! I had to see that. I started to cross the street. Half way I heard the car horn. I stopped to listen. Two short and a long. I started running down the sidewalk toward Dicky's. When I got there Elaine was standing on the sidewalk right across from the shop.

She turned her head toward me. "Something's wrong. A guy went in and then he disappeared. I don't think he came out and I haven't seen anyone out front."

"How long ago?"

"He went in about half a minute after you left."

I ran across the street and pulled on the front door. It wouldn't budge. I looked over my shoulder. "Elaine! Go call the police!" I ran around the corner of the building and tripped over some wood and cinder blocks. I made it to the back door and found it locked tight. I ran back up the alley toward the front. On the way I bent over and picked up a cinder block. I went to the front door, swung the block twice and let it go. The glass shattered and I stepped through, muttering, "Daddy's home…" I pulled my weapon out and slid along the counter with my left hand barely touching it as a guide. When I got to the swinging doors that led

■ ● ■

to the back room, I tried to look through the glass windows but it was impossible. They were filthy with flour dust. I kicked at the doors and they started swinging back and forth with a faint, little squeak as they slowed down, accompanied by a muffled cry. It was my day to do something stupid, so I slammed through the doors and went down on one knee. At the end of a long table I saw Sharon tied at the wrists to one of the legs of the table. She had rags stuffed in her mouth and Donut Boy had a handful of her hair, which he was using to yank her head back. She was bleeding from the lip and one eye was swollen. Her pants were down to her ankles.

Donut Boy's teeth were clenched so tight I couldn't tell if that was how he smiled, or if he was trying to imitate a wolf snarling. Either way I was going to break some of those teeth.

Then I heard another muffled sound to my left. I snapped my head and saw the kid who made the donuts tied up on the floor with rags in his mouth too. He started shaking his head violently. Uh-oh. I pivoted and threw both arms up in front of me just in time to get hit with a piece of wood that resembled a base-ball bat. Donut Boy?! There were two of them. Fucking twins! My gun flew out of my hands and landed somewhere across the room. Donut Boy 1 was trying to slide something over my head. I shot my left hand to my neck just as a piece of wire started to tighten. It was ripping into my hand , but I wasn't strangling. My right hand was trying to stop Donut boy 2 from getting a clean shot at my head with that piece of wood. Eventually he was going to connect if I didn't make something happen quick.

I pushed backwards as hard as I could until we ran into one of the tables. I heard Donut Boy 1 grunt when we slammed into it. I twisted my left leg around him, got him to twist his body a little and threw two quick punches to his stomach. The wire loosened and I pulled my left hand out, and managed to pull

■ ● ■

Donut Boy 1 in between me and his brother. Donut Boy 2 was jumping from side to side, winding up, trying to get an angle to hit me again but miss his brother. A big swing was coming. I grabbed a pan from behind me and tried to throw it. It didn't get very far. The pan was filled with flour and when the bat hit it, the air was suddenly almost unbreathable. The three of us were choking. The next swing hit his brother, who then dropped down to his knees and wrapped his arms around my left leg. Where the hell was my gun? I saw it over by the kid who made the donuts. I tried to hop toward it dragging Donut Boy 1 along with me. His brother saw what I was doing and ran toward the pistol. The kid who made the donuts rolled over on it. Donut Boy 2 started kicking him in the ribs. I grabbed a tray off a table and hit Donut Boy 1 in the head about five times before he let go. Donut Boy 2 was on his knees trying to get his hand under the kid's stomach. I dove on top him and drove his head into the floor. His twin dove on top of me and tried to scratch my eyes out. The one on the floor grabbed my hair and an ear that he was trying to rip off. The one on my back slipped one of his hands into my mouth.

Fuck this! I bit down as hard as I could. Blood filled my mouth. Donut Boy 1 was trying to pull his hand out while hitting me in the back of the head with his other hand. The harder he pulled, the harder I bit down. If it came off maybe I could win this. I don't know where it came from but another cloud of flour poured down on us. The one on my back finally managed to rip his finger out of my mouth. The one below me was shaking his head trying to get the flour out of his mouth and eyes. He had me by the hair with both hands and was pulling my head toward him. I slammed my face into his and then bit into his cheek like it was a hot dog. Blood spurted up into my face and Donut Boy 2 let out a scream that made his brother stop trying to punch me

■ ● ■

for a second.

Then the gun went off. I thought, 'Shit! They're triplets?!" I looked up and saw Elaine standing over us with her .38 pointed at Donut Boy's temple.

"Get up and sit on the floor over there. Make a stupid move and you are dead."

The Donut Boy on my back did as she said. I couldn't believe how hard I was breathing. I pushed myself to my knees and caught a glance of Sharon. I felt sick to my stomach. I stood up with flour falling off my shoulders and drifting into my face, and staggered over to her. I pulled her pants back up from her ankles. I took the rags out of her mouth and untied her hands. She had tears flowing down her face mixed in with snot and her hair. She started having dry heaves. I picked her up and sat her on a table. "You're going to be all right. You're going to be fine."

I went over to the kid. I started to bend down to untie him and I heard Elaine say, "I swear that if you get off your knees I will put a bullet right between your fucking eyes."

I turned around quickly and saw that Elaine had both of them covered. One was on his knees cursing. The other one was on his back crying with both hands on his face.

I got down on one knee to untie the kid. When I took the rags out of his mouth he said, "I'm hurt, mister. I'm really hurt."

"We'll get you to the hospital as soon as the cops get here."

"You dirty fucking cunt! I'll get out and I'll come for you, you slutty bitch. Just wait and see."

"Try standing up and repeating that, asshole."

"Fuck you, cunt. See if I don't get out. I'll get you, you bitch."

The kid said, "Mister, help me up."

"I think you should stay put until the medics get here. You were great covering up the gun like you did."

"Help me up, please." He was begging me.

■ ● ■

I helped him to his feet. Donut Boy 1 was still cursing Elaine. The kid walked like Frankenstein over to Donut Boy and kicked him in the face. "Shut up!" He kicked him again. "Shut up!"

Sharon yelled, "I think it was the other one. The other one." He took two steps like a sci-fi robot. It was obvious he wasn't going to make the next five feet.

I ran over to catch the kid before he fell. "Whoa there, Pele. Let's sit down, okay?"

The kid looked at me and tears started rolling down his cheeks. "I'm really hurt. It really hurts." It was almost a whisper.

"Your ribs?"

The kid nodded.

"You need to sit down."

I managed to get the kid on the floor just as two cops came flying in with their guns drawn. "Put your weapon on the floor." Elaine bent over slowly and put her gun on the floor. Then she raised her hands over her head.

The cops were staring at us like it was a freak show. "What the hell is going on in here?"

Donut Boy 1 started screaming. "They tried to kill us! They pulled us in here to rob us and kill us!"

Sharon started screaming, "Liar! Liar! You God damn liar!"

One cop had brown hair. "Everybody shut up!"

The other cop had blond hair. "I think we need an ambulance over here."

I said, "You better make that two."

The cop with brown hair looked at me. When he finally worked his way through the flour and blood, he said, "I told you to shut up. Get over against the wall with both hands on it. Don't move or say anything until I say so."

Behind me I heard Elaine say, "He's a licensed private detective. We were watching this building because of threats to one of

■ ● ■

the employees."

"Well ma'am, until I see some I.D. and I can determine he's not one of the perpetrators of a crime, he can stand right there. You can put your hands down, though."

From out front I could hear Andy holler, "Officers! Coming in." I looked over my shoulder and saw the blond point his weapon with both hands at the swinging doors. I suddenly wondered if these two cops had been on the force longer than the twelve minutes it took them to get here.

Andy's head popped through the door. He did a slow scan of the room.

"Is anybody dead in here?"

I said, "No. But they ought to be."

The brown-haired cop said, "I told you to shut up. You keep both hands on that wall or I will put you down."

"Officer, he's a licensed private investigator, as am I." I looked over my shoulder to see Andy displaying his identification to the blond. Sharp came through the door, looked at me and started laughing. As his eyes scanned the room he stopped.

The blond-haired cop looked at Sharp. "Who are you?"

"Me? I'm nobody. Ah just wanna' get some donuts." Sharp slid back out the door.

Andy asked, "Did anybody call in an ambulance or two?" The blond left the room in a hurry.

Then Elaine went off. "Can he take his hands down now? You've had him up against that wall for ten minutes and you already know who we are. What the hell is wrong with you?! Is this going to make you a better person some how?"

"Keep it up and you can yell at me downtown through some bars."

Andy was motioning to her to keep it down. The blonde came back in and said help would be here in about five minutes.

■ ● ■

Sharon was sitting on the table again, sobbing quietly. The kid started to say something, but Donut Boy 1 interrupted. "They were trying to rob and kill us. We…"

Sharon jumped down off the table and charged at Donut Boy 1. "Liar! Liar! You fucking liar!" She was throwing punches at him as fast as she could. The blond cop grabbed her and pinned her over a table. Then, to my utter amazement, he put cuffs on her.

Elaine's voice was too loud to echo in any room. "Are you kidding me? Those two try to kill and rape her and you handcuff the woman who's the target of the attack?! We're going to sue you, the city, the department." She was so out of control it was beautiful and the blond had to mention it.

"Ma'am, you can see this woman has lost control of herself."

"Wouldn't you lose control if someone had just tried to murder you and they sit there like they're the victims. Is he out of control, too?" Elaine pointed at me.

The brown-haired cop said, "You need to shut up, lady."

"What?!"

The blond looked worried. He noticed Andy taking notes. "Be quiet, Calvin."

"We need to keep this situation under control!"

"It is under control."

Elaine was waving her arms. "Tell dick-head to stop pointing his gun at my boss! He's obviously not going anywhere. What the hell is wrong with you?! Another couple of fascist cops! We're going to sue, goddamn it!"

"Ma'am, talk like that will get you put in jail."

"Like what? Like suing you?"

"No, like calling me a fascist. Calvin, let's put some cuffs on these guys."

Calvin took a step toward me. The blond stopped him. "Not

■ ● ■

him, Calvin. Those two."

Calvin looked back at Officer blond. "This is the one I don't trust."

"Calvin…"

Two uniforms came through the swinging doors and looked at everybody with wide eyes. One of them said, "What the hell was going on in here?"

Two detectives came through the doors. One of them waved at Andy. Andy nodded back.

"Who works here?"

I said, "The woman sitting there and this guy, who happens to need a doctor real bad." I pointed to the kid who was now lying on the floor. The way he was breathing, it sounded like maybe he had a punctured lung.

The brown-haired cop turned to me and his face couldn't have been more red. "Shut up. They want to talk to the people who work here. Not you."

I'd had it with this pig. "I wish I could say I don't know what your problem is, but I know exactly what it is and someday we're going to get part of it straightened out."

"Okay, shine. Up against the fucking wall."

One of the detectives said, "Livingston, let it ride."

My pal, Calvin, backed up glaring at me like a Buffalo blast furnace.

After that, we stood around giving statements to police officers for a good portion of the night. But when I finally said "I think you have your serial killers over there on the floor," the place went crazy. The detectives looked at me like I needed a straight jacket. They went up on their tiptoes dancing when I said the reason the women were beaten on opposite sides of the face was because one twin was right handed and the other was left handed. Then I said, "You never had four boxes, did you?

■ ● ■

But that one time you had three at two different murders. That's because the twins didn't know the other one was doing a murder at almost the same time. So each of them thought he was doing number three."

One of the two said, "How the hell do you know that?! Where'd you get that information?!"

"Doesn't matter, but those boxes represented caskets, I think. And one of them probably works second or third shift while the other one has a day job."

The same detective got a little condescending and said, "So then how are they both here tonight?"

What insight. "Jeez, I don't know. Maybe it's one of their days off, Sherlock."

He was coming for me and so was that jerk, Calvin. The detective who had nodded to Andy stepped between us and both of them stopped like they had hit the end of the chain at the doghouse. "We're going to need a formal statement from you down at the station." Andy stood behind them smiling.

When I was finally allowed to go over to the sink to wash my face I almost passed out. There wasn't a Halloween mask that could ever touch the way my head looked. I was covered in flour. I had blood running down my chin from my mouth. Flour and blood had mixed together creating an almost orange paste that covered a third of my face. I kept rinsing my mouth, but I couldn't get the metallic taste out.

Elaine came up behind me. "Do you need a doctor?"

"I don't think so, but my hands both hurt. One is swelling. I don't think it's broken or else I wouldn't have been able to hit them so many times. My back is sore. My shoulder is stiff. I have a foul taste in my mouth. I feel exhausted and I need some sleep, bad. But what I really need is a shower. Look at me. Just look at me."

■ ● ■

"I'll take you by your place so you can get some fresh clothes."

I was washing my face off when I said, "You called Andy when you called the police?"

"I thought we might need the guys, so I called them right after I called the police."

"Good thinking, but I needed you. Who else did you call? How many friends did you call before you came back? What took you so long? You call your mother?"

"What?!"

Elaine didn't know what to think. I got her good. "I'm teasing. Thanks for your help. I don't know if we would have made it out of this if you weren't here."

"It looked like you were winning when I got back."

"If I was, it was barely."

I went into the restroom for a few seconds. When I came out Sharon started her imitation of a sumo wrestler and threw a bear hug on me.

I felt bad for her all over again. "Come on, Sharon. You'll get flour all over you." She was weeping and I thought I heard her whimper, "I don't care."

Elaine smiled up at me like I was doing something wrong. Then Sharon stepped away from me and started hugging Elaine. Elaine's face lit up like the nose on that kiddy board game about appendectomies. Why was she so embarrassed? I wanted to laugh, but my shoulder and hand were starting to hurt so much, all I could do was smile. Then Elaine started hugging her back and said, "You're going to be all right."

The back room was finally quieting down. The medical people were gone. The Donut Boy twins were gone. All of us were going to the station. After that, Elaine and I would go to the hospital for the x-rays I didn't think I needed of my hand. Or was it the other way around? The hospital and then the station

■ ● ■

house?

When I went through the swinging doors, to my left I saw Andy sitting on a stool, his elbow on the counter, his head propped up by his hand. Mojica was next to him drinking coffee. I looked to my right and saw Sharp running the counter like he owned the place. Every stool and booth was occupied by Philco workers who had probably heard about the commotion when they were finishing their shifts and came over to see what was what. I wanted to ask Sharp what the hell he was doing, but I didn't have to. A man with a very confused and concerned look on his face walked behind the counter and said, "Who are you and what the hell are you doing?"

Sharp looked up from pouring a coffee. "Oh, you must be Barry. Glad you're here. It's kind of busy. Sharon is at the police station. The kid who helps with the donuts is at the hospital. We're out of glazed and there are two cops who want to talk to you out back." Sharp patted a glass jar. "And these here, are Sharon's tips."

Barry opened the cash register. Some bills fell on the floor. I could see how surprised he looked. It was packed with money. Sharp said, "C'mon, Barry, ah know it's late, but let's keep things together over on the register."

Barry looked at Sharp like he was going to say something. The toothpick was sliding in Sharp's mouth like he was daring Barry to open his mouth. Barry turned, looked at me and took a step back.

One of the detectives came through the doors and I said, "I think we have the owner here."

The detective introduced himself and guided Barry by his arm to the back room.

Down at the far end of the counter someone yelled, "Mr. Sharp, can I get a strawberry frosted?"

■ ● ■

"That's Sharp. Not Mister Sharp. Be right there with that strawb."

Two more guys came in. "Hey, Burdock. Is that girl okay?'

"I think so. She left with the cops a little while ago. I heard they might have the serial killer."

"No shit?"

"She looked a little banged up, though."

I watched Sharp work the counter for a few seconds. When I turned to Andy he said, "I'd say 'good work', but this was just dumb luck, wasn't it?"

Elaine piped up behind me. "Dumb luck, or good luck, business is going to be picking up whether you want it to or not. When this hits the papers it'll be like we're the only detective agency in town."

Andy stood up. "Bad timing, but we'll deal with it. Right?"

Elaine touched my arm. "We better get going."

Andy looked me up and down and said, "We'll pick up Helen. You better go change your clothes. You look ridiculous."

Elaine patted my back and we walked outside. I noticed the cinder block was holding the door open now. I looked up at the sky. "It's so nice out I wish we could walk. But it's too far isn't it?"

Elaine grabbed my arm. "Let's go get the car."

■ ● ■

Bridge

We were walking up onto the Hawley St. Bridge with our fishing poles. The bridge was deserted and dark. I'd thought there would be at least one or two guys out, but it was a Wednesday night.

We took a spot just about half-way across. I put my pole over the edge and leaned on the railing. The lights from the city were distorted, kind of drifting on the water. I couldn't seem to take my eyes off their reflections until I realized Elaine was actually putting bait on her line. I started laughing.

"We're not here to fish."

She didn't say anything. I looked around.

"Elaine, we're just here to meet Callahan and then we're gone."

She dropped her line in the water about thirty feet down.

"Maybe I'll get lucky and pull up tomorrow morning's breakfast."

"You're sure Callahan said 11:15?"

"Yes I'm sure Callahan said 11:15. It's only 11:05 right now."

I looked up and down the bridge. It was still empty, but I couldn't see much past either end.

■ ● ■

"Do you think about death much?"

I stood up straight and twisted my neck.

"Every single day."

"Really?"

"Yeah." I leaned on the railing again. "If I'm dead before 5 p.m. on any given day I know I won't have to come into work the next day to hear your bullshit questions. Wherever I am, I can do the big sleep and it'll be quiet."

"You afraid to give me a straight answer?"

I thought I saw her line twitch. "You just get a bite?"

"A nibble."

I was staring down her line waiting for it to jump again.

"Do you want to put something on your line and actually do some fishing?"

"No. I just want to see what Callahan has to say and then get the hell out of here."

"We're still early."

I started watching the lights again only to be interrupted by Elaine's next question.

"Why haven't you met someone?

"Jesus Christ, Elaine."

"Seriously. Why not? They were all over you in high school. Mr. Football. Mr. Basketball...Mr. Theater."

"Very funny. That was a long, long fucking time ago."

We were both silent, our thoughts drifting over the intervening years for a few moments. I was hoping that was the last question. Of course, it wasn't.

"Do you think it's because of the war?"

"What?!"

"Do you think you haven't met anyone because of the war?"

"I have a shrink now. As far as I know I don't need two."

It was quiet for about five seconds.

■ ● ■

"I'm asking as a friend."

"So you think we're friends now?"

"I thought we were."

"We work together. We weren't friends in high school. After six months we're not friends now."

"Oh…my mistake…Creon."

My skin went hot. "Fuck you, Elaine. You get pleasure in bringing that up? Or do you just think it pisses me off?"

"Both…boss."

She was clearly ticked off and 'boss' sounded like 'jerk.' I thought maybe I could turn the tables.

"So, Elaine. Why haven't you hooked up with anybody?"

"We only work together. Remember?"

"Oh, come on. Humor me."

"That's all it would be for you, is humor."

"Why do you say that? You shoot some poor bastard once? Or twice?"

She stayed quiet. I really didn't want her to be this pissed.

"Let's pretend we're trying to be friends."

She turned her head toward me, but I couldn't tell what the expression on her face was like. It was too dark. She looked back down at her line and started talking.

"I was with someone for about five years. He was a photographer who fell in love with one of his models. He moved out and about a year later I got a call from a hospital. He'd had a stroke and died."

"Why'd they call you?"

"He had no one else. His parents were dead. He had no brothers or sisters. So I took care of his remains and the funeral."

"That was kind of noble."

"I guess I wanted to have a 'she was noble' chapter in my autobiography."

■ ● ■

"Did the model show up for the funeral?"

"Eeyep. Turned out they were still seeing each other."

"Well why the hell didn't she take care of things?"

"I don't know. They called me and I guess I played the sucker. Maybe that will be a chapter, too."

"Asshole, maybe. But not sucker. You must have really cared for the guy."

I could hear her sigh like she was giving up. "You know, when you say something nice about someone, they'll like you better if you don't call them an asshole first."

I laughed. "I'll keep that in mind. But why haven't you snagged some other poor, unsuspecting bastard?"

"You're really on a roll tonight, aren't you? Your turn."

"My turn what?"

"Do you think you haven't met anyone because of the war?"

The reflections of the city lights seemed more wrinkled on the water now. The breeze was picking up and sometimes the lights seemed to float above the water.

Elaine was wearing me down. Now, I actually felt like talking.

"I don't know, Elaine. I mean, everything is because of the war. You go in thinking it's all about freedom and then one day you realize that's a cover. It's all about money. Somebody wants somebody's oil, or tin, or copper, or rubber, or gold. And you get sent off to make it possible for somebody to steal somebody's something. And your buddies die...or get maimed and you're afraid to tell them the reason they don't have a leg...or tell their sister why her brother is being dropped in a hole in the ground. And then I have this job that's kind of crazy sometimes. Feels like the same job I had in the military...but at least I don't have to salute or lie, if I don't want to...why would I want to try to find someone to be with me? This is not real. My whole story isn't real. Most times I feel like I'm a bauble from a sideshow.

■ ● ■

A cheap little throw away prize. Why would anyone want to be with me? Me and my friends…the Department of Discontinued Lives. I thought at least Andy and Heeks would be normal. And now Janie's not coming back…I thought she and Andy would get hitched…well, maybe fucking Mojica will be normal…even though he's not really normal."

"You're not a bauble. I think you could meet a great woman and lead a…a kind of normal life."

"Oh, come on. 'Normal' while I'm doing what I do?"

"Then why don't you quit this?"

"And do what?! Join the police force? Maybe I could start a rent-a-cop agency. Look…maybe I'm addicted to this. My friends…uh huh…"

I looked at him talking in the dark and wondered if we were really becoming friends, or if this was just providing him with a free therapy session. That was quite a ramble he was just on. He surprised me though, with his description of himself as a 'bauble.' He always seemed so full of confidence.

He started playing with his pole. Maybe so he could ignore me. "What are you doing? Did you decide you actually want to fish?"

"We're going to have to get out of here very quickly."

"What about Callahan?" I looked over the railing. "Your line's not even in the water and you managed to get it snagged on something."

He kept pulling on the line, and letting it go. Almost like a yo-yo.

"What the heck are you doing?"

"I guess Callahan made it here before us."

I looked around at the dark. "Where?"

"Elaine…follow my line."

I looked down to see what he was snagged on. Some shoes

■ ● ■

swung into view and then disappeared under the bridge. On the next tug the legs appeared.

I whispered, "Is that Callahan?"

"I haven't seen his face yet, but by the way he swings in the breeze, I'd say yes."

"Shit. What are we going to do?" He took a jackknife from out of his pocket and cut his line. Then he cut mine.

"We jump. Ready?"

"What?!"

"We're going to jump. As I remember it, you were on the swim team."

I stared down at the water. "It just rained yesterday. The water's going to be cold."

"Yeah. Frigid. Didn't you take senior life saving with Korte and that crowd?"

"How the hell do you remember that? How did you know that?!"

"Future detectives of America. I sent away for my ring in second grade. It's good to know your senior lifesaving skills will actually be valuable. It's time to go, Elaine."

"I'm not jumping in there!"

"It's probably not a good idea for you to walk to either end of this bridge."

"Why not? Did you see someone?"

"Nope. But I don't have to. I'm pretty sure someone plural is waiting at both ends."

"Oh, shit." I looked over the railing again. "How do you know if it's deep enough?"

"I jumped here many, many times when I was a kid. It's about eight to ten feet deep. If you're coming, bring your pole. No sense in leaving fingerprints."

"How is senior life saving going to help me now?"

■ ● ■

"Not you, stupid. Me. If I'm drowning you can save me. Look, when we hit the water we're going to swim over that way about twenty feet and then let the current off the center pylon drag us toward that point jutting out. We only have to end up doing some real swimming for fifty feet or so. Follow me. If you get out too far you'll end up like Jake Giambalvo."

"Giambalvo? Giam...didn't he drown..."

"Yep. He was on the swimming team three years ahead of us."

He climbed over the railing and held on to it facing me.

"Is that how I should jump here?"

"Huh? No. Doesn't matter. I'm turning around so I can see if it's Callahan on the way down."

"Of course it's Callahan."

"Oh, yeah? How do you know? See his face? Callahan might be over at one end of this bridge."

I started to pull my shoe off.

"Leave it on. We're not swimming mostly. And it's so rocky where we're going you'll want your sneakers on your feet."

He jumped backwards and it seemed like he dropped in slow motion. He hardly made a sound when he entered the water. I felt a little sick to my stomach until I saw him bob back up. I climbed over the railing and jumped. I really wasn't ready for how cold the water was when I hit it. But after a few seconds it didn't seem as bad as I thought it would be. When I came to the surface I could hear him whisper, "Elaine. Over this way." I did a breast stroke over to where I saw his head sticking out of the water.

"Was it Callahan?"

"Didn't you look?"

"No I didn't, shithead. Was it Callahan?"

"Yeah. It was Callahan. Stay close. In a couple of seconds lose the pole."

■ ● ■

I could feel the current pick up as we drifted. I looked back at the bridge to see if I could spot anyone. I squinted my eyes, but it was so dark up there. I could see the bridge, and under it, Callahan, swinging slightly in the wind.

"Elaine! You're over too far. You're too far over. Not over there!"

The distance between us had grown while I was looking back at the bridge. I tried to swim but I kept going sideways. I went into a crawl and then I started to panic because I was drifting away. I put my head down and really put my body into it.

He grabbed my arm and I lifted my head gasping at the air. "Kick, goddamn it! Kick!" We were both kicking furiously and then suddenly I could feel the current let up again. We had missed the point and now we were swimming for the shore about two hundred feet away. Now that my panic was over I could feel myself start to get a normal stroke. I began to pull ahead of him. I could hear his heavy breathing. He was laboring.

"Turn over on your back and put both hands on my shoulders."

He didn't say a thing. He kept swimming and I realized he wouldn't accept my help. "I'll see you on shore." I pulled away hoping he wouldn't drown.

When he raised himself out of the water and started walking toward shore, he tripped and fell.

"God damn it!"

He got up again and walked toward me with his legs far apart to maintain his balance. I was sitting on the bank shivering. I looked up at him.

"You okay?"

"Those swimming lessons didn't help you none, did they?"

"I'm sorry. I looked back at the bridge and the next thing I knew we were fifty feet apart."

"Let's get moving so we don't freeze to death."

■ ● ■

I got up and started walking next to him with a limp.

"What's wrong? Cramp?"

"I hit my knee on a rock when I got close to shore."

Yeah. Over on this side it goes from deep to shallow real quick. On the other side there's a gradual rise up to the bank. Are you okay?"

"I'll manage. Are we going to go get the car?"

"Yeah. Tomorrow. It might be better to walk for a while and then have one of the guys come get us."

We walked for about twenty minutes in silence except for the squishing sound from my sneakers.

"I'm sorry."

"For what now, Elaine?"

"My sneaks."

"Yeah. They are kind of noisy, aren't they? You should switch back to Cons."

"Recommended river wear?"

"See? That's why we're not friends. You got some wise-ass, condescending remark to make every time you do something stupid."

"Me?!" I started to tell him off and then realized he was joking. "You think that line up the whole time you were trying to drown yourself?"

"You mean while I was trying to drag your ass out of the Jake Giambalvo current?"

"Okay. One for you."

We were both quiet for a minute.

"Jake didn't really drown. He hit his head on one of the old railroad pilings and split it right open. He was above water when they found him. So really he didn't drown. But no sense in letting you replace a legend. 'The Deadly Elaine current'…sounds goofy."

■ ● ■

"Gee, thanks. I knew there had to be some ulterior motive for your attempt to save me."

We stood on a corner while a car went by.

"Why didn't they just come and get us? If they were waiting for us, why didn't they just come up and get us?"

He looked around as we crossed the street.

"Probably because they were waiting for someone else…who maybe didn't show…or saw what was happening and split… Yeah…someone else."

About ten minutes later we found a phone booth. I stood outside it wondering if I really was the jerk he thought I was. I could hear him talking to Sharp.

"No, man. I think we need to keep moving, so pick us up on Riley and Corcoran. We should be there in fifteen minutes…if Elaine will pick it up a little."

■ ● ■

Film

We were minor celebrities in town now. Andy and Elaine were anyway. It was probably good for Andy, since Janie decided she couldn't handle our life anymore. She told him that if he wanted he could come out there to be with her, but without saying so, he seemed to have decided to stay put. Right now he was a lot quieter than he used to be, except when the cameras or some reporters were around. Then he'd talk as long as they wanted.

Elaine would get accosted going in to work, going to lunch and leaving work. She was good about getting the free advertising that being on the inside of a case like the donut shop could give you. She always told the reporters she was just the secretary. Then she would follow that up with why we were such a great agency. She always vaguely mentioned some exciting case that we were working on. The second time I saw her do this on the news I got really upset, wondering why I didn't know about these jobs. The next day I realized the 'facts' she used were from a case we had closed over a year ago. It made me nervous that she could fabricate some "reality" like that day after day.

Mojica took to wearing black, thick-rimmed, fake eyeglasses

■ ● ■

and a Chicago White Sox baseball hat that was a little too big for him. Heeks gave pretty short answers to reporters, usually "yes," "no." Sometimes when he was feeling particularly verbose he would use "maybe." After a while the news people didn't bother with him too much. I think they wondered if he really spoke English.

Sharp just put his sun glasses on, a toothpick in his mouth and said, "Ah don't work here boys." Why they accepted that really wasn't a mystery. He said it with so much authority the news folks just stared at him for a second and moved on.

And me? I started going out the basement door as much as possible. Sharp would go with me sometimes, joking about how it was like being the Beatles. Not quite.

Basically we were trying to keep a barrier between us and the press. The way things turned out after the Haley field shooting and Callahan, we couldn't trust anyone in the news media. Even some of the people we knew and liked might have been in on creating some serious misinformation. Plus, we couldn't have our pictures in the papers every day for weeks.

So Andy and Elaine were the public faces of the agency. And Elaine was right. Business was booming. After the Donut Boys were taken in, potential clients came out of the woodwork from Duluth to Tuscaloosa. We were now turning jobs down flat out, or slipping them over to the few other agencies in town.

Today I had an unusual free moment and I was facing the window rocking in my chair, pondering. I spun around when I heard Sharp's voice. I looked out my door where I could see Elaine, busy at her computer, talking to Sharp without looking up. I stood up and strolled out into our new waiting room-reception area. Elaine had us set up with two new area rugs that looked expensive. Two upholstered chairs and a matching couch over by the window. They all looked expensive. There were cus-

■ ● ■

tom blinds that looked expensive. There were two parlor palms at each end of the room. Maybe they weren't expensive, but they probably were. There were prints on the walls by Monet, Kandinsky, Modigliani and framed posters of Frederick Douglas and Eugene Debs. As far as I was concerned, Douglas and Debs were the only real improvement to the office. All week I had wondered when the remodeling had been decided upon.

Sharp saw me coming and said, "Did you hear any of that?"

I shook my head.

"Dude wanted us to stake out his swimming pool to catch the kids who are jumpin' in during the night."

"Wow! You took that case, right?"

"Ah told him how much we cost and he told me how much he wanted to pay and ah said 'put up a fence.'"

"You could have sent him over to Willie Harrison."

Sharp looked shocked. "Why would we do that? You got a grudge against Willie?"

Elaine started laughing.

"I'm going to catch a slice at Carl's. You in?"

"I could use a snack. Ah'm in."

We took a couple of stools at the counter and Carl threw us a few slices off a fresh pie. I had one and Sharp had three. Carl and Sharp had their obligatory discussion of the state of boxing and the various new boxing federations. When Carl drifted away to wait on other customers, Sharp turned to me with a serious expression on his face.

"Ah, I wanted to ask you about the psychologist you're seein'. Is that off limits?"

"No. What do you want to know?"

"What's it like?"

"I don't know really. It's the second guy and he's very different from the ten minutes I spent with the first one."

■ ● ■

"Yeah. What happened with that? When you guys came back that day Andy was lookin' day-glo red."

"Bro, you should have been there. It was kind of like the Twilight Zone. I went into the guy's office and sat down. I didn't know what was supposed to happen so I just started talking about anything. He listened to me for about ten minutes, smiled and said he wanted to talk with my friend from outside for a minute. So Andy goes in to chat with this guy while I cool out with a Sports Illustrated. About five minutes later I hear Andy's voice, mad, coming through the door unadulterated. I stand up wondering what the hell is going on. Andy yanks open the door, comes out and says, 'Let's go.' The doc is standing in the door and he says, 'You both really need therapy.' Andy freezes and the secretary says 'Can I have your autograph please? I've seen you on TV.' Andy turns and I can see he's going for the doc. The shrink is standing in the door of his office, he looks at the secretary and he just says, 'Oh.' He slams his door shut and you could hear it lock. I'm holding Andy by the arm trying to calm him down. The secretary comes around her desk with a pad, a pen and some keys. She whispers to us, 'I'll let you in his office if I can have your autograph.' Andy grabs the keys and I'm trying to get them back from Andy while holding on to him. While we're playing tug of war the secretary says, 'And can you make that out to Louise?' Andy just relaxed then, looked me in the eye and took the pen. I looked over his shoulder and he wrote 'To Louise, just when I thought I had lost touch with reality I met you. Bernie Carbo.' When we got in the elevator Andy got pissed again. The shrink thought we were sharing a psychosis. He didn't believe we were really detectives until Louise asked for Andy's John Hancock."

Sharp burst out laughing. "What?! A folie à deux?!" Sharp was laughing so hard I thought he'd fall off the stool.

■ ● ■

"Is that French for a shared psychotic disorder?"

Sharp shook his head up and down and tried to get his laughter under control. "Kind'a. Whew! Andy must'a been hot. You know he won't put up with that kind'a incompetence."

Sharp's laughter calmed down and we both picked up a slice. We heard Carl talking to a couple of customers at the other end of the counter.

"I used to do some prizefighting…"

Sharp looked at me mid-bite with a smile surrounding his pizza slice. He put his slice down and shook his head slightly. The smile disappeared from his face. It made me feel like the sun went out for a second.

"I'm never going to forget this afternoon. Going to be etched in my brain like stone." He winked at me. "I need you to know something out loud. If you ever need me to go somewhere with you, or talk with you, or to someone else for you, you can always count on me."

My eyes locked on the orange and red liquid that was always swirling in that rectangular plastic box across from the counter. I could never get the guts to sip the stuff, even as a kid. But I always wondered how sweet it was.

I turned my head toward Sharp. "You didn't even need to say that, man. I know it. I just know it."

Sharp threw six dollars on the counter to cover our tab.

"The shrink I'm seeing now said he thought I had a traumatic stress disorder. And you know what? He said a lot of other shrinks won't even make that diagnosis. It's kind of controversial."

Sharp sighed. "Sometimes it feels like we're livin' in the Dark Ages, brother."

"Yeah. A little pestilence here. A little ignorance there. Throw in some blind faith."

"Ah didn't want you to get that gloomy. The sun still managed to shine in the Dark Ages."

We both stood up. From the other end of the counter Carl yelled, "Hey Sharp. When are you and me getting in the ring?"

Sharp laughed. "C'mon Carl. My body can't take your kind of punishment any more." Carl started laughing and waved us off.

When we stepped outside we both looked around, mostly at the sky. Then Sharp said, "You know, Andy mentioned that we should think about getting Elaine a license.

"Investigators?!"

"Yeah. You're already draggin' her ass all over town."

"It was only for the donut shop!"

"And swimmin' in the river…well, I think we should discuss it. It might be to our benefit to have a female workin' with us."

We started walking back toward the office. I started glancing over my shoulder and checking out reflections in store windows.

"Anything?"

"No. You?"

"Nope. Think we're clean…what made you start lookin'?"

"I don't know. What made you?"

Sharp laughed. "You did."

"Think I'm being paranoid?" I started to feel anxious and embarrassed.

"Shit no. In our situation? We both better be paranoid, brother." Sharp looked across the street and then muttered, "We sure as hell both better be paranoid."

When we walked into the office, Andy, Mojica and Elaine were standing in Andy's office with their backs to us.

Sharp hollered across the waiting room, "Hey folks, who's guardin' the gates?"

Andy half-turned toward us with an extremely serious look on his face. I realized they were all listening to the radio.

■ ● ■

I said, "What's going on? Cubs moving to El Paso?"

Andy turned all the way around, looked at Sharp and then me.

"There was an anti-Klan demonstration in Greensboro today. The Klan showed up with some Nazis and opened fire. They killed at least three people and wounded some. Seems everything was recorded by the local television stations."

Elaine walked out of Andy's office looking angry. "At least the bastards will go to jail if they were stupid enough to put their faces on video tape."

Sharp took the toothpick out of his mouth and threw it at the waste basket by Elaine's desk. "Ain't no one goin' to jail."

Elaine looked at Sharp like she had been slapped. "Of course they'll go to jail. They're on television."

Sharp pushed some hair back from his face. "Ah'll bet you a dozen donuts that unless the Justice Department is forced to get into this, none of them do a week. They come out to do a shoot-up in broad daylight, you gotta' believe either the FBI prodded them on, or knew what they was gonna' do. You don't think the FBI wasn't involved in this? Shit. Nobody goin' to jail. Not for a good long time anyway."

Andy shook his head. "Sharp's probably right. I wouldn't bet the donuts."

Elaine started to plead, "But God damn it all to hell, this isn't 1955 Selma."

"No, it's not. It's present day North Carolina and the points Sharp makes are valid."

Sharp said, "Anyone go to jail for killin' Fred Hampton in his sleep?"

Elaine looked like she might cry. "But that was Chicago."

Sharp pulled a fresh toothpick out of his pocket and said, "Uh-huh. And this here is North Carolina, not Illinois."

■ ● ■

Elaine bowed her head.

Mojica spoke for the first time since we got back. "They say its five dead now."

"Jesus fucking Christ." Elaine walked over to her desk, sat down and crossed her arms over her chest.

"Elaine, I…"

She slammed her palm down on the desk.

Nobody said anything. I glanced at the other guys. They seemed to be registering the same level of surprise as me. I think we viewed her as kind of unflappable.

Elaine crossed her arms again and scanned each of us. "I'm sorry. I shouldn't act like that in the office. It won't happen again."

Andy walked over to Elaine's desk and rested the fingertips of his left hand on her computer. "We probably all feel the same way you do. You don't have anything to be sorry for." Andy turned around. "We should discuss tonight's activity again and we should check out Mojica's microphone one more time.

There really wasn't much to discuss. We had matched up one of the phone numbers that Barthelme used to one of the names Bargas wasn't familiar with. Sharp was going to the "name's" house. He was going to play as Barthelme's replacement. If there was more than one guy, Sharp would leave immediately. If there was just one, and the situation deteriorated, we would all go in. If no one was home, we'd drive up and Heeks would get us in. We'd search and get out.

Elaine shook her head.

Andy said, "What's up? Why are you shaking your head?"

Elaine looked down at her keyboard, wiped off some imaginary dust and looked back up. "You don't know who you're dealing with. You have a name. Michael Ferris. And his number. You need a better escape plan."

Sharp leaned back in his chair. "If it starts to go bad, we drive

■ ● ■

away."

"What if it doesn't 'start' to go bad. What if you knock on the door and it's bad?"

I said, "I see your point, Elaine. But there will be four of us in two cars. I think we should be able to get out. Do you have a suggestion?"

"I think you should ask Raoul for another favor. I think you should ask him to help cover for you."

Andy stood up like he had sat on a tack. "No fucking way! I'm not going in there with him involved. I know you want him in on this, Mojica, but it ain't happening."

"Me?! What the hell are you talking about, Capitan? Raoul would make too many people. If Sharp gets in, he's in. If it's bad, we split. I didn't say shit about Raoul."

I looked at Elaine. She stared back at me and shrugged her shoulders. "I didn't mean to start an argument. I just thought Raoul might be good covering the road in some way. You said it was a dirt road back up to the house. If all four of you go in and something happens, then what?"

"Exciting, isn't it?"

Elaine looked around the room like she was seeing us for the last time. Maybe she was right and for some reason we were overconfident.

Sharp was staring at Andy as he paced on the other side of the room. "What's up Andy? Why'd you jump Mojica like that? I know he's a different man since he got his cast off, but is something bothering you?"

Andy stopped pacing. He was staring at the floor. We waited for a response and it started to get uncomfortable. Finally Andy said, "Heeks, I didn't mean to break on you for no reason. I guess I'm uncomfortable with the situation and I don't want Raoul in on this. Somebody will get killed if he's there. But there is only

■ ● ■

one way out of the place. What if something goes really wrong? There's just that one road."

"You been livin' like a city-boy too long, Andy." Sharp started playing with his toothpick. "We'll get out. I'll be miked up and you guys will only be a half-mile away."

Mojica stood up and slapped Andy on the back. "We'll be fine, Andy. You're just feeling the day, bro'. All that craziness in Greensboro. We just have to cool out for a while."

Elaine put both of her hands on her desk. "I'm sorry I created this tension. I'm just worried."

Sharp put his dark glasses on and turned toward Elaine. "You write the checks now, Elaine. You can still pay yourself if we don't come back. Right fellas?"

We all laughed except for Elaine. "Gallows humour will get you nowhere with me. Antonio, do you have a pair of very high-powered binoculars I could borrow? I want to go down to the lake tomorrow morning with Helen."

"Everything I got in 'nocs' is high-powered. Fix you right up."

The way Elaine asked for the binoculars made me feel like she wanted to borrow a blond wig.

Andy and Mojica were parked about a quarter of a mile away. I had my back to a tree, sitting with a pair of binoculars watching the front door of one Michael Ferris. In a few minutes I expected to see Sharp's car roll down the driveway.

We had all been concerned about the fact that Raoul couldn't find out who Michael Ferris was. We had his background, but it didn't match up with anything real until the past two years. Raoul found out in what year, and in what city he went to high school. But when he checked the school's yearbook, Ferris wasn't in it. No military service. 4-F, but no record of a problem. It went on like that. Never had a telephone until two years ago. No bills

■ ● ■

until two years ago. Somebody screwed up his cover.

Sharp's rental car bounced down the gravel driveway toward the house. To the back, and the right of the house were trees. A forest, really. To the left, almost as far as the eye could see for 1,500 yards, was a potato farm. Way out, I could see a line of trees and some farm buildings. The TOPO map I had checked out in the afternoon was pretty accurate, aside from some of those farm buildings way off in the distance.

I was looking east. The sun was right at the horizon and everything had a golden glow about it. I was scanning the fields and the woods for any kind of movement.

I watched Sharp get out of his car dressed in a suit and tie. I don't think I'd seen that since Cory's wife died. He knocked on the door and I wondered if Mojica could hear what was going on. There was a discussion at the door between Sharp and a gray-haired man. Sharp was jabbing at the man's chest with his finger like he was emphasizing a point. The man stepped aside and Sharp entered the house.

I scanned the field again and thought I saw a light reflect off glass, but I didn't see it again. I strained to see any movement in the trees and then I saw him. The figure who opened the door to Sharp was running away from the house across the field. I trained my glasses on the house but I didn't see any movement. A car was coming up the road. It was Andy and Mojica. They stopped and Andy said, "Get in, quick."

I hopped in the car and asked what happened.

Mojica turned around and said, "Sharp was chewing the guy out for not taking care of Barthelme's responsibilities. Apparently it was the wrong tack. Ferris went through a door, locked it and took off."

"Yeah. I saw him running across the fields."

"Sharp suggested we get up here fast and toss the place."

■ ● ■

As we approached the house the sunlight was disappearing. Sharp appeared in the frame of the front door looking like he owned the house and was welcoming guests. You had to admire his style. Andy parked behind the rental.

"Let's make this fast. I'm guessing we only have twenty to twenty-five minutes." Sharp and Mojica went upstairs. Andy and I started at opposite ends downstairs. The house was bigger than I imagined. I was rifling through a row of books in the den when I noticed a building out back that was almost completely shielded by tall shrubs.

"Andy! There's a building out back. I'm going to check it out." I turned to go for the kitchen door when the photos on the den wall caught my attention. There were about twenty random photos on the wall, all of them from Vietnam.But the three that caught my attention were of a general that Andy and I spoke to when we were charged with finding Lt. Roberts. I stared up at them and got real close.

"Sharp! Come down here, pronto!"

Sharp came down the stairs two at a time. "What's up?"

"You see these photos?"

"No. First time I've been in this room…uh huh…there's Ferris as a younger man."

"Andy! Need you! Sharp, have Andy check out these photos. I'm going to that building back there in the tree line."

The dusk was quiet. I crossed the forty yards thinking I heard rustling in the woods, but I thought it was deer.

The door to the outbuilding was unlocked. I went in expecting to see a couple of beds for visitors. Instead there was a screen on one wall with a super 8 projector on a table in the middle of the room. Next to it on the floor was some kind of projector I had never seen before. A simple folding metal chair was next to the table. On a shelf under the projector were three piles of super

■●■

8 film and some boxes that looked like they might be videos. I picked up an open reel and pulled out the film to hold it up to the window.

I started to sweat. There was a Vietnamese woman tied to a bed, gagged. My knees started to buckle. I was screaming to myself to keep it together. I stumbled back over to the projector. It was threaded. I flipped on the switch. A woman was manacled to a table. I stared. She wasn't Vietnamese. I hit the switch to turn off the projector. I turned away from the machine and the vomit seemed like it exploded out of my mouth. I put my hands on my knees and my eyes went blurry from tears.

"Okay. Okay. Stand up straight. Stop talking to yourself." I wiped my mouth with my jacket sleeve and then wiped my eyes with my t-shirt. I took a deep breath just in time to see them go by the window.

I squatted down and made my way over to the window. Where the hell did they come from? Four of them. They spread out behind the house about twenty yards from the back door. I moved over to the table. I ripped the film from the projector and started filling my pockets with as many reels as would fit. I had about half of them.

I was shoving one in my back pocket when the first explosion went off. I could see the light from the flames at the edge of the house. The second explosion made me go to the window. What the hell was going on? I went out the door of the building and stepped behind a hedge. One of the four turned around and then turned back to watch the kitchen door. Another one of the four pointed out into the field. I tried to look through the shrubs. Someone was coming across the field in a jeep. A local farmer coming to see what was going on? Two of the four looked like they were getting ready to welcome him with some automatic weapons. I could hear gunshots from the front of the house. I

■ ● ■

could hear someone on a bullhorn yelling. "Come out with your hands raised and your weapons above your heads where we can see them."

Sharp appeared at the back door and one of the four opened up on him. I fired and hit one. The other three turned on me. I ducked behind the building while branches of bushes fluttered and fell to the ground. A jeep flew into the yard and someone was standing and shooting.

Someone yelled, "Come on!" Elaine?! What the hell?! Who was driving? The guys would never make it to the jeep. I stepped around the building and started laying down cover fire. The three of them ran out the back door. They were diving into the jeep.

Andy was screaming, "Go! Go!" The jeep did a 180 and took off across the field. I was trying to keep the assholes at the back of the house pinned down. In between rounds I suddenly heard Elaine screaming, "No!" I kept firing and started drifting back into the woods. There were more of them coming around the side of the house. Out in the field the jeep's lights came on. A couple of these whoever they were started shooting at it but they were probably out of range.

I was moving almost blind through the woods. I had spent a couple of hours with a topographical map of the area. I hoped I remembered correctly. There was a stream about three hundred yards back in these woods. If I made it there I could follow the ravine to a small hamlet where they might have a telephone booth. I wasn't sure how determined these creeps were, but I'd probably have just as much of a battle with the mosquitoes as I would with the gunmen.

I walked for twenty minutes, bumping into ten or twenty trees, skinning my shin, before I heard the water. I doubted the bad guys would know what I was doing since they didn't know we were coming.

■ ● ■

After struggling through a blackberry patch and silently using every curse I'd ever heard, I stood ankle deep in water wondering what the hell I was doing.

■ ● ■

Fields

Helen and I were sitting at the edge of a farm in a borrowed jeep. Helen was behind the wheel and I had binoculars up to my eyes.

"Can you see anything?"

"Not really. I saw a car pull up to the house, but I can't see any activity from here."

"Maybe there's nothing to see."

"I hope there's nothing to see."

"This sunset is glorious. I'm going to miss this fall."

"Maybe we should move closer."

"How? There's no place to hide out there. If the guys find out we've been out here, Andy is going to get loud."

I looked at Helen leaning back in the driver's seat with her left foot up on the dashboard.

"What will Antonio say?"

Helen did a shallow laugh. "What the fuck, Helen?' That's probably all he'll say. Sharp will probably say 'Now you ladies'... hey...what's that?"

I looked out over the field to where a man was running. I aimed the field glasses at him to see if I recognized his face at all.

■ ● ■

Helen sat up straight and said, "That can't be good. What do you think is happening?"

"I don't know." I turned the binoculars to the house. Sharp suddenly appeared in the back door and then went back into the house.

"I just saw Sharp. He looked okay."

"What's he doing?"

"He went back into the house."

"Think we're going to see some action tonight?"

"I hope not. I hope the guys get out and we just drive on home."

I scanned the fields to our left to see if I could pick up the runner.

"There's another car coming down the driveway…It's Andy's car."

The sun was disappearing. Helen grabbed a black sweatshirt and pulled it over her head.

"Can you see anything?"

"Someone just came out the back door and is heading into the woods."

"Who?"

"I couldn't tell. Some lights came on in the house, but I don't see anyone." I kept staring through Mojica's binoculars, wishing the cars would just pull away and we could go home.

"That's funny. There was a light at the edge of the woods for about ten seconds and then it went out. It looks like there may be a building hidden back there."

Helen was leaning forward with both arms folded on top of the steering wheel. I put the binoculars in my lap. As soon as I did that the first explosion went off.

Helen said, "What the fuck was that?

I could see flames in the front of the house. Then there was a

■ ● ■

second explosion.

"They blew up the cars."

I looked over at Helen. "Are you sure?"

Helen turned the ignition. "Yes. The second one was definitely a car. Should we try to go over there?"

I raised the glasses again. "There are men at the back of the
house with guns. We have to assume they're in front, too."

Helen threw the jeep into gear, shifted into second and we
started bumping our way across the field. I could hear something
being said over a bullhorn.

"Do you think it's the cops?"

"The cops don't usually blow up your car before an arrest, do
they?"

I opened my bag on the floor and pulled out the Colt Andy
and Mojica gave me. "I have another pistol in my bag."

"No thanks. I'm going to have to concentrate on driving."

We were within one hundred yards now. Helen was driving
by the light of the burning cars. I was hoping the men in back
didn't notice us. When we got to fifty yards, two of them turned
our way. Then one of the others shot at the back door. Someone
started firing from the woods. The four men at the back of the
house started to scatter. One fell down, but got back up.

I stood up and grabbed the windshield with my left hand and
started shooting at the men trying to find cover. Helen floored
the jeep and we bounced into the backyard. Helen screamed,
"Let's go!", while she suddenly spun the jeep in a 180-degree
turn. I was falling out until Helen grabbed my leg. The guys
came flying out of the back door. Sharp was firing blindly. They
dove into the jeep with Andy screaming, "Go! Go!"

The four men in the backyard were shooting into the woods
and then one of them turned his gun toward us. Someone was
shooting from the woods faster than I thought was possible. The

■ ● ■

jeep bounced up in the air. We were literally flying across the field.

I could hear Andy yell, "Anyone hit?!"

"Good."

"I'm good."

Then it struck me. There were only three of them.

"No! Wait, Helen, wait! We have to go back!" I started to jump out of the jeep. Sharp's hand slammed me back down into my seat. Andy was hollering, "Keep going, Helen! Keep going! Elaine, sit still! He was laying cover fire for us. He was trying to draw them off us."

"What?! We can't leave him!"

Sharp said, "Elaine, even if we go back right now, he's not going to be there."

"What?! You think he's dead?! We have to go back!"

Andy screamed at me. "Calm down! He knows what he's doing. He's probably a half mile out in those woods by now."

I stopped struggling against Sharp's hand. He pulled it away. "He'll get out. He always does."

I was confused and now I was scared even though we were finally out of the field.

I could hear Antonio now. "Hey, Babe. Thanks for the lift, but you're going to have to do some driving because they're coming down that road to the left."

Helen yelled back, "Camaro hemi. Low drag."

We passed some farm buildings that went by in a quick blur. When Helen swung us onto the road she put the headlights on and we fishtailed. Helen straightened us out and ran through the gears. I could hear the engine of the car behind us suddenly roar. We were sailing down the road at 85. We were coming up on a slightly familiar curve, where earlier Helen had wanted to see how the jeep handled off road. So on the way Helen took the jeep out into an untended field. She had circled it slowly and I wondered why. But she was the expert driver, so at the time I kept quiet.

Helen suddenly yelled, "Hold on! Heavy brake!" She hit the brakes so hard I was squashed up against the windshield. Just before we completely stopped she spun the jeep so that we were perpendicular across the road. Helen took off down the dirt path that led off into a field. The Camaro was downshifting and when I looked back I could see it swinging in behind us. We went about fifty yards and Antonio yelled, "You got em!" I looked back and there were sparks flying up from under their car. Then I heard a loud metallic noise and their car stopped.

"Bottomed out. They're history."

Helen headed out into the field toward a tree line where I had seen a creek earlier. I started to wonder where she was going until I realized where I had just seen a creek, Helen had seen a spot where you could drive a jeep through it.

There was a popping sound.

I could hear Helen mutter, "Shit! Henry's going to be pissed about that."

As we splashed through the water Andy yelled, "Get us out of here, Helen! One of those bastards has a rifle with a night scope."

I looked at the hole in the windshield thinking that could have been one of us. We made it to the road and my head exploded with hundreds of thoughts all competing for attention. I wondered about my emotional reactions tonight. Why wasn't I scared until I realized we were leaving someone behind? Why did the other guys act like this was just the way things happen? What happened out there tonight? Why didn't Helen tell me what she was doing when we were riding around in the field? What am I doing with these people?

■ ● ■

The office was dead quiet except for Sharp's subtle snoring. Helen was asleep in Antonio's office. Antonio was upstairs at Caminiti's Photo trying to blow up the shot they took from the wall in the house. I had both arms crossed on my desk with my head laying on them. I was trying to sleep, but instead I found myself watching Andy on the monitor pacing back and forth out by the elevators. In an hour it would be light. I wondered how someone makes it out of a forest you've never been in before, in the dark.

When the phone rang, I raised my head and shook it. I reached for the phone but Andy's hand beat me to it. He raised the receiver to his ear and gave me a stiff smile.

"Okay. Okay...I don't know if we're clean or not, so stay sharp. Heeks hasn't gone over the lines yet today. Uh huh...a clip...do you have anything left?...okay, but stay sharp...what? A coffee...yep...a raspberry jelly donut?! Fuck you!...we left five minutes ago." Andy hung up the phone.

I couldn't help smiling. "Is he okay?"

"Is he okay?!" Andy looked at me in disgust. "He wants me to stop and get him a raspberry jelly donut!" Andy smiled.

Sharp was standing in the doorway of his office yawning. "We told ya he'd be okay, didn't we?"

I nodded my head and bit my lower lip.

"C'mon Andy, let's go get the boy."

"What do I tell Antonio when he comes back?"

Andy walked away from my desk without looking back. "Tell him to check the phone lines and come up with an idea for a new door. Glass won't cut it now." Andy turned to Sharp. "Take the Cuda?"

Sharp laughed. "Well you ain't got a car do you? It's either the little Cuda or a jeep with a 30 odd bullet hole in the windshield. Doubt we make the city limits in that. Wha'dya think?"

■ ● ■

Andy put his hands on his hips and stared at Sharp. "Are we going to leave today? I have to pick up a fucking jelly donut on the way, goddamn it."

"Lead the way, son. Lead the way."

"Elaine, keep your eye on the monitor."

The elevator came and took them down. I started crying.

■ ● ■

Chairs

Andy and Sharp found me squatting behind a dumpster at an Associated supermarket. When I got in the car, Sharp asked me if there was anything interesting to do out here at night. Andy actually handed me a coffee. I asked what happened to the donut.

"Go fuck yourself. Are you okay?"

"Yeah."

As we pulled away in the Barracuda, Sharp said, "Thanks for getting our asses out of there."

"I know you'll do the same should the situation arise again."

"Doubt it." We all laughed.

"Hey…who was shooting from the jeep?"

Andy turned around to look at me. "Elaine. Helen was driving."

"Jesus…I thought maybe Elaine was driving. I heard her voice. I suppose we'll be getting an earful from them later."

"We should. We screwed up last night and those two saved our collective butts." Andy was staring at my jacket. "What the hell do you have in all of your pockets?"

The feeling was immediate. It was like Pavlov's dogs. What

the hell was wrong with me? I felt myself getting sick. "Snuff films. Sharp! Pull over! I don't feel good."

I got out of the car and heaved in a ditch. Andy got out behind me.

"Snuff films? What the hell are you…"

"Mutilation! Women being mutilated and killed on film!" I threw up again and then leaned against the car.

Andy was squinting at me. "Vietnamese women?"

"Not only Vietnamese. Maybe Central American."

Andy leaned his head in the car window. "Sharp, do you have a bag in your trunk?"

Sharp got out and opened the trunk to find a brown shopping bag. I started emptying my pockets into the bag. My eyes went wet. I wiped my eyes with my jacket sleeve and felt sick again. I bent over and put my hands on my knees.

"All the way down that creek, all I could think about was those women…tied up and gagged and being cut up. All night I kept thinking about a picture of a woman with her eyes open and rags in her mouth. I couldn't stop thinking about the son of a bitch cutting her open while he stood there with a hard on. You know he loved it. He probably loved it every time she tried to scream!"

Andy whispered, "All right, man. All right. We're going to get the bastards."

Sharp came around the car to stand next to us. "Brother, we need to get back to town. Rinse your mouth out." He handed me my coffee and I just looked at it. Then I threw it.

"It's a business. It's a fucking business!"

"What?!"

"I had all night to think about it. It wasn't just the Vietnamese women. There's at least one film of a non-Asian woman. That's what made me realize this guy isn't just jerking off. There

■ ● ■

were videos, too. It's their business. They're selling this putrid fucking garbage!"

Sharp and Andy were silent for a minute. I was looking up at the clouds wishing it was a cloudy day. Sharp moved first.

"It's bad for us to stay out here in the open like this. We need to get back to the office, or at least get into town."

Andy was looking at me. "Bro, are you okay?"

"Yeah. Let's get the hell out of here."

When we got back in the car Andy told me to take a swallow of his coffee. I almost choked.

"What's wrong with you, Andy? Too much damn sugar. When did you start with all of this sugar?"

Andy laughed. "Quit complaining. Sharp pointed out the photos to me on the wall in Ferris's house. I remembered the secretary. Sharp said it was Ferris. Heeks took one of the photos and he's blowing it up so we can get his real name."

"Couldn't you just use a magnifying glass?"

Sharp laughed. "We tried that. Didn't really work. But Ferris is definitely the older version of the guy in the photo."

I said, "Andy, do you remember that general's name?"

"I've been wracking my brain over that all night. Corbett, or something like that."

"Damn…Corvell! It was Corvell."

"That's right. General Corvell."

We drove in silence for ten minutes. "That's the connection, Andy. Those guys think we're going to screw up their business."

■

When we walked in the office door, Elaine got up from her desk and walked straight at me. I thought she was going to hit me, so I put my hand up to block her. Instead, she wrapped her arms around me and gave me her version of a bear hug. Sharp

■ ● ■

patted me on the back twice before he went and sat on the new couch by the window.

Mojica came in about thirty seconds after Elaine told me I smelled like puke. Heeks told us the new door wouldn't be here for two days. Sharp thought we should make ourselves scarce until we found out who we had to go after. We all agreed, so we were back to living in hotels. Andy was in his office when I heard him call Sharp in. Mojica punched me in the shoulder while sporting a huge 'ain't you wonderful' smile on his face.

"Thanks for helping us get out of there last night." He leaned close to me, started sniffing and said, "Dude, what the hell you been doing all night? Rolling around in the sheep dip? You need a shower."

"Fuck you, Mojica." He punched my arm again and laid two 9x12 photos on Elaine's desk.

"Ferris's name in the army? Shea. I left a message for Raoul to see if he can get some background on him. Now look at the next photo."

I looked but I wasn't seeing what Mojica wanted me to see. I shrugged my shoulders. "What am I looking at? The general… Corvell… this Ferris guy, some…" I picked the photo up? "Bar-thelme?"

"Yeah. When he was still Holloway, I'll bet you."

Sharp raised his voice from the other room. He almost never raised his voice, so the three of us all turned. Sharp came out of Andy's office like all of North America needed to get out of his way.

Mojica looked at me. "Do you know what's up?"

"Yes. I found some films last night. I think they're what all of this bullshit is about."

Andy came to his door. "Heeks, you want to come over here?"

I couldn't hear Andy, but Mojica was talking very rapidly.

■ ● ■

"We need to find a place to stash these. She's a blond. Let me see that one. How many are there?"

Sharp was right next to me. "Bro, that shit is raw. Is that what you and Andy were investigatin'?"

I nodded.

Elaine got up and walked toward Andy's office. Sharp tried to catch up with her. "Elaine, you don't need to see all that."

Elaine turned on Sharp so fast, he kind of stumbled to a stop. "I've been shot at and almost killed over whatever you are all looking at. I will see that right now or I will walk out that door." Sharp raised his hand to grab her arm. Elaine swatted it away and walked into Andy's office. Mojica came out with his head down.

I looked into Andy's office. I could see him sitting at his desk leaning back with his hands clasped on top of his head. Elaine had her back to me. She was holding film over her head up to the lights. She put one reel down and picked up another. She looked at four or five and then started rolling the film back up.

When she came out she didn't look at me. I was sweating and I felt like I was standing in cement. Elaine sat down at her desk and put both hands flat on top of it. "There are no words to really describe those, those things, are there?"

Sharp said, "None I know of."

Andy hollered from his office. "We need to split these up and get them into safety deposit boxes. There are seventeen reels. How many do you think you left behind?"

I tried to speak, but I choked instead.

"Is this a business they're running?" Everyone looked at Elaine. Andy got up from his chair and came out to Elaine's desk.

"Why do you say that?"

"They can't all be for his sexual gratification. Could someone

■ ● ■

really afford to buy all of those? I mean, how much does something like that cost?"

I felt something like relief. Elaine was on my side. I was sweating. What did the others really think? "I believe it's a business, too. There were at least thirty or thirty-five tapes I couldn't fit in my pockets. There were also some larger boxes like Mojica has for our camera."

Sharp looked at Elaine. "That would be a pretty penny."

Andy shuffled his feet and put his hands in his pocket. "You saw the house. He has a penny and a few more to burn. But let's not jump to conclusions."

Sharp spoke a little pointedly to Andy. "Don't you think the odds are stacked toward this being a business? It makes sense, right? It makes sense that these films are what this is all about."

I felt excited. "The tapes probably pay for the house. And Barthelme's shoes. And...what are the chances of Ferris and Barthelme showing up in the same photo and this being just about wacking off?"

"Could you be a little less disgusting?"

"Disgusting?! You saw the films. Nothing is more..."

"In conjunction with the images on the film, what you said is fucking disgusting!"

Andy put his hand up. "Whoa! We seem to have a lot of tension in the air. Let's cool down a little. We have something to do and that is, get these films to some safe place." Mojica came out of his office with a few bags, one of which looked full.

Sharp started checking out the bags. "Heeks, what do you have in there?"

"Super-eight film. I only had twelve."

"Uh huh? To do what with?"

"I think we can use these as a decoy. Someone is probably going to try to follow us this morning to get them back. Maybe

■ ● ■

we sacrifice one real tape with the twelve blanks."

Andy looked around the office like he was searching for something. "I don't think we should give any of these up. If someone is intent on taking them back I think it'll be fast and furious. We might be able to use the blanks later, but we just have to get these into a safety deposit box, fast. What do you guys think?"

We all agreed with Andy. Mojica shrugged.

We split up the films into four piles. Andy picked out the four banks he thought we should use. Mojica and Sharp left first. Andy and I followed a few minutes after them.

We sent Elaine to a hotel in a taxi to register some rooms for us.

Two hours later we were at our next hotel. Mojica and Sharp went to pick up Helen from the hospital. I went to the shower.

It wasn't the best shower I ever had. The stink from the films kept clinging to me. I laid down on the bed and stared at the ceiling hoping the images from the frames I saw would fade and I could get to sleep. But they wouldn't and I couldn't, so I decided to walk.

When I got off the elevator downstairs, I bumped into Elaine and some guy in a suit. She had a sandwich and a cup that gave off the aroma of fresh coffee. I started to go around her with a strained smile.

"Where the hell are you going?" She glanced at the man holding the elevator door. "I'll get the next one, thanks."

I stopped and turned around. "For a walk, Mom. I need to clear my head."

"Wait. I'll go with you. You know, people not wandering alone?"

"I said I needed to clear my head, not play fifty questions."

She looked really hurt. "C'mon…I'm not that bad, am I?"

"Shit…okay. Go dump that stuff, or bring it with you, but

■ ● ■

get a sweater. It's not summery out."

"Be right back."

As soon as the elevator doors closed I bolted out the front. I turned left and just started walking trying to find a pace. I had just gotten into a good stride when I saw him. I almost did a double-take, but I walked right up to the bench and sat down.

"Scuzzie. What happened to your foot? Didn't you used to have a foot there?"

"Who…you…the guy from the park. Eeyep. Good to see you're still around. You're a good listener, that's why. Not too many around, ya know?"

"Scuz. What happened?"

"When? Oh, you mean my foot? Doc said I had some gain green. I hurt it and it didn't get better and I caught some gain green."

"Jesus, Scuz. You're lucky you didn't lose your whole leg, or die. Gangrene can spread quick sometimes."

"That's what the doctor said. But I been wonderin' if maybe he didn't just cut it off for a fee. For money."

"What?! The doctor didn't cut your foot off for money. Why would he do that?"

"Maybe for a transplant, or to study it. Besides, he got paid didn't he? The nurse didn't do it, did she?"

I reached into my pocket for some bills. I counted out five singles thinking this conversation was going to deteriorate rapidly. I tried to give him the money just as a couple of fire engines screamed by. I could see Scuzzie's mouth move, but I couldn't hear him at all.

"What did you say, Scuz?"

"You don't listen so good anymore." He grabbed my arm hard. "You use to be a good listener and I want to tell you something you better hear it."

■ ● ■

CHAIRS   301

"What's that, Scuz?"

Scuzzie looked up and down the street to make sure no one else heard his secret. He whispered in his scratchy alcoholic's voice.

"They're all around us today. You have to be careful. Think about hiding. They're all around us."

"Who?"

"You stay out here and you'll find out. They're all around us."

"Okay, Scuz." I pushed the money into his hand. "You get something to eat, okay? And thanks for the tip." He sounded like a fortune cookie. "And don't let anyone steal your crutches."

"Don't you worry about them." Scuzzie nodded his head like it was taken care of. I got up, and as I walked away I looked down and started laughing. Scuzzie had chained his crutches to the bench.

"Don't forget the combo to that lock, Scuz."

"Got it written down. Don't worry about me. Don't forget what I said."

I walked away wondering which would go first…his limbs or his brain.

I tried to get into a groove again but it wasn't working. I slowed down and made a right onto a street that was pretty empty.

"Hey!"

Holy shit. It was turning into 'people I hardly knew day.'

"Sharon, How've you been?"

"I'm good. Really good. I went to see Bryce yesterday. He's taking me to the movies tomorrow!"

She was so excited she couldn't stand still. "That's great, Sharon. What do you want to see?"

"Who cares?! He's gonna' take me to the movies and he said maybe we could get something at a restaurant after and I said we

■ ● ■

could come back to Eddie's or Dickey's and Bryce said he meant a real restaurant. Do you believe that?! He asked me!"

"Still working at Dick…" I never finished the sentence. The first gun stuck me in the small of my back. The second one pressed the side of my chest. A white van pulled up and the side doors swung open. Someone grabbed the hair on the back of Sharon's head and pushed her into the van.

"If you're smart you'll get in the van or we'll just drop you right here." They pushed me into the van and pinned me to the floor.

Suddenly there was a burning sensation in my leg. I could hear Sharon repeating, "I didn't do nothin', I didn't do nothin'," until I passed out.

■

Bernie and Bland were holding hands. Bland looked over the fence and pointed to the pile of cows. "You know, you could be with the cows. You're black and white. You see everything that way, don't you?" Bland looked right at me. "You should just keep going. Don't stop or we'll catch up with you." The man who walked backwards was out in the field. He took two steps toward me just to prove he could walk forward, too. I could hear Bernie. "This is going to be hard on you, Buddy. Really, really hard. Bland just smiled.

I lifted my head and tried to shake it. I was groggy and struggling to stay awake. I sensed movement to my right. Sharon and I were taped to a pair of wooden chairs, but apparently she had managed to get one hand free. She was tearing at the tape on her other wrist, breathing like she was frustrated. The room was gray. Most of the light came in through the vent over the door.

She was starting to get it off. She looked at me and didn't speak. She was getting frantic.

■ ● ■

I whispered, "Sharon, go slow. Take it easy."

She looked at me again and her eyes got big. The door opened and filled the room with light. I was feeling nauseous. Sharon froze.

"Hey John, look at this. The bitch almost got out of the tape."

John looked over his shoulder. "Who the hell tied her up?"

"There's no place for her to go, but what the hell? You know?"

"Tape her up again."

John moved behind me, tilted my chair back and dragged me backwards out of the room. We were in some kind of warehouse. The line of windows up by the peak in the ceiling made me think we were in the old Owego Bridge Company building. John dropped my chair in front of a work bench that had a vise on it. The sun was going down with rays shooting straight through the glass by the roof peak onto the wall behind me. Then Sharon's chair was dropped right next to mine.

There were about ten men milling around. Two men walked up in front of the work table. One of them, with graying hair, in a gray suit, blue tie and white shirt, leaned back against the bench. The other one folded his arms across his chest. His navy blue suit jacket barely wrinkled. The one in the grey suit smiled.

"So where are they?"

We were both silent. I could feel Sharon looking at me.

"Either one of you can answer, and then we can get this over with and go about our business."

Sharon was panicked. I thought she was starting to hyperventilate. "I don't know nothin'. I don't know what you're talkin' about."

"Now that's not exactly true, is it? I want to know where they are and how we're going to get them."

I suddenly had a weird feeling about this. For some reason, it struck me that they didn't know what they were looking for. But

■ ● ■

they knew it meant money. One bunch of these assholes didn't know what the other bunch was doing, besides pouring money into their little club.

Sharon was crying. I said, "Don't say anything yet. We're going to get untied before we have anything to say."

Sharon looked at me and shifted into heavy frantic real fast. I could hear it in her voice, when she wasn't gasping for air. "But I don't know anything. What can I tell them? I don't know anything. What do you want to know about?" She was sobbing, with those gasps little kids get sometimes when they're trying to stop crying.

The man in the blue suit was walking toward Sharon without looking at her. He pulled the gun so I fast I couldn't get "no" out of my mouth before he blew her brains out. Blood and flesh splattered on my face and dropped in my lap.

I was trying to catch my breath. The man in the blue suit walked back to the table putting his magnum back in his shoulder holster.

"She didn't know anything." He refolded his arms and calmly leaned sideways against the table. He said that like he had just paid the paperboy.

The man in the grey suit smiled again. "Can always get a new secretary. Now then, what is it that you think you're not going to tell us?"

I tried to jump up even though my legs were taped to the chair. The chair bounced a little. I started screaming, "Aieeee!" I was trying to slam the chair to break one of the legs. Someone grabbed the chair from behind and slapped me in the ear. My ears were ringing and I started crying. "No. Fucking no…"

A sound I hadn't heard in a very long time echoed through the warehouse. The man in grey looked to the far end.

"What the hell was that?"

■ ● ■

"Sounded like a concussion grenade." The man in blue pulled his magnum out and started moving toward the sound. Now there was the sound of gunfire and yelling. Behind me up high I could hear glass breaking. There was a shot and the man in grey fell down on one knee. The man in blue stopped and started firing toward the roof. Men were coming from the other end of the warehouse. Some were dragging other men behind them. The man in grey stood up. The side of his suit was leaking blood. My mind was screaming, "Die motherfucker! Die!" Men were running in so many different directions it was pandemonium. The man in blue came back to help grey. Behind me I could hear someone saying, "Get up, John! Come on! Get up, so we can get the hell out of here!"

Suddenly it seemed like all of the men were moving in one direction. It felt like an organized retreat. I heard the Thompson. I was still crying. I heard more gunfire in another room. Two men came out and one ran past me. The other one was shooting while running backwards. He tumbled into me, and my chair went over with him on top of me. I tried to bite him and missed. I tried again, got a mouth full of fabric, but he ripped it out of my mouth, got up and ran. I was lying on the floor crying, with shoes passing in front of my face.

Suddenly my chair got jerked upright so fast my head snapped. Raoul said, "Heeks!"

Mojica's blade was out. He cut the tape in a couple of seconds.

Andy said, "We have to move. Are you hurt?" I didn't respond. "Are you hurt?!"

I couldn't take my eyes off Sharon. Her head was misshapen. Half of it was gone. Her eyes were wrong.

"We got to go, Andy."

"I know that, Raoul!"

"Sharp and I will secure the far door."

■ ● ■

I looked at Raoul. "We can't leave her here like this."

Raoul frowned at me. "She gone, blood. She gone."

"We can't leave her tied up."

Andy grabbed my arm. "Let's go. Time to leave."

"But she's tied up."

Mojica pushed Raoul aside and cut the tape on her ankles and wrists. She started to slide down in the chair. Mojica grabbed my other arm and they dragged me out of the warehouse.

They threw me in the back seat of the Impala. Elaine was behind the wheel. Mojica told her to slide over. Mojica slipped in behind the steering wheel, hit the gas and tore out of the driveway with the tires squealing. As we bounced into the street, Andy, Sharp and Raoul came running out of the warehouse and jumped into one of Raoul's vans.

Elaine's eyes locked on mine. "Where's Sharon?"

I didn't want to answer. Instead I said, "How did you guys find me?"

Elaine looked like she was going to cry. She turned around and stared out the side window.

"Heeks, how did you find me?"

I heard Elaine say, "What happened to her?"

Mojica was slowing down. It seemed they weren't organized enough to come after us so soon.

"Did they shoot her?"

Mojica's eyes caught mine in the rear view mirror. I rubbed the top of my head and then slammed my hand on the car seat.

"Yes. They shot her. They shot her for no reason. They shot her because she didn't know what they were talking about. They shot her because she didn't know nothin.' They shot her because she had a chance to make herself and someone else happy. They shot her because she wanted someone to want to take her to the movies and a restaurant. They shot her because she knew me."

■ ● ■

Elaine had turned her head back toward me. I locked on her eyes and slammed my hand down on the car seat again.

"I was her charm…her bad luck charm. They killed her just because she knew me."

Elaine didn't say anything. She just looked at me.

"Yeah, they shot her. They thought Sharon was you."

"What?"

"They thought Sharon was you. Do you know what one of those bastards said after they killed her? 'You can always get another secretary.' Another secretary? It was a woman, AND HOW THE FUCK DID YOU FIND ME, HEEKS?!"

I started crying again. I was rocking back and forth on the seat. Elaine grabbed my arm and squeezed it. I took her hand in mind and tried to stop crying but I couldn't. I held on to Elaine's hand and watched the city go by. I wondered what movie she would have chosen if Bryce asked her to pick one.

Heeks started talking.

"So Elaine realized you were just going to take off when the elevator doors closed. She got out on the second floor and ran down the stairs. She said she would have missed you if you hadn't stopped to give a street person some money. She caught up and followed you. When she went around the corner she saw you being thrown into a van. She stopped a random kid driving by and offered him fifty bucks to follow the van. Then he took her to a phone booth and she paged us at the hotel. After that she called Raoul. Andy didn't say shit about that for a change."

We pulled up at the hotel. Mojica told us to go inside. As we got out of the car, Raoul's van pulled up. Sharp jumped out with a blanket covering the Thompson. Andy was carrying a box in one hand and had his jacket draped over a weapon he was holding in the other.

Andy waved. "We're going to get this parked. Go in and

■ ● ■

clean up." Raoul pulled away. Andy, Sharp and Mojica followed him in the car.

Elaine took my arm and guided me to the elevators. A man waiting for a car to come back down started staring at me.

Elaine blurted out, "What the fuck are you staring at?! A truck hit a dog and he tried to save it."

I looked at Elaine and I could feel a tear slide down my cheek. The elevator door opened. We stepped in.

Elaine looked at the man with a scowl. "You going up?"

"No. No. I'll take the next car."

Elaine slammed the button for 'door close.' We rode up in silence. Elaine had my room key and she led me to my room. We went in and I sat down on the end of the bed. I clasped my hands together, squeezing them.

Elaine stood in front of me. "Is there anything I can do for you? You'll probably want a shower."

I glanced up at her and then back at my hands.

"If you need someone to talk with, or just somebody to be around, I'm two doors down. Helen is next door. But don't go out alone again. Christ, I probably didn't need to say that…I'm sorry, but if you want to talk, I'm here. We're all here. I probably didn't need to say that either."

I glanced up at Elaine again and then I looked down at parts of Sharon's brains that had stuck to my pants.

■ ● ■

Steps

I slept for fifteen hours. When I woke up I laid in bed looking at the ceiling, trying to find a pattern in the plaster that looked like the face of any of my dead relatives. Nothing. I wanted to be asleep. For a change I didn't have any dreams that I could remember, so sleep would have been a good way to avoid my nightmare reality. I sat up and wondered what the papers would say about Sharon when her body was found.

I started to feel nauseous again. I got up, showered, drank some water and started to feel a little better. I was moving around the room trying to adjust to intermittent sweating and random shakes. I pulled the shades open and stared out into my future. There it was. All around me like a grey straightjacket made out of stone. I started to laugh and listened to the laughter drift away. I was still nauseous. If I could eat something and hold it down I'd probably be okay. I could deal with the sweats and the shakes. "The Wall," I bet'cha. Like that guy in Sartre's "Wall." Did I just do that yesterday? I shook my head and moved toward the door.

I made it to the elevator okay. When I got on I tried to push the button for the lobby. I missed twice, so I put my hand on

■ ● ■

the wall and slid it over to 'L.' I shook my head like I had spiders crawling on me but couldn't get them off. The door opened on 'two.' I started laughing. The man and woman that got on, smiled. I tried to stop but couldn't. The door opened at the lobby. They got out. I put my hand and forehead on the wall and started crying. The elevator started going up. I slammed my hand against the wall. "Pull yourself together, stupid. This thing isn't over. They're going to need you."

The elevator stopped on six. Two men in suits got on. The elevator started down and stopped on four. Andy and Sharp got on.

Andy gave me a look. "Where are you coming from?"

"Nowhere. I forgot to push the button."

"We thought you were still sleeping."

"Had a good sleep. Very restful…considering."

Sharp put his dark glasses on. He started whispering. "You get soap in your eyes showering? You know, you look so damn bad I hate being in the same elevator with you. Christ, you look so crappy it hurts my mother's feelings and she doesn't even live in this state."

The two men in suits started laughing softly. When the doors opened on one, the two men in suits just stood there watching us.

Andy shook his head. "Let's get something to eat, okay?" He said it more to the two voyeurs than to Sharp and me.

The two men walked out, one of them clearly disappointed. Andy held the door until we all got off.

I said, "You know, Sharp, your mother…"

Andy interrupted me. "We need to sit the fuck down and figure out how we're going to defend ourselves. They're going to make a move. We should go after them before they come after us. Right? Heeks called and said the phones in the office are

■ ● ■

tapped. He can't do anything about it. I want to talk to the hotel manager for a second." Andy walked toward the main desk.

I looked at Sharp. "Where's Elaine?"

"She's with Mojica and Helen over at the building. Heeks needed to go up to Caminiti's to use their dark room. Hey, meet me inside. I need to visit the john again."

I walked into the dining room and sat at a table by a window. There were only three other people in the room. The waiter came over to my table, looked around and then said, "We only serve people who can afford to take a room here. This is not a walk-in establishment."

"Well that's good because we wouldn't want any old riff-raff wandering in, would we?"

"Sir, I don't need to accept that kind of attitude, so if you don't mind..." He smiled. I stood up. He looked at me with a smirk like he had three hundred years of assumed superiority at his back. "Do I need to call the police?"

"Not unless you think they're going to pay the bill for my room."

The smile left his face. "I'll have to have someone check your room number at the front desk."

Sharp walked up behind the waiter. "Will you now. Will you need to check my room number as well?"

The waiter turned around and fell right into one of Sharp's more intimidating stares. He took a step back.

"Will you be checking that man and that woman's room over in the corner? Did you check their's."

"I didn't need to. I recognized them."

"Well, son, you need to recognize us, because we may be here a few days. Do you know what time it is?"

The waiter started to raise his arm to check his watch.

Sharp's hand stretched out like lightning and grabbed his

■ ● ■

wrist. "It is late twentieth century and you need to get your head right. You need to learn how to recognize everybody. Get my drift? It's late in the day for your kind of bullshit. Understand?" The waiter nodded his head rather vigorously. "Will you be taking our order?" He nodded again. Sharp let him go and the waiter said he could take our order right now. I could see he wanted to rub his wrist, but he didn't. He tried to flex it on his hip. He shook it a little. He put both hands together in feigned supplication trying to work the numbness out. Then he walked away.

Andy came over and sat with us after we sat down.

"So did you terrorize that arrogant prick enough?"

Sharp smiled. "Ah think we have made an adjustment to his social skills. Probably nothing more."

Andy looked at me and said, "How're you feeling? Bad day yesterday."

"Been having a string of them. Just have to survive."

Sharp slapped my arm. "You still look like shit, did you know that?"

"I think you mentioned that on the way down here. Yor' mama, Tex boy."

Sharp smiled and put his toothpick in the ashtray.

"It's on now, motherfucker. When we get this craziness shelved, it's you, me, some Jack Daniels."

"I prefer rum."

Andy tilted his chair back and crossed his arms. He slowly shook his head.

An hour later we parked the car about two blocks away from our building. When we were right across the street I looked down the block toward the Arcade. Funny how the center of the world could just disappear and the only things I could remember from it are the brightly colored shadows.

Andy grabbed my arm. "Hey. We need to get going. We

∎ ● ∎

shouldn't be out front like this."

I glanced at Andy, "Yeah. Yeah. I'm sorry. Let's go." I looked across the street. Sharp had already dodged four lanes of traffic and was standing on the opposite sidewalk with his hands out to his sides like he was asking us what we were doing. He was sporting a big ass smile that seemed to light up his entire side of the street.

As we started to step off the curb I looked up the street.

"Andy, did you see the black caddy two blocks up?"

He didn't turn. "Yep. I made them. That's why I'm trying to get you off the street."

As we walked through traffic I watched Sharp enter the lobby and head for the elevators. He waved at the news guy, then stopped and turned toward him. It was late afternoon. Andy and I both stepped up on the sidewalk and stopped. Men came out of both bronze doors shooting. The news guy pulled a weapon and started shooting. Sharp spun around. His legs gave out and he crumpled to the floor. Andy had drawn his piece and was shooting through the glass doors. I could see the elevator doors open and Ivars staggered out and hit the floor. The newsman walked over to Sharp and shot him again.

"SHARP!!"

I started walking. It was funny. I could hardly hear anything except for the roar in my head. I thought maybe I could get a good pace going. I went through the lobby door and as I was pulling it open, remembered to take out my Colt. I could hear Andy yelling, "No! No!" I kept walking with glass falling all around me. I started firing. Someone moved to my left. I shot him. The newsman was shooting at me. He got me. I could feel it. My leg was hit. It burned. I shot the newsman. He fell over a stack of papers. He looked up at me. I shot him again. Damn, I got hit again in the arm. It still worked, I could tell. I pushed

■ ● ■

another clip in and emptied it into the elevator and through one of the bronze doors. Glass started falling from the globe lights hanging from the ceiling. I bent over and grabbed Sharp's pony-tail, wrapped it around my hand and started dragging him across the floor. Someone fell out of a bronze door. I shot him. The door was kicked open and Mojica came out firing. He ran over to me and grabbed Sharp's jacket. Andy was in the lobby now holding his weapon with both hands. Heeks let go of Sharp. He started unloading on the telephone booths. Andy joined him. I didn't bother to look. We made it to the sidewalk. I saw Andy throw Mojica the keys. I started walking up the block. Two men with submachine guns came around the corner. I thought Andy was hollering something stupid, like take cover behind the cars. Screw it. I raised my gun and fired. I saw one face explode. The other face fell to the sidewalk with blood gushing from his knee. Up the street I could see a very large man coming down the next block right at me. Fuck it. I slid a new clip in and waited for him. He looked around in every direction and then walked quickly across the street. The street was empty. Where did everyone go? The driver's door of the black Caddy opened and the blue suit started to come out. He fired once and then took three hits in the chest. The Caddy's side window exploded out. The big man jumped to the rear of the car like he was in a ballet and shot once. Then he walked calmly to the driver's door, pulled it all the way open, stuck his arm in and I heard three more shots. The big man bent his body inside the car. He backed out after a second, stood up and walked away.

It was like a fog lifted. "Elaine?!" I ran back down the block to the office building. Where the hell were the cops?! Andy and Mojica were putting Sharp in the car. Andy turned to me. I said, "Go!" I could hear sirens now. I walked across the lobby to the elevators. I kicked someone's leg out of the way so that I could

■ ● ■

close the door and go up. As I pulled the door shut I saw the face. It was Ivars.

When I opened the doors on our floor, I got down on one knee and stuck my head out into the hall quickly and pulled it back. I saw feet with the shoe tips pointing into the tiles. I slowly peeked again. I stood and slid down the hall. Our office door was smashed open. I glanced in. Another man lay on his side on the floor with his eyes open. Over on the floor under her desk, I could see Elaine's Pumas.

"Oh shit! Elaine?!" I threw her chair out of the way. She had a shoulder wound. She was lying on her back. Her white shirt was one third soaked in blood. I got down on my knees to look.

She opened her eyes. They looked a little glazed.

"I think I got them."

"Yeah. You got them both."

"The camera wasn't working. I think they took the stairs."

I took my jacket off and made it into a press. "Elaine, this is going to hurt some, but I have to put pressure on the wound to help stop the bleeding."

I pressed down. She closed her eyes and winced. I could hear the second elevator door open. I trained my gun on the door.

"Emergency services. Anybody in here?"

"Yeah. In here."

Four men in whites started opening stretchers. They put one of the men lying in the doorway on one.

"Hey! Over here. Those bastards are dead."

One of the medics looked at me and then came over to us. I kept my pistol trained on him.

"Let me see the wound." He looked and then put my make-shift press back on it. "You've been in the service. She's going to be fine. If we don't get these two out of here we're going to lose them. You're going to need evidence."

■ ● ■

A cop came through the door. I kept my gun pointed at him while he put handcuffs on the two guys and attached them to the stretchers.

The one medic said, "We'll have someone up here for you in a minute." Then they were gone and it was like a dream.

Elaine muttered, "They weren't real, were they?"

I looked down at her. "It looks like the bleeding is under control."

I heard the stairwell door open. I stood up and it seemed like I hurt all over.

"Elaine?"

I frowned. "Helen?!"

Helen came through the door on tiptoes. She looked at me wide-eyed.

"I need your help. Elaine's been shot."

Helen stared for a second. "So have you!"

"I'm okay. Help Elaine. She's over here on the floor."

"You need to sit down."

I sat on the floor and leaned back against the wall. I kept a grip on the Colt even though I wanted to put it down. Anywhere. Helen said Elaine would be fine. She checked me out and said I had six superficial wounds that bled a lot. Then she asked me what happened downstairs. It was the first time since she came through the door that I saw any fear in her face.

"Antonio is fine. We were ambushed as we came into the lobby. Sharp was hit bad. Andy and Antonio are taking him to the hospital. Where did you come from?"

"Tony and I were up in Caminiti's dark room. We heard shots and Tony told me to stay there until he came back for me. When the shooting stopped I came down."

Elaine chuckled. "Disobeyed a direct order from a man."

"No talking, Elaine." Then Helen started laughing.

■ ● ■

A cop came through the door. "I have a license for this weapon." He definitely wasn't a kid. I saw his stripes and he was holding a walkie-talkie in his left hand.

"Uh huh. Push the weapon toward me." He raised the talkie. "We need medical personnel on floor four immediately." Two more uniforms came in. "Libous, you stay here until the stretchers arrive. Kimbel and I are going up. You ride down with them to the ambulance. Make sure they're okay and then work your way back up until you find us."

Elaine whispered, "They seem real."

"I said no talking."

"That's coming from a future doctor, so you better pay attention."

Officer Libous was gazing at me like I was specimen in his biology class. "How many times were you shot?"

I stretched and grabbed my Colt. Slowly got to my feet and put my weapon in my belt.

"Are you sure you should be doing that?"

"I have a license."

"I meant standing up."

Helen said, "He's very hard headed, officer, and apparently he runs in a crowd that doesn't shoot too good."

I leaned against the wall and noticed for the first time all of the blood on my clothes. "People don't realize that just because they have a gun and go to a range that they're not necessarily going to hit anything in a firefight. Most trained professionals hit a target with only about thirty percent of their shots. So some guy walking down the street thinks he's all taken care of because he has a pistol in his pocket. And…"

"And you got lucky. So sit back down. You're starting to lose it, Mr. Science."

I was starting to feel dizzy, so I slid back down the wall until

■ ● ■

I was sitting. I was hurting. I imagined myself with really nasty paper cuts all over my body. Damn, I hurt. The medical people were finally coming through the door.

I started to smile. "This ain't no day for no punks."

■ ● ■

Shadows

I was glad the sky was grey. I wished it was warmer out though. Ivars was being lowered slowly into the ground. The papers said Ivars was the only person killed in a mob-related grudge shooting directed at our agency. Sharp, Elaine and I were mentioned in articles as having been shot. The doctors said Sharp would be mostly fine in a few months. I knew he was lucky. We were all lucky.

Elaine was standing next to me with her arm in a sling. Helen suggested she stay home, but Elaine insisted on coming. Elaine said business would drop off for a while because the papers said it was an organized crime incident. People would be afraid to be around people who would associate with the mob. But she also said when things cooled off it would pick up again, but our clientele would be corporate. Corporations love doing business with people who could run in the same circles as the mob if necessary. She was probably right, but how the hell would she know that?

Andy was looking grim when I glanced at him. He was going out to California for a week. He said he wanted closure with Janie. He was also worried that our fairy tale wasn't over. The

Commission would want some sort of resolution. Some of them knew what they had. Some didn't. There, was the conflict. What was going to happen when everybody knew about the films and their sales network?

Fucking Mojica was going to pick up Helen when the service was over. They had planned a vacation a while ago and now it was a good time to take it. Helen would soon be going to medical school. I wondered if she would eventually wean Heeks off some of those drugs he dabbled in.

Raoul told me that he was worried about the size of the "action" that took place at our building. It bothered him that they were able to get in and take out all of their casualties and have them disappear. He told me he tended to agree with us that some of these people didn't really know what they had been looking for. Raoul thought they just knew it was a source of money.

I asked Raoul if he had taken out the men in blue and grey. He looked at me straight-faced and said he didn't know anything about that and neither did I. I just nodded. Then he added that it seems like most times the generals want to be able to see the action. Sometimes it's a mistake to get so close to the frontlines.

Me? I thought about going on a trip. That's as far as I got. Maybe I really was on that chain. I had quite a few appointments lined up with my doc. He was a decent guy and I really was looking forward to working with him. He said I had something called "Post Traumatic Stress Disorder." He said it was a somewhat controversial diagnosis, but that soon it would be recognized throughout the medical community.

The previous night I went to Eddie's to wait for Bryce to come in. I introduced myself and we talked about the war and the Cubs and the White Sox. I brought up Sharon and he stared at me like we hadn't just talked for half and hour. I told him that

■●■

Sharon had been killed.

"That'll happen to whores, won't it."

I was kind of surprised, but then I realized where his anger was coming from.

"Brother, she was a lost, young woman who I think wanted to fall in love with you. She was cleaning up her act and I think she just wanted to be wanted by someone she thought was special. I think she thought that was you."

I ended up telling him everything I knew about Sharon. He laughed about the new slacks.

Bryce said, "You ever notice how many shadows pass through our life?"

"Some we can hold on to."

"Not many."

We sat in silence for a while, watching the coffee drip. Then we went outside together. We shook hands. He went left and I went off to the right.

I watched the clouds race across the sky while someone said something about Ivars in Finnish. When I lowered my eyes my skin went cold. About forty or fifty yards away a man was walking backwards in between the tombstones. I could feel sweat start to form on my back. He stopped. I exhaled a little too loud. A couple of heads turned. I realized he was trying to read the stones. He moved over in front of one and stood still.

Elaine tugged at my arm and whispered, "Are you okay? What's going on?"

I whispered back, "Thought I saw someone. I didn't. I'm fine."

When the service was over, Elaine, Andy, Mojica and I started off toward the cars. A man with a pad and pencil started walking next to Elaine.

"You're the secretary, aren't you?"

Elaine nodded. "Now is probably not a good time to discuss

■ ● ■

anything with the press since a friend of ours is just being buried over there."

"Well, when you're up to it. I'd like to talk to you folks about what's been going on. I don't buy the stories the local news and the police have been putting out."

Mojica and Andy waved and split off from us. We stopped. Elaine looked at me for a brief second. She stepped toward the reporter. "You're not local, are you?"

"No. I'm not."

"Well maybe we can work something out in a few days. The trail won't go cold."

He held out his hand to Elaine. "Jim Colsen."

"Elaine Gottfried."

He looked up at me with his best "condolences" smile and held his hand out.

"And your name is?"

I looked back at him with a matching smile and shook his hand.

"Me? Nicky Carter."

"Nice to meet you Mr. Carter."

He walked away in triumph.

Elaine frowned at me. "Why'd you do that?"

I turned a real smile on for Elaine. "Do what?"

"Your name's not Nicky Carter. What the hell makes you act like that?"

I looked up at the clouds again.

"My panache."

■ ● ▨

Notes

Patrice Lumumba was a postal worker who became the first democratically elected Prime Minister of the Congo (Zaire). U.S. President Dwight D. Eisenhower ordered the CIA to arrange his removal from office to help stop the potential spread of "left-leaning" governments in Africa. The CIA funneled money to the Congolese military to gain support for a coup. Lumumba was arrested, tortured and eventually executed. The CIA then helped guide Mobutu Sese Seko to power and he ruled for three decades as a U.S. backed dictator.

■ ● ■

On November 3, 1979, at a rally against the Ku Klux Klan in Greensboro, N.C., four members of the Communist Workers Party and one supporter were shot and killed by members of the KKK and the American Nazi Party. In the attack, which was captured by four TV crews, ten other people were wounded.

In the first trial (1980) all six defendants who were charged with murder, were acquitted by an all-white jury. In the second trial (1984) there were nine defendants who were acquitted by an all-white jury. In subsequent legal proceedings it was determined by the courts that the Greensboro Police had co-operated with the Klan in the wrongful deaths of the demonstrators. It was also learned the FBI knew that the attacks were going to be carried out and did nothing to stop them.

Acknowledgments

There are a number of people I need to thank for their help in getting this little project to its conclusion. I should especially like to thank Linda Hanlon for all of her suggestions, many of which I ignored. Especially the grammar corrections. Linda knows her stuff. But I'm on a little different course from her, so if you saw some odd sentence constructions it was probably me not listening to what she had to say.

Amy Manso did a wonderful job designing this book and also giving me some suggestions about the story. I can't appreciate her efforts any more than I do.

I want to thank all of my readers, who spent so much time going over the writing and giving me great suggestions and criticism. Although I appreciate all the people who took the time to read and discuss the book, some folks I have to single out for their efforts .I need to especially thank Greg Mojica who always thought he was in the book. He spent a lot of time going over the 'action' chapters with me and kept encouraging me to finish the next chapter because he wanted to know what happened to 'Mojica.' I definitely need to thank sister-in-law Mary Brown for all of her written criticisms that came from an English teacher's perspective and that of a mystery aficionado. I want to thank my daughters, Kira Manso-Brown and Danika Manso-Brown, because they gave me honest criticism when I needed viewpoints I could trust. A big thanks to Len Warner who reviewed my "psychedelic city" twice and gave me a push toward finishing. I also want to thank my other 'family readers'; my brothers, Lance and Kris, and my sister-in-law, Marge, who all unhesitatingly told me what they didn't like…and what they did.

Finally I want to acknowledge all of the people who have stood up against fascism, many of who gave the ultimate sacrifice in order to defeat it. I worry about the future for the children of this nation. I believe they will be confronted by a serious fascist movement at some point in their lifetimes and I hope that we may give them enough education to defeat it when it raises its ugly face. If it comes sooner than I thought, I hope we have the backbone to crush it with a fury that will make the future for our grandchildren and their children safe.

About the author

LEE BROWN

- former musician
- former college basketball player
- past president of Local 994 International Chemical Workers Union
- union organizer
- community activist
- former owner of the Cubbyhole Coffeehouse
- father of Duke, Columbia and Harvard graduates
- read "Don Quixote" once
- his favorite authors are: Walter Mosley; Robert Coover; China Mieville; Milena Agus; Richard Brautigan; Patrick Modiano; Roberto Bolano; Natsuo Kirino
- plays less chess than he used to

CPSIA information can be obtained
at www.ICGtesting.com
Printed in the USA
JSHW021019210920
8028JS00004B/22